Torchship Captain

Karl K. Gallagher

Published by Kelt Haven Press, Saginaw, TX.

Cover art and design by Stephanie G. Folse at www.scarlettebooks.com.
    Editing by Laura Gallagher.
Audio Recording by Laura Gallagher.
Lyric from "Sam Jones" quoted with permission of CJ Cherryh.

To Robert Anson Heinlein

For a lifetime of inspiration

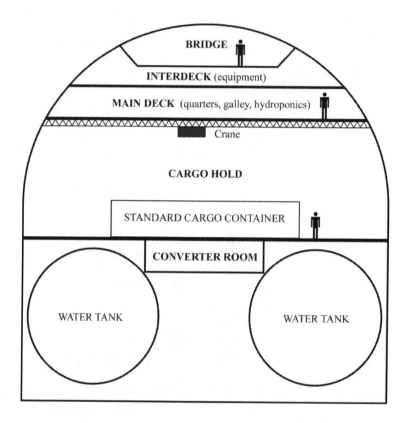

Cross section of 25m freighter *Joshua Chamberlain*.

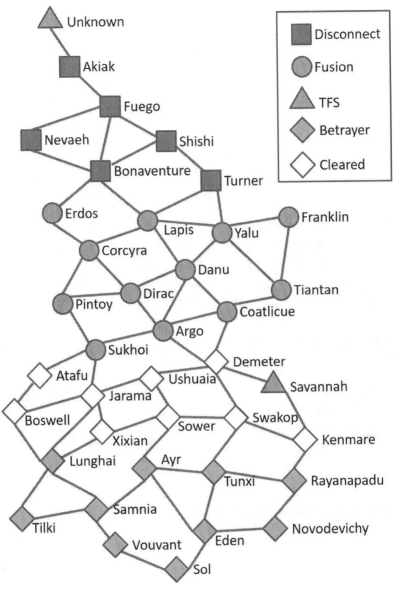

Interstellar Gate Map

Chapter One: Battlefront

Joshua Chamberlain, **Boswell System, acceleration 3 m/s²**

Mitchie thought the asteroid shouldn't be pretty. It was. The cometary ice dumped on the forward side gave it a smooth marbled appearance. A dozen rocket exhaust plumes glowed blue as the torch engines shaved its orbit. Together it looked like a vase of flowers.

It should be ugly, she thought. *Carving it into a skull would be overkill. But something destined to smash a world should be rough and grey.*

The asteroid would hit planet Boswell in four months. The impact should finish off the artificial intelligence who'd betrayed the humans living there a century ago. It would be the eleventh world reclaimed from the Betrayers since humanity began this offensive.

The torch Mitchie's freighter was delivering would cut two weeks off the time to impact. She thought of it as saving eighty lives. The human fleet was losing forty spacers a week as it fought the swarm of robot ships protecting the planet, keeping them pressed back so they couldn't intercept the rock until it was too late.

"Twenty klicks out and I have the beacon for our landing spot," said Centurion Hiroshi.

"Good. Take us in," ordered Mitchie.

"Aye-aye, Skipper." The pilot tilted the ship. The asteroid grew in the clear bridge dome.

The plumes springing from the back of the asteroid had irregular gaps between them. Their destination was in one of those gaps.

After covering half the distance Hiroshi pivoted the ship, aiming *Joshua Chamberlain's* plume to overlap the biggest plume in the ring. That torch must have been taken from a wrecked heavy cruiser.

Two klicks away from the rock Hiroshi cut the torch and let the ship drift on. He called the converter room to direct them to secure the torch, a mandatory safety measure when preparing to land on an inhabited body.

Mitchie thought the work crews tending the asteroid's torches were too few to count as "inhabitants" but didn't stop him.

Co-pilot Mthembu was watching for the landing point. "I think I see it. Ring of green lights."

"Green lights, aye," said Hiroshi.

The bridge was brighter than daylight with the glow from the mighty plume by their target. Mitchie found it too bright to look at directly. She focused on the side of the asteroid, tracing the pipes carrying melted ice back to the torches that would use it for reaction mass.

The light brightened.

Mitchie glanced at the plume. It was pivoting toward the *Joshua Chamberlain*. "Evasive!" she snapped. *The torch's support structure must be buckling,* she thought.

Hiroshi saw the threat coming, a blast of plasma that could destroy their ship. He fired all the maneuvering thrusters at full. The ship pushed closer to the rock. The plume kept sweeping toward them. Mthembu started praying.

She gritted her teeth. Yelling at Hiroshi for obeying regulations wouldn't make their last moments any better. And she didn't want to distract him from maneuvering away from the plume.

As the plume swept closer it changed color—yellow and orange of plasma not fully heated, multi-colored sparks where metal fragments were burning up in the exhaust. The torch was ripping its propellant lines apart as the structure collapsed under it. Debris was caught in the pipes. Then the plume faded out as the last pipe broke.

The ship pivoted as Hiroshi turned her to avoid hitting the asteroid. Mitchie glanced at the torch that had nearly killed them but her eyes were still adjusting from the glare. It was just shadows between the still-working plumes.

"Dammit. Anyone see the pad?" asked Hiroshi.

"I have it. Ten o'clock low." Mthembu pointed toward a shadowy spot with a few green flecks in it.

Landing took some finicky maneuvering. The pad was a shelf cut into the side of the asteroid, putting *Joshua Chamberlain's* flank only thirty meters from solid rock. It felt like a free fall docking. Even when the thrusters cut off, the rock's acceleration was too light for them to feel.

Mitchie unbuckled. "We'll have to chain down the landing legs. Hiroshi, stay at the controls. Mthembu, you're with me. I want to find whoever was in charge of mounting the torch that almost killed us and have words."

The co-pilot nodded as they suited up. At over two meters tall, he'd come in handy if the conversation went beyond words.

In the hold Mitchie saw Chief Mechanic Guo Kwan organizing the crew. Her shoulders untensed when she realized he was unharmed by the violent maneuvering. She knew someone would have reported to her if her husband had been injured . . . but she needed to see him to be sure.

"Once your suit has passed inspection, head out the airlock. Keep your safety lines hooked on. Finnegan, see if they have any tie-down chains already installed," he ordered.

Since they were on duty he limited his greetings to her to, "Suit inspected yet?"

"No." Mitchie hooked a toe into one of the rings in the floor of the cargo hold and spread her arms wide. A suit inspection could be fun, but there were too many witnesses right now.

Guo finished at the ankle seals. "Good to go, ma'am."

Bosun Setta had inspected Mthembu's suit. "He's good too," she said.

"That's everybody," said Guo. "Let's head out."

Mechanic Finnegan had found one of the pad's tie-down chains and was wrapping it around a landing leg with the help of the two deckhands. The rest of the crew spread out to copy them. There were only four chains, but Guo declared that secure enough.

"Good work, everyone," said Mitchie. "Chief Kwan, Coxswain Mthembu, with me. Everybody else back aboard."

From the landing pad they could see the wrecked torch now. The ring of thrusters was intact, but the platform to hold it in line with the other engines had collapsed. Torn pipes were growing strange ice sculptures as they leaked into vacuum.

The asteroid's work crew left guide ropes connecting the landing pad to other sites. Mitchie pulled herself along the one heading toward the wreck. The other two followed, safety lines clipped to her and each other.

"Chief, isn't that pack heavy?" asked Mthembu.

Mitchie chuckled, making sure her radio was off. Guo was wearing a thruster maneuvering unit on his suit, along with all his other 'just in case' gear.

"It is. But somebody might fall off this rock and I'd hate to go back inside to get it. You really wouldn't want to fall into those plumes."

She glanced at the circle of plumes pushing on the asteroid. Yes, even at the very small acceleration of this rock if you fell off it you'd eventually wind up passing through the plasma exhaust of the torch rockets. Mitchie shivered and kept both hands on the guide rope.

She flipped through radio channels. There were over a dozen space suited figures clustered around the wreckage. None working. It looked like they were discussing how to fix it, or fix the blame.

Channel seven had their conversation. Mitchie hastily turned down the volume. The argument was in a mix of English and Chinese. She knew Mandarin pretty well but her Cantonese was limited to space traffic control jargon and curses.

The latter was most of the conversation.

Mitchie switched back to four. "Locals are on seven. Sounds like they're having a meltdown. I'll have to sort this out so we can get them to unload our cargo. Switching."

She stopped a few meters from the crowd. "Who's in charge here? I have a bone to pick with you about almost pluming my ship," she transmitted at max volume. The guide rope let her brace her feet against the rock to stand tall. Not that her height would intimidate anyone. She was at least two hands shorter than everyone here.

The reply was multiple overlapping messages. But she had their attention. The ones in the middle stopped shoving each other and pivoted to face her.

"I'm Commander Michigan Long. Who's in charge here?"

The nearest suit was a Fusion Navy model. The wearer snarled, "Fuck off, we've got enough problems without more damn Diskers!"

He swung a monkey wrench, missing Mitchie, and hopped closer as he swung again.

Mitchie threw up her arm. She'd take a broken bone over a cracked helmet.

Guo flashed past her. Kicking off with both legs and firing the thruster pack on full made his punch to the wrench-wielder's center of mass strong enough to fling him off the asteroid. Someone yelled "Grab him!" but he was already soaring out of reach.

The guy's safety line didn't break. When he reached the full length it stretched, held, then pulled him back almost as fast as he'd left. He landed in the middle of the crowd, knocking more men in suits off the rock.

The sight reminded Mitchie of a living history team she'd seen demonstrate 'bowling.' Guo touched down next to her with a gentle puff of his thruster pack.

When the radio channel was no longer choked with screams she said, "I'm Commander Long. I'm in charge here. Officers, sound off."

There were two—a Fusion Navy lieutenant commander and a lieutenant from the Disconnected Worlds, home to Mitchie and her crew. The brawl had been over whether the Fusion construction crew had not braced the torch enough or the Disconnect operators had run at a higher thrust than intended.

"I don't care whose fault it is," Mitchie told the group. "Yes, the Fusion and the Disconnect were at war with each other a couple years ago. There's tension. And grudges. Such as my grudge over you nearly killing me with your damn collapsing torch. But we are fighting a common enemy. The Betrayers would kill all humans if they could. So let's focus on getting the job done. Put this torch back in operation. Then my ship has another one off a wrecked destroyer for you to install."

Part of why tensions remained so high was the war had been ended by blackmail. In her spy days Mitchie had found a secret that would shatter the Fusion of Inhabited Worlds. The Fusion government had abandoned their effort to incorporate the Disconnected Worlds into their rigid control system and allied against the Betrayer artificial intelligences as the price of keeping it hidden.

Guo joined in the discussions on how to fix the torch. Mitchie left it to him. She was a good spy and better pilot, but engineering she left to experts.

Most of the debate washed past her.

Guo said, "Fine, you're out of girders. You carved some damn big pieces of nickel-iron out of this asteroid to make that landing pad. Let's carve some pieces big enough to be pillars holding up the torch. Weld them in place and it'll hold."

She knew she could count on Guo to come through.

Four hours later she did pitch in, along with most of *Joshua Chamberlain's* crew, to help push still warm chunks of nickel-iron into place under the big torch assembly. Then everybody grabbed a rope to get clear as the welding started.

Guo bounced over and touched helmets with Mitchie for a private chat. "I figured out why this outfit is such a cock-up."

"Oh?"

"They're all survivors off ships too damaged to repair. No unit cohesion, lots of PTSD. I think command considered this a safe place to stick them while we're still going ship-to-ship with the Boswell Betrayer, but they need some moderating rods for this reactor core."

"Right. I'll call Logistics and see what they can send out. People without PTSD are in short supply though."

"Thanks. These guys need the help."

"No problem. Well, there will be a problem. As soon as I call in they'll have another job for us and we haven't even unloaded this cargo yet."

Logistics Ship *Hammond*, acceleration 0 m/s^2

Normal container ships carried neat stacks of standard cargo containers. The *Hammond* looked lumpy. A tight cluster of pressurized boxes was surrounded by empty slots. They isolated the laboratory. The rest of the ship wore irregular stacks of containers. Mitchie thought it resembled a chewed-on pine cone.

Joshua Chamberlain hung next to the pressurized section. It didn't have a docking port. The Fusion had insisted on no other ships being allowed to touch Pete's laboratory. They were terrified of the AI technology he was researching escaping into another ship's computers.

Which was why Mitchie's ship was working this assignment. It was an analog ship, built with no computers at all. The Fusion prohibited foreign computers from entering their space so the Disconnected Worlds built the analog ships to trade with their richer neighbors. A slide rule could not carry a computer virus, or rogue AI, or other cybernetic hazard.

With a war on the rules for analog ships had been waived. *Joshua Chamberlain* now had two digital boxes on the bridge, one for navigation and the other for communication. They had one advantage over a warship's integrated systems: if the artificial intelligences they were fighting subverted the box's code, the crew could smash the box and revert to analog methods. This had won the ship several initial reconnaissance missions.

Mitchie was content with doing rear-area work now. She just wished it wasn't so frantic. The overworked logistics fabricators tried to make enough parts and ammunition to keep the warships in action but her crew wound up spending as much time salvaging casualties and spare parts from wrecks as they did making deliveries to the combat zone. Helping the researchers was a nice break.

The research team crossed from the *Hammond* on their suit thrusters.

Mitchie waited in the cargo hold to welcome them. The Marines arrived first, grabbing onto a single safety line at parade-precise intervals. Pete Smith and his assistant scientists followed. They bounced off the deck a couple of times but found handholds before they damaged themselves or anything else.

Setta closed the hatch and flooded the hold with air.

The three scientists popped off their helmets as soon as they felt full pressure collapsing their suits against their skin. The rest waited until they heard Setta declare the atmosphere was good. Mitchie used the break to order Hiroshi to move out. They all settled gently on the deck as he used thrusters to maneuver to a safe distance from the

Hammond.

Once Setta took her helmet off and said "All clear" the military personnel followed.

Pete hopped over to Mitchie to offer his hand. "Mitchie—I mean, Captain Long, thank you for offering to help us out."

"You're welcome. It looks like an interesting mission." And more restful than running munitions to the front lines.

The senior Marine came to attention next to Pete. "Chief Warrant Officer Langerhans, commanding Commando Team 83, reporting aboard, ma'am."

Mitchie returned his salute. "Welcome aboard, Chief. Make yourselves comfortable." She waved at the dorm container used for injured rescuees.

She invited Pete up to the galley to give her a detailed briefing. Following him up the ladder let her see the shaved patch on the back of his head. Healing incisions lined the edges. "Did you have a head injury?"

"No, not as such. Decided it was time to upgrade my implant. Tripled the data storage capacity."

"Oh, okay." She shivered slightly. She'd much rather carry a gadget than give up a piece of skull to let it ride under her skin.

The situation was straightforward. Zeta 437 was an AI ship which had run out of missiles then had its torch blown clean off while attempting to ram. Now it was well behind the line of battle.

"The battle damage assessment showed the center section intact. There should be an undamaged brain unit. We're going to pull the memory and take it back to my lab."

Mitchie sipped her tea. "I see some hazards, but it's all stuff the Marines should be able to handle."

"Yes, they executed similar jobs for me in two other systems. Sharp guys."

"I'm surprised you're working with Fusion troops." Pete had been exiled to Mitchie's homeworld for violating the Fusion's harsh laws against computer research.

Pete added some sugar to his teacup. "That's . . . well, that's a compromise."

"Mmmm?"

"The Fuzies don't like my research. They're afraid I'll revive some AI and let it take over my lab. So the Marines keep an eye on me and my test material."

"Must be uncomfortable."

"Oh, they've been fine since I explained the goal of the research is looking for weaknesses and developing new weapons."

"Have you come up with any weapons?"

He shook his head. "I'm figuring out the evolution of the AIs. The original block of meta-control code is still being carried along but without the code police doing checks it's full of bit rot. None of the control mechanisms execute any more. I've been using the rot patterns to find which AIs descended from common ancestors."

"How does that help us?"

"It doesn't. But if we find a weakness in one type its relatives should also be vulnerable."

***

Zeta 437 spun violently in empty space. A Marine made a high-speed pass to put a thruster pack on the hull. A second pack was needed to completely stabilize it.

Chief Langerhans insisted civilians stay behind while his team opened up the wreck. 'Civilians' apparently included naval personnel.

Marines paired up on the hull, one with a saw, the other standing behind with a recoilless rifle. Cuts were extended to make a rectangle. An explosive charge sent the chunk of hull sailing into the dark.

A five minute wait saw no response from inside the wreck. The spiderbots didn't appear until the saws started cutting again. Two Marines were flung off the ship. The bots swarmed the next pair.

The saw-armed Marine carved open the bots grappling him. His partner passed out as the spiderbots twisted his limbs to the limit of the armored joints.

The rest of the team closed in, blasting the robot bodies with point-blank rifle shots. The metal tentacles held tight until the saws cut them into pieces.

It was over by the time the two Marines sent flying started up their thruster packs and landed back on the wreck. Chief Langerhans ordered them to take the casualties back to the *Joshua Chamberlain*. The conscious one protested he was still fit to fight the whole way back.

Cutting and blasting continued without further excitement. A few hours work exposed an armored egg shape with bundles of cables at each end. The Marines hauled the egg half a klick from the wreck before trying to open it.

They peeled it gently, not wanting to damage the contents. Even when a tentacle snapped out at a Marine they used the minimum force to cut it.

When the electronic yolk was revealed Pete and his assistants came out to inspect. He directed them to remove the processors, leaving only the memory arrays.

"Perfect," he said. "Let's get it back to the lab and I can start understanding the Boswell AI."

BDS *Patton*, centrifugal acceleration 10 m/s^2

"The admiral is in a meeting, Commander Long," said the receptionist. "Please have a seat."

Mitchie was precisely on time. She was certain the wait was planned to put her in her place. She wasn't worried. She knew where she stood with Admiral Galen.

Everyone else in the outer office had turned to look when the receptionist announced her name. *Ah, fame.* They looked away as she returned their gaze. She categorized the reactions.

The Fusion Navy officers hated her for being a spy before the war. The Marine major with them hated her for interrupting the fire support during the invasion of Demeter. The senior operations officer teaching a class on strategy with the admiral's holographic display wondered what trouble she'd cause next. The ensigns and lieutenants in the class admired her various heroics. And the receptionist hated her for her methods as a spy. *Well, at least she didn't say 'slut' out loud.*

The instructor resumed his lecture. "The fleet is executing the Boustrophedonic Plan. We're reducing the Betrayer systems adjacent to human-occupied systems first, one at a time. Then we'll sweep the next layer and continue until we've eliminated the Betrayers." As he talked the star map in the hologram showed a path going back and forth through the red stars. "Advantages of this strategy? Johnson."

The ensign said, "Eliminating the incursions into human space. Keeping our supply lines shorter."

"And disadvantages?"

"It maximizes the number of systems we have to provide security for. And gives the other Betrayers time to form coalitions against us," she said.

"What other strategies could we use?" asked the Ops captain.

A JG offered, "Go straight to Old Earth. Smash the toughest target. Split Betrayer space so they can't all unite. The resources of Earth would let us build a stronger fleet."

Another officer said, "We could go around the outside of Betrayer space. There could be humans on the other side. Descendants of people who fled the opposite direction from our ancestors."

Mitchie let a chuckle escape at that one. The students froze.

The Ops captain pivoted to face her. "Commander Long. Which strategy would you prefer?"

"The one which keeps the politicians from panicking and yanking our choke chain," Mitchie answered.

The captain let out a chuckle of his own. He turned back to his juniors. "That's not how I would phrase it, but Commander Long has captured the main advantage of the Boustrophedonic Plan. It keeps the fleet close to human space. We're always between our civilian leadership and any Betrayers that may try to attack them. This keeps the civilians calmer."

"Long!" Admiral Galen stood in the door of his inner office. As she started moving he returned to his desk. At his gesture she closed the door behind her.

Mitchie tried to report in properly but Galen interrupted her. "Skip it. I think you know my guest."

"Good afternoon, Michigan," said Stakeholder Ping. He was the Fusion's senior political representative with the fleet. Before that he'd received the blackmail threats Mitchie had delivered for the Disconnected Worlds. Which was more pleasant than their first meeting, when he'd wanted her tried for war crimes.

"Sir," was the safest thing she could say.

"The Fusion has only delivered half the reinforcements they promised," said Admiral Galen. He waved a datasheet displaying ship statistics. "The Stakeholder will meet with the Council on Pintoy to correct this."

"Apparently no Fusion ships are available to transport me," said Ping.

"The Stakeholder has requested your services. Is *Joshua Chamberlain* up to the trip?"

"To Pintoy?" Mitchie was slightly offended. "We wouldn't even need to top off the tanks. Sir."

"Do it anyway. Be ready to leave in twenty-four hours."

"Yes, sir."

"I'll come on board at 0900," said Ping.

Galen broke in. "Because of the urgency of this mission you are to go directly to Pintoy and return the Stakeholder directly to the fleet. Is that clear?"

"Yes, sir," said Mitchie. *That explains why he's not going on a Fuzie ship. They'd take him on a detour or not bring him back at all.*

"That's all, Long."

She saluted. The admiral waved her out.

An empty desk in the outer office had an intercom she could borrow. Guo and Setta answered her call.

"The good news is we're going to Pintoy," she began. "The bad news is our passenger is Stakeholder Ping."

"As long as it's not a combat zone I'll be happy," said Guo.

"We'll see. We need to be under way in less than twenty-four hours. Preferably by noon. Get us topped off."

"Aye-aye."

"Setta, pull everything out of my office. That'll have to be the guest cabin."

"Yes'm," said the Boatswain's Mate.

"Cheer up. We've earned this vacation."

Joshua Chamberlain, Atafu System, acceleration 10 m/s²

As they entered the Atafu system the picket ship informed them no Betrayers had been sighted there for over eight months. The crew felt their tension ease. They weren't back in human space yet, but at least they were safe from being attacked now.

With ten people aboard they were overflowing the galley table. Mitchie declared there'd be no all-hands meals. The bridge and converter room would have watchstanders at all times. With the Stakeholder coming to dinner she had plenty of volunteers.

To honor their guest Guo cooked Marshal's Chicken. The spicy sauce would flavor the ship's air for half a day. Mitchie wondered what Setta had traded to get the frozen vegetables from the depot ship's quartermaster. *Probably best I don't know.*

Mitchie opened the meal with a non-sectarian grace. The bowls of rice, chicken, and vegetables went around the table. It looked like the watchstanders would be having sandwiches instead of leftovers.

"This is delightful," said the Stakeholder. "If I'd known you treated passengers so well I would have found an excuse to travel with you before. Do you always serve traditional food?"

Mitchie knew "traditional" meant "Chinese" for him. Ping led the Sinophone autonomy faction in the Council of Stakeholders. At least he was polite enough to speak in English instead of Mandarin. Guo and Spacer Ye were the only members of the crew completely fluent in the other language. Hiroshi knew enough to deal with Traffic Control in Sinophone systems. Mitchie had been expanding her vocabulary since marrying Guo. Setta and Finnegan couldn't speak it at all.

Guo said, "We all take turns cooking. So you'll taste the traditions each of the crew grew up with. Spacers Ye and Wang should have some comfort food for you. The rest of the time I'm afraid you'll have to be more adventurous."

"Adventure is good. How much variety can I look forward to? I know the captain is from Akiak, and I noticed the Boatswain's Mate is from Bonaventure."

A tactful way for Ping to point out he hadn't been introduced to the rest of the table. Mitchie started on her right. "Pilot-Centurion Hiroshi is from Shishi. He's married to Boatswain's Mate Setta. You're correct that she is from Bonaventure, as is Spacer Finnegan. We have two spacers from Fuego, Ye and Dubois. Dubois is standing watch."

"North or South?" asked Ping.

Spacer Ye said, "I'm from North Fuego, Dubois is from the south."

Mitchie continued, "Spacer Wang is from Hainan. Our other watchstander is Coxswain's Mate Mthembu from Nevaeh."

"Who doesn't cook often," muttered Setta.

She wasn't quiet enough to keep Ping from catching it.

"Is Nevaeh's food so bad?" asked the Stakeholder.

Setta flushed.

Hiroshi said, "I've enjoyed the food there. But after eating his cooking a few times we've asked him to stick to sandwiches."

Ping laughed. "I like sandwiches. And I'm delighted to have so many of the Disconnected Worlds represented here. How did you assemble such a collection, Captain?"

She passed to Guo. "Senior Chief Kwan has been on the ship the longest."

"There was never a policy for it," said Guo. "We just took the best people we could find. When Captain Schwartzenberger fitted the ship out I was finishing a class on Bonaventure. The initial crew was me and five Bonnies. We'd have the usual attrition, people deciding they couldn't stand analog tech or not wanting to visit the Fusion any more. Next port we'd hire a replacement if anyone met the captain's standards. Which left us short-handed often."

Mitchie noticed sadness flashing across his face each time he mentioned her late predecessor.

"Becoming a Defense Force ship hasn't changed that," Guo continued. "When we need people, we find them. We don't worry about which planet they're from."

"I'm surprised you've never hired on a crewman from the Fusion," said Ping.

"We've had a couple over the years," said Mitchie. "They didn't work out." An understatement. One was locked up as insane. The other might still be on strong psychiatric medication.

"In the Fusion we make sure at least the enlisted crew of each ship are all from the same planet to promote cohesion. Even officers won't be exchanged until their third assignment."

Hiroshi said, "Disconnect warships are manned the same way. Shishi ships are all sponsored by a specific subpolity, so their crew is all from the same island or province."

"Interesting." The Stakeholder seemed pleased. "So even the Disconnected Worlds recognize the necessity of drawing people from homogenous groups for mission effectiveness."

"A Shishi duchy isn't homogenous, every barony in it could be a different culture," said Setta. "Bonaventure crews are drawn from all over the world. They may have nothing in common when they report aboard. But they form a good crew. BDF units regularly outperform Shishi Imperial Legion ones."

"Buying all the best gadgets helps with that," snarked her husband.

"But surely molding such disparate individuals into a crew must be harder than starting with a common background."

Mitchie waited to see if anyone else wanted to answer that before speaking. "I've found a common focus on the mission matters more than shared background. A homogenous group will completely fail if the members are all competing instead of cooperating." *For example, all trying to be the Academy honor graduate.* "We have a clear mission and everyone understands their part. Our performance proves our crew functions well together."

"Is that a team or just individuals moving together with no bonds between them?"

Setta took Hiroshi's hand. "Individuals can form bonds, sir. Professional and personal ones. Even if they come from very different backgrounds." They exchanged a kiss, still looking like newlyweds.

Mitchie wondered, *Did Guo and I ever look that sappy?* Reflecting on it made her admit, *Yes, until I blew things up trying to keep my undercover work from him.*

The Stakeholder applied himself to his food. The junior spacers at the table relaxed in the quiet. No one was eager to bring up a new topic.

Ping thought of a new approach. "Senior Chief Kwan."

"Sir?"

"I understand you are an enthusiast of the Confucian Revival."

Guo examined the statement for traps. Finding none he said, "Yes, I discovered it on my first visit to the Fusion. The lodges I've visited have been very accepting of Disconnect visitors."

"Did you ever visit the Confucian cities on Tiantan?"

"Three times, for a couple of days or weeks each. I studied in Hongmou. Beautiful city, beautiful people."

"Yes. They have the lowest crime and highest happiness statistics of anywhere in human space," said Ping.

"I was happy there myself."

"Have you been instructing your subordinate in the tenets of Confucianism?"

Spacer Ye looked up to find Stakeholder Ping pointing at him. He looked back down at his plate and froze.

"We've had a few conversations about it," said Guo. He sensed that this was the trap.

"But it's your duty as the senior philosopher present to instruct others."

"Forcing my personal beliefs onto my subordinates would be an abuse of my authority." Guo sounded angry at the suggestion that he would do that.

"Your philosophy requires you to do so."

"That would apply if I was in a Confucian society. The Disconnect military is not one."

"If you are so fond of Confucian philosophy why are you still wandering the galaxy as an individual?" asked Stakeholder Ping.

Guo did not reply.

"I guess you're not as enthusiastic about it as I'd thought."

***

Most ships would stagger the captain and first mate's sleep shifts so one was always awake in case of emergency. Mitchie stuck to that rule in hostile space. With Atafu officially safe she'd rearranged the schedule to let her sleep with her husband.

After months of missions in a combat zone sleep was all she wanted. She snuggled up to Guo as he stared at the ceiling and promptly fell asleep.

Spacers sleep lightly, especially captains. The steady roar of the torch or the hum of the ventilators doesn't bother them. But any unexpected noise will wake them as well as a siren would.

Mitchie sat up in bed, adrenaline surging, and tried to identify the sound which woke her.

"Oh, I'm sorry, I didn't want to wake you," said Guo.

"What was that?"

"Sorry, I closed a book hard." Guo had been wiggling a book back into its position under the restraining straps. He pulled it out, opened it in the middle, then slammed it shut.

Mitchie laughed. "That's louder than I thought they could be."

"Usually I'm gentler with them."

She glanced at the chronometer. They'd turned in four hours ago. "Did you get any sleep?"

"No. I've been doing some research." He traded the book for another.

"You need to rest."

"Too much on my mind." He dropped into the reading chair.

Mitchie watched him go through the index then start flipping pages. She rolled out of bed and walked over to him. She perched on the arm of the chair.

"You're in my light."

"I know." She studied the ideograms on the open page. "Duty to the community?" she said in Mandarin.

Guo nodded.

"Are you letting that manipulative bastard get to you?" In English.

He sighed. "Bastard or not, he's right. I am not living according to my philosophy."

"You're living well."

"I should be joining or forming a community."

"That's something for peacetime. We have to win the war first."

"I could have been doing it before the war."

She pressed her naked body against him. "You need to relax."

Guo moved the book away. Mitchie slithered down his body until she knelt before the chair.

"That is *not* relaxing."

Her reply was non-verbal.

***

Two nights later the shuffle of watch assignments put Spacers Ye and Dubois at the dinner table. To Stakeholder Ping's amusement they sat next to each other.

"I thought Fuegans didn't get along with each other," he said.

Ye ducked his head, eyes on his mashed potatoes.

Dubois answered, "He's a Northie. They get along with everyone."

"And Southerners don't?"

"We like our own clan. Other clans, there's usually a history of violence to give us reason to stay away." She cut her pork chop in half on the word 'violence.'

"Really. What if you were both from South Fuego?"

Mitchie said, "The S-1 shop would flag the transfer and make sure the second one never got to the ship."

"The chief network usually keeps it from getting that far," added Guo.

"The clan feuds fascinate me," said Ping. "Why so much hate for neighbors? Most peoples hate those who are different and far away. Why do the South Fuegans hate those most similar to themselves?"

Dubois clearly didn't like being the center of attention but she answered his questions anyway. "Northies never did anything to me.

People from other worlds never did anything to me. Now the Red Rocks killed my uncle and his son. The Drifting Sands kidnapped my sister and cut off two of my father's fingers. Them I hate."

"A classic revenge cycle. Does your clan attack them?"

"Of course. We want revenge. We need to prove we're tough targets or everyone will start raiding us. And the young men want to show off how fierce they are."

"But why is the South so violent and North peaceful?" Ping sounded honestly confused. "They're both as hot as humans can stand, both settled by African and equatorial Asian stock, both short on water. Why the difference?"

Dubois shrugged and looked at Ye. He swallowed his food and said, "I don't know. It's always been that way."

"Geology," said Mitchie.

"Please expand, Captain," said Ping.

"The North's bedrock is smooth, letting the whole polar region be one big aquifer. The Water Judges control it as a common resource. If a Northie stabs someone the victim's share of the water is divided among the whole population.

"Now in the South," she continued, "the bedrock is jagged and broken. There's dozens of small aquifers, each supporting two or three clans. Kill someone and their water goes from their clan to your own. It's a powerful incentive.

"The North uses capital punishment, mandatory birth control, and immigration restrictions to keep the population within limits. The Southies just murder people until they're at the same level." Mitchie took a sip of water.

"Interesting." Ping turned back to Dubois. "Is that the incentive for young men, Spacer?"

Her dark skin grew a little darker. "Well—they don't think about the water. Usually, it's, um, no girl will talk to a man who hasn't wet his knife."

"Wet?" asked Ping.

Mitchie picked up her butter knife and mimed slicing her arm.

"Ah. I don't think it's my place to say but it all sounds horrid. A pity there isn't some way to convince those lads they're better than the dry-knived scum without so many dead."

With that Mitchie realized Ping's point in dragging out all this anthropology. He wanted to convince them that the Fusion's vast array of virtual citizens, all losing status competitions with the stipend-collecting drones, were essential to keeping it a healthy society. *Maybe he's right. But I'd rather see the Fusion burning than healthy.*

Joshua Chamberlain, Sukhoi System, acceleration 10 m/s²

Mthembu was growing impatient with Traffic Control. Mitchie sympathized. Not enough to take the task on herself. But after more hours than she could count arguing with Fusion bureaucrats she did sympathize.

"No, we don't have a transponder. Analog ships are prohibited from carrying them by your regulations on electronics," said the coxswain.

She thought that was a tactical error. *Joshua Chamberlain* was an analog ship, but they'd added several pieces of gear the Fusion prohibited. They didn't like computers that weren't continually monitored by their network for signs of AI activity or other misbehavior.

"Yes, I am using a digital communications unit. We're a unit of the Combined Fleet. The military exemptions on network monitoring apply."

That was the better approach.

"We don't have a Fusion Navy transponder because we're a Disconnected Worlds ship."

The annoyance of educating every traffic controller was why Mitchie had delegated the task. They could have hidden the boxes and just flown as an analog ship . . . but she wasn't willing to give up the convenience.

"Yes, we're a freighter. Navies need supplies. We're still covered by the exemption for warships."

Mthembu's tone was becoming tense.

"Then complain to Admiral Galen, and he can put a missile in your control station!"

Mitchie turned around in her piloting couch, wondering if she'd have to take over the conversation after all. Then she saw Mthembu turn the microphone back on.

He said calmly, "Traffic Control, if you consult the Treaty of Lapis you'll see the exemption applies to all ships belonging to a Disconnect military force. The Bonaventure Defense Force is specifically listed."

He turned the mike off again. "Sorry, ma'am. I'll do penance later."

Mitchie laughed. "That's between you and God, Coxswain. I've heard plenty worse."

Chapter Two: Capitol

Capitol City, Planet Pintoy, gravity 9.4 m/s^2

Mitchie was fiddling with a datasheet. Her Disconnect-made one was confined to the ship because it wouldn't accept shutdown commands from the Fusion network. The loaner she'd been given at the spaceport, like all Fusion computing gear, would continually report on its activity so the Code Police could check for AI activity or prohibited programming.

She still couldn't get it to recognize her favorite swipe combinations. When the door chime sounded she tossed it on the table.

Mitchie opened the door to find Stakeholder Ping.

"Good afternoon, Captain. I wanted to make sure my aides found proper accommodations for you."

She stepped back to let him in. 'Captain' wasn't an appropriate address now that they were off the ship. Her undress uniform had the same rank insignia as the Fusion Navy, just in different colors. She wondered if his refusal to call her 'Commander' was a reminder of the promotion she'd been denied, or a hint of a bribe. *Or maybe he just wants to irritate me into overanalyzing everything.*

Guo was admiring the view from their 20th-floor window. Ping joined him. "Magnificent, isn't it?" said the Stakeholder.

"Yes." Guo kept watching.

The Council Acropolis was a building, not a hill. A clear dome at the top revealed the Council of Stakeholders' meeting chamber, two hundred stories off the ground. Stone from every Fusion world made a DNA-patterned mosaic as the column dropped straight for half the building's height. Then sloped windows alternated with terraces of trees and grass to the ground. The mountainous structure was surrounded by a wide circle of park. A loop of the Te River flowed through the park with gentle ripples.

Lights gleamed from the lower levels as skyscrapers cast afternoon shadows. More sparkled in the park.

Ping gave him several more minutes of contemplation before

interrupting. "I found something in my office that might interest you."

"Oh?" Guo tore his eyes away from the window and accepted the item from Ping's hand.

"It's just been gathering dust so I really ought to find it a better home."

Mitchie came closer to watch as Guo pulled off the tissue wrappings to reveal a book. The white cover was decorated with maple leaves. Some were seen edge-on, assembling into a set of ideograms. She worked out a translation. Guo confirmed her guess.

"Xi Wang's Falling Red Leaves!" he burst out in Mandarin. Opening it moved him to say, "An autographed first edition! I thought all of these were in museums. How did you find it?"

"It's been in the family. My cousin the history professor had it, but he'd analyzed all the notes and passed it to me as an inauguration present."

"Notes?" Guo answered his own question. Turning a few more pages revealed handwriting filling the margins. "Who was . . .?"

"My ancestor was the Communist governor of Shanghai. When the Rectification began he spoke for the people. Picked the right side every time until the very end. So instead of joining the Virtual Emperor's cabinet he won a retirement in a lovely mountain village in Manchuria."

"Your role model?" interjected Mitchie, speaking Mandarin as they were.

Ping shrugged. "I could do far worse. He was remembered fondly by many up to the Betrayal."

Guo held the book as if it was made of spun glass. "This should be in a university's library."

"It is. They've scanned the notes down to the brush pressure and ink density to evaluate the old man's mood as he wrote. They have the data. The physical object is just clutter to the academics. And I don't appreciate it as it deserves."

Guo nodded, eyes fixed on the pages.

After a moment of silence Ping caught Mitchie's eye and gestured toward the far end of the suite's living room.

"I apologize if I've deprived you of his company for the evening," he said.

"I'll be fine," said Mitchie. "Thank you very much. That is a perfect gift for him. Real history he can hold in his hands."

"You should have some compensation for the trouble of bringing me here."

"It was our duty."

"That is true." He took a chilled water glass from the coffee table, uncapped it, and sipped. "I would like you to accompany me to the Council session tomorrow. I have enough support to change the agenda to debate reinforcement funding."

"Do you want me to testify?" she asked.

"If necessary. There shouldn't be any need for you to speak. I just think some of my colleagues would benefit from a visual reminder of all the issues involved."

In less diplomatic terms, he wanted a symbol of the Disconnected Worlds' ability to depopulate Fusion planets if they didn't get enough cooperation. Mitchie was fine with that.

"I'll wear my best."

"Thank you. I'll meet you at the subway station at half past nine."

A few pleasantries were sufficient to see Ping out the door.

Guo hadn't said good-bye to the stakeholder. He sat in the chair with the best reading light. Every few minutes he turned a page.

Mitchie shook her head. She pulled out her datasheet. If she had some time to herself she might as well catch up on Fusion politics.

A few hours later she was hungry enough to order room service. She quashed the temptation to order for one.

The deliverybot arrived quietly. It left without Guo noticing. The scent of soup did break his focus.

"Is it dinnertime already?"

"No," said Mitchie. "That was two hours ago."

"Oh. Thanks." He put down the book. Halfway to the table he turned and sprinted to the bathroom.

Guo's dinner conversation was his favorite bits from the book. He was amazed by the pettiness of the motivations for some men to betray their faction. "Hardly anyone cared about the Virtual Emperor one way or the other, it was just a way to label the sides."

"Okay, I have to admit I haven't studied the Golden Age's history. Who was the Virtual Emperor?"

"Not a person. Software. One of the proto-AIs. It started as a polling program with secure anonymity. It would call everyone in the country, ask their opinion on something and whether there should be a law. If there was a consensus, say 90% wanting something, it would report the people's will as a decree of the Virtual Emperor."

Mitchie thought back to the opera Guo had taken her to. "That's what the fight was about? Opinion polling?"

Guo shrugged. "Everyone had been forced to repeat the official opinions, and the media was completely controlled by the Communists. So no one really knew what their neighbors thought. When they realized they could be honest safely all sorts of things came out. Sex, drugs, crime, foreigners—hating the Communists was the least of it. Rough time to be a minority in any sense."

"I can imagine."

Guo paused to take a few bites of his steak. Mitchie didn't say anything. She didn't want to set him off again.

He paused after finishing his potato. The Acropolis shone in the night. The lower windows were in a regular grid, but those in the tower followed the helices of its decoration.

"It really is a beautiful building," he said.

"Yeah. The Fusion of Inhabited Worlds' official dildo, ready to fuck us all."

Guo almost lost a bite of steak as he laughed. "Oh, my. It does look like one."

Mitchie glared out the window. *That's the real enemy.*

$$***$$

The Acropolis was served by sixteen subway lines, providing a smooth commute to the tens of thousands of politicians, bureaucrats, and hangers-on spending their lives there.

After leaving a boot knife and datacrystal at the security gate

Mitchie accompanied Ping through a series of conveyers and elevators until they arrived at the Council Dome. Her uniform drew puzzled glances if she was noticed at all. A few people did recognize it, or her. They were the ones acting as if a rabid dog was loose.

The Dome was familiar from news reports. Spectator benches ringed the outer edge. Lower rings held aides, staffers, and witnesses. Stakeholders had desks facing the speaker's platform on the north side of the floor.

Ping told Mitchie, "Enjoy the show," before heading off to confer with a colleague.

She looked around to pick a seat. One witness bench held three Fusion Navy admirals and a Marine general. She sat on the empty bench beside theirs.

The general gave her a polite nod. Then his eyes locked on her ribbons. "How the fuck does a Disker wear a Wreath of Virtue?"

"Sir, I performed a casualty pick-up from the Demeter spacehead." The Marine general who talked her into taking the mission had arranged the award after she'd pissed off her own chain of command.

"You're Long, then."

"Yes, sir." The Akiak Space Guard's dress uniform lacked a name tag.

"That was good work, Commander. Thanks for taking care of our boys."

"I was happy to help them, sir."

She was happy she'd helped them. The casualties had been young men, cannon fodder, with no choice in their orders once they'd enlisted. Not like the men and women in this room.

Mitchie looked over the Stakeholders sitting at their desks or chatting on the floor. These were the people in charge. The ones who'd given the orders to invade Bonaventure and take its people's freedom. Who'd ordered the bombing of Noisy Water because they didn't like the research done there. Who'd ordered her first love burnt to death just to keep the Disconnected Worlds intimidated.

Her fingers itched for the ceramic knife she'd hidden in her underwear. She would happily slit the throat of every Stakeholder in this room. Less painful than they deserved but she'd take what she could get.

The thought was ludicrous, of course. Even ignoring the security guards standing by in their ready room, most stakeholders were a third of a meter or more taller than her. They could knock her flat before she connected with the knife. She'd have to put them all to sleep before she could slit any throats.

And if she was going to gas the Dome poison would be just as easy as a sedative.

Mitchie realized she needed to calm herself. Focusing on the debate helped. The current topic was tax treatment of interest from medium-term corporate investments. Probably. The jargon flowed thicker than any military briefing she'd been in. Both sides of the argument claimed they'd produce better economic stability. She couldn't figure out what they were disputing. Finally she opened up her datasheet to look it up.

"Michigan?"

She looked up. "Pardon me?"

"It is you!" Suddenly a young blonde woman was hugging her. "What are you doing here?"

Mitchie recognized her as heiress Guenivere Claret, one time passenger on her ship. She said, "Ping wants me as a witness."

"Interesting choice," said Guen. She wore a sober black dress designed to make her look adult instead of not yet twenty.

"I'm sorry about your father," said Mitchie.

Guen lowered her voice. "Not here." She gave Mitchie another hug, and received a firm one in return this time. "When this finishes I'm going to carry you off for some girl time."

"I'd like that."

"Good. Damn, it's nice to see someone I can trust." Guen hurried back to her desk as the Parliamentarian called for a vote.

Mitchie dove back into her datasheet. *When the hell did she become a Stakeholder?*

The Parliamentarian stepped onto the speaker's platform. "There being no majority, the issue is tabled until the same slot next week. Next is CB 37, On Manning the Navy. Stakeholder Wang, please take the floor."

A stout Han man took the Parliamentarian's place. "I ask that the Council go into executive session. Is any Stakeholder opposed?" After half a minute he said, "The Council is now in executive session. Guests please depart."

Schoolchildren on the top bench whined as the ushers herded them to the elevators. Staffers headed for a different set of elevators. Mitchie noticed those near her weren't moving. She sat tight.

After the last elevator-load vanished Stakeholder Wang said, "Are all present cleared for this discussion?"

Someone on the floor, Mitchie couldn't spot who, shouted, "There's an enemy soldier here!"

Suddenly everyone was staring at her.

Stakeholder Ping stood, pulling the eyes toward him. "Commander Long is here as an expert witness, under my sponsorship. Allow me to point out a few facts.

"First, the Disconnected Worlds are not our enemies. We've allied with them against the enemies of all humanity.

"Second, Commander Long, by virtue of her own efforts as a spy and the data-sharing of the alliance, already knows all the secrets we will discuss.

"Third, she has sworn not to reveal those secrets to the general population, which is the reason we are in executive session."

Mitchie thought, *Fourth, I'm a naval officer, not a soldier.*

Despite some mutters no one demanded a vote on Mitchie. A few aides were expelled for insufficient security paperwork.

Wang took the floor. "Our ship production program has outpaced the number of volunteers for naval service. Already we have finished ships in parking orbits waiting for crews."

The Fusion's evasions suddenly made sense to Mitchie. They were ashamed to admit that with five times the Disconnect's population they were getting fewer recruits.

After some extended blathering Wang said, "Our proposal is to begin conscription from the stipend receiving population, choosing those whose profiles show the greatest aptitude for military service. In parallel with this conscription virtual citizens will be transferred to military units created to accommodate them. The stipend class must not feel they have been singled out for conscription."

That was staggering. Even after analyzing demographic data and stealing Fusion documents about them it had been hard for Diskers to believe in "virtual citizens." The Fusion gave its welfare class everything they needed: money, housing, medicine, and to save their egos from the strain of being at the bottom of society's pyramid, a steady supply of simulated victims to be bullied, out-competed, and beaten at every game.

In this room it was accepted as normal.

The admiral with the most braid stood.

"Admiral Vittelli, you may testify from the bench," said the Parliamentarian.

"Excellent Stakeholders," began the admiral, "the military cannot create virtual divisions. We do not have enough experienced personnel to staff such formations. We can't falsify such people without creating so many inconsistencies your great secret would be revealed."

He'd spoken in a rote tone. Mitchie inferred he'd given this testimony many times. Now he seemed to be responding to an objection.

"You could certainly fire me, and fire them," waving at the other brass hats on the on the bench, "and keep firing until you found some fool with more ambition than sense who'll carry out that plan. That won't make career sergeant majors and chief petty officers into talented actors. They can't lie well enough to pull off your plan. We've trained and selected them to not be able to lie like that."

Mitchie scanned the faces of the Stakeholders. No one was surprised. This had to be a well-worn debate.

Vittelli continued, "In my prepared testimony I attached recorded testimony from all predecessors predicting this policy would end in disaster. It seems we are about to see that disaster come to pass.

"We do have an alternative to offer. Recall the combined fleet. Use the troops as trainers. Conscript the entire stipend-collecting population. Train and equip them to fight the Betrayers. That will give us a force that can fight to Old Earth and beyond. We will also give purpose to people who are wasting their lives.

"Thank you, Excellent Stakeholders, for your time." The admiral sat.

A Stakeholder accused Vitelli of wanting mass conscription to enable a military coup. The Parliamentarian ruled him out of order with practiced ease.

Someone else took the floor to advocate offering cash bonuses to new enlistees. Another proposed property awards on discharge. More variations and combinations came from later speakers until they began to blur together for Mitchie.

A purple-haired one snapped Mitchie out of her daze. "Let's renegotiate with the Disconnect to reduce our contribution to only what people will volunteer to do. It's not like any of them would actually carry out an order to devastate an inhabited world."

The Parliamentarian interrupted. "Point of order. A request has been made that the Disconnected Worlds representative respond to Stakeholder Gonzales' assertion."

Mitchie considered diplomatic phrasings as she stood. *Screw it, I'm no diplomat.* "The Stakeholder feels that if an order to destroy a Fusion world came down it would be disobeyed. That no one would do it. But I assure you, people who had friends at Noisy Water would do it. Bonnies who lost their homes and children to your invasion would do it. I would do it. Hell, we could probably sell lottery tickets for the privilege of doing it and make enough to build a new fleet."

The Dome was silent. No whispers, no rustling of datasheets.

"Thank you, Commander Long," said the Parliamentarian. "Can you speak to the Disconnected Worlds' capability to carry out that threat?"

She thought a moment. "I can't be specific. Remember that right now the Combined Fleet is aiming an asteroid at an AI-controlled world. If the anti-missile defenses are down several missiles sent in at tenth-cee velocity would have a similar effect. That would destroy the biosphere. The weapon we used to disable the Fusion fleet in the Bonaventure System has never been deployed against an inhabited world. Simulations predict over ninety percent of the population would die if it was."

Mitchie sat down. *That was probably still classified. Oh, well. What's another reprimand on my record?*

"Thank you, Commander Long. Stakeholder Gonzales, you may resume."

The Stakeholder yielded the floor.

***

The debate was no closer to a conclusion when the Parliamentarian adjourned the session. A "see you tomorrow" message from Ping popped up on Mitchie's datasheet. She cleared the message and started a search for newly released romance novels.

"Mitchie!"

She looked up to see Guen—that is, Stakeholder Claret—approaching. Mitchie hopped down to meet her.

The non-security cleared aides were flooding back into the Dome. Most were bookish types. The kind eager to pass test answers to the popular kids.

Guen's aides were different. Mitchie read them as elite infantry stuffed into suits for camouflage. The two females looked as deadly as the rest. Careful study showed where their weapons—or some of their weapons—were hidden in the dresses.

The stakeholder closed for a hug before saying anything. The clinch was firm enough to reveal she also had a firearm under her dress. "Do you have to be anywhere now?"

"Nope."

"Good. Let's find a place we can talk."

The Dome wasn't such a place. The "aides" formed a wedge around them to open a path to the nearest elevator. Nervous wonks skittered aside.

No one else wanted to share the ride with them.

When the elevator started moving one of the killers-in-a-dress produced a scanner.

"Annie, she went through Council security," objected Guen.

"Yes, ma'am," said the bodyguard without lowering the scanner.

"It's not a problem," said Mitchie, sliding her feet apart and holding up her arms.

The scanner went head to toe without a beep. Mitchie went back to a relaxed stance.

Annie aimed it at Mitchie's hips. "What's that?"

Her training said she should play dumb in case they'd back off . . . but Mitchie was certain that would just annoy these people. "Ceramic knife," she said.

Annie held out her hand.

"Here?" said Mitchie.

The bodyguard smiled a little. "Boys, turn your backs."

Shoes pivoted and clicked together almost as one.

Mitchie sighed. Undoing the bottom four buttons of her jacket, unbuckling her belt, unzipping, and digging under the elastic produced the blade. She dropped it into Annie's hand and refastened everything.

Guen said, "That can't be comfortable."

"No. But sometimes you really need a knife."

"How often have you needed this one?" asked Annie.

"Once."

"Sounds like a three beer story. I've never seen one like this." The blade had no handle, just three loops on the back of the blade. They were sized for Mitchie's fingers. Annie could only fit her pinkie into one.

"It's a South Fuego hide knife." Mitchie mimed hiding the blade in a closed fist then slapping at a neck.

"That settles it," said Annie. "I'm retiring in the Disconnect. I like their attitude."

"Y'all can relax now," said Mitchie to the male bodyguards. "I'm dressed again."

When the elevator stopped four men went out to clear the area before calling for the rest. Mitchie stepped out to find Guen's private subway station. A courier waited with the items Mitchie had given to Security on entry. Annie took the bag and added the hide knife to it.

A ninth bodyguard waited in the subway car. Once everyone was aboard he started them out. The silence preyed on Mitchie's nerves but she didn't want to be the one to break it.

It continued through the subway ride, another private station, an elevator up, and foyer of an expensively decorated apartment. The guards fell behind as Guen led Mitchie through a large living room into a study with a vault-heavy door.

As the door thudded shut behind them Guen sighed in relief. "Safe at last! Let's get comfy." She tossed Mitchie a silk dressing gown and disappeared behind a screen with another.

Mitchie changed out of her uniform. She didn't know what was going on, but she wasn't going to refuse a suggestion from a stakeholder, trillionaire, and (hopefully) ally.

The room had six pillowy chairs and no display devices. She'd been asked to leave her datasheet in the foyer. Apparently they'd been isolated in here.

The silk settled on her skin as gently as a kiss. Mitchie decided she'd have to ask Guo to find her one of these.

Guen came out from behind the screen. "No, take your socks off. We're going to spa!"

Presumably this would make sense soon. Mitchie folded her socks and added them to the neat pyramid she'd made of her dress uniform.

"Sit, it's nail time." Guen waved her to the two chairs closest together.

As Mitchie sat the chair leaned back and adjusted to hold her arms at a comfortable angle. *It's like a very fluffy acceleration couch.*

Guen clapped her hands. "Nailbots, we have a guest!"

Pink boxes on wheels emerged from a cabinet. Mitchie glanced at her hostess. She was staying calm, so this must be a good thing.

Still, it took some willpower to hold still as her hands and feet disappeared into the open sides of four boxes.

"Oh, I needed this," said Guen.

Gentle rubbing started on Mitchie's hands and feet. Then pressure pulses in the cushions started working on the tensest muscles of her back and shoulders. Mitchie let out a slight moan.

"I know, isn't it great?" responded Guen. A few moments went by. "You said you heard about my father."

"I was shocked and sad. I'm very sorry for you. Um . . . the news said it was an accident."

A bitter laugh. "An automated delivery van turned off its transponder and accelerated straight down at full power. No accident. It was hacked."

"They couldn't track it back?" The upside of the Fusion's ubiquitous surveillance was quick apprehension of criminals. Or so she'd always heard.

"Pintoy's cops are in the pocket of the Sinophone factions. They've always hated us Dynamists." The Clarets were long-term supporters of the pro-growth faction.

That put a chill through Mitchie even with the warmth being applied to her hands and feet. "Do you have any idea who was behind it?"

"We have a list. Ping is number four on it."

"That's . . . yeah, I can see him ordering that."

"*Who* isn't the most important part. *Why* we know. The Sinophones want to keep the lid on, enforce every rule as is, even while everything's changing."

"That's why you wanted to become stakeholder? To change things?"

Guen let her grief show for an instant. "I didn't want it. Daddy didn't want the job either. But the Council was going to deny representation to the Demeter refugees, just dilute their votes as residents of wherever they wound up. Daddy was the only one with the clout to force his way in.

"Me . . . I only took the job because the rest of Demeter's politicians are cowards. We had a meeting to pick a successor. I was just there to make the donations. They kept nominating each other and declining. Then someone said me, might've been a joke, and I said, 'Yes, if nobody else wants to.' And here I am."

Mitchie studied the younger woman's face. Guen was nineteen, still a child by most Fusion rules. There were no lines. But tension pulled some parts tight enough for Mitchie to see where lines would appear in the future.

"You should have more friends in here. This is a really nice lair."

Guen tried to match the lighter tone. "I used to. All my friends who made it off Demeter would come over. But since the election their parents think it's too dangerous to be around me."

And they're probably right. "I don't know how long I'll be here. When the reinforcements are settled I need to take Ping back to the fleet. Until then I'm happy to come visit." *Guo's busy with his book anyway.*

"Great! There's a new Guianan place you have to try. I'll have them send some up. Have you seen *Fated Love?*"

***

"Sorry I'm so late, honey," said Mitchie as she came through the door.

Guo looked up from his new book. He was typing notes into his datasheet. The tabletop display showed multiple Chinese documents. He was in history mode.

He said, "Hi. I was wondering if the Stakeholder was going to keep you overnight. Did you eat?"

"God, yes. Guen was stuffing all these little delicacies into me. Shame you weren't there, you appreciate that stuff more than I do."

"Maybe I could come along some time." Guo's stomach rumbled.

"Did you have dinner?"

"Um . . . no."

"Lunch?"

"I've been reading. Ping's cousin published some papers based on the marginalia . . ." he trailed off. "I had breakfast."

"I know. I ordered breakfast for both of us." She pulled up the room service menu on her datasheet and ordered a meal. "When this arrives you close everything and eat it."

"Yes'm." He took his eyes off the book long enough for a hug and kiss.

"Go back to your project. I need to do some writing too."

"Who gave you homework?"

"Nobody. I want a log of everything happening here. Admiral Galen expected this to be a touch and go. Instead these people will be arguing for days."

"Crap. We need those ships."

"Agreed. And speaking of which I should. . . ." She inflicted a flurry of typing on her datasheet. "There. A message to Galen letting him know we arrived. No excuse for him to complain now."

Guo chuckled. Admirals didn't need excuses.

Eight Days Later

"Hi, *baobei*, I'm home," Mitchie called out as she entered their hotel suite.

Guo wrapped her in a hug. "Hey. Anything new today?"

"I wish. It's been a whole week of repeating stuff they said the first day. Nobody wants to tackle the real problem."

"They might have to. Let me show you something." Guo led her over to the suite's display wall. A wave activated a video labeled 'Recruiter Is a Sockpuppet.' Guo said, "This is four hours old."

A young male narrated over imagery of a player-vs-player battle in a virtual reality game. "Our rivals the Exurbs tried to raid one of our convoys. We kicked their asses. They whined at us. One got on my nerves by saying if we wanted to fight so much we should join the Navy. Well I checked. Four members of my guild have signed up and not a single member of the Exurbs has. So when that Akheeley guy started up again I told him the numbers and said he should make his own guildies enlist. He just logged off. After weeks of harassing us about that."

The view changed to the side of a typical Pintoy apartment building. "I was so mad I decided to confront him in person to make him save his recruiting efforts for his buddies." The camera view entered the building and took the elevator up. "We back-tracked his account to find his apartment." The apartment door yielded to boots when the buzzer wasn't answered. "And we found . . . nothing."

The camera swept through a fully furnished apartment. Three bots

stood idle. There were no clothes, decorations, clutter, or other signs of
an actual human presence.

"So we figured the hack gave us the wrong apartment. Then the
creepy thing happened."

The video showed a deliverybot piled high with food boxes
entering through the ruined door. It stacked the boxes in the kitchen
and left. A close-up showed the label had the supposed occupant's
name and address.

"We're all, he doesn't live here but he gets food delivered? What's
with that? Well, watch this."

The kitchenbot popped out of its niche. Its arms stripped the
packaging off a box and stuffed the wrappers in the trash. It held a pre-
cooked meatloaf in a metal grip as it moved out of the kitchen. The
camera followed it into the bathroom.

A second arm with a cutting blade sliced the meatloaf into tiny bits.
Every one fell into the toilet. The kitchenbot flushed then went back to
open another package.

"That is the creepiest thing I've ever seen," said the narrator. "We
kicked it around. Our best guess is a Navy recruiter made a sock
puppet identity and rented this apartment to back it up. Paying for
food for someone who doesn't exist is some serious devotion to
accuracy, dude. I don't know who you really are. Just seriously, stop
bugging us."

The video finished with an elaborate logo proclaiming it the work
of Death From Shadows. Mitchie wasn't sure if that was the narrator's
virtual identity or his guild's name.

"I'm pretty sure they can't blame that on the Disconnect," she said.

Guo pulled up an analysis of the video's dispersal through the
network. "They haven't figured out the whole secret. But some
observers are trying to find the creation date for the sockpuppet
identity. They've traced it back for years."

"If it's one of the Ministry of Social Control's virtual citizens it's
documented back to birth. Once they start asking why and how many
more there are . . . I need to make sure the big guys know about this."

Mitchie linked it to Guen and Ping with a vague but urgent

message. Guen's secretary bot promised that the Stakeholder would view her message as soon as she concluded her meeting.

Ping called back. Mitchie hastily switched it to her datasheet. His face was far too large on the display wall. "Yes, we know. My aides jumped me as soon as we left the executive session. It seems having all our virtuals become Navy recruiters was a strategic error. Now this building is full of Social Control experts infinite-looping."

"You don't have a contingency plan for this?"

"Nobody was willing to authorize executing the kids until they uploaded it, and then it was too late."

"Oh."

Ping looked very tired. "Michigan. If your husband has another brilliant idea, we would be very glad to hear it. Now I have to find someone not panicking so we can put him in charge."

The screen blanked.

"Why me?" demanded Guo.

Mitchie shrugged. "You suggested the alliance against the AIs."

"That was the obvious solution to the war."

"Wasn't obvious enough for somebody else to think of it first." She leaned close and locked eyes with him. "So, think of something, history-boy."

Guo dropped onto the couch. Mitchie cuddled up to him.

"This is functionally one of those situations where two social classes switched places or merged. Joshua Chamberlain's war was one of those. The working class outranked the slaves in every way. Freed slaves would be equal to the white lower class. And some of those lower class whites would have wound up on the bottom of the heap. They fought to prevent that. It was pure omegaphobia."

He paused. "The French Revolution was another. The nobles couldn't compete in the new economy based on trade instead of land. They were afraid of becoming peasant farmers with houses they couldn't maintain, so they enforced their privileges until the rest revolted."

"Do you have any examples that *didn't* lead to a million deaths?" asked Mitchie.

Guo reached for his datasheet and started paging through the history database.

***

The mystery of the automated apartment tantalized the puzzle-solvers among Pintoy's stipend collectors. "Who is Juan Anders?" discussions popped up in every form of social media. The virtual person's history was fully documented, down to an image from a hospital maternity ward security camera.

Someone using the handle Wayne Searcher rose to the top of the investigators by proving the video was a duplicate of one from a Tiantan hospital ten years before Anders' supposed birth. "Fake from birth!" brought in more amateur investigators. The new wave were less willing to accept "too overwhelmed with requests to answer" from Anders' family, friends, and guild mates. They announced plans to physically contact people.

Unlike the first investigation, that didn't lead to videos of empty apartments. The curious stipend kids were arrested on charges of privacy violation, trespassing, and conspiracy to commit breaking and entering. Political conspiracy theorists proclaimed the arrests proof that the government was hiding something.

Mitchie's comment on this development was, "That might be the end of it. Now it's a movement of fools."

Guo shook his head. "No, it's too big now. They're just followers, saying out loud what other people are thinking. Oh, you'll love this rumor."

Mitchie looked at the manifesto he'd put on the wall. "What is this crap?"

"An elaborate proof that the falsified identities are the stalking horses for an AI infiltrating the Fusion's network. It finishes with a call for the physical destruction of all systems storing the records of fake citizens since they must be under the control of the AI." He let out a morbid laugh.

"Good God. That would lead to riots. Hell, lynchings. How far has it spread?"

"Not very. You're looking at my local copy. The Code Police took down the site I found it on. But to a conspiracy theorist . . ."

"That's just proof the AI is covering its tracks," she agreed. "What else is going on?"

"It looks like this is going to break out into the general population soon. There's a guy who used epidemiology models to project the spread of the ideas."

In a moment the display bore a three-dimensional model of the population as nodes and pools. Mitchie cut Guo's explanation short. "I trust you. Don't give me the math. If I try to understand that I won't have room for astrodynamics. How much time do we have?"

"Probably less than a week before the entire secret is out, I'm guessing."

"I'll see if Guen's free for lunch."

***

"Of course I'm free. Annie's not letting me go anywhere now. Come on over. We can watch some more *Magic Princess Journey*."

'Coming over' wasn't simple. Mitchie followed directions to dress in lower-class fashion and meet one of the bodyguards at a park near Guen's skyscraper. She almost didn't recognize him. She expected the downscale clothes. It was the stipend kid 'I'm bored forever' pose that made her overlook him.

When he stepped toward her Mitchie backed away warily.

"Ma'am?" He changed to soldier in a breath.

"Sorry, didn't recognize you. Woon, right?"

He nodded. "This way, please."

The park was ten times as crowded as any Fusion park Mitchie had seen before. Gaudily dressed stipend collectors stood in tight clusters arguing at the top of their lungs. They weren't all discussing the virtual people scandal. Mitchie heard complaints about fashion and games. *I guess with so many false identities exposed they're only comfortable talking face-to-face.*

Woon led her out of the park to the utility side of a skyscraper.

The bot access tunnels for the building were tight even for Mitchie. Woon had to be miserable but didn't make any complaints.

Guen welcomed her with hugs and meat pastries. The cartoon princess distracted them with monsters, grand vistas, and extended soliloquies about her feelings for the heir of a rival kingdom.

Mitchie didn't bring up the crisis. Her value as a friend was based on being the only person on the planet who wasn't working for Guen, wanting something from her, or being a possible agent of rival Fusion factions. Playing Disconnect ambassador would ruin that.

When the show faded to black on a cliffhanger (actually the handsome warrior released the princess's hand, lest he pull her over the edge with him) Guen turned toward the window. "I feel trapped."

"They're not letting you go anywhere?"

"We did an evacuation drill to the country place two nights ago. Other than that I'm staying here or the Dome. I'm almost hoping there'll be a contested vote on something."

"Aren't there any votes about the crisis?"

"Pfft. Nobody has any proposal with enough support to be voted on. Conscript them all. Tell all and apologize. Tell all and bribe them. Impose martial law and a curfew. The sims say none of them will work. Social Control predicts riots in a week."

"Guo saw a crowdsourced prediction that said the same thing. Didn't have any way to prevent it."

Guen looked out her glass wall overlooking the parks. From sixty floors up the city still looked peaceful. "I don't think we can prevent it. We need the riots to make the stakeholders and bureaucrats see sense. They're convinced they can save the secret and stay the way we were. It'll take a riot to break them out of that."

"What's going to stop the riots?"

Guen laughed. "Passing the Dynamist Party platform would make the proles happy. I don't know if they'd be happy enough to enlist."

"How much support do you have?"

"A tenth of Anglophones, maybe three percent of Sinophones. Uncontrolled change scares people."

"I didn't think you were as scary as burning down cities."

"You're not Chinese." Guen grabbed a fruit tart and nibbled on its edge.

Mitchie wished Guo had thought of a plan to fix the disaster. This would be the perfect time to pitch it to the Stakeholder. "Want to watch the next episode?"

"Sure!"

***

"Oh, shit!"

Mitchie told Setta, "I'll call you back." She'd wanted the crew's shore leave restricted as tensions increased. If the latest development was enough to make Guo curse Mitchie wanted to know the details before making a decision.

"What happened?" she asked him.

Guo put a diagram on the display wall. "The cops are so overwhelmed they're arresting people, leaving them tied up on the sidewalk, and going after the next group. Police movements are public record. A friend of this investigating crew cut them loose and they explored more apartments. Which let them finish this." He waved at the display.

"It's a family tree."

"Yes. And every single one of them doesn't exist. They also proved that for this generation—" a row of boxes turned red "—not a single one of the people in their elementary school classes are real."

"The dam's breaking."

"In two ways. Enough of the secret is out that they can find the rest. And the government can't control people, which encourages more to dig into it."

Mitchie skimmed through the top-level official news to check on the crime trends. Then she told her datasheet, "Setta."

The bosun's face appeared. "Yes, ma'am?"

"Is Hiroshi with you?"

Her husband leaned into view. "Here, ma'am."

"New standing orders. If you don't hear from me or the mate for twenty-four hours, try to contact us. If you can't get hold of us in twelve hours, get a full news dump and head back to the fleet. Report to Admiral Galen. Do not let anything stop you. Clear?"

Hiroshi's face was grim. "Clear, ma'am."

"Next. New shore leave rules. No less than four together. Everyone must have a firearm."

Setta said, "Ma'am, our weapons are illegal in the Fusion."

"I know. Don't let anyone be arrested. Use force if you have to and get back to the ship. It's Disconnect territory, they can't touch you there."

"It's getting that bad?"

"Soon. These people are getting ready to burn down police stations. I don't want any of our crew inside when they do."

"Yes, ma'am."

After giving Setta permission to stock up on supplies Mitchie ended the call.

"I'm surprised you're allowing shore leave at all," said Guo.

"I don't want to. But they'll go nuts if they're locked in. Giving the option will let them stay sane longer. Taking the fun out of it should keep them from going out too often."

Mitchie's datasheet played the Interstellar Relay jingle. She grabbed it and slapped the alert. "Finally!"

A synthesized voice said, "Dear customer. We regret to inform you that your three messages are still being held at the Sukhoi relay station. They will be sent via the next ship traveling to their destination."

"Shit." She flung the gadget against the wall.

Guo looked up from his book. "What?"

"I was hoping that was a message from Galen with some guidance on what to do about this mess."

"If there were lots of reinforcement convoys going through we wouldn't have come here."

***

The spaceport stores had everything on Setta's list, but wouldn't send it to the ship. "Deliverybots out of service." The autocab service said it would be a two or three hour wait for a ride.

"Who's up for a walk?" asked the bosun.

An hour later six spacers exited the store laden down with bags. If this place was going to hell so badly Setta wanted the freezers full. Her crew grumbled about the weight but they were still happy to be out of the ship. Dubois and Ye bickered a little over what tonight's dinner should be.

To save time she led them through a short-cut past the chandlery. Its lights were dimmed. They were hours past closing time. The storage lockers behind it had the quickest way to the pedestrian gate in the landing zone fence.

As they passed the third shed some scruffy figures walked out from the shadows. "Gah, Diskers. Whatcha got in the bags?"

Setta didn't slow down. "None of your business."

"Yeah?" said the leader. "I think I want a taste." The others spread out to block the path to the gate.

She stopped. Getting into arm's reach of them would be bad. "Ingredients. Nothing you'd know how to cook, prole."

"I like raw. And you're going to give me a kiss to apologize for being so rude."

"No, I won't." Setta's bags crunched as frozen vegetables landed on the pavement. She slid her hand into her jacket pocket.

"Better learn some manners, bitch." The leader produced a chain and started it swinging over his head in a whirring disc. The others drew knives and clubs.

Lethal weapon, theft, blocking movement, sexual threat, I think that adds up to justification. Setta pulled the pistol from her pocket and fired.

"Bitch!" The head thug slapped a hand to his belly. Boxes and cans clunked on the pavement as spacers freed their hands to draw weapons.

The other thugs cursed and stepped forward. Setta pointed her pistol in the air. "Boys and girls, this weapon holds fifteen bullets. I only needed one for him. Why don't you pick up your friend there and take him to the hospital?" The leader had fallen to his knees.

Instead of taking her advice they ran off. "Cowards."

The wounded thug fell onto his side. "Who's best at first aid?" asked Mthembu.

"Doesn't matter," snapped Setta. "None of us are touching him. Walk around, don't get any blood on you."

The trickle of blood from the thug looked black in the yellow security lights. It streamed toward the spaceport fence.

Finnegan picked up some of Setta's bags. Mthembu grabbed the rest.

"You don't have to take my share."

"Best you have your hands free, bosun," said Finnegan.

"Fine. Anyone hear a siren?" Their first night on Pintoy Setta had seen a fistfight outside a spaceport bar. The sirens had sounded before the fifth punch. Now the night was quiet.

"Come on." She led them past the body on the uphill side to keep their boots dry. Once past the sheds she spotted a hovering security bot. Setta waved the spacers toward the gate and walked toward the bot.

Once she was under it she waved her arms until the bot turned to face its main camera at her. "Hey! I just shot a guy! He's bleeding to death over there!"

Security bots had speakers to allow police operators to address anyone at the scene. This one stayed silent.

"Fuck." Setta shot the bot. It bounced twice on the pavement. "Maybe that'll make someone check out this area."

She trotted back to the gate. "Don't wait for me, dammit. Get back to the ship."

"What about that guy?" asked Mthembu.

"Ain't our planet. Ain't our problem."

Four Days Later

The hotel was emptying out as guests and staff found excuses to avoid the capital downtown. Mitchie and Guo took advantage of the privacy by vandalizing the cameras over the hot tub and pool. After several hours of thoroughly prohibited activities they staggered back to their suite to sleep.

They slept late. No debates were scheduled in the Council. Guen's security had convinced her to avoid visitors. And this was no time to play tourist, no matter how good Guo thought the museums were.

A rising series of beeps dragged Mitchie out of bed to shut up her datasheet. Guo muttered a protest.

"What the hell?" said Mitchie.

"Huh?"

"Message from Ping. One line of text. Marked high priority, urgent, Stakeholder business, maximum interrupt. He must've spent more time flagging it than writing it."

"What's it say?"

"Just 'Stay away from the Acropolis.' It's not like I go near there unless he invites me." She walked over to the window.

Guo watched her walk. This completely justified opening his eyes. "Damn."

When she didn't elaborate Guo joined her to see for himself. The ring park around the Acropolis was full of people. More were streaming in on foot.

Guo studied a small part of the park, then did some mental math to extrapolate. "That has to be over a hundred thousand people."

"At least," said Mitchie. "If someone said half a million I wouldn't doubt it."

He said "news" to the display wall. It became a mosaic of articles. "Let's see . . . our top story is hologram star Kimmie Z breaking her engagement because Rocko made bad jokes while she was in labor with their newborn. Top interstellar news is the Trade Board cutting the tariff on perishables by one point five per cent."

"Censorship?"

"Absolutely. Here's some real news. The Council of Stakeholders passed a conscription law this morning."

"There were no votes scheduled," said Mitchie. She picked up her datasheet.

Guo pulled up a summary of the new law. "Conscripts everyone arrested for trespassing, privacy infringement, restricted data accession . . . it's going after the people researching the false identities."

"Ping didn't vote for it," said Mitchie. "He wasn't even there. Guen was absent too." She skimmed through the list of votes. "Every Stakeholder I know by name missed the vote."

"DISPERSE." A distant shout came through the window. A security drone equipped with large sound projectors was drifting past the hotel. "RETURN TO YOUR HOMES. YOU ARE ORDERED TO DISPERSE." It repeated the command as it passed out of audible range.

They looked out at the park again. The incoming streams were thicker.

Now that they were looking for them dozens of drones were visible over the crowd. One folded in half and dropped into a tree.

"The cops are going to be pissed about that," said Mitchie.

"I think they have bigger problems." Guo braved the open net to look for the drone crash. The normal chaos of open discussion had become a maelstrom, without any time to sort facts from rumor from deception.

One video's popularity stood out. Guo played it on the wall.

A stipend kid in an orange shirt with teal collar tassels waved a rifle over his head. "I shut up that damn drone! And I'm going to shut more up." An inset played the video from the rifle's built-in camera of the bullet breaking the drone's spine. "I'm not going home. I'm not going anywhere until we get the truth."

"That kid isn't afraid of the cops," said Guo.

"No." Mitchie looked for other videos from the crowd. Was it a protest? They weren't waving signs. Not enough damage done to be a mob yet.

Though there was damage. Mitchie put a video on the wall. A subway car with its doors jammed open by chairs and park benches.

"Which station is that?" asked Guo.

"One of the ones just outside the Acropolis." She flicked through similar scenes. "It looks like they have all sixteen lines serving the Acropolis shut down."

"I wonder how many of the Stakeholders are still inside."

"Good question," she said. Though she only cared about one.

Guen answered the call promptly. "God, no. I wasn't invited to that disaster. Oh, are they still censoring it? Go read *Sausage Casings*, they have most of the facts. The Minister of Social Control made a quorum call, but he left out the faction leaders and committee chairs. He had a bare quorum, just backbenchers. His speech panicked the hell out of them and they passed his law. You can see the results."

"From our window," Mitchie agreed.

"You're still there? Better be packed. I'm, uh, can't say anything."

"I understand. Stay safe, Guen."

"You too!" The connection dropped.

Guo was packing. He produced two backpacks from one of his suitcases. He tossed the smaller one at Mitchie. The other he loaded with underwear, socks, and drab civilian clothes. His precious book went in a side pocket.

"I don't think I can fit my dress uniform into this."

Guo added some water bottles to his backpack. "In the course of a long life a wise man will be prepared to abandon his baggage many times."

"I don't think Confucius actually said that."

"No, but it's still good advice."

She started going through her own luggage. Civvies, underwear, and a spare jumpsuit went into the pack. A sharper-looking jumpsuit went on the coffee table along with three knives and a pistol. Guo was still sneaking glances at her as he sorted gear, so she put a bra and panties on the table instead of on her person.

The chaos on the display wall grew an island—a few related video feeds were gaining enough popularity to stand out. Guo expanded one to the whole wall. A double rank of riot-geared police marched down a street. The watching securitybot paced them. Their batons waved in threat. No one lingered to be hit, most fleeing into the cross streets to watch the marchers pass.

Mitchie studied the metadata along the edges of the image. "That's Golden Leaf Street." She moved to the window and checked a map on her datasheet. "I can see it. Not the whole thing, lots of buildings in the way. But it's obvious where the cops have cleared the road." After a minute she added, "There they go. I see them between two skyscrapers."

The action in the video feed matched what she could see of the distant specks. Convinced it was valid, Mitchie turned to the wall to watch the action.

The police formation was almost to the end of the street. Ahead of them it split into paved pathways spreading through a grassy portion of the ring park. Grass and pavement were hidden under the crowd. Thousands of people awaited the police.

The formation didn't slow as it marched into the open. A gazebo to the left disintegrated as young men pulled apart its balusters to make clubs. People shifted aside to avoid the batons, then moved behind as they passed.

"Refuse your flanks," muttered Mitchie. "Refuse your flanks."

Guo looked at her. "Are you rooting for the cops?"

"No. But I hate incompetence." She checked her map. "They're heading for the subway station. Guess they want to reopen it to evacuate the Acropolis."

"That explains the formations on the other radial roads. This one's made the most progress."

The overhead view disappeared as the securitybot died. Guo looked at the other feeds from the site. One was a hatcam labeled "Jozzy." He put it on the wall.

***

Jozzy had the best arm. His buds brought him stones and he threw them. A good throw would make a cop stumble. Most hits just bounced off their armor. A bounce still made the crowd clap and cheer. Girls were blowing Jozzy kisses.

He had to keep moving forward to keep up with the cops. His boys grabbed the rocks he'd already thrown and brought them back to him. Some strangers in the crowd were gathering rocks too.

The cops had two ranks of twenty-five men and three more behind them. The middle rear guy had a gold stripe circling his helmet. Jozzy aimed most of his throws at him.

The next throw was perfect. Just under the helmet, right on the back of his neck. Gold-stripe went to one knee and had to push himself back up with his big transparent shield. The crowd screamed in triumph.

A bare-breasted girl gave Jozzy a kiss on the lips. "Do it again!" she said.

A few second rank men looked back at their commander in concern.

"Eyes front!" yelled Goldstripe. "Keep your line straight!"

The crowd kept melting away in front of the marching cops. Then a couple dozen men in the crowd stood fast, bunched up around their leader. They lined up facing the police formation. Jozzy recognized them. Thun's Boys. Big, strong, nasty, and no sense of style.

Thun waved the top half of a lamppost at the cops. His boys all had weapons. The back of a park bench, metal handrails, a sapling with dirt still falling off the roots. They waved their clubs in the air and accused the cops of complicity in the great deception.

Even Goldstripe was silent as the formation marched up to the gang. Shields held overhead absorbed the long clubs' impacts. A couple of cops were knocked down. The rest moved past swinging batons. Each time a baton struck home there was a crackle of electricity and a truncated scream.

In a few breaths the formation was straightened out, marching on as twenty-some bodies lay in their wake.

A few twitched and groaned. Most lay still. Thun was obviously dead. A boot had crushed the side of his skull. Blood welled up in the tread marks.

Jozzy felt cold. Thun was an asshole, always had been, but he didn't deserve that. He dropped a rock and picked up the broken lamppost. "Boys!" he called out. "Grab a weapon. No more playing with these bastards."

He raised his voice. "Everybody! If you have a weapon come

forward. If you don't get out of the way! Move!"

The bare-breasted chick gave Jozzy a glowing look as she skipped back into the crowd.

Men with sticks and other things were coming forward. Jozzy waved them forward as he trotted to catch up with the formation.

More kept appearing. About forty men had matching white wood beams. Others pulled apart park benches. Jozzy kept trying to count them.

When a few more pushed his estimate over two hundred he thrust the lamppost straight up. "Brothers! Now we fight! Punish their lies! Punish their murders! Charge!"

Jozzy ran at Goldstripe.

The commander snapped, "Squad halt! About face!"

Goldstripe held his shield in front of him, sloped like a roof. Jozzy had used a polearm in the Struggle for Shaping virtual reality game. It wasn't his favorite weapon, but he'd learned some tricks.

Jozzy hooked the shattered lamp onto the edge of the shield and pulled.

Goldstripe staggered several paces forward before he could twist the shield out of Jozzy's grasp. Behind him three cops broke formation to rescue him.

Repeating the same move almost let Goldstripe land his baton on Jozzy's arm. Hammering on the shield didn't do any damage but distracted the boss cop enough for another rioter to club his knee. Goldstripe went down on his back.

Another cop leapt over his commander. His baton glanced off the lamppost and brushed Jozzy's arm.

An instant later Jozzy's head and heels were digging into the grass. He tried to fill his lungs to replace air lost to screaming. Amazingly, he was awake. The baton hadn't connected well or was running low on charge.

A boy in a lemon tunic scooped up the lamppost and yelled, "Liars!" as he charged the cops.

Jozzy struggled to prop himself on his elbows. That gave him a view of the battle.

Half the cops were still standing. They were back to back in two rough lines, proving their training was effective. Rioters pounded them with sticks or tried to pull their shields away. A few rioters wielded batons from fallen cops.

Someone found a pistol on a downed cop. He couldn't fire it well. Only half his shots hit cops. But every rioter who fell was replaced by two more. Wounded cops stayed down.

In a couple more minutes it was over.

* **

Guo closed the hatcam feed. Looking at a few others he said, "The other police units have halted."

Mitchie said, "It's officially a riot now."

Next Day

Two hours before dawn the mob was still chanting "Liars" loud enough to hear from the hotel. Mitchie glanced out the window. The bonfires were still burning. She wondered what they'd found to fuel them. The government cut power to the park after the police strike force was killed. Fire had substituted for the electric lights. But there couldn't be that much dead wood in the park.

She went back to perusing *Sausage Casings*. Guen was right, these guys had a much better grasp of reality than the official news services (still censored). A couple of their contributors were trapped inside the Acropolis.

They called it a siege. Video of dead rioters shot down by the security guards made Mitchie believe it. A rough census found over fifteen thousand bureaucrats and politicians in the structure, including a bare quorum of the Council of Stakeholders.

No one had the presence of mind to impose rationing on the cafeterias. *Sausage Casings* had a page with the latest black-market prices for hamburgers (only triple pre-Siege prices), crackers (in demand among those expecting a long stay), and whiskey (not quite its weight in gold).

Rumors said support staff defecting to the mob had equal chances of being accepted or beaten to death.

Guo woke from his nap. He took a moment to appreciate Mitchie's datascreen-lit figure before asking, "Any changes?"

"No. I'm amazed it's gone on this long. Back home we'd have orbital artillery taking out the mob followed by hardsuited infantry."

Guo stared at the bonfires. "If these people could make a decision they wouldn't be in this mess."

The Acropolis glowed at every window. The light it shed probably lit more of the ring park than the fires. Then it went dark.

Mitchie and Guo grabbed for their datasheets. He found a gloat, stipend kids posting video of themselves taking out the power and data feeds to the Acropolis one by one.

Sausage Casings confirmed it. One of their inside men had expected this. A military-grade comm unit let him send out text. His only news was panic among the occupants.

Mitchie thought she could have guessed that. She lay down for her nap.

When she woke the sun was high. Plumes of smoke dotted the park. She guessed they were burning green wood.

Guo extracted brunch from room service. Mitchie was amazed it still functioned. They tipped heavily. Leftovers went into the suite fridge for dinner.

Around noon Mitchie noticed movement in the park. "There are people moving toward the Acropolis. Anything in the feeds?"

"No," said Guo from the display wall. "But with the shutdown only people on the outer edge of the park can link anything."

"Wish I'd grabbed the telescope from the ship."

Her naked eye was sharp enough to recognize people climbing up the 45-degree slope of the Acropolis' outer rim. Their goal was the terraces providing leafy lunch spots for the office workers. Presumably they hoped to by-pass the armed guards at the official entrances.

They looked like foraging ants at this distance. When a scout found an opening the swarm converged on it. Then a thick rope of reinforcements formed, drawing more rioters out of the mass in the park.

Mitchie's datasheet chimed. One of her alerts had triggered. *Sausage Casings* had a new report from their inside man. "Rioters in the Acropolis. Security counter-attacking. Can hear gunfire and grenades."

"Bad place to use grenades," muttered Guo.

"Friendly fire?" asked Mitchie.

"No. The whole thing is built of carbon weave. If the fire suppression system is down any fire will spread."

Two hours later a video of the fighting appeared on the net. The uploader claimed he'd walked out of Ring Park after his arm was broken by Acropolis Security.

The beginning showed rioters spreading ant-style into the building. Any staffers encountered were clubbed down, or taken aside for worse treatment. A trio of security guards emptied their guns at the rioters, then charged with batons.

The video after that was chaotically cut. Running from Security. Assaulting a barricade defended by maintenance and cafeteria workers. Overwhelming a Security patrol by sheer numbers. Setting fires for smokescreens or to block a flank. Looting fancy offices. Another brawl with Security—the one where the cameraman was injured.

Mitchie turned back to the window. Trickles of smoke were coming from a dozen terraces.

"It's started," she said.

By sunset smoke plumes rose from all around the Acropolis' perimeter. They left the lights off in their suite so they could make out faint lights. There were fewer bonfires in the park tonight. Some of the tree-filled terraces were burning. Some of the windows had red flickers behind them.

Rumbling stomachs reminded them to eat. Guo didn't bother heating up his leftovers. He sat on the couch poking at an egg with his fork.

"Hey." Mitchie leaned against him. "Don't feel so bad. It's not our problem."

He laid the fork on the plate and wrapped an arm around her. "Yes it is. We're supposed to bring back a few hundred warships. That's not going to happen if a civil war breaks out here."

She could feel him relaxing as she pressed her skin against his. "It's not going to be a war. Any minute now the Marines will show up, evacuate the Stakeholders, and kill all the rioters."

"Yeah? Why didn't they do that already?"

"It's the Fusion. They had to have all their committee meetings."

That brought a bitter chuckle from him.

They cuddled on the couch. Mitchie prodded Guo to finish his meal. Sleep was reaching out for them when a yellow flash caught their eyes.

From the couch only the upper third of the Acropolis was visible through the window. It had been dimly reflecting the lights of kilometer-distant skyscrapers. Now a brighter light brought out the decorative mosaic along the tower.

Mitchie and Guo dashed to the window. Terraces high on the Acropolis' steep slope vented gouts of yellow flames. Swarms of fleeing ants showed clearly in the light. Windows higher in the structure glowed.

They could track the spread of the fire in the windows. The base was completely engulfed. The flames marched slowly up the tower.

A stone panel separated from the tower as its connectors turned to ash. The perimeter flames illuminated it as it spun down. It smashed through the roof, releasing a burst of flame and smoke.

Flames poured out of the hole it left behind. More panels followed.

Two hours later the flames were at the top. The clear dome was dark in the night. Now a yellow glow illuminated the dome from within.

"Oh, God," moaned Guo. "They're trapped there."

The flames silhouetted ant figures rushing along the edge of the dome.

Mitchie laughed.

"They're dying," said Guo.

"Good," she answered. "Stakeholders deserve to burn. I watched as we poured Derry's urn into the grave. There was more of his spacesuit than of him. The Stakeholders voted for it. They can burn."

"What about everybody else in there?"

"Accomplices." Mitchie kept watching the fire. As a curtain of flame hid the dome she laughed again.

Guo backed up to the edge of the window. He looked back and forth between the fire and his wife with equal horror on his face.

Chapter Three: Ashes

Capitol City, Planet Pintoy, gravity 9.4 m/s^2

The Acropolis' skeleton was black in the noon sun. The Dome survived, dull black with soot. Sixty-four diamondoid beams descended from it, straight down as the tower had been, then curving toward horizontal as they reached the base's perimeter.

The layer of ash underneath looked paper-thin but was many meters thick with bits of bone and metal. Wisps of smoke still rose from the ash.

The mob surrounding it was quiescent. Victory dancers had mostly fallen asleep. Some had left. Many were searching the crowd for friends who'd been caught in the fire.

Mitchie's datasheet played the *Magic Princess Journey* theme music. She leapt out of bed to grab it, but held it up to her face before answering. "Yes, Guen?"

"Hi, have you—sorry, is this a bad time?" Guen's face turned red.

Mitchie about-faced. She'd just shown *far* too much of Guo to her friend. "No, we're just sleeping in. What's up?"

"Have you heard from Ping?"

"Not since this all started."

"We're trying to organize a committee to restore order. Ping promised he'd be there. A bunch walked out when he didn't show. His flunky just promises to have him call me. Can you go bang on his door?" An address popped up at the bottom of her image.

"Sure."

"Thanks!" Guen ended the call.

"Did I just flash a Stakeholder?" asked Guo.

"You should be honored. Given Uncle John, her father, and the current security crew I bet that's the first penis she's seen in her entire life."

"I have enough problems without a Stakeholder imprinting on me."

"You have my permission to show it to Ping. Let's get in the shower."

Fifteen minutes later they were washed, dressed, armed, and exiting their building. Ping's Capitol apartment was in a skyscraper less than two klicks west of their hotel. The road between them had a mix of greenspace and shops, both nearly empty.

A few gaudily-dressed youngsters seemed to be looking for trouble, but the two Diskers weren't the kind they wanted.

Ping's building had an actual human guarding the entrance. He looked up as Mitchie shoved on the locked door. "Authorized access only."

Mitchie said, "This is Combined Fleet business. Open up." Her jumpsuit was the Space Guard undress uniform. It had enough stripes and decorations to make it clear she was military, especially with Guo wearing a matching outfit.

"You need an invite from a resident." The guard sat in a clear booth. It had a small opening for passing in forms or cards. It was more than wide enough for Mitchie's pistol.

"Don't you dare! You're being recorded!" yelled the guard as he pressed against the back of the booth.

"Ten thousand people were just murdered with the whole world watching and the police didn't do a thing. You think they'll care about you? Besides, Combined Fleet orders override civilian law. It's perfectly legal for me to kill you in the line of duty."

The door popped open.

Once they were in the elevator Guo said, "You used to be more subtle than that."

"You don't like those methods. And I was in a hurry."

"Just let me do the talking next time." He hitched up his tool belt. "I'm sure they need something fixed."

Ping's apartment took up a quarter of the 48th floor. The door chime brought the voice of a flunky. "I'm sorry, the Stakeholder is not receiving visitors. I'll be happy to take a message for him."

"This is Commander Long on Combined Fleet business. Open up."

"I'm afraid I can't do that."

Guo's hand caught Mitchie's just above her holster.

"Let me," he said.

A pouch on the opposite side of the tool belt from the hammer produced a plastic box with metal rods tucked into its underside. Guo unfolded them and touched them gently to the door jamb. Pressing the big red button caused a pop and a whiff of smoke.

"Fusion fire safety regulations require all locks to fail open," he said. He pushed open the door and waved Mitchie in.

The flunky was elegantly robed in Traditionalist style. His flusterment would have drawn severe criticism from any Confucian Revival master. "You can't come in here! The Stakeholder isn't seeing anyone. He's ill. You must leave!"

The front room was finely appointed with cushions, seats, and tables set out for conversation groups and individual meditations. The walls held ancient artworks spaced far enough apart to let each one be admired without distraction from the others. Guo recognized one as a calligraphed rendition of a Warring States Era poem.

Two carved wooden arches decorated doorways leading farther into the apartment. Mitchie chose the left.

The flunky scurried to block her way. Her boot flicked out. The flunky fell to the floor, clutching his knee and screaming.

"Shut up," she said.

The screams became whimpers.

The apartment didn't take long to search. Two secretaries and a legislative aide were herded back to join the flunky. Despite the many comfortable servant quarters there were no cooks, maids, or valets.

Mitchie focused on the aide. "Hong, isn't it?"

"Yes," said the young man. "And I know who you are. The Stakeholder told us all about you." He tried to be defiant but his voice quavered on the end of it.

"Good. That saves us some time. Where is the Stakeholder?"

"None of us will tell you anything." Hong looked up at the chandelier to avoid meeting Mitchie's eyes.

She stepped forward and stood tip-toe to whisper in his ear. "You know what I can do. You know what I will do. You're going to talk. So why be miserable when it won't change anything?"

Hong swallowed. Looked at his feet. Looked at the prone flunky, still whimpering. "He's not here."

"I figured that out already."

"He left yesterday morning. He wouldn't tell me where he was going. Said it was better if I didn't know."

The secretaries showed a mix of anger and relief at this confession. Mitchie decided he was telling the truth. "Fine. Y'all sit over there."

Guo spread his datasheet out on a table and began some searches.

Mitchie called Guen to break the news. The young stakeholder was getting better at using profanity. *I guess I'm a bad influence.* After venting Guen used her as a sounding board for who else could represent the Traditionalists on the Order Committee.

"Ha! Got him," said Guo.

"We might be able to catch him," said Mitchie. "But get the other guys anyway." She disconnected and stepped over to Guo's table. "What?"

"The gossip channels are still going. Someone saw Ping boarding a torchship." Guo played a video of Stakeholder Ping walking up a gangway.

"Yep, that's him."

He typed some more. "That ship lifted last night for Sukhoi."

Mitchie promptly called Hiroshi.

"Yes, ma'am?" he answered.

"Anyone on shore leave?"

"No, we're all on board."

"Good. Prep for launch and a high acceleration run."

"Yes, ma'am."

"I'm heading back with the Mate. I want to lift as soon as I'm in my couch."

"Aye-aye."

The autocabs weren't operating. Mitchie and Guo walked half an hour before finding someone who could be hired to take them to the spaceport. Riding in the backseat gave them time to think.

Guo asked, "Why are we chasing him?"

"Orders," answered Mitchie. "We're supposed to bring him back."

"Since when do you let orders run your life?"

She looked out the window. The robotic factories passing by offered no change of topic. "It's what's left."

"Mmmm?"

Mitchie met his eyes. "I have my revenge. I have true love. We have more money than we know what to do with. I have a ship of my own. That's everything I've ever wanted. So I might as well obey orders. I don't have any reason not to."

Guo pulled her in for a snuggle.

Slightly muffled by his shoulder, she said, "Besides, Ping is such an asshole any plan he comes up with we should wreck on general principles."

He laughed. "I'll go along with that."

The port did have autocabs running within the fence.

"It's good to be home," said Mitchie as she climbed the cargo hold ladder.

"Agreed," said Guo from a few rungs below.

Hiroshi was on the radio with Traffic Control when Mitchie entered the bridge.

"This is a Combined Fleet mission. We are launching. So divert your damned traffic or we will blow your shipload of orphans to hell."

He waited a few moments.

"Thank you, Control. *Joshua Chamberlain* acknowledges clear for immediate launch." He switched to PA. "Up ship!"

Fifteen gravs pushed Mitchie firmly into her couch. "Orphans?"

"From the chatter I overheard it was a tanker hauling plastics feedstock. I was going for intimidation value." Hiroshi thought a moment. "You're a bad influence."

Mitchie laughed. "If you're tired of me we should get you a command of your own."

"And miss out on all the excitement of this ship? Never."

Her tone turned more serious. "You're more experienced than a lot of destroyer skippers. If you're willing to work a Bonny ship I could probably swing you a light cruiser."

"I appreciate the confidence, ma'am. But warship commanders

have to sleep alone."

"There's that." She was stretching the regs to operate *Joshua Chamberlain* as a civilian ship. Technically she should have been declared an auxiliary.

"So what is the excitement?"

"We need to catch the freighter *Zhang Jue* before it reaches the Sukhoi gate."

Joshua Chamberlain, Pintoy System, acceleration 15 m/s^2

"Merchant Ship *Zhang Jue*, cut thrust and prepare to be boarded," Mitchie transmitted. "This is an order from the Combined Fleet."

"Negative, *Jay Cee*," answered the other freighter's radioman. "We have too much velocity to transit the gate. Safety requires us to maintain deceleration."

"You can hand over Stakeholder Ping and still have enough time to reach safe velocity. Cut thrust." She glared at the other ship. It was clearly visible a few klicks away. She'd managed to match vectors without even pluming it, which had been an impressive demonstration for her pilots.

The *Zhang Jue* didn't answer. Mitchie ordered, "Cut thrust or you will be fired upon."

Still no answer. She turned off the microphone with a curse.

Co-pilot Mthembu said, "Um, ma'am? We don't have any ship-to-ship weapons."

"Some of our defensive toys are multi-purpose, coxswain." Mitchie activated the PA. "Captain to Mate. Take out their torch."

In the cargo hold Guo supervised as three spacers hauled a countermissile into the airlock. It was nearly as long as they were, narrow enough for a hand to wrap around it, and still heavy enough to need all three. When it leaned against the outer hatch Guo said, "Finnegan, keep it in position. Rest of you, out."

Guo stepped into the airlock and closed the inner hatch. When the air was too thin to talk he leaned his helmet against Finnegan's. "Keep it braced, I'm opening the hatch."

Zhang Jue posed against the stars in the open hatchway, balanced on its torch plume. Guo tapped on the countermissile's control display until it acknowledged its target. "Finnegan, I'm taking the bird. You take the hatch. As soon as the bird is clear, slam it."

The mechanic nodded, the gesture clumsy in his spacesuit. As Guo took the weight of the countermissile Finnegan let go. He wrapped one hand around a bracket in the airlock, the other took the hatch's handle.

Guo keyed his radio. "Cut thrust." Suddenly he weighed a tenth what he normally did. His muscles protested as he sent the countermissile out with a mighty heave.

CLANG. SLAP. The airlock hatch closed an instant before the countermissile's plume blasted *Joshua Chamberlain's* hull.

"Oh, God, I hope I don't ever have to do that again," said Finnegan.

Guo laughed. "Kid, if you wanted to be safe, you asked for the wrong ship."

"I didn't ask for it. Chief said, 'A freighter needs a new mechanic, grab your duffle.'"

"Tough."

The bridge had a clear view of the countermissile. All Mitchie saw was a blue streak connecting the ships. The other ship was rising above her as it continued to thrust.

It hit the outer ring of *Zhang Jue's* torch. The blue flame turned green and orange as fragments of metal burned in the plasma. The curtain of flame parted as nozzles ceased to fire, spinning the wounded ship with asymmetric thrust.

Mitchie braced for the partial plume to sweep over the *Joshua Chamberlain*, but the torch cut off as the ship was halfway through the first rotation. *Yay for automatic cutoffs*, she thought. Her ship needed mechanics to turn valves to shut down a damaged torch.

The comm box squawked with outrage. "You've killed us! You killed us all! Oh, God, we're dead."

She lifted her mike. "*Zhang Jue*, take the spin off your ship and prepare to abandon. We will take on all survivors."

"What survivors? We're going to overspeed the gate! We're doomed!"

"There's plenty of time to decelerate. Get the spin off and get everyone into bubbles so we can pick you up."

The crippled ship's thrusters fired, reducing the spin. Mitchie brought *Joshua Chamberlain* closer.

When the ship stabilized Mitchie ordered, "Get everyone into bubbles or suits. Open your upper airlock. We'll come get you."

By the jaded standards of Mitchie's crew it was an easy retrieval. Spacer Ye took a line over and hooked all of them up to it. An easy tug had them drifting into *Joshua Chamberlain's* cargo hold. As soon as the hold doors were closed Hiroshi fired the torch for a standard ten gravs.

Mitchie led the reception committee in the hold. The one in a spacesuit was a mechanic. His arms were vacctaped to his sides. Mitchie checked the bubbles until she found the captain. She unzipped it and dumped him onto the deck.

"Why aren't you accelerating?" he demanded. "We'll die if we hit the gate at this rate."

Mitchie squatted down to look him in the eye. "Do you know who I am?"

He gasped. "You're Michigan Long, the torturer and spy."

"Close enough. For some other introductions, this is Bosun's Mate Setta. She's killed three men with that pistol. One took days to die. The guy with the hammer is Senior Chief Kwan. He crushes skulls. So if you don't tell me what I want to know you're going to suffer. If you annoy me enough you go out the airlock in your bubble. Clear?"

A spastic nod.

"Good. Where is Stakeholder Ping?"

"I don't know."

"Wrong answer."

"I really don't! He, he came on board, made sure people saw him do it. Then he got into a crate and was offloaded with some of our cargo. He didn't lift with us."

Mitchie glared at him.

"He didn't! I swear!"

"Don't piss yourself, we've had enough of that already." She straightened up.

"You believe him, Captain?" asked Guo.

"Yep. It's Ping's kind of trick. Setta, get these guys some cushions for the hard boost."

Setta waved her deckhands forward. "We're set, ma'am."

Mitchie called the bridge on her handcomm. "Can we get enough side vector to miss the gate and stay in-system?"

"Fuck, no. Uh, ma'am," blurted Hiroshi.

"Right. Take us to forty gravs as soon as we have the prisoners secured. I'll be up in a few minutes."

"Don't have time for that, ma'am." The pilot switched to the PA. "All hands, secure for high acceleration in thirty seconds."

In thirty seconds Mitchie would still be climbing up the ladder to the main deck. She cursed.

"Here you go, ma'am," said Setta. She pulled the cord on a box and stepped back as it expanded into an acceleration mattress.

"Thanks."

Guo was already in his. "So back to Pintoy after we jump?" he asked.

Mitchie lay down. "Maybe. I have to think through his options and see if we might be able to cut him off in another system."

***

The roar of the torch went silent. Instead of three people lying on top of her Mitchie felt herself float.

Hiroshi's voice came over the PA. "All hands, we are safely in the Sukhoi System."

The prisoners traded expressions of relief and complaints about their captors.

Mitchie's handcomm chirped. "Yes?"

"Where to, Skipper? Back to Pintoy?"

"No. Head for the Dirac gate. I think this shell game means Ping is planning something fancy. So he'll head for Tiantan. It's the base of his movement. Pick a station. We'll dock there and check traffic records."

She looked around at the prisoners. "And it'll give us a chance to offload our guests."

Capitol City, Pintoy, gravity 9.4 m/s^2

"Where the hell are they?" demanded Stakeholder Vones.

"I took an evasive route to get here," replied Guen. "So did the rest of us. We've already heard stories about having to double back to avoid a pack of rioters." She waved at a pair of Stabilist stakeholders. "I'd expect someone to be delayed. This is exactly the sort of chaos we're meeting to put a stop to."

Murmurs of approval went around the room. Vones threw up his arms theatrically and went back to sit with his Structuralist comrades.

Guen hid a sigh of relief. *I can't keep them together much longer. Everyone's too nervous.*

Annie appeared in the doorway. Guen's chief bodyguard pinched her chin to indicate urgent news. It would have worked better as a private signal if all thirty-some stakeholders hadn't turned to stare at her.

"What's the news, Annie?" said Guen.

Annie stood at attention. "Ma'am. Honorable Stakeholders. I regret to inform you that Stakeholders Singh, Martinez, and Chang have been killed."

"How solid is this information?"

"The murderers uploaded video of the deaths."

"Let's see it," demanded Vones.

Annie looked to Guen, who gave a confirming nod. She activated the conference room's display.

The video opened on a kaleidoscopic group of stipend kids. Someone yelled, "Hey, I know that guy!" The camera swung to track a dozen men in suits running from one alley across the boulevard to another. The crowd stampeded toward them.

Two suits stopped in the opening of the alley as the rest ran. They disappeared under a pile of bodies. The camera went past them with the baying mob. The running suits made it two blocks before encountering a different band of stipend kids. Fear and fancy dress attracted predators like flies to sugar water. The men went down under stomping boots. By the time the camera wielder forced his way in for close-ups stakeholders and bodyguards were indistinguishable.

"That's it," said someone. "I'm going to my country house."

"Country hell," snapped Vones. "I'm getting off this planet."

In a minute Guen was the only one sitting in the room.

"Orders, Miss?" said Annie.

Guen wiped her eyes. "You were right. This was a bad idea. I don't know what to do now."

Annie waited patiently.

"Okay. Let's get out of here. Find a safe place."

Annie nodded. "Have to move before one of those fools leads the mob back here. Then we need to get you some clothes."

The stakeholder looked down. She'd chosen this dress to look more mature to the other politicians. The black silk was fully opaque but slinked across her curves in a way that was very revealing in the right light. In any light it was something no stipend kid could afford.

The other bodyguards came in at Annie's call. They changed into their outer perimeter gear, clothes designed to blend in with office workers or tourists. None of their outfits would fit Guen. Even the shortest bodyguard was a hand taller than her.

Annie shook her head. "You're dressed exactly like the kind of people who are staying off the streets now. We all need to look like we're in the stipend set."

"Any stores nearby?" asked Roger.

A couple others laughed. "The nearest one like that is probably ten klicks from downtown," said Woon.

"We'll just have to scavenge what we can. If you see someone your size pass the word and we'll cut them out of the herd." Annie briefed the team on tactics for moving dispersal. "Memorize the key points on this map. We can't pick a route. Things are too unpredictable. Our goal is the safe house here. If we're broken up the rally point is the gazebo in Doolittle Park. Alternate refuge point is this apartment building. It's one of Social Control's ghost warehouses. There should be a reaction squad based there. If we see transportation that can take the Stakeholder out of the city we grab it. Any questions?"

"If we see a stipend kid wearing puce, I have dibs," said Woon.

No questions interrupted the laughter.

"Ma'am, any words?"

Guen could only manage, "Thank you all."

Annie wanted to use 'disaster tourists' as their cover. Guen tried to act the part by being fascinated by damage instead of horrified. It was harder to ignore her guards as they went past, jogging or strolling ahead then loitering until the pair passed them.

More than half the guards were out of sight at any one time. This made sense. They were watching out for trouble. Moving independently kept them from being associated with Guen. But it felt lonely. Very lonely. She was used to being surrounded when out in public. This felt naked.

The stores had been looted. Or maybe just vandalized. All windows were broken. Merchandise lay in the street as if looters had become bored with their booty less than a block after taking it.

Annie twitched. "Don't react. Just got bad news. Be ready to run."

Guen looked around. Nothing had changed. There was some shouting in the distance. She stopped to wait for Annie as she fiddled with some jewelry lying on the sidewalk.

"Here, take this." Annie slipped three sparkly bracelets onto Guen's wrists. "It's fashionable."

Only true by stipend kid standards. Guen thought they were cheap and flashy. *But I guess that makes them good camouflage.*

Some people, stipend kids by their dress, ran around the corner, panting with fatigue. "Pee-kays! Pee-kays!"

"Player killer" was virtual reality slang for someone who attacked other players in the game. The label had been hung on those who used the collapse of order to let them murder, rape, or otherwise abuse other lower-class folk instead of just members of the government.

Annie burst into a run, yanking painfully on Guen's arm to drag her along.

Guen stumbled. They'd changed direction, heading toward Doolittle Park instead of the safe house.

Annie added to the "Pee-kay" shouts.

Woon's voice came from behind them. "You think you're tough? Who's up for some one on one? Who's a tough guy? You? Think you're tough without that iron bar?"

Annie kept them running too fast to look back.

Doolittle Park swarmed with stipend kids. A band played vector baroque in the gazebo. Hundreds of nude dancers gyrated around them.

Shouting "PK" brought tall armed men running.

"Fuck that! This is our park!" shouted the biggest. "Where are they?"

Annie pointed. She didn't need to. The PK mob approached with bloody weapons. The big defender ordered his men into a line.

The PKs smashed the formation. Fighting spread all over the park.

Annie cursed. She dragged Guen to a public restroom. "In here." She shoved Guen into a stall. "Lock it, then put your feet on the seat. Crouch down. Don't let yourself be visible. I'll get you some safer clothes."

Then she left Guen alone.

Guen waited. She decided she was stuck here until the riot died down or her surviving bodyguards figured out a way to get her out. Heavy feet clomped into the room. Probably a man. She tensed.

"Put this on," said Roger. Oh, good, he was still alive. Some clothes came over the door.

She stripped out of her thousand-key dress. It was trash now, the mob would kill anyone wearing something that fancy. The wad of clothes she caught included some underwear, fortunately stretchy. The pants didn't stretch. They were the latest fashion in the stipend set, shiny polymer fabric studded with metal stars. Exhaling, tensing muscles, and pulling hard on the belt loops let her pull them up to her hips. Her thighs were painfully compressed. The lower half of the legs was slashed into ribbons, dangling to her ankles. Metal mirrors at the end of each ribbon tickled her shins. She hoped she could walk in this without it cutting her. Roger hadn't tossed over any boots.

Roger led her to the rally point. Everyone had changed. Some of the clothes had blood on them. Annie must have mugged a man for her outfit. The scarlet shoulders had black metal spikes on them.

The fight with the PKs was over. Guen couldn't tell who'd won. Dead and bleeding bodies were everywhere. Even the walking wounded hadn't been bandaged.

Woon and three others were missing. Annie said, "This is everyone now. We're going north through the park. Bounding overwatch flanking primary pair. Move."

The bodyguards slouched off.

Annie and Guen started strolling.

They passed the gazebo. Smashed instruments surrounded it. Dead dancers made a ring outside them. The survivors must have dressed. No one in sight was nude.

"Hey, I know you."

Annie muttered, "Look down," and walked a little faster.

"I know you! I do."

The stranger was coming closer.

"You—you're a Stakeholder! Everybody, the blonde girl is a Stakeholder!" She was shouting loud enough to get attention through the crowd.

Annie looked around at the converging crowd. "Dammit. We're fucked."

The other bodyguards recalled into a defensive ring. It made a nice visual confession of Guen's status.

Guen made a snap decision. "I'll talk to them. I need a platform."

A lamppost was the only option. Roger stood next to it and made a stirrup of his hands.

A quick boost put Guen halfway up the lamppost. The decorative ring held her feet while she clutched the top. The movement attracted even more of the mob than the hostile ring confronting her bodyguards.

"Good people! I was a Stakeholder! But now I'm a revolutionary like you! I found out their lies and I reject them!" She projected her voice firmly. Any quaver would mark her as a victim. Speeches in Council had given her practice in talking to hostile crowds but this one was different. As she extemporized on the evils of the Fusion's government she threw in all the stipend-kid slang she could remember. Fortunately her Demeter accent didn't sound like Pintoy's upper class. She let her vowels blur instead of trying to make them crisp, the opposite of how she'd talk in Council.

Her rhetoric fell on eager ears. Confirmation that they were right to riot, proof of their suspicions, and denunciation of their enemies soothed the void in their souls. Applause, cheers, and echoes of her key phrases filled the air.

All that was left of their needs was leadership. When they called on her Guen answered, certain that denying them anything was death for her and her people. When they asked for a target she gave them Social Control's apartment building.

Roger guided her onto his shoulders. Most of the mob followed her. Some ran ahead. When she arrived at the building it was already a battleground. The Ministry had sent staffers there to hide. Now they were being flung out of tenth-story windows. The mob cheered and chanted Guen's name.

Hebe Station, Dirac System. Centrifugal acceleration 5 m/s²

After a week of extra shifts as prisoner guards the crew enjoyed being released for shore leave. Hebe Station was barren compared to Pintoy, but it wasn't work and no one wanted to kill them.

Not even the ex-prisoners. After finding the local law unwilling to intervene in a 'political' matter *Zhang Jue's* crew sought berths on whatever ships were leaving soonest.

Mitchie and Hiroshi used the station library to analyze the list of ships entering the Dirac System from Pintoy. *Shuai Xi* stood out.

"No stops between the gates. No public flight plan. And the timing's right," said Mitchie.

Hiroshi looked up from his datasheet. "It's also owned by Tall Mountain. That's his cousin's corporation."

"Right. Let's get everyone back aboard and chase it down."

Capitol City, Pintoy, gravity 9.4 m/s²

There hadn't been a food delivery to Doolittle Park in two days.

Everyone was cranky.

Guen tried to boost morale by wandering about and chatting with people. Hunger left her too weak. After walking a quarter of the park she went back to their gazebo and collapsed on a bench.

Not many other people were standing up. Even the perimeter guards let their sticks and pipes rest on the ground. Most weren't even sitting. They just laid on the ground.

One young man was fiddling with a datasheet and some other boxes. Guen couldn't see the point. When she turned on her datasheet it just said "NETWORK VERIFICATION NOT FOUND—OPERATION PROHIBITED" and turned off again.

The tinkerer let out a whoop. "It works!"

A friend next to him sat up. "Do you have news? Is food coming?"

"I'm looking. There's no net. Not much message traffic. All I'm finding is military."

Two young women ran over to him. "Are they going to help us? Are the Marines coming?"

"I'm not finding anything yet. Wait." He kept tapping on the datasheet. "Here's something. General Order: All naval and Marine units are to remain in their bases until orders are received from responsible civilian authorities."

"They're not going to help us?"

"Sorry, no."

The dejected women wandered back to their blankets.

An older man walked up as the tinkerer kept typing. He waved a datasheet. "How did you get a connection? Mine says the network still isn't working."

"Oh, it isn't. I have some connection units programmed to simulate the network permission signal. That let my datasheet function. I'm trying to find out what is working."

"That's an unmonitored computer?" The man's voice rose.

"Well, yes," said the tinkerer. "But it's perfectly safe. If—"

The big man's muddy boot caught the tinkerer in the ribs. "You bastard! We have all these problems and you want to bring a Betrayer down on us!"

The shouting brought more people over.

Big man's accusations made them angry.

Tinkerer gasped out an explanation that made things worse.

"Think he's working for a Betrayer?" asked someone in the crowd.

Another answered, "Careless or traitor, he's just as dangerous."

The tinkerer's friend jumped up. "Hey, he's just trying to help."

Fists silenced him.

The boxes attached to the datasheet were stomped into pieces.

Guen stood up—or tried. Annie's hand on her shoulder pushed her back down to the bench.

"I have to do something, or they're going to hurt him," said Guen.

Annie said, "It's too late."

Someone had found a ten meter long cable. The crowd dragged the tinkerer and his friend toward some lampposts.

Guen whispered, "I just wanted to help."

"So did he. Look where it got him."

Joshua Chamberlain, Danu System, acceleration 10 m/s^2

"All hands, successful jump. Prepare for high acceleration in thirty minutes." Mitchie put down the mike. She'd take a break for personal needs herself but first she wanted to make sure they were on the correct course.

Hiroshi reported, "Nav box has our location. Producing a vector for the Yalu gate. And . . . we're inside the error cone. Need to run for a bit before we can do any corrections."

The navigation computer retrofitted to the bridge had precise sensors, but *Joshua Chamberlain* was still flown by hand. Trying to make tiny corrections would just waste fuel in repeated overshoots. Mitchie wasn't worried about it. Wasting a few percent of the delta V budget on large corrections was the price of being an analog ship, and they had plenty of fuel and reaction mass on board.

Mthembu babysat the comm box. It worked well enough as an independent system if someone could tell it "give up and start over" occasionally.

"I have a news dump from the relay buoy," he said.

"Shipping status?" asked Mitchie.

"Sent the request. May have to get it all the way from Traffic Control Central." He fiddled with the box's screen. "Huh. *Shuai Xi* is in the news dump."

An announcer's voice came on in mid-sentence. "—leaving the Steeplechasers in an excellent position to win the Planetary Cup. In racing news, a new space speed record has been set for the Danu System. The luxury yacht *Shuai Xi* reached a speed of four point three eight percent of lightspeed, breaking the old record of four point oh three set by *Shining Hermes* twenty-three years ago."

"Gosh, Bill," said another voice. "Is there a race going on this week I didn't know about?"

"Nope. When we asked why the rush *Shuai Xi's* captain replied, 'Sometimes you just have to stretch out her legs.'"

Both laughed.

"I'd hate to try stretching my legs at forty gravs," said the second voice.

Mthembu cut off the recording as they moved on to a player's contract negotiations. "Forty gravs?" he asked. "Can they handle that for day after day?"

"If they have hydraulic couches, yes," said Hiroshi. "Much better support than these things."

"And if they can afford that they can afford the best high-grav drugs," said Mitchie. The drugs strengthened the walls of blood vessels to keep them from rupturing under higher pressure. The run through Argo had already made a dent in *Joshua Chamberlain's* military-issue supply.

She activated the PA. "All hands, we are discontinuing high acceleration. Rest of cruise will be at ten gravs. That is all."

"You think he's deliberately evading us, ma'am?" asked Hiroshi.

"If he set up a decoy at his apartment and a decoy ship he's serious about not being followed. It wouldn't be much extra effort to have a spy send word ahead about a pursuing ship."

"So he'll get to Tiantan a week or two ahead of us."

"Yes. And there's no point killing ourselves to cut that lead in half."

Capitol City, Pintoy, gravity 9.4 m/s²

Annie didn't want her to go to the party. Guen overruled her. Staying alive meant keeping the mob happy. Part of that was avoiding 'hoity-toity' behavior such as going to cocktail parties. But another part was being friends with other people the mob liked.

The mob loved Professor Corday. So when he sent an invitation Guen accepted.

The mansion used to belong to a stakeholder. Now "The People's House" was painted over the door. Clear plastic covered the smashed windows.

The furniture inside was ripped. Holes spotted the walls. But the floors were swept clean. Everything was neatly arranged. Guen noticed all the chairs were usable. Broken ones must have been cleaned away.

Professor Corday met them in the foyer. "Stakeholder Claret. Thank you so much for coming."

"I'm not a stakeholder any more. It's just Guen now." She shook his hand firmly. "This is my aide, Annie."

"Pleased to meet you. Everyone's in the buffet room. Please, enjoy yourselves."

The buffet grabbed their attention. Food at Doolittle Park varied among real, none, and basic synthetic paste. Fresh fruit and cooked meat were spread on ping-pong tables around the room. It felt like a flashback to two weeks ago, before the uprising.

Once they'd eaten enough to take the edge off Guen surveyed the crowd. Corday had kept his guest list secret. She was certain he had an agenda, but there hadn't been any hints.

One guest was instantly recognizable even through the swarm surrounding her. Guen pushed through to her. "Kimmie Z! I loved you in *Heartbreak Beach.*"

"Miss Claret. Thank you so much. I had so much fun making it."

"Just Guen, please."

"Then I'm Kim." They shook hands. The crowd backed off a bit. "You had such *chemistry* with Blake."

Kimmie turned her head in an artfully practiced bashful look. "*Too much chemistry according to some.*"

Guen remembered that had triggered one of her many break-ups with Rocco. "And *Night In the Woods*, that's another favorite of mine."

After a few minutes of mutual appreciation of Kimmie's holos Guen stepped back to let someone else have a turn with the actress. This left her next to a tall young man with fresh scars on his face.

"Hi, I'm Guen."

"Jozzy." His handshake was tentative, as if he was afraid of hurting her.

"Nice to meet you." Guen realized she had no idea how to talk to a total stranger. She normally had a full briefing on every attendee before entering a party. If a stranger approached her in public he'd have something on his mind, and Annie would do an identity search and whisper key information in her ear.

Fortunately Jozzy wasn't as tongue-tied. "How did Kimmie Z know you? Did you meet before?"

"No, this was our first time. She'd heard of me because I was in politics before."

"Oh. Is that why you were invited to the party?"

"I don't know. The Professor didn't say. Did he tell you why he invited you?"

"No. I figured it's for killing those cops. It's the only thing I've ever done."

"That was very brave of you." Guen had been horrified when she saw policemen dying in the riots, not admiring. Saying so would be a quick way to die at the hands of the mob.

Jozzy shrugged. "I was just angry at what they did to Thun and his boys."

Handclaps caught their attention. Professor Corday stood at the far side of the room. Wide doors had been opened onto an equally large room.

"Could the primary guests please join me in the next room?" he said. "Friends and aides are welcome to keep enjoying the buffet. You'll be able to hear everything."

Jozzy and Guen joined the parade into the next room. There were no tables, only a ring of chairs facing the center. They were spaced widely enough to walk between.

Professor Corday stood in the middle.

Guen took a seat on the far side. Jozzy sat to her right.

The professor began, "Thank you all so much for coming. I've heard you wonder why you were chosen. It's simple. You are all the most popular people among those who matter. It used to be the Stakeholders and the rich mattered. Now it's the stipend kids. We are the ones who matter now.

"The old government is gone. Some dead, some fled, the rest ignored. The Navy refused calls to intervene because the people asking had no authority. They were remnants. The police are hiding in fear of the stipend kids, or protecting the richest neighborhoods for under the table payments. There is no government on Pintoy.

"Now the old order made anarchy sound good. But it's not working well for us. People are in danger. We need to keep the public safe.

"I propose that we become a Committee of Public Safety. Our personal followers combined will give us the full support of the stipend kids. With that the middle class will endorse us to restore order.

"Are you willing to take on this burden?"

The silence hung heavy. Even the buffet room had hushed, listening for the answer.

Someone spoke up. "Yeah, I guess. Somebody has to."

More murmurs of assent spread around the circle. Guen said, "Yes."

A contrarian said, "*Can* we do it? I think it's a good thing if we can, but I don't know how to run a committee. None of the people I know here do either."

Professor Corday nodded to him. "Wayne Searcher, you make a good point. Does anyone here have experience in government?"

Kimmie Z said, "Guen Claret was a stakeholder."

The professor turned to Guen. "Did you learn how to run a committee meeting?"

"Yes, the Council had a class on the procedures," answered Guen.

Before she could get to the "but" someone said, "I nominate Guen for chair."

Jozzy seconded.

"All in favor?" said the professor, raising his hand.

Guen was the only one without a raised hand.

"Congratulations, Guen," said Corday, taking the only empty seat.

Everyone waited expectantly.

Well, you wanted to do this with stakeholders. Now you're doing it with rebels. Guen stood. "When we ask people for their support we have to tell them what we're going to do. Two things have to come first: stopping the pee-kays and food distribution."

Committee members nodded in approval as she continued.

An itch traveled between Guen's shoulder blades, like a knife point seeking a place to sink in.

Joshua Chamberlain, Tiantan System, acceleration 0 m/s²

"Traffic Control has cleared us for a parking orbit," reported Hiroshi.

"Good. I'm sure Ping's been informed of our arrival by now. I'll see if he'll come along quietly." Mitchie had to admit she was whistling past the graveyard on that.

She kept her initial message to the minimum. MUST MEET TO ARRANGE YOUR RETURN TO FLEET. LONG, CMDING J.C. The comm box forwarded it to Tiantan's relay satellite.

Tiantan shone ahead of them. Some considered it the Terraforming Service's best work. No deserts, no swamps, no uninhabitable plateaus. The small ice caps gave way to forests then grain fields followed by rice paddies in the equatorial zone. The mountain ranges were thin, shaping weather patterns with the least loss of usable land. The shallow oceans supported abundant life. The night side glowed with the lights of small towns and cities focused on learning.

Too damn manicured, thought Mitchie. *It's like living in a greenhouse.*

The response came from Traffic Control. "Ma'am, they want us to land. Specific coordinates on the planet. Should I comply?"

"Yes. That's the meeting I requested." *I hope.*

A terse reply from Stakeholder Ping invited her to join him at the Mansion of Contemplation. That sounded like a good place for a quiet chat. She didn't mind the direction to come alone.

Joshua Chamberlain, Tiantan, gravity 8.7 m/s^2

The landing pad was less than half a klick across. Most worlds wouldn't let a cutter land on something that small, let alone an analog ship. Hiroshi placed them exactly on the crossing stripes in the center.

Before debarking Mitchie called Guo and Setta to the bridge. "I want to clarify the chain of command. First Mate, Pilot, Bosun." Guo, Hiroshi, and Setta nodded in turn. "Our orders are to bring Stakeholder Ping back to the Combined Fleet. Our mission is to make the Fusion supply its share of reinforcements."

She considered ordering them to return to the Fleet if anything happened to her. But Guo wouldn't let an order get in the way of rescuing her. That's why she'd put him in command over the more qualified Hiroshi. No sense adding the extra step of hitting the pilot over the head to Guo's rescue plan.

"If anything happens to me take whatever action best carries out the mission."

A chorus of "yes, ma'ams" came back.

A driver waited in a four-seat scooter at the base of the ship. "I will take you to the Green Place," he said in Mandarin.

"I'm supposed to go to the Mansion of Contemplation," she replied, stumbling over the last phrase. Her Mandarin was still weak.

"Same. Green Place is nickname."

She sat in the seat next to him. Both hands grasped the front rail as he accelerated. The speed was insignificant compared to her ship's peak velocity but it felt very fast down here with all those things to bump into.

The scooter screeched to a stop where the pavement changed to gravel. She had a third of a klick to walk. She thanked him politely anyway.

From there the structure looked a pure, bright green. Her niece had a plastic toy frog that color. As Mitchie walked up the gravel path she started to pick out dark and bright spots, placed next to each other to fool the distant observers. Then the broad patches of grass-green became mosaics of slightly different shades. She stopped as it sank in. The entire four-story building was covered with jade. Stones of different shades, some striped, all selected and fit together to look identical from a distance. Knowing how they did things on Tiantan it had probably all been done by hand.

The Mansion didn't have the look she'd expected. Mitchie studied the doors and windows. As the Sinophone movement's headquarters it should have a classical Chinese architecture. The two pagoda roofs did draw on that. The walls below them were curved, not straight, almost if the building was trying to be a bubble under a hat. The doors were marked with decorative arches that didn't match the rest. Then it hit her—the walls were imitating a Mongolian yurt. The doors had Japanese torii arches. The clashing windows must draw on another tradition she didn't recognize. The Sinophones were trying to draw all the Asian descendants into their faction by representing them in this building.

A middle aged Chinese woman met her inside the doorway. "Welcome to the Mansion of Contemplation," she said in, thankfully, English. "Please come with me. You must prepare for your meeting with *Daifu*."

So Ping had a new title. Mitchie tried to remember what the word meant as she followed the lady through narrow hallways to a small room. Unlike the works of art decorating the rest of the building, the contents of this room were fully modern machines.

"You must be dressed properly for your audience. Please remove your outer clothes and stand under the measurement arch."

As she peeled off the jumpsuit Mitchie realized why she was instinctively obeying someone she disliked. The woman looked and sounded like Shi Bingrong, Guo's predecessor as first mate.

Standing under the arch was insufficient. The woman made an impatient twirling gesture with her finger. Mitchie obediently turned around. *I would have saved this hassle if I'd gone back to get my dress uniform.*

But no, I had to rush after him.

The big machine started to purr. Mitchie accepted a cup of tea to be polite. Before she finished it a drawer slid out with clothes.

It wasn't an Akiak Space Guard dress uniform. The grey fabric was a shade too dark. The command and pilot badges were embroidered in silver thread instead of being metal pins. And it hadn't produced shiny low-quarter shoes to replace her boots.

"Thank you. That's impressive work," said Mitchie as she started dressing.

"I apologize for not replicating your ribbons. I couldn't find a good enough image."

"That's fine. Everyone who needs to know what I've done already knows."

She led Mitchie to a large circular chamber. Flunkies of various types lined the walls. A round table held a dozen Chinese ranging from double Mitchie's age to decrepit. Given Fusion tech the oldest might be nearly two centuries.

Stakeholder—now *Daifu*—Ping swiveled his chair to face Mitchie. "My fellow teachers, I present the famous and infamous Michigan Long. Our liaison to the Disconnected Worlds."

An interpreter stood behind the table, translating their conversation for whichever of the leaders didn't know English.

Ping wore a conventional suit, though the fabric bore a semy of butterflies and bamboo leaves instead of pinstripes. The others wore Confucian Revival robes except for one in the uniform of a Fusion Navy admiral.

Mitchie decided to ignore the rest. "Mr. Ping. Admiral Galen ordered you to return from Pintoy to the Combined Fleet with no detours. You will return to *Joshua Chamberlain* with me."

The flunkies chuckled.

"And if I do not?" asked Ping. "Your ship is unarmed."

"Your dossier on me is thorough. But you missed the incident where I killed a recalcitrant man by hovering over him on my ship's torch. He was baked into the soil."

Ping thought for a moment. "Murtaza?"

"Yes."

"It had always seemed odd to me that a man died in your presence without it being your fault."

"Then you're coming."

"No. Please contact your ship."

Mitchie pulled her datasheet from her pocket. "Hiroshi. Any news?"

"Uh, ma'am, three warships just touched down around us. Two destroyers and a light cruiser. The Fusion Navy markings are painted over. They say Protectors of Harmony now. Each one has a laser pointed at us."

"Sit tight. Long out." She shoved the datasheet back into the pocket. "Firing on my ship would be an act of war. Your last war with the Disconnect didn't go well for you."

"I doubt the Defense Coordinating Committee would go to war over a clearly documented act of self-defense. I'm prepared to bet my life on it."

The flunkies also being wagered were silent.

"If you're not going to obey Admiral Galen's order why are you talking to me?"

"You are Disconnected. A very useful thing right now."

Mitchie watched warily as Ping stood and began to pace.

"We have order here. The stipends have ended. Everyone works for their keep. The riots were suppressed."

"How many deaths did that take?" interrupted Mitchie.

Ping looked to the admiral.

The officer shrugged. "The obedient lived. The rebellious died. We didn't count them."

So thousands dead at least, thought Mitchie.

"We are grounding our society in traditional principles so everyone may lead a happy and fulfilled life. Our best teachers will lead us toward a proper understanding. Then we will have harmony.

"But to truly live in harmony we must have peace with our neighbors. Other worlds are in chaos. Murder in the streets goes unpunished. They must restore order to be good neighbors. When we have that the volunteers training for the militia can join the Fusion Navy and resume our fight against the Betrayers.

"An ad hoc group has seized power on Pintoy. As a Disconnected Worlds representative you are a neutral party. I wish you to deliver the Harmony's statement to them. The sooner a new order is established the sooner we may deliver the ships we promised to the Combined Fleet." Ping held a data crystal out to Mitchie.

"I presume you included a complete copy of the Master's works?"

"No. Pintoy has libraries if they want to emulate our success. But there are many European-derived social philosophies. We don't care how they organize their society. Just that they do organize it, in accordance with human nature, and not force people into unnatural patterns until they explode."

Mitchie took the crystal.

"Safe journey, Commander Long."

On the way out the Bing-lookalike handed her a neat bundle tied with a pastel ribbon—her jumpsuit.

Guo took Mitchie's hand to pull her up the last few rungs of the ladder.

"We're leaving," she said.

"Nice outfit." Guo reeled in the rope ladder, securing it in the cargo hold airlock. "He's not coming, then."

"No. He's covered every angle and is willing to be violent. So he's maneuvered me into being his messenger. I hate that."

"Messenger duty isn't that bad."

"Not that. Everything I've done Ping saw coming and blocked. Now I'm doing a job for him because that's the best way to try to do our mission."

Guo sealed the airlock. "He has a lot more resources than we do."

"It wasn't that." Grudgingly. "He outsmarted me."

"Good. That should happen sometimes. Humility is good for you."

Her fist hit his triceps hard enough to bruise. Guo only grinned.

"I'm going to the bridge. We need to get off this rock."

Chapter Four: Disorder

Joshua Chamberlain, **Danu System, acceleration 10 m/s²**

The comm box grabbed a daily news dump whenever they were close enough to a relay buoy. The news from Pintoy had been 'Planet In Chaos, Nobody Knows What's Happening' the whole trip. Today there was actual news.

An oversized datasheet hung in the galley for when the crew wanted to watch a show together. Now it displayed the new rulers supervising executions.

Guo complained, "Guillotines? And a Committee of Public Safety? Did they have a coup by historical reenactors?"

"Couldn't be," answered Hiroshi. "We got them all."

"Looks like you missed the French ones."

Mitchie looked up from her datasheet. "Damn, that is Guen. How the hell did she wind up in charge of this?"

No one answered. On the big screen more heads went into baskets.

Guo said, "It's a revolution. Anything can happen. At least we know she's alive."

"If she hasn't been assassinated since this footage."

Mthembu yelled down the open bridge hatch. "Ma'am, can you come up?"

Mitchie joined him on the bridge. "What's up?"

"Traffic Control sent out a notice about a naval convoy transiting the system. It's not Fusion Navy. Bonnie ships. I thought you might want to know."

"I would. Thank you, Coxswain's Mate."

She fed the data feed from Traffic Control to the nav box. The convoy's course went straight from gate to gate. Clearly headed for the front. A wide cylinder marked an exclusion zone. The Fuzies were afraid to let any civilian traffic pass close to the warships.

Joshua Chamberlain was not civilian traffic.

"Mthembu, plot a course. I want to make a close approach with option to rendezvous."

"Yes'm. How much accel can I pull?"

"See if you can keep it at ten gravs."

While the co-pilot wrestled with the navigation computer, Mitchie took out the telescope. She could see the convoy. Eight ships in a sloppy formation. She meditated on the sight.

"Ma'am, I can do it at fifteen gravs. They have too much of a head start for ten gravs."

She secured the telescope and looked over his work. "Do it."

He gave the crew two minute's warning of the acceleration increase. Then they had three days of thrusting to match position with the convoy.

Mitchie intended to wait until they were inside ten light-seconds from the warships to contact them. That much lag made a conversation only irritating instead of impractical. The convoy spoiled the plan by sending a voice-only message at fifteen light seconds.

"Convoy Three-Zero-Eight to unknown torchship. Maintain your distance. Ships violating the convoy security zone will be fired upon."

She made a verbal reply. "Akiak Guard Ship *Joshua Chamberlain* to Convoy Three Oh Eight. I must speak to the convoy commander."

The thirty second delay gave her a chance to remember that *Joshua Chamberlain* was chartered to the Bonaventure Defense Force rather than the Akiak Space Guard. *Oh, well. They won't know any better.*

"Stand by," said the comm box's speaker. Then its screen lit up. "This is Lieutenant Commander Sheu, commanding the cruiser *Audie Murphy*. Who am I speaking to?"

Mitchie activated the camera. "This is Commander Michigan Long, commanding the *Joshua Chamberlain*. I need to speak to the squadron commander." She managed to not end her transmission with "kid" even though that was the youngest lieutenant commander she'd ever seen.

Sheu left his camera running while waiting for an answer. He almost jumped out of his seat when her image appeared.

"Is that really Michigan Long?" said an off-screen voice.

"I think it really is her," answered Sheu. "My God."

Curious—and youthful—faces peeked into the edge of the screen.

Ah, fame, thought Mitchie.

Sheu waved them away and composed his features. "Ma'am, I'm commanding the squadron as senior captain. It's a temporary unit, we'll be broken up when we reach the fleet."

With that face the word "senior" should mean graduation parties, not command. Mitchie would rather do this next part as question and answer but the time lag was too long. She'd have to make a speech.

"Commander Sheu, I don't know how closely you've followed recent events in the Fusion. The Council of Stakeholders is mostly dead. A new group has seized power. And another faction is preparing to wage civil war.

"My mission is to ensure the Fusion provides its promised reinforcements to the Combined Fleet. We also need to make sure whatever new government arises respects the peace treaty with the Disconnected Worlds. All of that will require more firepower than just my ship. Do you understand?"

Turning the camera off would be an expression of weakness. So would fidgeting, nail chewing, or humming. Mitchie had polished her acting skills in years as an undercover intelligence agent. Now she used them to project calm interest in Sheu's answer.

"Yes, ma'am. I'm not sure how we can help. Our orders are to proceed directly to rendezvous with the Combined fleet."

"And they need your support. But this is a major crisis that will determine if the Combined Fleet will get any reinforcements from the Fusion or if humans will be at war with each other again. We need to brainstorm the best way to respond to this as the Disconnected Worlds units on the spot.

"I'm inviting your squadron captains and XOs aboard for a meeting to determine the best course of action. *Joshua Chamberlain* has the most room for everyone. Coordinate with my co-pilot on maneuvers."

As a higher-ranking officer her 'invitation' would be considered an order. A meeting wouldn't conflict too much with their existing orders. Bringing them onto her ship would establish psychological dominance.

"Yes, ma'am. We should be able to report aboard in less than an hour." The kid actually saluted.

She snapped one back. At least the guy wasn't green enough to hold it until he saw her return it. Sheu dropped it after five seconds. She turned away from the comm box.

"Mthembu, take care of the rendezvous. Make them do the hard part. I need to prepare a reception."

***

Sixteen visiting officers overflowed the galley. She'd considered briefing them in the cargo hold but sitting the captains at the table added a useful formality. They'd been in free-fall since the ships rendezvoused so stuffing the executive officers in odd corners wasn't a strain on them.

Setta and her deckhands passed out free-fall friendly snacks. Feeding them was another way to bond them to Mitchie as a new leader. Fresh fruit, sandwiches, and pastries managed to tempt all the visitors into eating something.

Sheu wasn't as young as he'd seemed on the screen. He was almost exactly Mitchie's age. He just didn't have the I've-lost-count-of-how-many-times-I've-almost-been-killed lines she was used to seeing on the faces of ship crews.

A couple of JG's did have those lines. Chit-chat while waiting for the rest to arrive confirmed they were mustangs, enlisted men commissioned after serving in the Third Battle of Bonaventure. Neither minded being staked out as bait for Mitchie's trap, or possibly they hadn't made the connection.

The other light cruiser was the last to send its command staff over. The senior was a Lieutenant Commander Zimmerman, apparently only junior to Sheu because same day promotions handled seniority in alphabetical order. He gave a bitter laugh as he explained it.

Once everyone was introduced Mitchie plunged into the briefing. The Fusion's deceptions and the resulting carnage shocked them. The Harmony's restrictions on individual freedom offended them. She cut short the video of the Committee of Public Safety's executions—a couple of lieutenants looked ready to vomit.

Her crew hadn't been bothered. *Which may be because my crew was pushing body parts out of the way during search and recovery missions.*

"This is the part of the briefing where I tell you the plan. The situation is too fluid for a plan yet. We will have to assess what's happening on Pintoy and respond appropriately. We need to all focus on our goals.

"First goal: make sure whatever new government arises isn't a threat to the Disconnected Worlds. There are too many historical precedents for a weak government trying to unify its people by starting a war. A prompt show of force could prevent us from having to missile a city. Destroying one city could avert a war which destroys multiple planets.

"Second goal: make them abide by the peace treaty. Free transit for our ships, fair treatment for Disconnect citizens.

"Third goal: make them deliver reinforcements to the Combined Fleet. The Fusion built hundreds of warships it couldn't crew. They're sitting in parking orbits waiting for some revolutionaries to grab them. We need those ships attacking the Betrayers, not the Disconnect or rival Fuzies."

That left the officers looking grimmer than the videos of Pintoy had.

"Right now the available resources are my unarmed ship and your squadron. Clearly some have to continue on to the Combined Fleet. You're not just needed as warships, you need to inform Admiral Galen of the situation here."

The body language of the captains let her judge which way they wanted to go. Sheu's hero worship of her wasn't shared by everyone else. Zimmerman was suspicious of the entire situation and resented the interruption in their flight. The lower-ranking officers were worried but didn't seem to have useful ideas.

"We do need to have a presence in Pintoy," said Sheu. "Something more intimidating than, pardon me, ma'am, a freighter."

"I agree," said Mitchie.

Zimmerman snapped, "You can't abandon your command to go

off like this."

Mitchie said gently, "If Commander Sheu's ship goes to Pintoy, command of the remainder if the squadron would devolve to the next highest ranking officer."

He tried to keep a poker face, but she could tell Zimmerman liked the thought of taking command.

One of the mustangs asked, "How many ships do we need to make a difference?"

"Just one warship would be a significant presence," said Sheu.

"Yes," agreed Mitchie. "A second and third would let us show the flag in more than one place if we need to, or send messages."

Lieutenant Snyder, commanding the destroyer *Walking Rollo*, asked, "Has any of this been reported to the DCC?"

Everyone looked at Mitchie.

"No, I'd only planned to report to Admiral Galen," she said. Even Sheu's expression turned down at that. "I hate to give up another courier, but you're right." *The one time I try to follow the chain of command somebody talks me out of it.*

"Then I'll volunteer to take that message back, ma'am," said Snyder.

"Good. Hopefully they can send some diplomats back with you."

"Ma'am?" One of the XOs was too shy to ask her question straight out.

"Go ahead, Ensign."

"It sounds like you need intel types more than warships."

"Yes," agreed Mitchie. "But y'all are who I have. I want you all to check your crews for anyone with useful experience or aptitude. We need intelligence agents, Mandarin interpreters, open source analysts, and covert operatives. If you have anyone like that transfer them to here or one of the ships going to Pintoy."

"Which are the *Joshua Chamberlain* and *Audie Murphy*," said Zimmerman.

A lieutenant spoke up. "We should have a second warship at Pintoy. I'll bring *St. Aubrey*."

Another volunteered his destroyer as well.

"Very well," said Mitchie. She wanted to thank them but it would damage the little bit of authority she'd managed to hold over the group. "Commander Sheu will lead the Pintoy squadron. Commander Zimmerman, take the remaining ships to the Combined Fleet. I'll have data crystals with this briefing and some other files for you and Lieutenant Snyder. Everyone check your crews for special talents and transfer them to the Pintoy squadron before we boost."

Bosun Setta waved a covered basket as she floated in the corridor. "And feel free to take some more cookies on your way out."

A wave of "Yes, ma'ams" came back as the officers started moving.

Joshua Chamberlain, Dirac System, acceleration 10 m/s²

Guo looked up from his datasheet as Mitchie entered their cabin. "Have you read this ultimatum of Ping's?" he asked.

"Just enough to convince me I didn't want to read the rest. It's huge." She leaned on the back of his chair to see what he was looking at.

"Yes, they buried the key bits under piles of philosophy and pleas for reconciliation. But it means war. War with the insurrectionists, and war with us."

Mitchie moved to the bed to face him. "Ping sounded like he wanted peaceful coexistence when he handed me this thing."

"I'm sure he did. And he's not demanding political control. He wants to impose bottom-up social controls. Any world that doesn't exercise enough control he's threatening war on."

"What kind of controls?"

"No stipends."

"Sounds like home." Akiak's impoverished children and invalids were assisted by private associations. The able-bodied could work or starve.

"Yeah? Does providing mandatory government make-work sound like home?"

"Hell, no. That sounds like it would violate the anti-slavery clauses."

"It would. Along with the rule that everyone have a supervisor responsible for his decisions."

She gave that one a moment's thought. "What about small businesses and freelancers?"

"They don't exist," said Guo in grim tones. "Everyone is part of a chain of command, tying the whole planet into a single organization."

"Whooo. Yeah, he does want war. Guen would go down fighting over that. What else is in there?"

"Family rules. Fathers have supervisory control over kids until they're transferred to a new supervisor as an adult. Research restrictions. Closes a few loopholes in the old Fusion rules. And there's the 'Good Neighbor Policy.'" Guo gave the phrase a sarcastic lilt. "All worlds complying with the Harmony's rules are required to enforce them on worlds that aren't."

"Shit. He wants to renew the war with the Disconnect."

"Oh, we can be disconnected at the political level if we implement his social rules."

"Sure. I don't think any one of the Disconnected Worlds could enforce that without civil war. And I'd be one of the rebels." Mitchie fingered the empty spot on her belt where her holster would go.

"I can pull the excerpts of the bad stuff into a file for you," Guo offered.

"No, I'd better read the whole thing. I need to be a player in this argument. Have to make friends with the Committee of Public Safety, keep them on our side. Or with whoever's in charge when we get there."

Guo chuckled.

Mitchie looked up at him. "How Confucian is this?"

"What do you mean?"

"It's your philosophy. How well does this plan implement it?"

He thought for a few moments. "The structure fits well. People are happier when they're integrated into a family or a strong group. Forcibly incorporating people who don't believe in it is a huge shift from tradition. Confucians are supposed to educate people, not coerce them."

"So this isn't appealing to you?"

"No."

She kept her eyes locked on him, wanting more of an answer.

Guo said firmly, "I swore an oath to protect our people's freedom. If this was better for all of them, and I'm not sure it is, I'd still fight to keep it from being forced on them."

Mitchie walked over and kissed him.

Pintoy System, acceleration 10 m/s^2

"*Joshua Chamberlain* to Traffic Control. Request clearance for Pintoy landing." Mthembu sounded frustrated. They'd been in the system for hours without a peep from Traffic Control. Sheu's ships had completed their jumps and gathered into a loose formation behind the freighter.

The comm box picked up a transmission. "*Lyke Star* to *Joshua*. Give it up."

Mthembu picked up the mike. "*Lyke Star*, what happened to Traffic Control?"

A minute went by. "Don't know but they're gone. We're all on watch and avoid. So be careful."

"Oh. Thank you, *Lyke Star*."

Another minute. "Good luck, *Joshua*."

The Coxswain's Mate turned to Mitchie. "What do we do now, ma'am?"

"We keep going. Fire up the radar and do visual checks. We'll just have to dodge if anyone gets in our way."

There wasn't much traffic in the system. The ship-to-ship bands had a steady chatter of ships announcing their intentions. Nobody complained about getting plumed.

"*Audie Murphy* to *Joshua Chamberlain*, come in please."

It was Sheu's voice so Mitchie answered it herself. "*Chamberlain* here."

"Ma'am, I think we found a solution to the parking problem."

Both leaving the squadron in orbit and landing it on Pintoy had hazards. Mitchie had delegated the decision to Sheu, who'd postponed it.

"Glad to hear it. Where?"

"We heard an ad for the ski resort on Matsu. They sound hungry for business, so they'd have plenty of room for our ships."

Pintoy's moon was a methane-atmosphere iceball. If this was the place Mitchie had heard of before, 'ski resort' was a euphemism for casino. As a base for the squadron it had the advantages of proximity, shore leave, and safety from revolutionary mobs.

"Sounds worth a try."

"If you land with us we can transfer the specialists over without an EVA."

"Agreed."

Matsu, moon of Pintoy, gravity 2.2 m/s²

Joshua Chamberlain's turbines spun harder to get full thrust from the lighter atmosphere. The exhaust blew ethane snow off the concrete landing pad. Once the flurries settled a crawler came out from the insulated tunnel extending from the resort domes. An accordion tube expanded behind it. At the ship the crawler's cab lifted off its chassis to meet the cargo hold airlock.

Ensign Jones met her in the dome. "Volunteer detail ready, ma'am!" she said with a salute. The spacers formed up behind her in two lines.

"Good morning, folks. I'm Commander Long. Stand easy." Not that standing at attention was a strain in this gravity. "I'll chat with each of you before we go down to the planet."

Jones had files ready for each one with a summary of their applicable experience. Most had tours in Intelligence or Shore Patrol before the fleet expansion pulled them onto ship duty.

Mitchie approved them all. She was in no position to be fussy.

After a Gunner's Mate led the enlisted to the ship Mitchie turned to Ensign Jones. "That was a solid audition for adjutant. Good work."

Jones flushed. "Actually, ma'am, I want to be a covert operative."

"How much intelligence experience do you have?" Not that an ensign could have experience unless she was a mustang. Jones looked far too young to be one.

"I was selected for Intel my senior year at Academy," said the ensign. "They sent me to Tactical at graduation."

"Analyst or operative?"

"They had me tracked to be an analyst. But you need operatives more."

Which was true. "How much tradecraft training have you had?"

"No formal training. I've read several books." A visible blush—she was as pale as Mitchie. "Including everything I could find about your career."

"Most of that is bullshit."

"I'd be glad for any training you can give me, ma'am."

"You wouldn't be able to use my special methods."

Another blush. "How could you tell?"

Because you didn't say 'fuck you, bitch' when I said you couldn't. "Gut instinct."

"Even so, you mostly used conventional methods. I've studied how to do them."

"That's not the same as practical training." Still, only one of the other volunteers was willing to do undercover work, and his background was police, not intelligence. If this butterbar could do the job Mitchie could use her results. "What would you use as a cover identity?"

"Stranded tourist. Captain sold my ticket to a rich guy fleeing the mob and left me here. Gives me a reason to hate Pintoy's upper class."

"And if I need you to infiltrate the upper class?"

Jones thought a moment. "I'd do it openly, as your aide. You have connections to the old and new governments. They'd suck up to me to get access to you."

Mitchie stared at her junior. *That's . . . actually a good idea. Maybe she does have some talent for this.* "Very well, Ensign. Welcome aboard."

"Thank you, ma'am."

"That's enough ma'ams for now. We'll be working together too closely for that. What's your name?"

"Heidi, ma'am. Uh, sorry."

Mitchie chuckled, not at the mistake but the name. It fit her blonde braids too well.

Capitol City, Planet Pintoy, gravity 9.4 m/s^2

Guen was waiting as Mitchie slid out of the car. "We're already in session. They're waiting for you."

There went Mitchie's hopes of actually getting a briefing on what the Committee of Public Safety was other than 'those guys who set up the guillotines.'

"Don't be formal. We don't use parliamentary procedure. It's all first names." Guen took Mitchie's arm and led her into the building. They passed by the stairs and headed straight for the door flanked by six armed guards. "Just belt it out. If anyone asks a question give them a one line answer and go back to your pitch."

The guards opened the door for them. They marched into the meeting room, followed by Guen's bodyguards. "Damn, we need to find some private time soon. Here we go. Good luck." Guen led her to the center of the room.

A half-circle table held the important people, presumably the Committee by body language. They were dressed in a range from thug to worker bee. Flunkies lined the wall. The empty seat in the middle must be Guen's. Conversations died as they watched Mitchie's arrival.

"Everyone, this is Michigan Long," proclaimed Guen. "She's an officer in the Akiak Space Guard. You heard of her as the hero of the recapture of Demeter. Now she has urgent news of our enemies." Guen turned and began walking to the end of the table. She glanced back and made a 'start talking' gesture.

'Ladies and gentlemen' was too formal for this crowd. Mitchie opened with, "My friends. I bring harsh news. Stakeholder Ping has organized a revolt against the Fusion of Inhabited Worlds. His supporters have formed a new polity called the Harmony. They are enslaving the stipend collectors and threatening war against the rest of humanity."

People seated at the table cursed and made other exclamations of outrage. The flunkies confined themselves to echoing whoever they were standing behind. Mitchie used the interruption to reorder her thoughts.

"I am under orders from the Combined Fleet to bring Ping to the high command to answer for the Fusion's failure to meet its obligations under the Treaty of Lapis. Ping refused and threatened my crew with lethal violence. He demanded I serve as a messenger for him. Rather than endanger my loyal crew I cooperated."

Mitchie held up a data crystal. "Here are his demands. Put the stipend kids to laboring at useless make-work. Assign watchers to double-guess the decisions of every freelancer, entrepreneur, and businessman. Give parents control over their children's decisions on where to live, what to do, and who to marry. And wage war against anyone who doesn't comply with those demands."

This time she talked over the curses and grumbles. "Which means he's demanding you make war on us, the Disconnected Worlds. We want to be friends with you but anyone who attacks our people's freedom is our enemy."

Guen declared, "The Committee of Public Safety supports the Treaty of Lapis," from her seat in the center of the table. An uncertain stir went through the other committee members but no one replied.

"Then the Disconnected Worlds will stand by our friends and allies," answered Mitchie. *I wonder if the treaty covers internal conflicts? The DCC is going to be pissed if I just dragged them into a civil war.*

"Can we see the details of the Harmony's demands?" asked a committee member in a shiny lime green jacket and blueberry beret.

"Of course." A technical-type flunky scampered up to Mitchie with a datasheet. He accepted the data crystal from her and plugged it into the datasheet.

"You'll find most of it is philosophy, explanations for why their system of total control is the only acceptable choice for society and best for individuals . . . in the long run." Mitchie watched as the committee members began fiddling with their datasheets.

The meeting devolved into a general argument about the horribleness of Stakeholder Ping, his Harmony, and the ultimatum. Mitchie drifted toward the wall to avoid attracting more attention. She studied the dynamics of the Fusion's new rulers. Guen confined herself to shutting down personal attacks between committee members. Most of the speeches were competitions over who was most outraged.

An older man stood out by his silence. Mitchie noticed he didn't participate in the debate but his terse comments would steer it in new directions. His fingers stayed busy on his datasheet, presumably passing private messages to one or another grandstander.

Proposals to attack the Harmony were side-tracked into arguments over the state of the Navy. Apparently a wave of new recruits were in training. That was good news, if they would actually be available to support the Combined Fleet instead of being ground up in a civil war.

"That's enough for now, people," broke in Guen. "There are subcommittee meetings in half an hour. Chairs need to make sure they have their agendas ready and I want everyone there on time." Apparently that was a formal adjournment for this body. "Commander Long, thank you for your help today. I will follow up with you to coordinate our response with the Disconnected Worlds."

Mitchie nodded.

***

Guen arrived in a three truck convoy. They pulled up next to the *Joshua Chamberlain* in a flurry of dust. Brightly colored thugs jumped out of the front and rear trucks and formed a loose perimeter around the ship. A squad of professional bodyguards dismounted smoothly from the middle one. They formed a corridor to the gangway. Mitchie recognized some from Guen's old security crew.

The Chairwoman hopped out of the middle truck's cab. She strolled calmly up the gangway into the open hold.

Mitchie had most of the crew lined up to honor their guest. Guen swapped hugs with Mitchie. She hugged Guo until he squeezed back. The rest of the crew received handshakes and polite greetings.

When that was done she whispered, "Privacy?" in Mitchie's ear.

"Let's go up to our cabin." Mitchie led Guen and Guo up the ladder to the main deck. When she closed the door of the double cabin behind them and announced "Privacy" Guen flopped on the bed.

"Oh, God, I'm safe. At least for a few minutes. It's been a

nightmare."

"You keep wanting to wake up?" asked Guo.

"Worse. The kind where you wake up, and think it's over, but it's another nightmare, and you wake up again, and it's still nightmare." Guen pulled on her hair.

"Well, you're safe here," said Mitchie firmly.

"Thank you." Guen sat up on the edge of the bed. She twisted her back to relieve the pinch from her top.

"That outfit looks uncomfortable," commented Mitchie.

"Oh, it's terrible. I'm doing this woman-of-the-people routine so I have to wear stipend kid fashions. It's all catch-the-eye crap. I have creases on my boobs when I take this off."

"No one's watching now." Mitchie unlatched a drawer. "Try this on." She tossed Guen a nightshirt.

"Oh, yes."

Guo turned to contemplate a poem on the bulkhead.

Mitchie had to pull the knee-high lemon boots off.

"That is *so* much better." Guen bounced a little to enjoy her freedom.

Guo asked, "If you're up to talking about it, why are there so many historical references in the revolution? Committee of Public Safety, guillotines, political sentencing?"

"Oh, that's Professor Corday. He always has a suggestion when we need an idea and half the Committee loves him. Sometimes he'll throw a fit and we can't get anything done until we agree to do it his way."

"Why isn't he the Chairman?" said Mitchie.

Guen's smile was too cynical for such a young face. "The Chairman is first one to be executed when things go wrong. Wish I'd known that before he maneuvered me into the job."

"Wait," said Guo. "Georges Corday, author of *Bloodlust as Politics: The French Revolution?*"

"That's him. He gave me a copy of his book. I'm only a third of the way through it. Every page has something I have to spend an hour reading about to understand."

"Good God. I'd think he'd remember how that revolution came

out."

Guen shrugged. "He's testing his theories on the mob. Sometimes I think he's just doing it all to write another book. He's constantly taking notes. But it's useful. The guillotines are providing more satisfaction to the mob with fewer executions. It's a better show than firing squads."

"Hey, you must be doing some good." Mitchie spoke brightly to keep Guen from noticing the shocked look on Guo's face.

"I'm trying. The economy's going again, even if some sectors are running on barter. I put a lot of the family fortune into that. Oh, and there's millions of volunteers training for the Navy. Turns out the Navy had a virtual reality boot camp program. They wouldn't use it because it's only 80% effective."

"That must make Admiral Vitelli happy," said Mitchie.

"No, he was dead before I heard about the training software."

"What happened?"

Guen let out an unhappy sigh. "He told the Committee we were a bloodthirsty junta. Which we are. But a dozen committee members immediately moved to execute him. Nobody voted against it. I wanted to, but I was afraid they'd execute me if I was the only one opposing them."

"You are way too stressed," said Mitchie. "You need to relax. Lie face down."

Mitchie and Guo traded massages often enough to be well-practiced. They started on Guen's arms, Guo on the left, Mitchie right. After rubbing her legs from toes to top they split the back. Mitchie took the shoulders and upper back. Guo stroked the lower back, and after Mitchie nudged him, below.

When she was done on that side they flipped her over. Guo worked neck, scalp, and face, while Mitchie stroked pectoral and abdominals.

"Better?" asked Mitchie.

"Oh, yes. Well, better physically. I still have all my worries."

"Maybe we can help. What's the biggest one?"

Guen laughed. "Just one? I don't know enough to do this job. The military hates us almost as much as they hated the Stakeholders. Half the stipend kids want to beat people up as a personal dominance display. Everyone who was doing well under the old regime would kill us all to put things back the way they were. And I have no idea how to fix it."

She shivered. The couple enveloped her in a warm joint hug.

"Oh, that's better."

"What have you been doing?" asked Guo.

"Treading water. Approving everything with majority support so I don't piss off the Committee. Offering food and entertainment to the stipend kids so they won't riot again. Supporting people who stand up to Professor Corday so he doesn't get complete control."

Mitchie slid closer, following Guen as she leaned into Guo's side of the cuddle. "What's Corday after?"

"I don't know. His supporters go in different directions. He talks about an 'improved status quo ante' but I don't believe it. There's just too much sneaking around for that. I keep thinking if I knew more history I could figure it out."

"I can recommend some books to start with," said Guo.

"I'd like that. I don't know when I'll have the time. If I wasn't here I'd have a line of people waiting to talk to me."

Mitchie chuckled. "It would take three years to read all the books he'd give you anyway. You don't have time to learn everything."

"I know. I hate being so ignorant. And I can't ask questions because that's showing weakness. Or the answers I'd get would just be to manipulate me. At least I have some basics in economics from working in Dad's company. That let me get food distribution going again."

"That's good," said Mitchie. "What do you need to know the most?"

The younger woman paused. "This is embarrassing."

Guo tightened his hug for a moment. "We're good at keeping secrets."

"It's . . . I don't know anything about sex. It makes me feel like a child working with all those adults who know everything."

"Surely you've seen holos," said Mitchie.

"Yeah. But there's violence in holos too. I've seen people beaten and killed. It's nothing like the holos. So I can't trust holo sex to be accurate. And I can't ask anyone to demonstrate for me."

Mitchie had been watching for a vulnerability she could plant hooks into. This was it, if she could get Guo to cooperate. She chuckled. "Maybe you can't ask. But someone could volunteer."

Guen suddenly looked hopeful. "If . . . if you wanted to."

"Oh, if you weren't here we'd be screwing anyway. This guy won't pass up a chance."

"Kettle," said Guo. "We should really talk—"

He broke off as Mitchie knelt before him and undid his fly.

"Isn't that uncomfortable?" asked Guen.

"Mmmmm. Depends on the guy. This one is a perfect fit for me." She went back to what she'd been doing.

Guo tried to say something, but it was incoherent.

Mitchie had peeled her jumpsuit most of the way off while on her knees. She kicked it the rest of the way off as she stood. Guo's only took her a moment to take off. "Come on, lover. Let's be educational."

She flopped back onto the bed, pulling Guo after her. Any resistance he'd had to the project was gone now. "Ooh, that's right. Lift up your chest, let her have a good view."

Guen scooted closer to find the best viewing angle. A hand disappeared under her nightgown.

Mitchie moaned in appreciation of her husband's efforts. She turned to study Guen's fascinated face. "If you're feeling warm you can take that off."

The nightgown flew away.

Mitchie leaned up to whisper in Guo's ear. "Doesn't she look kissable?"

They both looked at Guen. The teenager looked very kissable— eyes wide, cheeks flushed, lips barely parted.

Mitchie twisted her hips to make Guo lean toward Guen. Lips met. Guen whimpered. Mitchie said, "Kiss her right." Mouths opened.

She slid out from under Guo. A hand on his ribs pushed him toward Guen. He rolled her onto her back.

Guen froze in a moment of panic.

Mitchie took her hand and stroked it, whispering, "Relax. Just lay back. He knows what he's doing. It'll be good," into Guen's ear.

Guo managed enough self-control to start slowly. Guen gasped, then began to pant. When Guo sped up she pulled her hand out of Mitchie's grasp and clutched his shoulders.

They finished with shouts and moans. Mitchie fought down an urge to applaud.

She joined in the cuddle behind Guen, laying her arm on Guo's where it rested on the girl's waist.

Neither fell asleep, though it was close for Guo. Guen explored him with her free hand, growing bolder after Mitchie whispered, "You can touch him anywhere."

When he responded Mitchie guided her to kneel above him. His attempt to help was quashed by, "Hold still. It's her turn to be in charge."

After some fumbling and shifting a moan from Guen announced that she'd made it work. It worked well. He was quieter this time, she was louder.

They'd actually fallen asleep when a gadget in Guen's discarded clothes began beeping.

"Crap. Meeting."

Guen rolled off the bed and grabbed her clothes. Mitchie had to help her with the boots again. Guo was the last to finish dressing.

Guen wrapped herself around him with a deep kiss. "Wow," she said. "That was—wow. I love you."

"I love you too," he replied.

Guen gave Mitchie a quick hug. "Thank you. For everything."

"Hey. Friends help each other."

Once outside the cabin they kept a casual demeanor. They handed her off to the bodyguards at the gangway.

When the trucks pulled away Guo said, "We need to talk."

"Agreed," said Mitchie. What she needed was for it to be *her turn*. But Guo would want to talk first.

***

Guo sat down in the reading chair, legs crossed with a foot resting on his knee. Not willing to let her change the subject, Mitchie decided. She sat on the edge of bed facing him.

"I've known non-monogamous married couples," he said. "They make a big point of everyone communicating so they're all working from the same assumptions."

She nodded.

"This kind of, of spontaneous fun could bite us in the future. Hard. It's probably going to bite Guen harder. How's she going to feel when she realizes she's falling in love with a man who's always going to pick another woman over her? And that's not even considering dealing with diseases or pregnancy."

"You're worried about catching a sexually transmitted disease from a virgin?"

"This time, no. The next time we land on Pintoy who knows what she'll have been doing. And there's still pregnancy."

"Until two months ago Guen regularly received the best medical care the Fusion could offer. I'm certain she has a contraceptive implant and immune system boosts."

"But you didn't ask."

"No."

"And you wouldn't let *me* ask." Guo was annoyed over that.

"I was worried about breaking the mood. If we'd started going over ground rules and medical checks she would have gotten cold feet and we'd all have wound up watching *Magic Princess Journey*. Then you'd claw your eyes out."

"It's not that bad."

"You've seen it?"

"You met my sisters. Stop changing the subject."

Talking about his sisters wouldn't get her what she wanted. "Okay."

"Yeah, breaking the mood would have ruined the chance of having that fun today. And I'll admit that was incredibly fun. But she could think about whether the mob would kill her for sleeping with Diskers or if she was ready for this or whatever. And we could discuss how to handle a teenager with a crush trying to get between us. You noticed she did put herself between us?"

"I was fine with her having the middle of the cuddle. She's lost some weight, probably gets cold easily."

"I'm not worried about her being cold. This is about you and me and protecting what we have."

"We're here, safe, and talking openly. That's a solid relationship."

"Yeah? How solid is it going to be with Guen asking me to meet her one on one without you? Because she doesn't seem to have that much interest in you."

"No, she has to be the most hetero woman I've ever—never mind."

"So you're fine with me going off to see her? I'm not sure that's such a good idea."

"If she asks I think you should. I don't know that she will. She did get nervous at one point, she may not be up for more."

"Wait, nervous? I didn't notice her being nervous." Suddenly he sounded nervous.

"You were being, mmm, focused. I coaxed her through it. She didn't say anything."

"You didn't *ask* her?"

"No, she relaxed and enjoyed it."

"That is *exactly* the situation where you should ask someone! Especially a virgin, for God's sake."

"She left happy. She's fine. And if you think it should've gone differently why didn't you ask her?"

Guo stared at the bulkhead as he ran through his memory of the encounter. "You manipulated me. You actually pushed me into doing it."

She shrugged. "Somebody had to or you two were just going to look at each other all afternoon."

"No, you didn't have to. Looking at each other was just fine. That could have turned into something horrible."

"If it was rape, who did the raping?"

"Don't goddamn try to pin this on me. Why? Why were you so obsessed with me screwing her?"

Mitchie took a deep breath. This was not going to go over well with his romantic nature. "She's the chairwoman of the CPS. It's a powerful position. I wanted to make her like us as much as we could."

Guo needed a moment to assimilate what he'd been told. "That's it? Not doing your friend a favor or a treat for your husband or adding some excitement because you're bored? This was *politics?*"

She kept her voice level instead of shouting back. "Guen is the figurehead for millions of bloodthirsty revolutionaries who are about to board hundreds of warships. They could go anywhere. I want to give Guen every reason to not aim them at the Disconnect."

"You manipulated me into popping a teenager's cherry for political advantage?"

"It's not politics. It's a war. Fuzies against Diskers, with a truce that can't survive this civil war breaking out. One Fusion destroyer carries enough missiles to kill everyone on Akiak. Our *duty* is to keep that from happening. We're protecting our families, mine and yours, and everyone else on the planet."

"Fucking to protect the planet. Including the penguins and sheep?"

"Yes, and the goddamn terraforming lichens too." She was shouting back now.

"So now I'm a whore for Akiak too."

"Fuck you." Mitchie walked over to his chair. She grabbed his hand and pulled it between her legs. "This is a weapon I will use to do my duty and protect our world. Just like this ship is a weapon." She leaned in to stroke his crotch. "And I'll use that as a weapon if I see a way to get the mission done."

"You'll destroy our relationship for political advantage."

She sat on the bed again. "I'm willing to die for my duty. I'm willing to let you get killed. We've come closer than I like to think to that a dozen times. If either of us dies that's the end of the relationship. There are a hundred million people on Akiak. I will trade the two of us to protect them. DO THE FUCKING MATH."

"That's a great attitude for a captain," Guo said.

They'd been married long enough to start completing each other's sentences occasionally. She heard the rest of this one clearly: *But a terrible one for a wife.*

"I guess I'll go do some captain stuff then."

As she closed the cabin hatch behind her Mitchie saw four crew at the galley table, halfway done with lunch. The flinches belied the we-weren't-listening-poses. *Crap. So much for soundproof bulkheads.*

She met Hiroshi's eyes and pointed at the bridge hatch. He followed her up the ladder.

On the bridge Mitchie told Mthembu, "You're relieved."

"I still have two hours left on my shift, ma'am," said the coxswain.

Mitchie said nothing.

Mthembu unstrapped, went down the ladder, and locked the hatch behind himself.

"Y'all heard that I take it?" said Mitchie.

Hiroshi stood at attention. "Couldn't make out words, ma'am. Just that there was angry shouting."

"All right then. Married couples all have fights." The twitch on his face brought out a small smile on hers. "Enjoy your honeymoon while it lasts. Go finish your lunch. I have the con."

"Yes, ma'am."

Mitchie climbed into her acceleration couch. A long silent shift of watching the cameras for nonexistent intruders was just what she needed right now.

***

"Ma'am?" Ensign Jones popped up in the bridge hatch.

"Come on up, Heidi."

Jones climbed onto the deck and stood at parade rest.

"Relax," ordered Mitchie. She sat on the edge of her acceleration couch and waved the ensign to the other one. "How are the troops?"

"Settled, ma'am. We found a building abandoned during the unpleasantness. The security guard said the landlord skipped town, so we're paying rent to the guard. They're setting up bunks and offices."

"Good work."

"I've also set up virtual and physical dead drops for the chief and myself. We're ready to go undercover as soon as you give us a target." Ensign Jones waited eagerly.

Mitchie took her time replying. She still felt doubts about Jones' aptitude for covert work. Chief Morgan was better suited, but his experience made him expect armed back-up close at hand. Mitchie might not be able to give them any support in an emergency.

The target she was sure of.

"Professor Georges Corday. He's on the Committee of Public Safety. Does a lot of behind the scenes manipulation. Very influential. I need to know his ultimate objective, what he wants, and why. Don't rush. Work your way in slowly. Read everything the analysts can find you on him before you deploy."

"Yes, ma'am!" Jones saluted before disappearing down the hatch.

Good luck, kid, thought Mitchie.

Capitol City, Pintoy, gravity 9.4 m/s^2

The virtual reality parlor looked like all the others Mitchie had seen before. Rows of transparent bubbles holding people in tactile feedback suits. The difference was that these VR junkies were doing push-ups instead of miming swordplay.

"How do you promote team-building in a solitary experience?" she asked.

"They have a squad of fictional people as buddies. The better they do, the better the buddies do. Then they have four drill instructors taking turns yelling at them." Commodore Strittmeyer waved at his trainees, each lost in their personal boot camp.

"Four? Why not just one?"

"Immersion," answered the Fusion Navy officer. "Having the same sergeant yelling at them continuously without getting tired or sweaty eventually triggers their disbelief. Instead every time they switch training stations one is waiting for them in a crisp uniform."

"Just like real boot camp. The staff is rested and trainees

exhausted."

"Exactly," said Strittmeyer.

A bubble split open. The trainee inside dashed to the corner of the building. Mitchie raised an eyebrow at her guide.

"Bathroom break. The biosensors tell us their exact physical state so they're allowed just enough for what they need."

She laughed. "I didn't always get that much time as a plebe."

He shared in the laugh. "Neither did I. But we individualize to keep their focus."

"Doesn't letting them out of the bubble break immersion?"

"It does. We use physical conditioning exercises to get them back into the mindset. Once the sweat is rolling off we can do real training again. Also we have headsets on them. Yelling at them in the latrine keeps their minds from wandering."

"I see. What's your graduation rate?"

"Over ninety-five percent of the ones who make it through the first week complete the six-week course. The big losses are in the first four hours. Almost one in three quit then," said Strittmeyer.

"And then the graduates go to tech school?"

"The very best do. The rest go to ships for on the job training."

"Training from who?"

"Their supervisor. We've been spreading out the crews of the operational ships to provide experienced cadres."

Mitchie did mental arithmetic on what she knew of the Fusion Navy's dispositions. "How experienced? You'd have to put first-hitch spacers in supervisory roles."

"They may not be *experienced*, but they're fully trained. There's also augmented reality scenarios to take them through routine maintenance and operations tasks. That was the predecessor to the virtual boot camp."

"That'll get them through day-to-day but how will they learn trouble-shooting and damage control?"

Strittmeyer grimaced. "The hard way. We can only do so much."

"Of course."

Walking through the rows of bubbles she'd seen trainees doing physical conditioning, marching drill, and some contortions that might have been an obstacle course or unarmed combat. Their eyes were covered by VR goggles. The mouths wore expressions as serious as any trainee she'd seen before.

The commodore used an obstacle-climber as an excuse to blather about the group problem-solving exercises. Mitchie cut him off. "How are you getting officers?"

"From everywhere. Headquarters is pretty lonely now. Most of the Academy faculty were assigned as ship commanders. All the midshipmen are ensigns now."

"Good God. Even the freshmen?"

"Yes. Well, the Commandant had a blackballing party the last night. Thirty-odd middies went out on the street instead. The rest are on ships now."

"Officers that green must be driving the chief petty officers mad."

"If they complain we commission them."

Mitchie laughed. "Sneaky. What do you want out of me?"

"Inspiration. One of the rewards for passing a milestone is a pep talk from a hero. A few were recorded for the prototype test. Some more from troops sent back for long-term hospital treatment. Your record exceeds everyone we've recorded so far."

If running away and herding refugees counted he was probably right. At least the public affairs people found ways to make that sound heroic.

"All right. Let's do it."

"We'll show you an example first."

Techs waited by a pair of empty bubbles. They dressed the visitors in full feedback gear. A few minutes of checks in the bubbles had them ready for VR.

"This is a typical instance," said Commodore Strittmeyer.

Mitchie turned on her heel. They were in the obstacle course area of a boot camp. Trainees and instructors ran everywhere. Most were marked "scenery" in her interface, which possessed privileges no trainee could access. The one actual human was marked with his full name, performance rating, and physical status. More trainees surrounded him, bearing the labels "slug," "brute," "weasel," "joe," and "brain."

"We're invisible to him," said Strittmeyer. "You can talk freely."

"Weasel?" asked Mitchie.

"There's forty-some squadmate simulations. We select them to match the trainee's personality. Weasel encourages him to cheat."

"And another acts as his conscience?"

"No. He has to learn to be his own damn conscience or we don't want him."

"I see."

The human reached the end of the course then turned to cheer on the rest of the squad. As the last one crossed the line a virtual Marine walked up to the group. He congratulated them, told a summary of his medal story, and promised the trainee would do great things when he got to the fleet.

"That's how it works," said the commodore. "We can pair you with a live trainee to do your speech, or you can do it with a virtual one. Give me a moment and I'll find someone about to finish."

Mitchie shook her head. "Don't bother."

The VR controls were standard. Once she filtered for instances with someone active in this spot she could flip through and look at each one.

One trainee was tilting to the side as he struggled to crawl along a log. The display put "RYAN" in glowing letters over his head. Mitchie flipped her invisibility setting from a hundred percent to zero.

He slid off the log and hit the ground spinning. His mouth twisted as the feedback suit squeezed him to simulate a four meter drop onto dirt. At least he was spared the traditional mouthful of mud.

Mitchie went to one knee by his head. "Hard landing, spacer."

Trainee Ryan looked up at her.

"I'm Michigan Long, the Disker. I landed an unarmed cargo ship on Demeter during the invasion to pick up a load of wounded and flew out through a storm of Betrayer missiles. You might have heard of that."

He nodded.

"What you didn't hear about is the times I ran like hell. Or when I was punched in the jaw so hard I blacked out. Or before all that, when I fell off something like that and got so much mud in my nose and mouth I nearly choked."

She leaned toward his face. "But you know what I did? I got up. I got up, and I got back in the fight, and I kicked some ass."

Mitchie stood. "So get up, spacer! The Betrayers are out there. I want you with me when we kick their electronic asses."

Ryan scrambled to his feet. "Ma'am, yes, ma'am!" He trotted toward the beginning of the course to try again.

She turned away. The label "Strittmeyer" hovered over empty space. She set herself to invisible as she walked toward him. "How's that?"

The commodore said, "It's not what we wanted. But I think it's what we needed."

***

Returning to the *Joshua Chamberlain*, Mitchie found Guo and Guen sharing a late lunch in the galley.

"Oh, hey," said her husband with a welcoming grin. "There's some left in the wok if you want to join us."

"Thanks." She checked the wok. It had a half meal's worth of something broccoli-based. She poured it into a bowl.

Behind her Guo was saying, "With all the historical references he's drawing on I'm surprised Corday doesn't have people calling each other Citizen Smith and Citizen Wang."

"Oh, he tried that," answered Guen. "But the second time someone called me Citizen Chairwoman Claret I told him to just say Guen. And we've been on first names ever since. Except Corday's first name is Professor."

"Now that was exercising personal power." Guo's voice was warm with praise. "You didn't need to hold a vote or give an order. You set an example and people followed."

"I guess so." Guen wrenched her eyes from Guo as Mitchie sat next to him. "What did you think of the training?"

Mitchie decided an honest report would be best. "I think one percent of the fleet will blow up from incompetent maintenance. Another percent will be lost to friendly fire. But we're still going to come out ahead on firepower with all those ships manned."

"Good." Guen scraped the last grains of rice out of her bowl. "I'd better be going. There's a Food Subcommittee meeting this evening."

"I'll walk you out," said Guo. He slid out of his seat away from Mitchie and went around the table to take Guen's chair as she stood.

Mitchie said, "Good-bye."

"Bye," said Guen. She snuggled into Guo's side as they walked toward the hatch.

Mitchie looked over the dirty dishes, wondering if Guo would come back to clear them or if she should just wash them all now.

***

"I'm not asking for the whole fleet," said Mitchie. "Just some reinforcements to help them out. The Combined Fleet is tired and worn. They need some hope. One squadron would give them that."

"The Harmony could attack at any time," countered Guen. "We need to concentrate our ships to defend ourselves. That's an important strategic principle, concentration of force, isn't it, Admiral?"

"Well, yes, Madam Chairwoman." Admiral Selig had expected to present a status report on the readiness of newly constructed warships. He was not happy to be dragged into a top-level policy dispute.

Mitchie wasn't impressed. "The Harmony is making noise but what are they actually doing? Nothing. They're probably putting all their effort into redoing their internal structure."

Guen looked down. Then she turned to her aide. "Annie, can you put that report from Danu on the wall?"

Annie fiddled with her console. The view wall shifted from an autumn landscape to a spaceport. Text labeled it as Ballyshannon Port on Danu. Thousands of protestors lined the chain-link fence waving signs.

In the corner of the room Guo put down his reader. He'd been waiting for the meeting to end. Now he stood behind Mitchie for a closer look.

Two dozen spaceships descended to landing pads inside the fence. They wore the elegant calligraphy of the Protectors of Harmony. Mitchie counted eighteen troop transports escorted by destroyers with one heavy cruiser for intimidation.

An English translation of the announcer's speech scrolled along the bottom. A quarter of the planetary council had petitioned for membership in the Harmony. The Harmony had accepted this request and declared a majority council vote rejecting them invalid. Now the new order would be backed with force.

The camera switched from watching the off-loading troops to moving along the line of protestors. "What do the signs say?" asked Mitchie. She knew over a thousand ideograms but the sign-makers were not drawing from the vocabulary of navigation, engineering, or spaceport safety.

Guo translated. "Slave masters go away. You are not welcome. Freedom for stipend kids. Choices for individuals."

"Notice they brought children along," said Guen.

The troops formed up facing the protestors. Thin lines of infantry were broken by armored vehicles mounting heavy guns. Drones hovered overhead. An officer strode forward. He began reading a document through a megaphone. The scrolling text translated it as a formal order to disperse.

"He's talking in Mandarin," said Guo. "Danu's Sinophones speak Cantonese. Even the announcer did."

A few people in the crowd translated for their neighbors. Some of those began to back away. Most of the crowd chanted back against the megaphone.

The officer finished reading, about-faced, and barked a command. The infantry dropped to kneeling stances, rifles ready. Another command. The rifles and heavy guns fired as one. A few of the explosive bullets struck the fence, blowing it into stray wires. Most passed through and shredded the sign-holders. The heavy guns put some angle on their shots, blasting holes in the rear of the crowd.

The officer barked again. The second volley tore into the middle of the protestors. A few of the survivors broke out of their shock to start running as the third volley hit them.

More orders turned the formation to the left. It advanced at a slow march. The news report changed to a split screen. One side showed the Protectors proceeding through the spaceport's main gate. The other, crippled survivors crawling over piles of torn flesh.

"We heard about this," said Mitchie, "but assessed it as a rumor because there wasn't any confirmation. Where the hell has this report been?"

Guen answered, "A trader brought it in four days ago. We asked them not to share it."

"You're censoring the news?"

"Not censoring. We just . . . asked for a delay."

Mitchie laughed. "Guen, when you say 'please pass the salt' everyone hears 'or I'll send you to the guillotine.' Asking is censorship."

"We're going to release it when the first battleship is on line. Then the mob will feel safe instead of panicking and burning down the Sinophone neighborhoods."

Guo was still contemplating the video. "I bet they're going to put Mandarin speakers in all key positions. They're exploiting the fault lines inside the Sinophone community."

"Not my problem," said Guen. "I need that battleship. How soon will it be ready, Admiral?"

"We'll be at initial operational capability this week, ma'am," answered Selig. "She'll be able to help defend the system. The *Dread* will need a couple of months to get her crew trained to where she can participate in offensive operations."

"Try to speed that up. I want to take the offensive against the Harmony before they commit many more massacres like that." Guen shifted her gaze from Selig to Mitchie. "And once we've crushed them the entire fleet can go fight the Betrayers."

Three days later

Taking his wife out to the Capitol's suburbs cost Hiroshi some extra keys but it was worth it. Walking through a shopping district with no visible riot damage and no thugs loitering about was relaxing for Setta.

"So are we going anywhere in particular?" she asked.

"No, just exploring. I thought we'd have dinner then see what else there is around."

Someone was coming toward them in a bright fuchsia jacket and lemon pants. Stipend kid clothes. But just one wasn't a threat.

"Think there's a place with spicy food?"

"I'm sure it's spicy for me."

The stipend kid stepped into their path. "Sir, ma'am, please support the Committee for Public Safety."

She shoved a flyer into Hiroshi's hands. He lifted it to his face to cover the shock of recognition. This was Ensign Jones, one of their undercover agents.

"The Committee is protecting you from the mobs by restoring order. They need your support to have new elections for honest Stakeholders to replace the ones who lied us into this mess."

"I'm all for new elections," said Hiroshi. He needed not to say anything that might break her cover.

"The Committee is working hard for you. They're restoring system monitoring as fast as possible to prevent rogue AIs from forming."

"Oh, good," he said.

Setta interrupted the propaganda pitch. "Are you eating enough, child?"

Jones outranked Setta and was only a year younger—but her head came only to Setta's nose and she was scruffy enough to pass for a teen.

"I have a good meal waiting for me when I'm done passing these out," said the undercover agent.

Setta took another flyer. "Thank you. We will support the Committee."

Jones nodded and moved on in search of her next target.

"You think mint is spicy," said Setta. "Let's keep looking until we find someplace the food has taste."

They held onto the flyers and headed in search of dinner. There were too many observers about to discuss the encounter until they were back at the spaceport.

Nine days later

Joshua Chamberlain, **Capitol Spaceport, Pintoy, gravity 9.4 m/s²**

"Ma'am, is this Ensign Jones?" asked Spacer Ye.

Mitchie looked at the image on the spacer's datasheet. It was the ensign, asleep. No, dead. The peaceful face was belied by the "Do you know this woman?" caption. The seal of the Capitol Police Department rested in the corner. "Yes, it's her. Do you have any more information?"

"No, I was looking for trending news and that popped up."

"Thank you. I'll take care of it."

***

This police station had survived the riots unscathed, or been thoroughly cleaned up. Some chipping on the entryway floor pointed toward the latter. The desk sergeant watched Mitchie approach. His bored expression didn't change.

"I'm Michigan Long, the Disconnected Worlds Liaison to the Committee of Public Safety." The last few words put everyone on alert, including the civilians sitting on the foyer bench.

"Yes, ma'am. How can we be of service?" said the desk sergeant.

"I'm here to see your Jane Doe." Mitchie turned her datasheet to him to display Jones' picture.

Someone in a more formal uniform, ascot and flowing collar, approached. "I'm Major Tong. I'll take you down to the morgue, ma'am." As they descended the stairs he asked, "Did you recognize her?"

"No. But if she's not in your database I thought she must be a Disker."

"A few months ago that would have been true . . . but we didn't have enough backups to keep our data intact."

"I understand."

The morgue wasn't as chilly as she feared. An attendant stood by a sheet-covered gurney.

"Let's see her," ordered Tong.

The sheet pulled back to reveal Ensign Jones in a new set of stipend kid fashions. Mitchie pulled out her datasheet and scrolled through images of the Diskers who'd contacted her wanting a ride off this planet. "She's not on my list. And those are local clothes. But they're new. Let's check something."

Flipping up the other end of the sheet revealed spacer boots. "Those have some wear on them."

The attendant blocked her hands from the boots. "Allow me, ma'am." She deftly unlaced one and wiggled it off the foot.

Mitchie took it and checked the markings inside. "This was made on Bonaventure. She's one of mine, then." She handed the boot back. "What happened to her?"

Tong rolled the body onto its side. A bullet wound showed clearly on the back of skull. Burns surrounded the hole. "Looks like it was a standard self-defense pistol. They're supposed to upload imagery and fingerprints of the user, but . . ." He shrugged.

"Not your fault. I presume this had to be intentional?"

"Oh, yes, ma'am. There's no evidence of a struggle. The body was cleaned before we found it. And she was left in a park. Could've been murdered on the other side of the city from here. Clearly premeditated, likely took an organized group."

"I wonder who she pissed off." *Dammit. Professor Corday understands security, and he's as vicious about that as everything else.*

"If we find anything on the case, we'll be sure to let you know," said Major Tong.

"What would you like us to do with the body, ma'am?" asked the morgue attendant.

"Cremation would be simplest . . . but I should check with her family. Sending the picture to Bonaventure and identifying her would probably take months. How long can you hold the body?"

"For a friend of the Committee we will spare no effort," said Tong.

"I can analyze her DNA and give you an identification dataset," offered the attendant.

"Yes, that would be very helpful, thank you. Please hold her until I find out the family's wishes."

"Yes, ma'am."

Walking out of the station into the sunlight didn't take the chill off. Mitchie started walking back toward the spaceport. A scruffy man approached on the sidewalk, staring at the ground. Then he looked up to meet her eyes for an instant before looking down again.

Damn, what's his name? The figure had been in her year at Intelligence School. *Marven, that's it.*

Marven circled around her on the sidewalk with a muttered, "'Scuse me."

Not a brush pass. But he's trying to make contact. She spotted a piece of paper wedged between bricks in the police station's corner. Scratching her back against the corner let her pocket it.

The feel of the paper in her pocket burned at her but she wasn't going to open this until she was sure she was in private.

***

It said only, "Surveyor Park. Like the drizzly March Tuesday." If she remembered the training exercise Marven meant correctly the dead drop would be under a park bench. One was in roughly the same position as the one she'd trained on. She sat on it and read her datasheet for a quarter hour before standing. A seeming accidental drop of the datasheet let her reach under the bench as she picked it up. *One message item. Successful exercise, ten points.*

Back on the ship she checked the crystal. Encrypted, as it should be. She dropped the task of opening it on Guo with a few catchphrases from her class to start with.

Then it was time to break the news about Jones to her crew. Afterwards she passed around a whiskey bottle and shot glasses. "Space is wide and good friends are too few." They echoed her and drank.

Guo looked up as Mitchie came into their cabin. "Perfect timing." He copied a few more lines from a messy worksheet onto a clean copy.

She read through it. "Straight forward meet. What was the password?"

"It was 'got an eraser.' Okay, what's so funny?"

Mitchie stopped laughing. "Punchline of an old joke."

He looked expectant.

"Right. Miner is taking a shuttle flight. He's a real foul-mouthed guy, every other word out of his mouth is fuck or shit. A priest sits down next to him. Miner has enough manners to not want to cuss in front of a priest. He nods, priest nods back, priest takes out a paper crossword puzzle and starts working on it. Miner's happy, he won't have to say a fucking word all flight.

"Halfway there the priest gets stuck. He asks the miner, 'What's a four letter word for woman, ending U-N-T?' Miner panics. He doesn't want to say that word to a priest. He prays silently, 'God, please don't make me say that.'

"And God answered his prayer. Miner says, 'Aunt. A-U-N-T.' Priest says, 'Oh, of course. Got an eraser?'"

"Heh. So why is it a password?"

"It became our official class euphemism. We used it a lot."

Guo shook his head. "Aren't officers supposed to behave better than that?"

"Nice people don't volunteer as covert intelligence operatives."

"Heidi was nice."

Mitchie poured herself a cup of plum wine. "Yes, she was. I should have realized she wouldn't cut it. Not let her go out and get killed." She drank half the cup.

"You couldn't have known she'd fail. And you didn't know Corday's people were that rough."

"Oh, no, why would I have guessed that Professor Guillotine

would be willing to commit a secret murder? All the thousands of people he killed lost their heads in public."

Guo kept his voice level. "You needed the information. You still do."

"Yeah. Next decision is whether to pull Chief Morgan out." Mitchie drained the cup.

"He'll be fine. He's a total asshole."

She laughed.

***

Mitchie saw Marven walk up to the edge of the duck pond. A few of the park's fat ducks paddled toward him to see if he'd offer anything interesting. He tossed something into the water, producing wing-flaps and splashes as they raced for it.

Her stroll along the water's edge brought her to him. "Hi."

"Hello, Commander," said Marven. "Congratulations on surviving your many adventures."

"Thank you. Congratulations on surviving the events here."

More ducks were arriving, quacking at each other to get out of the way. The noise should interfere with any eavesdroppers. He tossed out some more to encourage them.

"Is the stuff the news says about you true?"

"About three-quarters of it. As usual." Mitchie held out a cupped hand.

He poured his bag into it. It wasn't bread. They were green wafers, with raised lettering declaring they were ideal nutrition for ducks and most waterfowl. She tossed one into the mob of ducks, sparking more commotion.

"Now the important question. Who the hell appointed you the Disconnected Worlds ambassador to the new government?"

"Liaison. Nobody did. I'm senior officer present. Unless you've been promoted?"

"No, I'm still a lieutenant senior-grade. I haven't been grandstanding in front of admirals."

Mitchie bit back an angry retort. She needed Marven's willing cooperation. "There's a destroyer on the way to Bonaventure and a squadron carrying my report to Combined Fleet Command. Until orders or a new boss return from either one, I'm it. We can't ignore this mess. What if some demagogue convinces them to go attack the Disconnect?"

Marven threw more wafers to the ducks as he contemplated that. "What are your orders, ma'am?"

"Start with a status report."

"There are five of us with solid covers. We have separate safe houses and homes for our covers. We have lots of data on the Fusion Navy, which the Combined Fleet now has from the Fuzies. We collected lots of data on Stakeholders who've since been burned alive, beheaded, or fled the planet."

"Anything on Guen Claret?" asked Mitchie. A double-check on her personal assessment would be useful.

"She had zero seniority and the Dynamist party had hardly any clout so we didn't bother. Now it's too dangerous to try to get close to her. Or anyone on the Committee of Public Safety. As both your agents found."

"Both?"

"The other fought his way out of an ambush. Killed three of Corday's men, wounded two, and broke contact. We found him and took him to a safe house."

"Good for Chief Morgan. How is he?"

Marven shrugged. "He'll be back on duty in a couple of weeks. When he gets home he'll need a chunk of lung and some intestine regrown."

"That may be a while. What are your current collection targets?"

"You and your amateurs. We've mostly been sitting tight. Figuring out how to make contact without blowing our cover was hard." Marven sounded resentful.

Mitchie tossed more to the ducks as she thought. "The primary target is Professor Corday. He instigated the CPS and most of its atrocities. We need to know what his goal is and if it's a threat to the

Disconnected Worlds. Second goal is to detect any agents from Ping's Harmony."

That provoked a burst of laughter from Marven. "Not asking much, are you?"

"The good news is I can get you support staff. As you said, amateurs, but they're loyal Diskers with security clearances. You can staff up the safe houses and stop being your own janitor."

"That'd help." He up-ended the bag to shake broken wafers over the ducks. "But you're asking us to go to the well too many times."

"We're all going to the well too often, Lieutenant Marven. All of us."

Chapter Five: Conspiracy

Six days later
Capitol City, Pintoy, gravity 9.4 m/s²

"Enjoy yourselves," said Mitchie as she closed the door.

The hotel hallway was empty. She started walking toward the elevator. Giving Guo and Guen privacy left her at loose ends for a few hours. She had no idea what to do. They were only in the hotel for the weekend because Guen feared her frequent visits to their ship would look suspicious.

On the ground floor the elevator faced the bar. She walked straight in and took a stool. The menu gave everything "revolutionary" names. She ordered a "Head In a Basket."

It was rum and fruit juice. Mitchie drank it slowly. Married life had cut down her alcohol consumption. She wasn't used to something with this much of a kick any more.

The bartender made eye contact once. Then he polished glasses at the far end of the bar. *Do I look that cranky? I guess I am that cranky.*

Six empty bar stools made a line between Mitchie and the next customer. Someone sat down on the one next to her. "Buy me a drink, sugar?"

Mitchie said, "You're dialing the wrong number."

"You're ignoring the boys. I thought you might be in the mood for some . . . girl talk."

She looked the whore up and down. "Thanks, but I couldn't afford you."

"A cutie like you I'd give a discount to." The stranger studied Mitchie's face. "You look like you need to vent."

Sigh. "You're right. But you're not a therapist."

"I keep secrets better than they do."

That broke her resistance. Mitchie shoved her glass away. "Let's do it. This place have any good wine?"

The whore waved at the bartender. "Franz. Bottle of house Merlot."

He looked to Mitchie. When she nodded he produced a bottle.

They exited the elevator on the eighth floor, only halfway to where Guo was introducing Guen to ecstasy.

The whore said, "I'm Iroth," as she closed the door behind them. "You're welcome to cry on my shoulder, or whatever else you like."

"I'm Michigan."

Iroth took two wine goblets out of a cupboard. "You do have the look. But if you're going to pick a fake name it's better to use one that other people aren't already copying."

Mitchie didn't argue. She pulled her Space Guard identification card out of her pocket and handed it over.

Iroth read it out loud. "Michigan Long, Commander, Akiak Space Guard . . . you're really her."

"Yep."

"Ohmyohmyohmyohmy—can I call my friend Blythe? Can she come join us? Blythe will kill me if she finds out you were here and I didn't tell her." Iroth's professional façade fell away, revealing a star struck fan.

"Why Blythe?"

"She, um, well, she does you."

"What?"

"Well, there are guys, who've heard of you, and, um, obsess, and she, um, scratches that itch for them."

This was an aspect of infamy that had never occurred to Mitchie before. "Yeah, call her."

***

Blythe was scary.

She wasn't a perfect mirror-image. Just a bit too tall, the face was too narrow despite Fusion medicine's best efforts, and just looking at the breasts made Mitchie's back ache.

The clothes didn't match either. Mitchie wore a blouse and slacks in don't-notice-me grey and brown. Blythe's outfit might have started as a jumpsuit, but it was tailored to follow every curve. She wore it only partially zipped, leaving her navel as anchor to the bare skin above.

"Oh, my God, it is you, it is!"

"I told you," said Iroth.

"Oh, wow."

"Hi," said Mitchie. "So what exactly do you . . . do for these guys?"

Iroth gave Blythe a goblet and topped off Mitchie's. Three armchairs made a cozy circle for them to sit in.

"Usually he'll have a case in mind. I just follow the script and bam, he's happy."

"A case?"

"One of your documented interrogations. Fusion Counter-Intelligence back-tracked all your operations. There's weeks of public surveillance video of you, detailed transcripts from everyone you targeted, even simulations of some incidents."

"How do you know all this? Isn't that classified?"

"It's an interrogation fantasy. I have to ask them about *something* classified."

"Your customers are FCI agents?"

"Sure. That's how it starts. They go through your surveillance file, start doing themselves at work, then at home. Finally they go looking for a short girl."

Iroth quipped, "And we send them to her."

"Good God," said Mitchie. "FCI is using their database as a pornography library. No wonder they're so bad at catching spies."

"It's not all agents. The Wentworth interrogation is public. There's a lot of guys who see that and your pictures and come to me."

Mitchie's face scrunched up as if she'd found half a worm in her apple. "They want to be suffocated?"

Blythe shrugged. "I try to give them what they want."

Boys are so strange. "Why?"

Blythe looked helplessly at Iroth. The older whore said, "We make our money figuring out *how* to give them what they want. There's no money in why."

"Okay, I believe you, I just can't wrap my head around it."

"Speaking of how." Blythe was suddenly shy. "How do you make a guy pass out without killing him? I strap him down and put my hand over his nose and mouth but I always lose my nerve before they pass out. Some of them demanded their money back. But they thrash so much I'm afraid of a heart attack."

Mitchie swigged down her wine. "I couldn't do it by holding my hand on his face. That's too intimate." She felt her boot knife slide into a heart, chilling her spine.

Shop talk was more comfortable than the conversation she'd planned on having here. "I had him in a pressure suit. Airtight, I just turned a valve to cut off his air. He could still breathe in and out, just got bad air. So less stress than covering his mouth."

Iroth topped off Mitchie's wine again.

"You need to have medical sensors. Full set. Pulse, blood pressure, oxygen fraction, carotid and jugular velocity, neurotransmitter levels, all that. The readouts will tell you if he's hitting a danger level on any of them. So just sit back and wait for him to pass out."

"Perfect. Thank you. That's exactly what I needed to know. What book were you reading?"

"Book? When?"

"Wentworth said you were reading a book but he didn't remember the title."

"Does it matter?" asked Mitchie.

"For what they're paying I should get every detail right."

"Um . . . probably *Marooned on Akiak*. But I don't recommend it. It's terrible. Kind of a guilty pleasure."

"That's okay, I just need the cover."

Blythe went on to demand more details, some on incidents Mitchie barely remembered. Iroth ordered two more bottles from room service. Mitchie used the time Blythe spent typing in notes to sip more wine.

"Next. There's a recent rumor that you hide a knife in your pussy."

"Ow. Hell, no. It's in my underwear."

The whores looked hopeful and expectant.

"Fine." Mitchie unzipped her slacks, pulled out the hide knife, and dropped it on the coffee table.

"Oh, that is sneaky," said Blythe.

Iroth laughed. "I wouldn't want to stick that inside me either."

"If you want every detail right you need to fix your belly button."

"This is my original. There are no naked pictures of you at all. Do you know how rare that is? What does it look like?"

Mitchie pulled up her blouse.

Blythe leaned forward to study the navel. "Right. I can describe that to the doc. Fixable."

"How much did you already get fixed?"

The whore shrugged. "Usual amount of work for a professional."

"The eye color work was the worst," said Iroth. "I was living with her for a week until the bandages came off."

"Boys notice details like that. Especially if they've spent who knows how long staring at a picture."

Mitchie snarked, "You'd think they'd notice the breasts are the wrong size."

"Some do. But they react anyway. It's an instinct." Blythe twisted in her seat, dropping the pseudo-jumpsuit to her waist. "I had them get the shape right, I hope."

"Um." Mitchie glanced down. It was a lousy angle to compare them. "Guess so." Looked back up. "Nipples are the wrong color."

"Oh? What should they be?"

"Pink." Mitchie regretted her last two glasses of wine.

"Blythe's are pink," said Iroth.

"Yeah, but a darker pink. Oh, hell." It was easier to unsnap blouse and bra than to try to find the right words.

Iroth pulled a make-up kit out of her purse. She spun the dial before holding it up to Mitchie's chest.

"That's it," said Blythe.

"Rouge LM," Iroth read off the gadget.

"Now you know everything you could possibly need to know," said Mitchie.

"There is one more thing."

"What?"

"The sounds you make when you climax." Blythe flinched back from Mitchie's glare. "They tell me I'm getting it wrong!"

"How the hell would they know?"

"There's an audio recording. It's highly classified, nobody's willing to let me hear it."

Mitchie cursed at length. "Who did that?"

"I don't know his name. A fighter pilot."

"Housefly Seventeen. Yeah, he's enough of an asshole to do that." Iroth giggled. "Going to kick his ass?"

"Can't. He's already dead."

That alarmed the whores. "I didn't think you did much of that," said Blythe.

"I didn't do it. Combat loss. His squadron was destroyed trying to protect a freighter full of refugees from a Betrayer attack." Her freighter. Being grateful to him for that didn't mix well with being angry over the recording.

"So you understand why I need to know." Blythe was kneeling in front of Mitchie's chair now.

Crap. I didn't zip up my pants after taking the knife out.

Iroth leaned down for a kiss. "Relax, sugar. We know what we're doing."

***

Pillow talk was a chance for Mitchie to unload the rant she'd come to this room to give. The whores listened attentively.

"You're pissed at him for doing what you asked him to do?" said Iroth.

"I'm not *pissed*. It's . . . the guy was always paying attention to me. I thought it was just high situational awareness. Didn't even realize he liked me. Now she walks into the room and it's like I'm invisible." Who 'she' was had stayed vague in her story.

Blythe asked, "When did you realize he liked you?"

"He killed two guys who'd taken me captive."

"That's not in your file!"

Mitchie threw her hands into the air. "Thank you, Lord! There's one part of my life that FCI isn't using for entertainment."

"Have you talked to him about the invisible thing?" said Iroth.

"I haven't tried to talk about it much. After the first time he was mad at me for rushing things. When he found out I wanted it for politics he blew up. Now we sorta tiptoe around it."

"But he's still fucking her."

"They've probably fallen asleep by now."

"You need to talk to him," pressed Iroth. "Explain what you need. Ask him to give it to you. You're not asking much. Just attention, recognition. Acknowledging you exist while she's there."

"How can I demand more for me while I'm insisting he give so much to her? She's so damn needy I think he's at his limit as it is."

"Is he getting what he needs?"

Blythe laughed. "He's getting a hot teenager. What more could a guy want?"

Iroth stayed focused on Mitchie. "Seriously. Is he?"

"I don't know. He's not a complainer."

"Then you'd better check."

Mitchie thought on this.

Iroth had her own chain of thought. "Guenivere Claret was a virgin?"

"How the fuck did you—I didn't say that!" blurted Mitchie.

"Only person in the CPS or Active Groups who fit the description. But I thought a trillionaire's kid would have partied harder than that."

"There's Lorraine Q," interjected Blythe.

"Lorraine is using her Active Group to hunt down the guys who gang-raped her and send them to the guillotine. She may need to learn what good sex is but she's not naïve."

Mitchie pleaded, "Between her mother's murder and the kidnapping attempts Guen was locked up tight until now. Please don't share this, it could get her killed."

Iroth said, "These days anything can get someone killed—"

"Or nothing," quipped Blythe.

"—but the first one to die is always the whore who talked too much. She's safe from us. And so are you."

The "Conscript's March" from *Three Wars In Five Generations* set Mitchie's datasheet quivering. She crawled over Blythe to grab it from her pants. Before answering she made sure nothing but her face and the wall would be visible.

"Hi, *baobei.*"

Guo looked tired. "Hey. She just left. I miss you. Can you come back soon? Where are you?"

"I ran into a couple of fans in the bar. We've been chatting."

"Oh, good. Glad you weren't bored. I need a shower."

"Go ahead. I'll probably be back before you're done."

They exchanged kisses.

When Guo disconnected Mitchie said, "Are there towels in there?"

"Of course," answered Iroth.

"Right. I need to rinse and run."

Iroth followed her into the bathroom.

"I don't have time for anything, I need to run," snapped Mitchie.

"You want to let me do a lipstick check."

***

The whores pointed out joining Guo in the shower would be easier than drying off completely. He didn't hear her come in. With his head immersed in the spray he might not have heard a gunshot. She pressed her torso against his back.

"Hey! You're back."

They pivoted to both stand in the spray.

"All clean now?" she asked.

"Mmmm. Haven't really washed. Just wanted to get the sticky feeling off."

"Did you?"

"Everything except my conscience."

Mitchie grabbed the soap. "Let's see if getting you all the way clean helps with that."

Once she soaped him head to toe he wanted to return the favor. Which led to other things. Eventually they collapsed on the bed wrapped in towels.

Mitchie finally broke the cuddle. "How's your conscience?"

"Still unhappy."

"You regret fucking her?"

"The sex isn't the problem. However we started this," —yep, he was still mad— "she knows what she's doing now. It's listening to 'boo-hoo, I signed death warrants for a thousand people half of whom are innocent, but I'm afraid to say no,' and then I have to kiss her and say it's all right."

Guo glared at the ceiling. "It's not all right. It's a Goddamn atrocity. She's enabling it. And now I'm enabling it."

Mitchie had to admit Guo wasn't the best fit for this kind of influence operation. "Did you tell her that?"

"Hell no. You're right, we need her in charge and liking us. So I made her happy and gave her a pep talk about power growing as she uses it."

She wriggled out of her towels and sat cross-legged facing him. His eyes locked on to her, easing her heart a bit. "How are you handling the stress?"

"I don't know that I'd call it stress. I'm okay. I just hate having to lie. It's worse lying with my whole body."

"The sex?"

"Sex is the easy part. It's when we're cuddling and she talks about some atrocity. Keep my voice sympathetic, easy. Fake smile, fine. But I have to keep my arms and legs wrapped snugly around her like I'm holding a pretty girl instead of a venomous snake."

"Sounds like you're doing a good job at it."

"Mostly I think she's too clueless to realize I'm screwing up."

Mitchie laughed.

"I'm handling it," Guo said firmly.

She squeezed his shoulder muscles, feeling the tension. "How long can you keep it up? Do we need to get you out of this?"

"No. I can keep doing this. She's someone we need to keep on our side."

"So she's a decent lay," teased Mitchie.

"She's learning fast." He wasn't amused.

"Are you getting what you need?"

"I think so. Letting me vent helps. Seeing you're not mad helps. How about you?"

She shifted position closer to him. His eyes flicked down as her breasts jiggled. "Just having you look at me helps."

"I always look at you."

"Eh . . . not while she's in the room."

Guo looked upwards in thought, then back at Mitchie. "Yeah. She wants all of my attention. If I look at something else, even a clock, she moves into my line of sight or says something I have to answer."

"I hadn't realized it was intentional."

"I'm not sure it is. She's just insecure. Probably just subconsciously trying to hold my attention. I've been going along with it to keep her happy. I'll make sure I keep looking at you while she's here."

"No . . . no, focus on her. Better that I'm insecure than Guen. You can make it up to me later."

"I'll work on that." He gripped her hand. "Tell me about those fans you met."

"Oh, that's a story. I wound up doing professional consulting for them."

"Piloting or captaining?"

"Worse. They poured a bottle and a half of wine into me and asked me how to torture people." Mitchie explained about Blythe's clients. Seeing Guo look as boggled as she felt reassured her about men in general and him in particular.

"Sheesh," said Guo. "This sounds like the opening of a porn holo."

"Yeah, well, um . . . they're whores. They have only one way to say thank you."

He burst out laughing. "If I wasn't so drained right now I'd be angry. With someone you just met?"

"We'd gotten to know each other. And Blythe is just like me so that makes it masturbation not sex, right?"

"Hmmm. Looks just like you . . ."

"No. Fuck no. Absolutely not. Never. No fucking way." In the back of her head a mocking voice quoted, *I'm completely confident in my body. My breasts are the perfect size.*

A broad grin spread over Guo's face. "That's why we should talk about it before screwing other people. What if I'd met her first? I'd be telling you, 'Sorry, honey, I didn't realize she wasn't you until—'" The pillow cut off the rest.

There were plenty of pillows in Guo's reach but he made it a tickle fight instead.

***

An invitation to join Guen in 'pressing the flesh' was considered a high honor by the other CPS members. To Mitchie it felt like a good way to get shot.

When Annie urged her to bring a pistol Mitchie asked what the rules of engagement were.

"I trust you to use your judgement," said the bodyguard.

My judgement says to stay home.

The Van Rijn Plaza was a popular gathering spot for Capitol City's upper middle class. Post-revolution it became a "members only club" but the armed guards only checked stipend kids for membership cards.

Guen bought memberships for herself, Annie, and Mitchie. The dozen bodyguards were left in the greensward by the drop-off zone. Annie didn't complain. The set of her jaw said it took effort to not complain.

Once in the covered plaza they fit in better. Guen and Annie were in elegant dresses, a notch above what the patrons were wearing. Mitchie's Space Guard undress uniform wasn't too far from the men's suits. It looked a decade behind fashion instead of a class below.

A wandering wine seller decided it was safer to accept the three women's custom than avoid them. He poured them each a glass of his "finest red."

Mitchie thought the taste was excellent and color ominous.

The crowd was thinning out in front of them. The patrons were drifting to the far side of the plaza.

Guen made a show of enjoying herself. A stand-alone kiosk sold desserts by the slice. Mitchie found herself with cheesecake covered with sliced strawberries. It was delicious. *I wonder how they're getting their luxuries in when there's so little real food the tenements are eating synthetic carbohydrate paste twice a week.*

The trio sat at a little round table as they ate. Annie had nudged toward one in an open area. Mitchie thought she'd be happier by a wall she could put her back to.

The crowd was drifting back toward them. People wanted to peek at the infamous Chairwoman of the Committee of Public Safety. In this neighborhood they called her the Queen of Guillotines.

But not where a stipend kid could hear it.

Mitchie did her part to keep the table conversation going. The story of how she'd broken her arm as a little girl by climbing on top of a cow and trying to make it gallop provoked real laughter from her companions.

Guen put her fork down with her peach pie half-finished. She stood and faced the thickest part of the crowd watching her. "Hello, friends!"

The front row flinched back.

"I know you're worried about what's going to happen next. Everybody is. We're restoring basic infrastructure. When that's done we'll have elections for open local offices. Then we can elect a new Council of Stakeholders, one that will be honest and take care of everyone."

The crowd wasn't moved by Guen's speech. They'd heard it before in the CPS's official propaganda broadcasts.

She switched her approach. "Feel free to ask me questions."

Someone too far back in the crowd to identify yelled, "Will you cut off our heads if you don't like them?"

Her tone was firm. "No. Execution is for criminals, not curmudgeons."

Mitchie kept her face still. Everyone knew the CPS had killed people to appease the stipend kid mob. Even the trials being held now put the burden of proof on the captive if the right people laid accusations.

An older woman stepped out of the crowd. "Why are you wasting time with unimportant things when Betrayers are running loose?"

"Ma'am, the Combined Fleet has destroyed every Betrayer for two or three systems from here."

"We mean the Betrayers that could be forming here," said a man in a pastel orange opera suit.

"There's gaps in the monitoring everywhere!"

"All those kids are running around with systems that keep operating in unmonitored areas!"

More people talked over each other.

"Please!" Guen threw up her hands. "We're working on it!"

The crowd settled down, remembering to be afraid of her.

She continued, "There's engineers working right now to restore monitoring. It's a top priority along with water, power, and sewage."

"I'd rather crap in a bucket than be killed by a Betrayer," said the man in the orange suit.

"I agree. Even the Diskers agree." Guen waved at Mitchie as she said it.

Mitchie smiled and nodded. *Just a visual aid, that's me.*

"But think how it looks to the underclass. If they're using buckets or bushes while work goes into network connections, they get mad. They think the network is just to give you people deliverybots and autocars. When they get angry they go out to snap antennas and smash cameras and cut cables. Then we have more work to do. So please be patient. And I assure you every report of potential Betrayer activity is promptly investigated."

There were mutters of "damn stipend kids" but no one contested this.

Guen pointed at a man in pink. "Sir, you look like you have a question."

"Well . . . when are we going back to cash taxation? Confiscating in-kind materials is killing businesses."

She smiled. This question she was ready for.

BDS *Patton*, Boswell System, acceleration 0 m/s²

Two Betrayer ships blew apart as missiles hit home. A third

smashed into the asteroid. One of the rock's engine plumes went out. A moment later a second shut down on the other side to maintain balance.

"That's the last of them, sir," said the tactical officer. "The enemy has nothing left but its planet-side forces."

"The rock is still on course for impact in a week," reported Astrodynamics.

The flag bridge crew was too tired to cheer but the relaxation was obvious.

"Wonderful," said Admiral Galen. "Pass the word for all combat units to go to minimum manning."

Before the admiral could sneak off for some rest of his own his chief of staff approached datasheet in hand.

"Can't this wait?" groaned Galen.

"Most of this has waited for days," replied Commodore Deng.

"Fine."

"First item. The last reinforcement convoy brought another dispatch from Commander Long."

"Let me guess. The Fusion is a shambles and she's asking what I want her to do about it."

"Yessir."

"I don't know, any orders I give will be obsolete by the time they reach her, and she'll ignore them if she doesn't like them anyway. I'm not going to waste a ship to deliver that message."

"Yes, sir." Deng checked off the item. "Two. Logistics wants to stop missile production to do maintenance on the fabricators."

Joshua Chamberlain, Capitol Spaceport, Pintoy, gravity 9.4 m/s^2

When *Walking Rollo* returned from the Disconnected Worlds with a Defense Coordinating Committee courier Mitchie was delighted. This lasted until she heard his message.

"Appreciate my efforts? What the fuck does that mean?"

Mitchie's office on the *Joshua Chamberlain* was cramped with her, Guo, and the courier all in it. He leaned against the locked hatch as she yelled.

"The DCC voted to recognize that you're doing great work here."

"I don't need recognition. I need decisions. Is the Disconnect going to take sides in the Fusion's civil war? Are we recognizing the CPS as a legitimate government? Are we sending ships?"

"Yes, well, all those questions were voted on. But the DCC can only act when there's a unanimous vote. There isn't a full consensus on how to handle the situation."

Guo shook his head.

"Then why didn't they order me off Pintoy?" Mitchie demanded.

"That vote also failed."

"Okay." Mitchie took a deep breath to calm herself. "By how much did those votes fail?"

The courier slid toward the latch side of the hatch. "DCC voting records are strictly confidential. I don't have access to them."

"Fine. You're useless to me. Get out."

"Do you have any message for the DCC, ma'am?"

"No. And you're not going back to them. Report to Chief Morgan, he'll have some work for you."

The courier opened his mouth, possibly to point out he was a civilian, then closed it again. He shut the hatch behind him.

Guo waited for Mitchie to stop cursing before he said anything. "The DCC only worked well because they were facing a Fusion invasion fleet. Take the predator pressure away and they're just a bunch of politicians with different agendas and no accountability."

"It's not just them. I've sent six messages to Admiral Galen and heard nothing back."

"He probably can't spare a ship for courier duty."

"He's going to court martial my ass."

Guo said, "Maybe not. I found a precedent."

"Oh?"

"This guy named Wendell Fertig. He was the same rank as you when the Second World War started. When he was caught behind enemy lines he promoted himself to general and led a rebellion among the locals."

"Did he get court-martialed?"

"No. He received a medal and a promotion. They didn't promote him to general, though."

"We'll see if the court accepts it. I doubt pre-Golden Age precedents will go over well."

***

Weather Control scheduled the heavy rain for late in the evening. That made it the best time to stroll to the safe house without being seen. Mitchie's umbrella didn't survive the walk. Her coat was soaked through.

"Cook" and "butler" weren't among the skills Mitchie had looked for in the squadron volunteers. The ones staffing the safe house still managed to put her in a dry robe with a cup of hot chocolate for her sit-down with Marven.

"Sorry you got so chilled, ma'am," said the head spy.

"Not your fault. I always get cold easy. Don't put out the heat big people do. What do you have?"

His notes were on paper for security. "We have inserted two people into his organization but they're in the outer rings. There's some inner members we've made contact with. Nothing useful from them yet. Our best success is in penetrating their datasystems. We've analyzed their physical facilities and found an isolated system."

Mitchie sipped hot chocolate. "So you don't have anything on his plans yet. Why did you want the meeting?"

"I think the best approach is to brute-force the airgapped datasystem." He shuffled the papers to put a building floorplan on top.

"You want to break into his headquarters?"

"If we time it right we can get in and out without anyone noticing." She waved the cup to encourage him to go on.

"He's throwing a party at his townhouse next week. That's an all-hands operation. Almost all his people will be doing perimeter there or playing servants. The headquarters will just have a handful of watchmen."

"How many do you have available?" She drained the cup and put it on the only uncovered part of the table.

"That's the problem. Most of my people have been hanging around that building. The security system has enough data to recognize them just from their walks. That leaves me and Quang. We need a third to be sure of success."

"I'd have some qualms about letting one of the support crew attempt an infiltration."

"No, none of them have the training we need. The only other person who does is you."

Mitchie laughed. That sounded like more fun than another round of diplomacy with imbeciles and maniacs. "Can't. I'm going to be at that party."

"Say you're sick."

"And then someone my size shows up on their security sensors? Doesn't need a professor to figure that out."

"Figure something out. We need you. You have the most hands-on experience with Fusion secure systems." Marven refilled Mitchie's cup from a thermos.

She took a sip, not needing the warmth so much now. "I might be able to establish an alibi."

***

They circulated for fifteen minutes before encountering their host. "Commander Long, Senior Chief Kwan. Thank you for coming. We need closer ties with the Disconnected Worlds."

"Thank you for inviting us, Professor Corday," said Guo. "We're glad to get to know our neighbors better."

Blythe said, "Your drink's almost out, let me get you a new one." She disappeared with Guo's quarter-full glass.

"Did I offend her?" asked the professor.

"Oh, everyone has," said Guo, projecting an air of a husband weary of his wife's quirks. "I have to tell you I greatly admire *Bloodlust As Politics*. I just re-read it—I read it when it first came out—and it's still a powerful telling of the Revolution."

"Thank you. It's good to know I have one reader who isn't being forced into the book to pass a test." He followed the rehearsed witticism with a real chuckle.

"I've been reading your others, on Germany and Rwanda. Fascinating. Though *Dripping Machetes* isn't as good as the other two."

"That was my dissertation, and I had to keep bending things to make the committee happy. They demanded changes even though the documentation clearly—anyway, academics have their own politics."

"Academic politics must seem amusing compared to what's happening today."

The professor laughed. "It was even more angry and bitter. Now conflicts are *solved* instead of locking two rivals into a room with each other forever."

By 'solved' Guo assumed he was referring to decapitating the loser. "Do you have any time for writing now?"

"Hardly. I can barely take notes on what's going on around me. Hopefully someone not in the line of fire will write this up properly."

"I was thinking of writing laws. The Fusion needs a new constitution, something the Harmony worlds can agree to as well."

"Perhaps we do. But I don't have time for one. Perhaps you should draft one, you're well-read enough. Ah, Wayne Searcher has arrived, you must excuse me."

"Of course." Guo looked after Professor Corday as he disappeared into the crowd.

Blythe arrived and handed him a margarita. "Here you go, dear."

"Thank you. That was . . . interesting."

"You found up what he's up to?"

"No, ruled out one possibility for it. Let's find a quiet spot."

The ballroom overlooked a sunken garden. An open door to a balcony made a nice nook for them to hide in.

"I've been saying hello to people," said Blythe. "Is that enough showing the flag for the night?"

"No, we need to stay here until I get the word."

"Well. Silver lining. Should be long enough for you to tell me how good a job I'm doing at it."

Guo gave her a hard look. "You're doing a terrible job."

"What? How?" The bewildered expression was one Mitchie would never wear.

"You're only paying attention to me."

"Well, of course. You're my husband."

Guo shook his head. "Mitchie would have her attention spread over the whole room, watching for anyone she should be targeting. She'd be tracking anyone close enough to grab her. That guy behind you? She'd know if he had a concealed weapon and which hand he'd draw it with. Yes, she pays attention to me. But never only me."

"Oh."

"Let's go hit the buffet. And look around this time."

***

The youth spasmed and fell to the ground. Quang ran up and pulled the stun bag off his victim's neck. He added a few dance steps that practically shouted, "It worked! It worked!"

Mitchie followed behind, sweeping the suppressor beam over anything that looked like it might hide a camera or other sensor. *That's why we need pros for this*, she thought. *An amateur would've said something and given Corday a voiceprint.*

Behind her Marven stared at the screen of his sensor/jammer box. The spy had pulled out all his gadgets for this mission. They'd decided there was no chance of concealing that the break-in had happened so they were using all their tools to finish the job before reinforcements arrived.

Marven walked ahead of Quang, making an 'all clear' gesture. His box must not show any watchmen beyond the three they'd already knocked out. He led them to the emergency stairs and stood aside to let Quang disable the alarms.

The steps had a thin layer of dust. Nobody bothered with fire drills in this building. Mitchie carefully put her feet in the marks left by the others.

At the top floor Marven ran the scanner for two minutes before stepping into the hallway. Mitchie forced herself to hold still despite envisioning a carload of Corday's thugs arriving below. Fidget patterns could be distinctive, if any motion sensors penetrated the jamming field to record her.

The lock on the computer room resisted Quang's first attempt. Marven opened it with a hammer and chisel.

Workstations and datasheets of all sizes lined the walls of the room. An oversized view screen clung to the ceiling, ready to be lowered down for meetings. All were connected to tendrils of the building's data network.

A wooden table in the center held a high-powered workstation with a holographic display. Only a power cable penetrated the smooth case. Their target.

Mitchie squeezed a chair to its maximum height and set to work. The palmlock wasn't fooled by twists and wiggles. The names and passwords they'd brainstormed were rejected. The hammer and chisel came out again to take a side off the workstation's box.

A portable memory bank came out of Mitchie's bag. She popped the workstation's array of memory crystals out of their slot. The bag produced a bunch of cables, one of which mated to the frame holding the crystal array. Another connected it to the memory bank.

Then Mitchie pressed a button and sat back. Brute-force copying of all the data on the workstation would work. It would just take longer than using the workstation's own system to select the interesting bits.

Marven circled the room, inspecting every workstation to see if it was unplugged.

Quang paced aimlessly. The second time he looked over Mitchie's head to check progress she put a hand on his shoulder and pressed until he stopped jittering. After that he waited by the door at parade rest.

The memory bank's 'beep' sounded painfully loud to the trio's frayed nerves. Mitchie unplugged the crystal array and stuffed everything else in her bag.

Halfway down the stairs Marven froze. He scribbled on the

scanner's screen and held it up. "Camera shows flyer landing in street. We go out back." Mitchie and Quang nodded.

They kept going at the same pace, trying to stay quiet.

On the ground floor Marven led them left from the stairs, the opposite direction from how they came in. Echoes of boots sounded through the halls. Corday's boys must have split up to search.

"Hey, I see them!"

Mitchie's goggles turned black as Marven tossed a dazzler at the thug. She ducked as bullets whined past. The thug couldn't aim, he just emptied his pistol down the hall.

"Shit!" barked Quang.

She grabbed a bandage from a belt pouch. The goggles didn't have to clear all the way for her to see the blood coming from his arm. She wrapped it tightly, more worried about blood leaking out than treating the wound. Quang hissed.

Marven threw a smoke grenade and some toe tappers down the hallway then grabbed a can off his belt. He sprayed organics cleaner on the floor and wall, then sprayed Quang. It wouldn't do him any good but they couldn't afford to let the blood on his clothes drip as they ran.

More thugs came around the corner as the smoke grenade popped. Curses mixed with the first thug repeating, "I don't know, they blinded me." The trio stepped lightly along the corridor.

They turned a corner as the first toe-tapper was stepped on. It skittered around making pop-pop-pop sounds. Deeper pops indicated a thug panicked and fired into the smoke. Another toe-tapper went off.

Mitchie worried the noise would conceal another group of searchers closing in on them. But they went out the back door without seeing anyone else. A block away they gave Quang some much-appreciated medicine.

The support staff had cached changes of clothing in four alleys near Corday's HQ. They took an evasive route to the northern one. The old clothes, along with gloves, galoshes, goggles, and hoods, went into a squeeze bag to be destroyed. Marven took the databank.

Mitchie shook his hand. "Excellent mission. Well done."

"Thank you, ma'am," he replied. "I appreciate your help."

She stopped herself before offering her hand to Quang. He waved his uninjured left arm. "Stay safe, ma'am."

"You too. Let me know if you need a doctor."

"We have everything he needs at the house," said Marven.

"Good. See you soon." She stuffed the bag under her shirt and started toward the spaceport. She had to make another stop to change into the outfit Blythe had worn before making the switch.

Joshua Chamberlain, Pintoy Spaceport, Pintoy, gravity 9.4 m/s²

"Welcome home," said Guo with relief.

Now that's fidelity, thought Mitchie. *Normally a husband chatting with a big-titted hussy flinches when his wife gets home.* "Hi, *baobei*." She kicked off the borrowed high heeled shoes and draped the pink raincoat over a chair. Blythe would wear them off the ship to finish the switch for any observers.

Blythe straightened up. "Hello, Michigan." The way she'd been leaning across the galley table must have given Guo quite a view. He was opposite her, looking almost cornered against the counter.

"Hi, Blythe. How was the party?"

"Um, okay. I didn't talk much. Some people might be offended."

"I'll deal with that. Let's get you paid." Mitchie walked into her cabin, crooking a finger to bring Blythe along.

An electronic transfer from a shell account covering half the agreed fee went directly to her. Mitchie covered the rest with gold and silver coins in a mix of Akiak and Bonaventure denominations.

"Whoa," said Blythe. "These are worth lots more than they used to be."

"That's why we use them. And a little extra. You can't spend these anywhere but you can use them as props." Digging in her shirt drawer unearthed a bundle of flimsies held together by an elastic.

Blythe riffled through them. "Bank of Eden, One Thousand Rubles." Her face lit up. "Is this from Old Earth?"

"Eden. First system on our way back. If anyone asks you'll have to say you bought them from a collector."

"Oh, wow. Something you brought back from your trip to Old Earth."

"That covers what we agreed on, yes?"

The whore jerked her eyes away from the cash. "Yes. Thank you. Let me know if you need me to do it again. Or do . . . anything for you."

"If I ever do I'll contact you."

Blythe turned to go, then paused with her hand on the open hatch. "Just so you don't have to worry, Guo and I didn't, didn't anything."

"I know."

***

"Look, there's been three weeks of changes to the file," said Marven. "We copy the new version and compare them. That gives up patterns of data structures, positioning, time trends." Quang chimed in with more cryptographic technobabble.

Mitchie leaned back her in her seat at the head of the galley table. The dataraid had found backups of Corday's routine correspondence and one large encrypted file. It had defied their efforts to crack it. Marven had grown desperate enough to give a copy to Guo in hopes his limited code training might find a weakness. Now he was trying to talk Mitchie into supporting a second dataraid on the same target.

Guo emerged from their cabin, secure datasheet in hand. "I don't think that will help."

"Oh?" Marven glared at him.

Mitchie couldn't tell if the anger was over his plan being challenged, an enlisted man questioning an officer, or an amateur contradicting the specialist. Possibly all three.

"I tried an old troubleshooting technique, working the problem from the opposite end. Encryption tries to make data look like noise. Instead of looking for the data I analyzed how random the noise was."

He slid his datasheet onto the table. Quang peered into it eagerly.

"Mathematicians have tests for random number generators to see if their output is truly random. As they say, it's too important to be left to chance. I copied a set of tests to the secure system." He stroked the datasheet to bring up an array of results.

Quang studied the data. Marven just snarled, "Well?"

"Your mystery block is pure, total, casinos would pay good money for it, randomness. No patterns at all."

"You mean I got shot for nothing?" said Quang.

Mitchie laughed. "You got shot for bait. Corday set it out where someone spying on him would find it, and we fell for it."

Marven let out a string of curses.

"If he's set up that level of data security, he probably has multiple layers of personnel security. Analyze your infiltrators' contacts. Check for honeytraps and overwatchers," she ordered.

"Yes, ma'am. God damn it. We've totally wasted our time," complained Marven.

"No," Mitchie corrected him. "We proved he's expecting intelligence operations against him. We know he's diverting resources to security and deception. We can infer his plans are tightly held in his inner circle. He may be keeping them entirely to himself."

Marven thought a moment. "It's negative data . . . but, yes, if he was doing more than that we'd see signs."

Mitchie wrapped up the meeting and saw her spooks off the ship. Guo still sat at the table when she returned.

"What bothers me," she said, "is I was an idiot and led Guen to expect I'd have a breakthrough for her. Guess I was too excited about getting through the mission alive." She filled a cup from the sink and drank. "Which raises the question of how much I should tell her."

Guo answered, "No specifics. Just say we took something, it turned out to be cheese, and if he's setting traps it means such-and-such."

"That works. She's going to be pissed though."

He smirked. "Then I'll cheer her up."

Guen accepted the news calmly. And accepted Guo's cheering up.

***

Mitchie flung herself onto the bed.

Her husband looked up from his papers. She'd just come back from checking on the analysts, which wasn't tiring duty. The fall had been too theatrical to be real exhaustion. She was probably just trying to distract him from his project.

And it had worked.

Guo left the papers on the chair as he climbed on the bed. "Rough day, *wo de airen?*"

"No. Just frustrating. We're helping the new fleet get trained up but not getting any ships to send against the Betrayers, which is our real mission. Admiral Galen probably thinks I deserted."

He chuckled. "He might be happier if you had."

"True. Involving the Disconnect in a civil war is excessive initiative." She snuggled into his chest as his arms tightened around her.

"Want to see something that might end it?"

Mitchie looked into his eyes. "I finally get to see the secret project?"

"Now that it's done, yes." Guo pulled some sheets out of the stack on the chair and handed them to her. "My proposal for a peace treaty between the Harmony and CPS."

She sat on the edge of the bed to read. "This isn't a treaty. It's a constitution."

"If they're going to live together it's the same thing."

Mitchie went through the second page with a mutter of, "Bicameral, nice." After the fourth page she re-read the second and third. She looked up at Guo. "The representation and protections for underpopulated worlds . . . are you thinking the Disconnected Worlds would join this?"

Guo shrugged. "Whether they join the Fusion or not, they need to have some structure. The Defense Coordinating Committee can't be a real government, it's too weak."

"Don't I know it."

She read the rest. "I like it. God knows what the Fuzies will make of it."

"I'll show it to Guen at our date tomorrow."

Pasteur Park, Capitol City, Pintoy, gravity 9.4 m/s²

The cheers almost deafened Mitchie even without electronic amplification. Guen continued her praise for the new boot camp graduates. The latest wave to pass through the VR training was the largest ever. They now filled Pasteur Park for a public ceremony. Tomorrow they'd be shuttled up to their ships.

"You will bring us victory! Victory over the Harmony! And victory over the Betrayers!" Guen's close brought more cheers, shaking the stand holding the dignitaries. She stepped down from the pulpit.

Professor Corday took her place and launched into his speech. Mitchie wondered how Guen had maneuvered him into such a visible position. The speech wasn't bad. He'd avoided making a lecture of it. The historical examples were amusing or inspiring.

A wave of laughter covered the sound of the shot. Mitchie saw blood spurt from under Corday's shoulder. He swayed back and fell as his toes just caught the edge of the pulpit's step.

Mitchie dropped flat.

Panic began, some people jumping off the platform or running for the ramp. Guen flung her arms around Corday, crying, "Professor! Professor!"

Rapid shots sounded. Mitchie lifted up to see. The action group lined up in front of the platform was firing. She traced their aim to a purple laser dot marking a skyscraper overlooking the park. Part of the façade fractured and fell off under the rain of bullets.

Two med techs ran up to the pulpit. "Ma'am, ma'am, you have to let us take care of him." They pried Guen's arms off the shooting victim.

Guen turned to Mitchie and seized her in a bloody hug. "Oh, God, it's so horrible," the younger woman sobbed. One arm held Mitchie tight. The other slid down her side. A hand went under Mitchie's uniform jacket then poked into a pocket.

Then the hand withdrew, leaving a small object behind.

What the hell? thought Mitchie.

The med techs cursed as more blood sprayed them. "Get another cauterizer!" yelled one.

Someone else was shouting, "Cease fire! We have people in the building now. Cease fire! Cease fire!" The gunfire tapered off.

Guen kept her head tucked into Mitchie's chest, letting out the occasional sob. Mitchie looked at the blood covering both of them. This uniform was a loss. Guen's bodyguards formed a line to shield them from any further shots.

Another line protected Corday and the med techs. A doctor arrived and examined their efforts. "Keep the synthblood going. We're going to have to collapse the lung and replace it later. I'll shut down the affected pulmonary arteries."

"Yes, ma'am," said a med tech. He started cleaning off Corday's chest, adding chest hair to the shredded clothing on the floor.

When the doctor started cutting through ribs Mitchie looked away. Even her goriest moments had been neater than that.

Guen looked up. "Where's the MC?" she demanded.

The master of ceremonies hurried up.

"Play some music," she ordered. "The crowd's getting restless."

Mitchie could hear the mutters even over the curses of the medical team.

"What music? I don't have any ready," babbled the MC. He was almost in shock from the disruption of his well-planned event.

"Anything! Have that redhead sing the anthem again."

The MC flinched and hurried off. The redhead, a soloist in the Pintoy Planetary Opera Company, was more composed than the MC. She stepped over the splashes of blood to the pulpit, asked for prayers on Corday's behalf, and launched into an aria of a daughter praying for her father's recovery. Repeater screens showed her image around the park at ten times life size.

The doctor stood and turned until she spotted Guen. "I'm sorry. We did everything we could. The shock wave from the bullet left leaks in every blood vessel in his chest. We couldn't stop the bleeding." She looked anxiously over her shoulder as Corday's bodyguards snarled.

Mitchie frowned. The exit wound she'd seen hadn't matched the exploding bullet needed to cause what the doctor had described.

"I'm sure you did your best," said Guen, taking the doctor's bloody hands. "You and your men go rest. You—" to the bodyguards "—will take the Professor's body to a mortuary. He will receive a martyr's funeral and lie in state for all to pay their respects."

The soloist finished her first song and began a lament.

Guen's datasheet buzzed. "What? Good. Hold on, I want to make this a public report." She stood next to the pulpit and made a cutting gesture. The soloist ended the song with the current refrain.

Guen took the singer's place. "My fellow citizens! The assassin has been discovered!" A swipe on her datasheet transferred the call to the repeater screens. Instead of Guen they now showed Lorraine Q, leader of the Committee of Public Safety's most vicious Action Group.

"Chairwoman Claret. Citizens," began Lorraine. "The assassin is already dead, thanks to the response of Action Group Trey." The gunmen lined up in front of the platform cheered themselves.

Her camera turned to show a room stippled with bullet holes. A dead man lay against a wall. His multiple wounds had already stopped bleeding. A rifle almost as long as he was tall lay across him, its barrel pinched where a bullet had struck it.

"Biometric identification revealed him as Vo Wang, a known agent of the Harmony," continued Lorraine. "After failing at subversion and sabotage he moved on to murder."

The crowd roared in anger. Guen shifted the repeaters back to herself. "This is an outrage. The Harmony has demanded our submission, attacked peaceful worlds, now they spill blood on our own world? No! We will not tolerate this! We will crush the Harmony and force them to respect our freedom! Spacers, to your ships!"

With cries of "To ship!" knots of training graduates ran out of the park, heading for the shuttleports.

Guen shut down the repeaters and pulpit. She whispered to Mitchie, "Best get your people inside. This could get ugly."

Mitchie just nodded. No one got in her way as she left the speakers' platform. She ducked into the first public restroom she saw.

A stall provided privacy to check her pocket. Poking from outside revealed Guen's present as a small cylinder with a spike on the end. She reached in carefully to avoid stabbing herself.

It was a standard single use injector, one dose of medicine with a needle and pressure cartridge. The label declared it had contained 'clotase,' a standard treatment for heart attacks, strokes, and other clotting problems.

Mitchie remembered a first aid instructor finishing his lecture on clotase by threatening to strangle anyone who gave it to a bleeding victim, even a nosebleed. With no ability to clot even trivial wounds could bleed out.

She pondered how to destroy the injector. Flushing it would only lead to an intact injector arriving in the sewer lost and found with its description posted on the net. Not a good way to cover up a crime. Destroying the evidence would take running it through a converter.

Mitchie had to admit Guen had chosen the best qualified person to act as her accessory to murder. No, two murders. The 'Harmony agent' fit his role too well. He had to be a plant or dupe.

Mama Mitchie's little girl is all grown up now.

***

Guo hugged Mitchie as she came through the cargo hold airlock. "I'm glad you're back. It's going crazy out there."

"More than you know." She led him below decks to the converter room. After chasing out mechanic Finnegan she produced the injector. "We need to destroy this."

"Easy enough." Pliers tore it into small pieces, then they went into the inspection port for the start tank. Next time *Joshua Chamberlain* fired up the converter they'd be disintegrated. "Why?"

"Proof of premeditated homicide."

"Who did you kill?"

"Not me. Guen knocked off Professor Corday."

Guo sat on a cross-pipe. "Really? It wasn't the Harmony?"

"She had someone shoot him, then dosed him so he'd bleed out. First I knew about it was when she planted the drug injector on me."

He let out a string of Mandarin words she didn't know. Profanity, by the tone. "That's it. I can't see her any more."

She considered the possible repercussions. "I kill people and you still sleep with me."

"You're following orders. She's just blowing where the wind takes her. No more."

Mitchie gave him a long hug. He clung to her for comfort. "I'll take care of it. Not sure how, but I'll think of something."

The PA speaker came on. "Captain to the bridge! Captain to the bridge!"

"But it'll have to wait."

***

Mitchie climbed through the bridge hatch then bent over, hands on knees, to catch her breath.

Mthembu closed the hatch behind her.

"What?" she panted. Maybe she shouldn't have taken all those ladders at top speed.

"Ma'am, the comm box says you have a secure message for your eyes only," he reported.

Password and retina scan let the box divulge the message. It was from Marven. "Safe house in danger. Fire spreading this way. Rioters in street. Need rooftop pick up or armed ground escort to evacuate."

The latter option would be the safer one if she had a platoon of infantry. She didn't. She sent "Rooftop" back to Marven.

Mitchie turned to Mthembu. "Are Hiroshi and Setta on board?"

"I think they're in their cabin, ma'am."

"Get them up here." She strapped into her pilot couch. The converter answered as she spun up the turbines. She called "Up ship" over the PA as Hiroshi came through the hatch followed by his wife. "Mthembu, take the con. Keep us heading north-east."

The co-pilot took the controls without any questions. Possibly he'd given up on getting answers.

Mitchie stood up. "Okay. There's riots all over the city. Stipend kids blaming Sinophones for Corday's assassination."

The bridge dome gave them a good look at Capitol City. Any direction they faced smoke rose from burning buildings. Drones flitted about watching them spread. Firefighting bots clustered by the river, picking up tank-fulls of water and dumping them on the nearest fire.

"This place is going to be ashes when the revolution's over," said Hiroshi.

"Not our problem. What is our problem is a dozen of our people trapped out there. We're going to find them waiting on the roof, hover next to their place, and take them on board."

Her subordinates were clearly combat fatigued. They didn't even flinch.

"Hiroshi, I'll want you on the controls with me. Mthembu, take comm, let me know if someone is going to do anything about us busting traffic rules. Setta, figure out a way to help them board. Borrow the mechanics to help. The Mate can ride the converter by himself for this."

She let Hiroshi steer them to the safehouse. Finding it in the ship was harder than when she'd walked there. Plumes of smoke kept obscuring their view. Her datasheet's map function was confused by being a klick high in the air.

"We could just go there at walking height," suggested Hiroshi.

"That wouldn't be neighborly of us." The turbines blew cool air instead of superheated steam but the pressure needed to keep over a thousand tons of spaceship in the air was fierce. Even at this height people below had to feel the breeze.

"That's it! Not on fire yet." Hiroshi had to add the 'yet.' The buildings on the other side of the street were all burning.

"Right. Mthembu, get Marven on an unsecure channel and ask if he's ready to go."

She could hear his answer from the box. "Hell yes! We're stomping on cinders so this one doesn't catch. We have some neighbors tagging along, do you have room?"

That was terrible security practice, likely to blow the covers of everyone in the safehouse. She said yes.

As *Joshua Chamberlain* closed on the pick-up point they had to switch to the cameras in the ship's base and sides. The dome wouldn't let them see below the ship.

"Ma'am, the street's too narrow," said Hiroshi. "We won't fit."

Mitchie studied the screen. They'd aimed for the south side of Marven's building, away from the raging fire. The street on the north side wasn't any wider.

"I have the con," she said. Hiroshi released the control. She slid the ship north. "Tell them to go to the south edge and take cover if they can."

In empty air the turbines held the ship up like four legs. When they descended the air jet would reflect off the ground and push against the base of the ship. The 'ground effect' just provided extra lift when they were over a flat surface. When over something asymmetrical, such as a hillside or building, ground effect could push the ship off course or even flip it over.

Keeping *Joshua Chamberlain* upright would require rapid adjustments of all four turbines to match changes in the ground effect. Mitchie had done it before . . . and come far closer to crashing than she liked to remember.

The camera screen showed the roofs of the burning buildings on the north side of the street. They only varied in height by a few stories. As the ship settled toward them the flames blew out. They'd certainly reignite as soon as the wind from the turbines died down.

The ground effect wasn't too asymmetrical. Gentle tugs on the turbine throttles kept the ship level. Mitchie nudged them all in together to descend.

The jetwash of all four turbines spread out until they merged in one huge wind. The closer the ship came to the roof the more the jetwashes narrowed. At a few hundred meters up the force of the turbines was concentrated on four spots, each holding over three hundred tons of force. As *Joshua Chamberlain* descended they narrowed even more.

The inevitable happened. A roof caved in. Mitchie pushed up the throttle for the turbine over it to balance the loss of ground effect pressure. A little extra drifted the ship east, the jetwash chewing away at the edge of the open hole.

More roofs collapsed. Mitchie shifted the ship to tear down the remaining intact structure along the street. Already weakened by fire, the buildings crashed to the ground in a cloud of smoke and embers.

Joshua Chamberlain dropped a dozen meters, then bobbed up as ground effect established itself at the new ground level.

Mitchie heard a whimper on the bridge. Probably Mthembu, she decided. Hiroshi had done stunts almost this reckless before coming on board.

"Tell them to come to the north edge," she ordered. Then she used the PA to tell Setta to open up the hold.

The side cameras showed they were too low. Mitchie boosted the ship a little. They wobbled as the base crossed from the ruins to the street. Setta began a running narration on the intercom to guide Mitchie in. "Four meters away, down two . . . two away, one up . . . one away half down . . . hold it here."

"Hold it here" would be an easy instruction if there was no wind. The large fires in the city were disrupting wind currents. Mitchie gritted her teeth, countering every gust as she felt it.

In the hold Setta yelled, "Throw the net!"

The mechanics and deckhands threw the cargo net across. Smoke-stained men on the roof grabbed it.

"Pull it tight!" she yelled.

The roof men pulled it back, hooking loops over vents and antennas. The other end of the net was anchored on fittings in the hold. Setta and Ye carried forward a wide panel and threw it over the gap.

The improvised gangplank wobbled. The ship was moving side to side a hand width, and up and down about that much. It would have to do.

"Come aboard!" Setta called, adding arm waves. Then she coughed. A lungful of hot smoke hurt.

Finnegan ran across the gangplank holding a rope. Wang braced the end behind him. "Hold this as you cross," said the mechanic.

The Disker intelligence agents urged some civilians ahead of them.

Two pregnant women followed by an elderly couple crossed the gangplank.

With them across the rush began. The younger ones crawled over on the net. When the last civilian crossed Marven walked up to Finnegan.

"Back aboard, son," he said. "I'm last off."

"Yes, sir." The mechanic ran back into the ship, coiling the rope as he went.

Lieutenant (SG) Marven looked around the roof for anyone left behind, saw only embers starting flames, and crossed into the cargo hold.

"All the way to the back, sir," directed Setta. "We need you off the net."

With their guests clear the crew unhooked the net. "Clear to lift, ma'am," said Setta to her handcomm. "Everyone's aboard."

Joshua Chamberlain moved straight up. The net slid out of the open hatch, taking the gangplank with it. Setta started the hatch closing.

It was still open wide enough for them to see the roof disintegrate as the turbines rose high enough to blow on it.

Mitchie smoothed the bucking as the ship ascended above the broken, burning building. She tapped the intercom. "Confirm we have all our people."

Setta replied in a moment. "Lt. Marven confirms everyone from his house is on board. No major injuries."

"Thank you."

Joshua Chamberlain now hovered high enough to see over the immediate fires, revealing more fires. The riots had spread throughout the city. Murder, rape, and arson were too much fun to be restricted to Sinophones. Mitchie snarled as she viewed the damage.

Just beyond the local fires a park held swarms of rioters. They danced in swirling lines.

Mitchie's jaw tightened. *Celebrate this.*

She tilted *Joshua Chamberlain* to accelerate toward the park, giving up altitude for speed. The turbines blasted leaves off trees and sent rioters tumbling away from the ship's wake. More thrust was needed to safely clear the apartments on the far side. Mitchie went up a klick and hovered.

Another pass was tempting. Firing up the torch and blasting them with five hundred degree steam was more tempting. But that would panic innocent people. And Guo would refuse to enable the torch anyway.

"Hiroshi, take the con. Back to our landing pad."

"Yes, ma'am."

He flew a gentle course back to the spaceport, avoiding fires and traffic. Apparently he'd had enough excitement for the day.

Mitchie's datasheet played the *Magic Princess Journey* theme. The city network was holding up well under the riot damage. She pulled it from her thigh pocket.

Guen's face appeared. "You just put most of two action groups into the hospital, or worse."

"Oops." Mitchie didn't feel up to faking an apology.

"I need those guys. The action groups protect the Committee."

"If you need them so badly you shouldn't let them riot."

Guen glared. Mitchie wondered if they'd have another repeat of the militia-needs-discipline versus volunteers-resist-control argument.

"Goddamn arrogant professional." She cut the call.

Chapter Six: Ambassador

Joshua Chamberlain, **Planet Pintoy, gravity 9.4 m/s^2**

Mitchie said, "I have an idea for getting you away from Guen. But I don't like it."

Guo was washing grease off his hands at the sink in their cabin. Damage to the ship from the rooftop rescue had been his excuse for being too busy to see Guen. He knew that dumping her could lead to violence. "What is it?"

"If the CPS endorses your peace treaty somebody will have to deliver it to the Harmony. If they make you ambassador you'll be off planet for a month or two. Long enough for a nineteen year old to fall for someone else."

He scraped under his fingernails. "That would work. I don't know how good a diplomat I'd be."

"You know enough philosophy to talk to the Harmony. You know what's going on here. Guen trusts you. I doubt there's anyone who'd do better."

"Maybe. I'd hate being away from you for so long. The ship will be okay. Ye and Finnegan are both up to working the converter room solo. And I can drop the first mate duties on Hiroshi. It's just going to be a lonely trip."

Mitchie stood behind him and wrapped her arms around his waist. "That's what I don't like about it. Oh, Guen will probably want one more time with you before you go."

Guo ran water over his hands to the wrists to get all the soap off. "I can handle that."

"And I want more than one." She pulled him toward the bed.

"Hey! Can I dry my hands off?"

"No."

Committee of Public Safety Meeting Chamber, Capitol City, Pintoy, gravity 9.4 m/s^2

"Intervention by the interstellar government is only authorized when a planetary government has violated one of the enumerated rights. Otherwise the planets are autonomous."

The Committee member nodded to accept the answer and sat.

"Next question?" asked Guo. His proposed constitution seemed to be going over well. Some of the questions displayed real understanding of the concept. Others were just attempts to get digs in at rival CPS members.

A man in a shiny copper skullcap seized the floor. His 'question' was an involved speech about the traditional powers of the Fusion government. Guo smiled and nodded, waiting for a question.

Guen cut the speaker off. "Thank you, Tony. That's very informative. Let me remind the committee that we are not here today to define the final government for the Fusion. That will take a long time with many amendments. Today we must decide if this shall be our counter to the Harmony's ultimatum demanding total social control. Something for your spacers and the other worlds to fight for. Are we ready to vote?"

A few formalities led to a show of hands. When the outcome was clear the laggards lifted their hands to make it unanimous.

"Good. Now we need to choose an envoy to carry our response to the Harmony."

Annie, Guen's former bodyguard and aide, was now a CPS member in Corday's place. She said, "As a Disconnected Worlds citizen, Guo Kwan is a neutral in our civil war with the Harmony. I nominate him as envoy."

With very little discussion the appointment was approved. Guen adjourned the meeting.

Guo drifted back to a corner to stay out of the way of the politicians and their hangers-on.

Mitchie came up from the spectator seats to join him. "That went well."

"Thanks. We'll see what Ping and his buddies think of it."

"They'll hate it if you do your job right."

He laughed.

Guen came up trailing a dozen flunkies and lobbyists. "Congratulations, Mr. Envoy."

"Thank you, ma'am." Guo gave her a slight bow.

"Oh, crap. How are we going to get you there?"

Mitchie said, "I'll handle that."

"Good, thank you. Mr. Kwan, please come back to my office. I need to brief you before your departure."

Mitchie suspected Guo would be debriefed. The meeting room was emptying as the rest of the committee members left. She decided it was as good a place as any to make a call.

Relaying an ordinary call to a spaceship required going through a person. The network control software had broken down as laws changed or were overridden by men with guns. Saying she was calling from the CPS building skipped past questions of authorization and payment.

Commander Sheu's face appeared on her datasheet. Mitchie said, "Hi, I hate to bother you but I need to borrow a ship for courier duty again."

She expected a five second wait for his reply. Matsu was not quite a million klicks away. Instead it took over forty seconds for Sheu to answer.

"Yes, ma'am. I can have *Walking Rollo* on Pintoy in thirty hours. Is this going to take her into a combat zone? If not I'll want to keep her electronic warfare ratings to stay here to support training operations."

Mitchie realized she should have been supervising Sheu and his squadron more closely. "That's fine. No combat, it's just diplomatic transport. But what's she doing that far out? And for that matter where are you?"

Forty three seconds.

"We've been helping train the new Fusion ships. Their experienced spacers are so dispersed everyone's learning their job. I've put the squadron on opfor, mentoring, and sometime search and rescue. Gives us a lot of insight into their capability. I've been sending weekly reports to the analysis group."

"I'll take a look at them. Keep up the good work. We'll meet *Walking Rollo* at Capitol Spaceport. Long out."

***

Walking Rollo massed as much as *Joshua Chamberlain* but stood more than twice as tall. The long narrow hull provided room for weapons, sensors, and extra heat radiators. An elevator box dangling from a cable hauled them up to the main airlock.

The ship's commander met them. "Welcome aboard, Commander Long, Senior Chief Kwan. I'm Lieutenant Commander Max Snyder, and this is my longboat."

"Thank you," said Mitchie. "I should let you know Guo Kwan is the diplomatic envoy you're transporting. For this mission he's a civilian, addressed as Ambassador."

"My apologies, sir."

"Don't worry about it," said Guo. "I'm trying to get used to it myself."

"I want to make your priorities clear for this mission," said Mitchie. "One, keep the Ambassador alive and unharmed. Two, bring him back here, or if this place goes completely to hell, to the Disconnect. Three, support delivery of the message and other diplomatic activity. Is that clear?"

"Very."

"Then I hope you enjoy the trip."

"I expect we will."

After some small talk Snyder offered a tour, which Mitchie declined. "I want to get this mission into the black before the CPS comes up with any new ideas."

"Of course, ma'am. I'll get our lift clearance as soon as you're off."

"Right. Give us a minute?"

Snyder closed the hatch behind him.

Mitchie squeezed Guo and pulled him down for a fierce kiss.

"Hey. Relax. I'm just going on a trip. You're the one who does dangerous stuff."

She chuckled. "Yeah. But I worry. Promise me something?"

"Yes."

That was so like him. She'd never make a promise without knowing what she was committing to.

"If they try to subvert you, convince you of . . . whatever, let them think they succeeded. I know you like to argue philosophy, but let them win. Convince them that you're a useful asset for their side."

"Ping's not going to hurt an ambassador."

Mitchie said nothing.

"I promise I'll give them every reason to keep me alive."

One more kiss, then she stepped back into the elevator.

Guo pressed the down button.

***

Mthembu's voice crackled on the intercom. "Ma'am, Commander Sheu is on the commbox."

"On my way." Whatever he wanted, it had to be more fun than reading reports.

Mitchie could see Sheu's face on the commbox screen as she climbed onto the bridge. "Long here," she said. She started a timer to measure the lag to his response.

It only took four seconds for the image to react. His ship had to be inside the orbit of Matsu.

"Ma'am, did the Committee of Public Safety order an exercise? Most of the squadrons we've been supporting have received new orders. I haven't been able to get an explanation from anyone. If they're not going to let us participate I'd like to give my crews some shore leave."

"I haven't heard of one. I'll ask around. Go ahead and take shore leave. I think you're overdue."

"Thank you. Sheu out."

Mitchie sat at the comm console to write a terse but polite query to the chairman of the Naval Subcommittee. As she sent it a white streak crossed the sky.

When it touched the horizon a white flash dazzled them. Mthembu shouted a prayer.

Mitchie blinked to clear her eyes. It didn't help. As her vision cleared she looked out to the source of the flash. A mushroom cloud rose on the horizon.

"Crap. Missile attack. What's the target? That's the wrong direction for the city center."

"Dunno." Mthembu tried to pull up a map on the navigation box but it wasn't responding. He started a power cycle.

Mitchie tried to get a map on her datasheet but it only displayed snow.

Spacer Ye came up the bridge ladder. "Ma'am, there's been a major explosion in Stony Brook Wilderness Zone."

"How many casualties?"

"Nobody knows yet. Lots of network disruptions. Hundreds dead at least. Some refugees from the city were camping out there."

A Fusion "wilderness zone" was more controlled than some Disconnect gardens. It would have been a safe place to hide from the chaos.

"You still have net connection?"

"The wireless is down but we're still getting full capability on the spaceport wire."

"Look at that!" Mthembu pointed out the top of the bridge dome. Torchship plumes hung in the sky over Capitol City.

Mitchie cursed. "Whose ships are those?"

Neither man had a guess.

"Right. Mthembu, get the boxes back on line. Ye, let's see what we can find out about them."

Her guess was a squadron incited to mutiny by the Harmony. By the time they reached Ye's workstation the ships had revealed themselves. Their announcement was broadcast on a loop.

"Citizens of Pintoy! This is the Restoration Executive, Admiral Parata. The Committee of Public Safety is now disbanded. The Restoration Executive will oversee the election of a new Council of Stakeholders. Once the Council has assumed control the Restoration Executive will resign all power. The so-called Committee of Public Safety must declare their surrender in no less than six hours or further demonstrations of force will be made." It began again.

The workstation presented quick reports from the analysis group. They'd identified several of the ships overhead and listed the resources available to respond.

The crew of every planetary defense battery had been granted five-day passes yesterday.

Most of the fleet was headed to dispersed points in deep space.

Civilian ships started fleeing when the missile struck.

The Marine units around Capitol City were only equipped for riot suppression.

When Mitchie's datasheet recovered she gave the workstation back to Ye. She checked the froth of the net to see what the reactions were. The middle-class, now subordinate to ex-stipend kid thugs, wanted the old order back. Those pissed at the Stakeholders' lies vowed to fight. Everyone who'd come out ahead in the big reshuffle was panicking. The stipend kids stuck on the bottom just wanted their easy money and games back.

The opening chord of the *Magic Princess Journey* theme sounded. Mitchie muttered, "Thank God," and answered it before the second bar.

"Are you following this?" demanded Guen.

"Yeah. What's your response?"

A bitter laugh. "I ordered the Committee to disperse. Half of them were running already. Annie made me relocate." The background of her image was a moving vehicle.

"What about a counter-attack?"

"The only force I can find is your squadron of Disconnect ships."

"Um. Let me get Sheu into this." It took a couple of minutes to arrange. They asked the squadron commander if he could attack Admiral Parata's force.

The reply took longer than four seconds.

"Yes, ma'am, we can attack them. But that's two destroyers and a light cruiser against a battleship and eight heavy cruisers. We might have surprise, but I bet they're tracking us. Plus every shot that misses will be hundreds of dead civilians. Hell, if we hit one the wreck will land on this city, kill thousands."

Mitchie gave a confirming nod.

"Dammit." Guen pulled on the hair behind her ears. "I don't want to destroy the city. I don't want to wreck the ships, we need them. Most of the crews are there because I asked them to volunteer. If they knew what the admiral was up to they'd stop him." She hissed in frustration.

"What if we launched a high-intensity EMP attack?" asked Mitchie. "We could overwhelm—"

Sheu had started talking as soon as Guen finished. "If you want to talk to the crews we might be able to put you on their speakers."

"You can hack into a warship's PA?" said Mitchie.

Guen let go of her hair.

"Not exactly hack, ma'am." Sheu was grinning. "We've done a lot of tech support for these green Fuzies. Sometimes it's easier to remote in and fix it ourselves than explain it. They've been using common passwords across squadrons because of personnel turnover—"

Mitchie blurted, "Holy shit."

"—so we have access to most of their fleet. I'll have to check with my other ships to get the passwords they've—" He heard the curse. "Yes, ma'am. That is on my list of issues to complain about before we go on the offensive. But it's a big timesaver in a training environment. We can pull together the how-to up here but you'll want to execute on the ground. I'll need the techs from *Walking Rollo* at the spaceport phased array control center. They'll need security. Should only take two three hours."

"Good. Let's do it. Mitchie, I'll need your help making a speech customized for spacers." Guen started another call. "Hey, Lorraine, I have an escort quest for you."

***

The converter room of FNS *Dread* could hold a missile frigate, if there weren't so many pipes in the way. Five separate converters were humming as they powered the battleship's torch to keep it hovering over Pintoy. A full fifty spacers were monitoring the systems and plumbing.

Ensign Vicario was the only officer present. He didn't know why the Chief Engineer hadn't shown up, the bridge just said he was "indisposed." He didn't mind being in charge. It was what being an officer was all about. He strolled along the rim of the room listening to his spacers work.

"Sir? I have an overheat reading."

Vicario leaned over the spacer's shoulder to look at the display. "Where?"

"The outer regenerative loop is hotter than it should be."

The schematic displayed the pipes in yellow to indicate the temperature variation. The ensign pulled up a reference chart. "That's in the safe range. The nominal is calibrated for vacuum. Sitting in atmosphere like this is warming everything up. We're getting plume heat conducted back through the air."

He traced the limit of the safe zone with a finger. "That's where you need to worry." The torn stitches on his cuffs caught his eye. He dropped his arm before the spacer could notice it. *I need to replace my midshipman jacket next time I get planetside.*

"Oh."

He clapped the spacer on the shoulder. "Good eye, Pucharty. We'll be fine as long as we're not here for days."

"Thank you, sir."

Ensign Vicario returned to his wander. The PA speaker crackled with an incoming message. He looked up in concern. The ship was at Condition Red. This wouldn't be anything routine.

"Spacers of the Fusion!"

The ensign tried to place the voice. It wasn't a Pintoy accent, or Sukhoi. Didn't sound like any of the bridge officers.

A rating exclaimed, "That's the Chairwoman of the CPS! What's she talking to us for?"

"You have put your lives on the line to protect our people from the monstrous Betrayers and the tyrants of the Harmony. The whole people honor you for your sacrifices and will welcome you with open arms when you return victorious."

Vicario scurried over to his control console. A command to shut down the PA resulted in an "AUTHORIZATION DENIED" error.

"But your officers are not attacking the enemies of the people. They've launched a coup to restore the old order. Admiral Parata wants to put the complacent Stakeholders back in power."

The converter room crewmen had stopped working and were listening to the PA. Some were shouting in alarm at the message. The ensign took a deep breath and shouted, "Ignore that! Everyone get back to work! This is a performance critical situation."

"He wants the lies back. He wants to punish those who found out the truth. He wants you to live a false life again."

The nearest spacers glanced at him and then back to the PA speaker. No one turned back to their console.

Ensign Vicario reached into his pocket. The XO had ordered him to carry his pistol on shift today without giving an explanation. He hadn't wanted to alarm the crew by carrying it in a holster. Now he pulled it out and shot the nearest speaker.

Guen's speech continued from three more speakers spread around the room. "Admiral Parata has already killed hundreds by ordering a missile attack on Pintoy. He has struck at the people of his own homeworld."

"Get back to work, dammit!" Vicario pointed the pistol at a cluster of spacers.

At the second converter station Fireman's Mate 3/c Ryan realized the officer was about to shoot. He decided not to wait. He yelled, "No more lies!" and flung a wrench at the ensign.

"Spacers, rise up! Stop this attack on the people. Stop this attempt to bring back the lies. Fight for your freedom! Fight for the freedom of all the people!"

The wrench hit Vicario's ribs, making the first shot miss. The ensign fired twice more as the spacers rushed him. By the time Ryan reached the fight there was just a pile of bodies wrestling with the officer.

"Okay, we got him," ordered Ryan. "Get up so we can finish it."

All the spacers but one stood. Ensign Vicario had made a headshot before the crew broke his neck.

"What're we gonna do with the bodies?" asked someone.

"Airlock. You and you—" Ryan pointed "—carry them to the lower lock. You two, swab this mess up."

The PA was silent. The babble among the crew grew louder. "What do we do now?" "Let's march up to the bridge!" "No, tell the Admiral to come down here." "He won't come. Let's boost the drive and take the ship up to orbit." "We can't steer from here, you ninny." "Shut down the drive, we can wreck the ship so he can't attack the planet." "You fucking idiot."

Ryan raised his voice. "Shut the torch for one second. That'll tell them we're in charge now."

Given a plan neither futile nor suicidal the crew moved back to their duty stations. Ryan counted down to the synchronized shutdown of the five converters.

The ship dropped five meters then began thrusting again.

"That's rougher on the tummy than plain free fall," muttered Ryan.

The command console intercom flared with the red light of a priority call. The spacers near it stepped back.

Ryan realized people were staring at him. He walked to the console and accepted the call. "Converter room."

"This is Captain Fechner. What the hell was that?"

Killing the ensign already made them mutineers. He couldn't be in any more trouble. Still, it was hard to tell the captain, "We're taking over the ship, captain. We're stopping the coup."

"Who the fuck are you? Put Vicario on the line!"

"Vicario's dead, sir. And you will be too if you don't give in to our demands."

The ship's commander hissed. "I'll give you sons of bitches one chance to be brigged instead of shot. Surrender to the Marines I'm sending in there or you're all dead."

"We fought the Stakeholders. We'll fight you to keep you from bringing them back. Converter room out." Ryan pressed the off switch. He looked up to see spacers staring at him with looks ranging from admiration to horror. "What are you standing there for? Let's get the hatches blocked and scrounge up some weapons."

The converter room hatches were designed to lock securely against battle damage. Spanners and pipes were hammered into the wheels to keep them from opening.

Other spacers tried to reconfigure some of the back-up systems for defense. The task would be much easier if they didn't have to keep the torch running while they worked on it.

Ryan discovered even the higher-ranking petty officers deferred to him. Witnesses spread the story of the thrown wrench. He approved every idea brought to him, only intervening when two groups squabbled over using the same power line.

A hatch blew off its hinges. It landed seven meters away, crushing a spacer against his console.

"Wait for them to come in!" ordered Ryan.

A dozen unarmored Marines ran through the hatch, spraying frangible rounds at the spacers who hadn't taken cover.

"Now!"

A fireman second class activated a valve on his console. A pipe aimed at the hatch blew thousand degree steam at it. Marines screamed as they tried to roll out of the blast. The next squad died in the hatchway.

Ryan had entrusted the ensign's pistol to a machinist's mate who claimed expertise with firearms. The MM quickly finished off the surviving Marines. When the steam jet was stopped they could hear scalded troops crying in the corridor.

"Can we use their weapons, Branson?" Ryan asked.

"A few," answered the machinist's mate. "The heat ruined most of them. Cooked off the ammo too."

"All right. Get some volunteers." Ryan went off to check on the wounded. Most of the injuries were superficial. The Marines had used light bullets to not risk destroying the converters. Two spacers were dead, seven more out of action.

Branson called, "Test shots," as his three gunmen fired bullets into the pile of dead Marines. When they'd each tested their new weapons he dispersed them around the converter room.

Ryan whispered to Branson, "I'm trying to come up with a plan for if they try sleep gas. Any ideas?"

"I doubt they have any. This ship is configured to fight Betrayers. Gas doesn't work on robots."

"I hope so. Let me know if you think of something, just in case."

"Did you come up with a plan?"

"Shut down all the converters before I pass out."

"I'll try to come up with something better than that."

Ryan took a turn around the room, boosting morale with encouraging speeches. At least, he hoped they were boosting morale.

Another hatch blew open. A few objects bounced after it.

Ryan yelled, "Take cover!"

The grenades exploded, killing spacers and ripping consoles free from the deck. Smoke obscured the open hatchway.

Two Marines ran into the converter room, moving opposite directions from the hatch.

"Wait for the group," ordered Ryan.

Branson's gunners sprayed bullets around the Marines. The Marines ignored them, firing armor-piercing bullets at the pipes over the hatch.

"Shit!" The spacer handling the valves for that hatch cut pressure to the line as superheated steam sprayed out over the defenders.

"Wet the floor," ordered Ryan. A firefighting hose sprayed cold water toward the opening.

The gunners finally took down their targets. Two more came out to replace them.

"Zap 'em." A spacer energized the cables lying in the puddle with direct current from a converter. The Marines fell down and twitched.

More grenades came out of the hatch. One landed on Converter Number Four. Its detonation breached the reaction vessel, spraying molten radioactive metal into the air.

FNS *Dread* tilted as one fifth of her torch went out. The puddle sloshed against the wall. Some went through the hatch, electrocuting Marines waiting out of sight. Some spacers slid down the deck into the puddle and joined them in death.

Ryan held onto a console to steady himself and pulled up the cross-connection interface.

The ship came back to level. The helmsman must have adjusted thrust to compensate.

As Ryan diverted power from converters Three and Five to Four's torch plumbing a status update from the bridge came across his screen. 'SECTOR ONE AND TWO THRUST REDUCED. LOSING ALTITUDE.' He marked it acknowledged and kept switching valves.

More Marines stormed through the hatchway, met with gunfire, water sprays, and catapulted bolts.

When he had the new configuration set up and water heating the pipes Ryan typed, 'SECTOR FOUR FULL THRUST ETR TWO MINUTES.'

The helmsman acknowledged it then typed, 'CAPT PROMISES PRISON ONLY IF YOU SURRENDER.'

Ryan replied, 'WILL LET OFFICERS LIVE IF SURRENDER TO CPS.'

Half the Marines went down as another steam pipe blasted them. The spacers tried to shift it to spray the rest but were shot down.

'YOU CAN'T WIN.'

'WE CAN SMASH ALL THE CONVERTERS.' Ryan walked away from the console. He picked up a weapon from a dead gunner, aimed at the Marines, and found it was empty.

A blast of automatic fire from the hatchway killed the remaining Marines. A hand waved in the opening. "Don't shoot! Friends!"

Ryan ordered the steam and electricity traps secured. "Who's there?"

A stranger in a Damage Control uniform leaned into view. "Fighting for the People, Jock O'Grady, at your service. Got these bastards from behind."

Jock came through the hatch and looked around. "Good Lord they made a mess of y'all."

"That they did." Ryan shook his hand.

"I'll leave a few men here to help with your wounded. The rest of us want to get in on the fight for the bridge before it's over."

A trio of sick berth attendants began triaging the converter room survivors. None were unwounded. Ryan had a bullet hole on his thigh he hadn't noticed until the antiseptic spray hit. Twenty two were alive, though half would need a hospital visit to stay that way.

Damage control shoved everyone to the starboard half of the room so they could decontaminate the spillage from Converter Number Four.

Ryan fell asleep.

He woke to Jock shaking his shoulder. He promptly leapt to attention. Seeing an admiral had that effect. Even when Admiral Parata had his hands tied together and was guarded by grinning one-stripers.

"We thought you should have the honor," said Jock, "seeing as you struck the first blow."

"Thanks. Uh, honor of doing what?"

Jock shrugged. "The honor of deciding what to do. There's a lot of argument over that. So we're leaving it to you."

"Oh." Ryan thought a moment. He was still tired from the battle. "Let's get this over with."

He led the parade out of the converter room. A public affairs rating steered a floating camera ahead of him. Jock, the admiral, and the guards followed. More spacers crowded after.

This low on the ship the airlock was nearly horizontal. Ryan opened the inner door. The guards shoved the admiral in.

"Any last words, sir?" asked Ryan.

"I'd rather die than live under that collection of thugs," snarled Parata.

"Wish granted." Ryan closed the inner door. With full atmospheric pressure on the outside there was no delay in opening the outer door.

***

There were five empty seats at the Committee of Public Safety's table. Some of Corday's supporters had endorsed Admiral Parata's coup. Mitchie skimmed her analyst report. Two of them were already dead. The other three had been taken away by Action Groups. The analysts expected them all to be dead within forty-eight hours.

Mitchie wondered if some more committee members might be dead sooner. She'd been listening to accusations and counter-accusations of treason for an hour now. Some of the screamers looked ready to get physical.

Guen had sat out the arguments. Now she looked out of patience. She tapped her gavel three times. The two members screaming accusations didn't notice. She dropped the gavel and fiddled with her datasheet.

A horrid feedback squeal came from the room's speakers. Mitchie jammed fingers in her ears. Most of the people cringed. When it cut off the room was silent.

"I hope you've gotten that out of your systems," snarled Guen. "We will not consider any charges based on having the wrong friends or wrong opinion. Only hard evidence, recordings, or neutral witnesses. Now. Does anyone have any *evidence* that a committee member has committed treason?"

Guen let the silence last two full minutes.

"Then let's get to work. First item. Establishing control of the Navy."

Chaos broke out again. A cry of "Abolish the Navy!" shouted down by "Betrayers!" and "Harmony!" In a bit the shouting died down and people actually took turns speaking in calm voices.

The suggestions were still terrible. Civilian loyalty monitors in crews, continuous surveillance of officers, banning warships from a million klicks around Pintoy, and worse. There was always someone who could explain why they were stupid so Mitchie felt no need to speak up.

Then Kimmie Z suggested appointing a civilian to replace Admiral Parata as Fleet Commander. That received only token objections and many approving comments. Someone asked what qualities they should look for in candidates for the position.

Mitchie had picked the seat at the left end of the spectator section because it let her make eye contact with Guen. Now she raised her hand.

Guen tapped the gavel. "The Liaison from the Disconnected Worlds has advice for us."

Mitchie stepped forward. Not to the focus of the semi-circular table, as a witness or pleader, but at the end of it as if she was another member.

"My friends. Fleet Commander is not an entry level position. It requires years of experience and formal training to do well. There needs to be civilian oversight, yes, but the Fleet Commander must be a naval officer."

Annie said, "I nominate Commander Michigan Long as Fleet Commander."

Kimmie Z seconded.

A chorus of ayes made it unanimous.

Guen said, "Congratulations, Commander."

Mitchie kept her face calm. *You bitch. You set me up for this. You didn't even ask.* She decided she'd have to share that thought with Guo so he could laugh at her for being upset over not-asking.

***

She'd called ahead to order Hiroshi, Setta, and Mthembu to wait for her on the bridge. She jumped straight into the news. "The CPS decided to put me in charge of their fleet. I expect this to be temporary. For now Centurion Hiroshi will be acting captain."

None of them looked surprised.

"I haven't had a chance to check the legality of this. It might technically be treason. If any of you has been wanting to shoot me now's your chance."

Hiroshi broke the silence. "I think it'd count as an exchange officer. Are you wanting to be shot?"

"No, no. It's just the only way I can think of to get out of this."

The pilot grinned. "Look on the bright side, ma'am. How are all those admirals feeling?"

Don John Station, Pintoy System, centrifugal acceleration 10 m/s²

The admirals came to their feet as Mitchie walked into the room. She said, "As you were," carefully modulating it to sound calm and in control.

The front of the conference room was devoid of lectern, chairs, tables, or any other useful cover. The admirals all had desks to sit behind. She stood front and center, hands on hips.

"For anyone who hasn't been paying attention, I'm Michigan Long, your new Fleet Commander. Some of you may be wondering if the reports on my career are accurate. I'll give you the summary.

"Akiak Guard Academy grad. Intelligence operative. Many years of covert operations. Cover identity as a freighter pilot. When war broke out I was needed more as a pilot than spy. Still flew the same freighter."

Admirals nodded as she confirmed what they'd read.

"I've never commanded a warship. Never been to Fleet Tactics School. Never taken offensive action in a space battle." The last wasn't true, but the infoweapon attack was still classified, and it wasn't useful experience for her new job. "And I'm not even a Fusion citizen.

"So why am I in charge?"

No admiral volunteered an answer.

"Apparently I'm the highest-ranking officer trusted by the Committee of Public Safety. Which is a tremendous insult to every one of you. You should feel insulted." Beat. "Unless you feel you're to blame for this mess and the Committee is right to not trust you."

"What if we think the Committee is to blame for the mess?" came from the back.

Mitchie spotted the speaker. He was one of the half-dozen commodores who'd squeezed against the back wall.

"I don't think that's a productive topic," she said. "Why don't we blame the politicians who built Fusion society into a time bomb? They're dead, they can't complain."

No one laughed, but she saw some lips twitch.

"We don't have time to argue about blame. There's a war on. More than one. The Harmony intends to impose its order on all the worlds they can reach." She switched from English to Mandarin. "Can you define the most important virtues in descending order?"

That forced smiles from the Sinophones in the room. One was bold enough to answer, "Not well enough."

She returned to English. "We can expect conflict with them soon. The Combined Fleet is fighting the Betrayers and desperately needs reinforcements. Getting them that is my official mission here. And let's hope the war with the Disconnect doesn't resume."

A Vice Admiral in the front row—Sunil, if she remembered her briefing sheets right—said, "You think there's a chance we'd attack the Disconnected Worlds in this condition?"

Mitchie stepped forward to look Admiral Sunil in the eye. "You think only the Fusion can start wars? Let me tell you a story about what it's like in the Disconnect right now."

She'd heard this from the late Ensign Jones. It happened only weeks before her squadron left.

"Some people on Bonaventure decided to put on a play. Central character was a man who'd lost his wife and children in the invasion. So he stole a torchship. Planned to boost it up to one-tenth lightspeed and smack it into Pintoy."

That sent a shudder through her audience. Planetary defenses trained for out of control ships more than they did enemy attacks. The impact would equal a million megaton bomb. No humans would survive.

"The hero stole a courier and chased him. Most of the play was them arguing over the radio about revenge and innocents and consequences. At the end the hero snuck aboard the other ship, sabotaged the engine, and made it miss the planet."

She'd wandered back to the front wall while telling the story but could still see relief on some faces.

"The crowd booed. Some rushed the stage. The stagehands and ushers had to use force to get the actors out the back door. Police came with riot gear. The play was never performed again."

Dead silence and poker faces.

"That's how much the Bonnies hate y'all."

She let the silence stretch out.

Finally Mitchie shrugged. "Now me, I'm from Akiak, and I have work that needs to be done. So let's get this over with."

She pulled her pistol from her pocket as she walked back to Vice Admiral Sunil's desk. They were too disciplined to flinch from it, but the tension made it clear they thought she might shoot. She placed it on the corner of the desk, not aimed at him, but with the muzzle pointing through the middle of the audience in a very unsafe manner.

"If anyone thinks the next person the Committee of Public Safety will appoint will be an improvement over me, go ahead and shoot me now."

No admiral or commodore moved. Sunil leaned over in his chair to avoid the weapon.

"Anyone?"

Mitchie looked from one admiral to the next, making each one drop his eyes. She hated playing this kind of dominance game but if she was going to run this outfit she needed gut-level respect, not just a symbolic title. Especially with the men.

She stared down the two female admirals just to be safe.

By the time she worked her way back to the commodores they wouldn't even meet her eyes. She pocketed the pistol.

"All right. We have a lot of work in front of us. The recent unpleasantness left holes in the command structure. We need to fill those, assess fleet readiness, and make plans for taking the offensive."

Tiantan, gravity 8.7 m/s^2

As the elevator cage descended along the side of the destroyer, Guo saw a groundcar approaching. The passengers emerged just before he reached the ground. The first was Stakeholder—no, *Daifu*—Ping. A woman he didn't recognize exited through the door on the other side.

He mentally rehearsed his greetings to Ping. Establishing the proper tone as a neutral messenger was crucial to the success of his mission. Then the third person exited the groundcar.

"Master Su!" Guo flew past Ping, then stopped, unsure if he should bow. The old man spread his arms to demand an embrace.

When they released the hug the old man said, "It's good to see you again, boy. I wasn't sure I'd live long enough."

"It's been too long. And I don't know if you ever received my last letter."

"I have the one you sent after returning to the Disconnect from Earth. Congratulations on your wedding. I sent the reply to Akiak."

"It must have been lost in the war." The invasion of Bonaventure had disrupted much more than mail service.

"I'll resend it. But we must remember our manners."

Ignoring Ping had been rude of them. Guo turned to face him.

"Welcome to Tiantan, Ambassador Kwan." Ping accompanied the greeting with a firm Disconnect-style handshake. "Is this your fourth visit here, then?"

"Yes, the *Fives Full* let me take shore leave when we traded here."

"I hope this visit won't be as abbreviated as the others," said Su.

"I'm to help clarify the Committee of Public Safety's proposal to give the Elders a full understanding. I will stay until they've formed a reply for me to carry back."

"And I promise you, Master Su, we will consider our words carefully," Ping said with a smile. "Now let me introduce the Ambassador's guide and liaison to the Elders. This is Chang Lian, a staffer in the External Affairs Advisory."

The woman stepped into full view. She made a demure bow.

Guo strove for self-control. Her face was perfection. He'd only seen such beauty in advertising holos or on stage. To see it in person, up close, without warning—he made himself take a breath. "Miss Chang. I'm pleased to meet you."

"Please call me Lian, Ambassador. I'll be handling all your needs for your visit."

"Of course."

Ping announced plans for dinner. Guo found himself in the back seat with Lian. She filled his silence with tour guide chatter, leaning into his personal space when pointing out landmarks on his side.

As the shock wore off Guo analyzed her appearance. It was too perfect. Only holodrama stars and professional models would invest in the precision surgery to achieve that look. She looked to have pure Han ancestry, which made her height only a little below average for her stock. But her torso curved more than the Han average.

She could wear Mitchie's clothes without a wrinkle. That couldn't be a coincidence.

He interrupted Lian's praise of an irrigation canal. "Were you born on Tiantan?"

She welcomed the question with a smile that made his wedding ring feel tight. "Yes, in Weihai. My parents came here from Franklin to join one of the Revivalist villages being founded. They're scholars at the Zengxi Academy now."

"My family had no interest in Confucian theory. But their behavior has always been close to it in practice."

Master Su interjected, "While you are brilliant at theory and terrible at practicing it."

                              ***

The groundcar delivered them to an elegant building with no sign. After a few words from Lian the hostess took them to a private room. Four cushions ringed a low table.

The meal was family-style in presentation, platters brought out for them all to take portions from. The food was not family cooking. It was exquisite. Salmon with no sauce, cooked to bring out the full flavor of the meat. Pork with a sauce deliciously scented as he brought it to his mouth, another flavor on his tongue, and an aftertaste different yet equally fine. The tea would have been the highlight of any other meal. Dishes kept coming with varied delights.

In peacetime Guo had splurged on gourmet meals on a dozen worlds. Few equaled even a part of this one. The totality was such perfection—the only superlative he could compare it to was Lian's beauty.

"You never lift with your chopsticks," said Lian. She balanced a piece of chicken on hers to demonstrate.

Guo looked down at his next bite, clamped firmly between two pieces of bamboo. "I hadn't thought about it. I guess I developed the habit eating in free fall. You have to keep everything under control or it can fly off."

"Cooking must be impossible under those conditions."

"Some kinds. Boiling and frying are out. But you can broil and bake. I used to put dough on skewers, shish kabob style, and make perfectly spherical muffins."

"We'll have to encourage someone to open a restaurant on the highport," said Ping. "Who knows what pleasures we're missing by only eating in gravity."

"I'd visit it," said Guo. "But don't ask me to run it. I've had a lifetime's worth of freefall time already."

"It would keep you out of the mines," said Master Su.

"There's lots of ways to stay out."

"Are you claustrophobic?" asked Lian.

Guo chuckled. "The converter room of a spaceship is just as cramped and windowless as a mine tunnel. It's worse when your ship is in combat. But when you come out of the mine you're always in the same place. Walk off the ship and you're someplace different. Bonaventure, or Demeter, or here."

He waved at the window of the room. It overlooked a small lake. An island in the center held a shrine.

Master Su said, "In your traveling, have you found a way to obey your family's will?"

That provoked a burst of laughter. "If I had I wouldn't be here," said Guo.

"Yet you've gotten married, as they wished."

Ping and Lian busied themselves with their food.

"I'm married, yes. But it didn't happen as they wished. I followed my wishes. And hers."

"Have they met her yet?"

Guo nodded.

"How did they like her?"

Guo looked at the other two. If he was talking privately with

Master Su he'd want to answer honestly. But—he was an ambassador now. All his conversations would be monitored unless he went back to the secure room on the warship which brought him here.

"Their feelings were . . . mixed," he answered.

"Daughters in law often receive a wary welcome. That changes with the first grandchild."

"She's a naval officer in the middle of a war."

"And when peace comes?"

"We've talked about it." And he shouldn't be talking about it here, in front of the target of his mission. Guo was a messenger, dammit. They shouldn't be talking about him at all.

Master Su turned back to his plate, lifting a spike of broccoli on his chopsticks.

Lian filled the silence. "We have a tai chi session in the morning. Would you like to join us?"

"Yes, I'd be delighted," said Guo.

"After that I'm afraid you'll have to play tourist for a few days," said Ping. "We've barely had time to start looking at the documents you transmitted. I want to be fully studied up before we meet to discuss the proposal."

***

A white gi and trousers were laid on the chair in Guo's room when he woke to gentle music. He dressed and left the room. Lian was in the hallway in a similar outfit, also barefoot.

They walked out of their quarters. It was one of five buildings making a loose hexagon. The open side faced east. A glow on the horizon hinted that dawn was close. Dozens of people were standing on the lawn east of the covered walkways connecting the buildings.

Lian began introducing Guo to the others. Everyone wore exercise clothes. Some in gis, some in loose tunics. One was in a Fusion Navy PT uniform. Guo recognized him as the admiral on the Elder Council.

Looking over the crowd he recognized several other Elders. He'd studied their dossiers on the trip here. Ping was here. It looked like all of them might be in the gathering.

When the first light of the sun peeked through the trees a young woman walked east a few meters then turned to face the crowd. People began forming into evenly spaced lines. All conversation had stopped. Guo wasn't sure where to stand. As the grid formed around him there was an obvious space left. He stepped into it, now a double-arm interval from Lian and a judicial expert on his other side.

The exercise leader stood relaxed, almost at attention. Everyone matched her. She swept her arms up, then pivoted on her feet to face south. Guo mirrored her, a beat behind the rest. They held the pose for a long ten-count, then bent knees and leveled the arms. That pose was held for a ten-count as well.

Lagging behind the others frustrated Guo. Everyone else seemed to anticipate the leader's changes, matching her precisely. They knew which pose would be next. He'd taken T'ai Chi classes on multiple worlds, including this one, but they were classes. The instructor would tell students what to do. He'd also chosen ones focused on the self-defense side of the art. This . . . was hardly even exercise. More a whole body meditation.

The thirteenth pose was a repeat of the first one. The one after was also a repeat. Guo realized there was a cycle, which is why everyone could anticipate it so well. This would have been useful for him if he'd tried to remember the earlier poses. Instead he was starting each change late and jerking his movements to catch up to the rest. Everyone else moved as a single being with many bodies, and he was twitching inside it like a tumor.

The start of the third cycle eased him a bit. He half-remembered the pose which let him anticipate some of the motions. More importantly he'd learned to watch whoever he was facing at the time and let his body match theirs. Eyes guided limbs, while the brain stayed out of the way.

That left him free to fret about looking bad in front of the people he needed to impress. But at least he wasn't looking as bad now.

Three or four more cycles went by. He'd stopped counting, just flowing with the motions. He'd learned to not anticipate, just to flow, being one cell in the being. His arms moved with everyone's arms. He turned with everyone. They were all together.

It was a shock when the young woman returned to standing straight and bowed to everyone. The practitioners all bowed back. Guo only lagged an instant in his bow. The grid dissolved, some trotting off to work, others resuming conversations.

He'd broken a sweat at some point without noticing. However long they'd been at this—the sun was well clear of the trees—it had added up to real exercise. He was tired, but without the ache of calisthenics.

"This way, Ambassador Kwan," said Lian. One of the tables by the walkways had been set up with a light meal of rice and dumplings.

"Please, call me Guo. I'm just a temporary ambassador."

"As you wish." She broke open a dumpling and took a bite.

Guo sipped his tea. "Do we do that every morning?"

She gave him a demure smile, still dazzling in that face. "Yes."

Dammit, I'm at war with these people. I need to not think of them as 'we.' I'm a terrible ambassador.

***

"I can't see arranged marriages working in modern times," said Guo, dubious about the latest Revivalist custom.

"My parents' marriage was arranged. Not by their parents, by the leaders of the local Revivalist group," countered Lian. "They're very happy together."

"Marrying someone not knowing anything about them has to be a handicap." Guo'd come closer to that than he liked to think.

"Oh, we know lots about each other. My sister was reading profiles and work portfolios for every candidate our parents suggested. She's comfortable with her husband."

"Doesn't leave much room for chemistry between people."

"The heart gets a veto. But it's an important decision. The brain should have the first vote." She looked out the window of the autocar. "Here we are."

The car stopped well clear of the gardens. Guo stepped out, then held Lian's hand to help her out after him.

The ground between the buildings was crowded with people. A few were stacking the last of the sod slices by the corner to be taken away. Some men with sledges and picks were breaking up the sidewalks. Others were taking plants off pallets and tucking them into holes in the bare ground. Another group with trowels was preparing for the next batch of plants.

"They're certainly enthusiastic," said Guo. "Who are they?"

"Brand new apprentice gardeners. Formerly stipend collectors with no reason to leave their rooms." Lian waved at the two brick-shaped buildings. At five stories tall they were as big as any Guo had seen on Tiantan.

He couldn't spot a foreman. "Who's in charge?"

"No one. They had two weeks apprenticing elsewhere and then came home to create their own garden. It's a completely collective project, consensus driven. Look."

A bucket held HUD glasses for anyone who needed them. Lian put one on Guo then took one for herself.

He looked over the site. As Lian pulled up the consensus, multicolored lines and labels appeared marking out a mix of flowers and vegetable beds. The strength of lines varied, with the thinnest overlapping unreadably.

"What's that spot?" Guo pointed at a tangle.

"That's a dispute over the final design. It's being left unresolved while they work on the agreed-upon parts."

"Just postponing the decision?"

"More that they're working to increase their weight in the consensus." Lian highlighted the overlay of the flowerbeds being filled in. She expanded it to show who supported that decision. Each name further expanded to what work they'd done and how difficult it was.

"Interesting. The more dirty your hands are the more of a say you have." Guo appreciated the elegance of the feedback mechanism.

"Yes. But it's diluted by how much you've pushed for different parts, so if someone tried to control the whole garden they'd wind up with little influence on each bit."

Guo dropped his HUD back in the bucket. He caught one of the
flower planters as she headed back to the stack of pallets. "Excuse me,
do you have time for a few questions?"

"Of course, sir." She kept her eyes low. Likely his ambassador suit
was intimidating her.

"I'm visiting from off-world and I'm curious about this project.
Did you volunteer for this?"

"Oh, yes. There were more volunteers then they had openings as
gardeners. And not all the volunteers chosen passed the gardening
class. I'm very fortunate to be here."

He wasn't sure how to get at what he was looking for without
offending his eavesdropping hosts. "Do you like the flowers you're
putting in?"

"The peonies are a symbol bringing success for our venture." Her
voice lowered a bit. "I didn't pick them, but working to put them in
gives me more leverage on the third stage plan. I want some carrots to
supplement our rations." She went on to explain the bargain she was
negotiating with the other vegetable fans in detail.

When she paused for breath Guo quickly said, "Thank you, I wish
you all success in your plans. I should let you get back to work."

"Thank you. It's nice to be doing something that makes a
difference in the real world. Enjoy your stay on Tiantan, sir." She
trotted off to get more peonies.

"Convinced we're not enslaving them?" said Lian in a teasing tone.

"Mostly," said Guo seriously. "It's so damn inefficient doing this
kind of work by hand though. Look, you've got the gardenbots that
used to maintain this just sitting out as junk. You could recycle those.
Or send them to Akiak. We'd pay good money for bots that are sturdy
enough to handle our weather."

She led him back toward the autocar. "They're not there as junk.
It's a statement. We value the former stipend receivers more than we
do robots. We'd rather have them do the work and throw the bots
away than use bots and let their tenements be a trash heap of people."

"This isn't value. They're destroying value. They're probably
burning more calories doing the work than they'll grow in their garden.

We'd starve on Akiak if we grew food like this."

"You're too poor to waste people's labor. This is a rich world, and we've been wasting those people's labor their whole lives. We shouldn't measure the wealth of Tiantan in tons of food produced but the character of our people." Lian waved behind her at the gardeners. "They're building character. They have pride now. A work ethic. Results they can show to others. To hell with efficient production of vegetables."

"Are you putting all the stipend kids to gardening?"

"We're finding work for all of them. There's a whole department devoted to finding useful, fulfilling work. Until then some are doing make work, yes. They're earning their meals."

Guo opened the door for her. "What about the ones who refuse to work?"

"Their meals aren't very tasty."

"Coercing stipend kids into service is what blew things up on Pintoy."

"When society is attacked it has a right to defend itself."

The autocar started moving as soon as Guo had his belt fastened. "How many died when society defended itself here?"

"I wouldn't know."

A blatant lie. Lian was more like Mitchie every day.

***

That night was the banquet honoring the winners of the annual Tiantan poetry competition. All the Elders attended. Guo discovered his ambassadorial rank made him *ex officio* an Elder for such events.

Lian gave him enough warning to read all the winners and most of the finalists. It didn't help him as much as he'd hoped. Guo appreciated good poems. Critiquing them had developed into a profession with its own dialect. His dinner conversation stuck to polite praise. Expressing his honest opinion of the pretentious microanalysis of his tablemates would be . . . undiplomatic.

After dinner and the awards Guo found a chance to buttonhole

Daifu Ping.

"Yes, I've read it all. It's a fascinating proposal. But I can't open any negotiation on it until the Elders have come to a consensus. Many of them are busier than I am. Once they've gotten through it and formed their opinions we'll meet and discuss it. Then we'll be ready to talk to you."

"Surely you have some initial reactions of your own," Guo pressed.

Ping took a sip of his wine. "Well. One issue I will be bringing up with my colleagues: extradition. As written someone can commit a crime and escape punishment by fleeing to another jurisdiction. We need to bring back those due punishment, or in debt, or committed to perform a service."

"Thank you, I'll think on that," said Guo.

"Remember, it's not the loss of the individual that matters. It's the loss of trust. If a group can't count on its members to stick around, none of them will bond strongly to each other." Ping turned to greet an approaching scholar, who promptly began lobbying him to support a pet project.

Guo thought on the *Daifu's* words. Incorporating some version of the Fugitive Slave Act into the treaty violated his principles. But if the alternative was the Harmony feeling it needed to establish control over all its neighbors for its own survival . . . maybe he needed to convince the Elders they could win when people vote with their feet. Though offering Shishi's tradition of pedestrian elections as an example would not win them over.

***

"Welcome aboard, Mr. Ambassador," said Lt. Commander Snyder. "Making sure we haven't left without you?"

"No, just wanted to have an hour of not being lied to, and maybe practice my English a little." Guo shook hands with the destroyer's commander, then the XO and bosun.

"Well, no stories from you, Chief. He's not in the mood," the XO said.

The bosun sniffed in disdain.

Snyder led them to the wardroom.

Guo perked up at the scent of coffee. After two weeks of nothing but tea even the Defense Force's coffee was a pleasant change.

Once they all had cups the XO asked, "What kind of lies are they inflicting on you? Desires for peace and coexistence?"

Guo sipped his drink, enjoying the sugar's softening of its bite. "Haven't gotten to those yet. They're still giving me a runaround on why they can't respond to the proposal. Latest is that the Elders are too overscheduled to find time to discuss it together."

He stared into the cup. "They're stalling and I don't know why. They should be moving fast to strike before the Committee of Public Safety has its ship crews trained up."

"Maybe they're planning a strike instead of negotiations?" asked Snyder.

"That's what I expected when I arrived. But they're putting too much work into softening me up if they're not going to talk to me at all." He took another swallow. "I hope the wait isn't too frustrating for you."

"Not at all," said the commander.

"The men are enjoying their shore leave time," added the XO.

The bosun translated that as, "The whores are cheap."

"I'm sure," said Guo. "They're charging just enough to maintain their cover identities."

"You think they're all intelligence agents?" asked the XO.

"Everyone you talk to in Porttown is a professional agent or is accepting a retainer to report all their observations. They've been wrapping me in continuous surveillance."

"We've enforced a strict policy against locals coming on board."

"Good." Guo drank down the last of his cup. "If you gentlemen will forgive me I need to consult the references in my cabin."

Once in the locked stateroom Guo didn't touch the shelf of books or secure datasheet. He sat at his desk with blank paper and a pen.

Any message he sent through interstellar mail would be read by Harmony Intelligence, and multiple factions of the CPS. He didn't have any news to report on his mission but he wanted to reach out to his wife. Writing her a letter then burning it in a candle felt romantic but there was undoubtedly a camera which could read every stroke of his pen in the guest quarters.

Here he could write a private letter to Mitchie, even though he'd have to hand deliver it to her. He filled three pages in English with complaints about Ping, descriptions of the better tourist spots, and a professional critique of Harmony Intelligence's methods.

Then he switched to a calligraphy pen and took a fresh sheet. Mitchie appreciated his love poems for the effort he put in rather than the beauty of their language. But there were some feelings he couldn't express in English.

The characters flowed down the page as he poured out his passion. The brushstrokes were perfect with no need for thought. Then he stopped in horror. He'd written "soft brown eyes."

Mitchie's eyes were green.

He tore the poem into tiny bits.

***

Elder Wang kept his remarks brief. Guo nodded at the paean to virtuous behavior. Instead of calling for dessert to be served Wang gave his place to Admiral Chang, the Harmony's Minister of War.

Chang ordered, "Brigadier Li, front and center!"

A middle aged officer strode forward from a table in the back.

Guo noted that the only change they'd made to the Marine uniform was replacing the Fusion's lithium atom with the Harmony's yin-yang.

Admiral Chang read from a scroll. "Brigadier Li inspired his troops to end dissention on Franklin. Former Planetary Director Walter Sponaugle was tracked down in his marshy lair, captured, tried, and executed. The rebel guerrillas have been dispersed. Franklin now looks forward to peaceful membership in the Harmony. Therefore Brigadier Li is declared a Virtuous Exemplar."

The Marine bowed as the red ribbon was draped around his neck.

Guo did not join in the thunderous applause. Lian clapped with the rest for a moment, stopping when she noticed his expression.

When the officers returned to their seats Guo muttered, "The son of a bitch should be court martialed for incompetence."

Master Su raised an eyebrow. "You think he lost too many men in the pursuit?"

"Oh, it's bad enough he lost hundreds to ambushes in the swamps. I'm talking about turning the man into a martyr."

Lian and the others at the table stared at their empty plates. Treason was not what they expected for after-dinner conversation.

"Having their leader killed will demoralize the rebels."

Guo shook his head. "Li turned Sponaugle into a legend. They'll be singing about him generations from now."

"As a villain," countered Su. He thanked the waiter placing a bowl of sherbet before him.

"Think on how this looks in Anglophone culture. He was born to wealth, used it to gain power, then lost it all. Rather than give up he learned to fight, bled the invaders, then died as a martyr for his people. That's a combination of Robin of Locksley and Jesus of Nazareth. You couldn't ask for a more powerful inspiration to young Anglophone men."

Su put his spoon down. "I don't know the Locksley story but I'm certain Sponaugle was not much like the Nazarene. We will take control of the schools of Franklin. In two generations they will all be properly instructed in the Master's teachings."

Guo's tone was cold. "And after a day reciting the proper answers they will go out to the woods, sing Sponaugle's epic, and murder some official."

Lian mustered the courage to intervene. "Ambassador Kwan, your dessert is melting."

Master Su looked down to his own bowl.

Guo picked up his spoon.

***

The Xiasi Chorus was six hundred strong. They rehearsed in the same amphitheater they performed in. Guo and Lian sat in the nearly empty stands with some parents and teachers.

The complex harmonies stirred his emotions directly. The exultant sopranos sent his pulse racing. The left and right flanks of the chorus waged aural war. Then the baritone tragic aftermath brought grief. Guo wiped his cheeks, startled to find tears flowing.

The others had all heard it before. After a brief critique from the director the singers dispersed, taking their personal audiences with them. Lian waited with him.

The assistant director came over to their front row seats. "Mr. Ambassador, thank you for honoring us with your presence. I hope you enjoyed our rehearsal."

"Yes, very much."

"Shall I arrange tickets for the official performance?"

"Yes, if my schedule allows." He cast about for some actual conversation. "Do the soloists rehearse separately?"

"Soloists?"

Lian explained, "In the Disconnect, the most skilled member of a chorus will perform the most difficult parts individually."

"Ah. No, sir. All members of our chorus perform every part in their range."

"And they do it very well," said Guo. A bit more praise for the chorus let them escape.

Back in the car Lian said, "I'm sorry. I didn't realize that would be so hard on you."

"It wasn't hard. Just . . . more powerful than I expected."

"Well. I should find something to relax you." She pulled up the weather display. "There's something I've been wanting to surprise you with. This would be the perfect time for it. But I'm worried about getting you home before the storm breaks."

Guo laughed. "I'm not afraid of rain. What is it?"

"A surprise." She told the car a street address.

The destination was a greenhouse. Discreet ideograms labeled it 'The Scent Garden.'

"We're going to look at flowers?" asked Guo.

"No, they're not all flowers. Flowers are chosen to look pretty." Lian led him inside.

The proctor had to repeat the rules.

"Blindfolds? Seriously?" demanded Guo. "I thought you were joking."

"Mr. Ambassador, to have the full experience one must focus one's senses. The walkway and railings are perfectly safe to navigate by feel. Every specimen is on the left as you walk."

He entered the maze ahead of Lian. The pathway curved to mark the edges. The handrail reinforced where to walk. Textured pads on the railing marked where to lean over to sniff.

The first was a rosebush. Pressing a button with his toe produced a brief recording confirming the plant's identity.

Guo felt Lian lean in to sniff the flowers. Even with her dazzling face hidden he couldn't help being aware of her. She was far too graceful to bump into him, but his skin felt the breeze of her movement and the heat of her skin hovering just far away to not touch.

The garden wasn't all sweet perfume. Some were musky, others bitter. As they moved through the pattern the scents became complex combinations. A glasswort smelled salty, though Guo suspected that might have been the water it sat in rather than the plant.

Going around a corner Guo took Lian's hand to keep her from stumbling on the irregular path. It seemed natural to keep holding hands as they went along. The layout encouraged side-stepping. They started flanking each plant and leaning in to sniff it together.

Being almost cheek to cheek with Lian over plant after plant made Guo notice the scents that weren't changing: her hair, and skin, and breath. He paused over a weakly scented cactus, trying to pick out what was her and what was her subtle soaps and cosmetics.

She whispered, "Are you liking this one?"

The warmth of her breath against his ear sent goosebumps down both his arms. "No, no, just woolgathering."

They went through the remaining plants a little faster. He still paid more attention to Lian than the flowers.

***

The Akiak dialect of Mandarin had many words for snow, some stolen from other languages over the objections of traditionalists. Rain was the gentle weather that came after the thaw.

This left Guo unprepared for the distinctions among 'rain,' 'lots of rain,' 'monsoon,' and 'typhoon.' The incoming storm was on the higher half of that scale.

Lian interrogated the autocar on its stability rating. Only when she was sure it could handle the forecasted winds did she allow it to start back to Elder's Rest.

Discussing the Xiasi Chorus and the Scent Garden kept them occupied as sheets of water darkened the sky. The sunset disappeared behind black clouds. The car shivered under the wind but stayed on all four wheels.

Conversation dragged to halt as it became harder to be heard over the storm. Lightning strikes came often enough to keep them from being bored.

The autocar had slowed as the storm grew more violent. Now it stopped. The car announced, "Traffic Control has declared erosion around Culvert Carp 57 is now at unsafe levels. Proceeding along alternate route." The car turned about and retraced its path.

The next announcement came five minutes later. "Traffic Control has declared erosion around Culvert Carp 54 is now at unsafe levels. Destination is now unreachable." It kept moving.

Lian raised her voice to be heard over the wind. "Car, what is the current destination?"

"We will stop at highest elevation point of accessible roadway. Emergency Management has been notified." Pause. "Emergency Management requests priority for rescue."

Lian flashed a smile barely visible in the glow of the dashboard. "Tell them your rank and they'll send out a convoy of tracked construction vehicles."

Guo scoffed. "Low priority," he ordered.

The wind eased off. The rain came down harder. The front had passed over, putting the heart of the storm over them. Guo could feel the temperature dropping as cold air flowed in.

The lightning was gone, or at least out of sight. Flickers to the east showed someone else was getting the show.

The car declared, "Contact with Traffic Control lost. Initiating emergency shutdown." The dashboard lights went out.

It wasn't hard to talk over the storm now. "I'm glad I leaned my seat back already," said Lian.

"Me, too."

She turned over and began feeling about in the back. "I should check what we have in the emergency kit. Four water bottles. Some emergency food bars."

"Tasty?" asked Guo.

"Hell, no. The storm will be long gone before we're hungry enough to eat this stuff. And . . . oops."

"What?"

"I used the emergency blanket for that picnic last week. I forgot to replace it."

"You didn't put it back?"

"It had bugs on it."

Guo laughed.

"Fine, give me the lecture about how the Disconnected Worlds are so poor you can't afford to waste anything."

"Don't need to. I'm surprised your weather engineers let the storm grow so violent."

"The ecologists insist on it. Heavy rains wash away silt and dead plants and such. This was only a three-year storm. If it was a twenty-year one I'd have kept us inside playing cards."

She sounded distracted. Her normal tour guide spiels were ten times as long.

"Guo?"

"Yes?"

"I'm cold." The words were shaky, as if she was suppressing a shiver.

"Um . . . do we need to share warmth?" He turned onto his side.

She slid between the seats. She turned onto her left side to match him and pressed her back against his chest.

Guo put his arm around her, his hand accidentally, mostly, landing on her breast. "Oh, sorry."

"It's all right. I'm cold there too." She laid her arm on top, locking his in place. Her bottom pressed firmly against his erection. Her legs slid against his.

He took deep breaths, trying to calm his racing pulse. He was immensely attracted to Lian. That pull combined with a push from enormous frustration. Life with Mitchie made him accustomed to frequent sex. When he was away from her he'd take measures to relieve himself. On Tiantan he was inhibited by the surveillance. He didn't want some agent writing a report on his nighttime habits. Or worse, Lian reading it.

This left his body aching to take Lian right now.

Guo's mind still had control.

He thought through the situation. Trapped together, with privacy, after a tour that had them pressed close together. Two bridges out with perfect timing to strand them. Topped by the detail-obsessed Lian sabotaging their emergency kit.

Logically this had to be a premeditated seduction. Or an attempt to provoke him into seducing her. Which would compromise his diplomatic mission.

His hand gently squeezed her breast. He didn't care about his mission right now.

Guo thought about Mitchie. She'd used this exact technique against her collection targets. She'd given him advice on dealing with it. But what came to mind was her advice for this trip. "If they set a trap for you, fall for it. If you avoid it the next one will be nastier."

He lifted himself on his elbow. Lian rolled onto her back at his nudge. He lowered his lips to her. She returned the kiss warmly. Her hand grabbed his shoulder and pulled him close. His free hand slid up and down her curves.

Guo broke the kiss to take a breath.

Lian said, "Yes."

He exposed her skin to the cold air. She didn't complain. His own clothes were cast to the floor. His body was in command.

Lian slid her hands along his back, encouraging his passion. There was only one moment of resistance. "Ow. Keep going, I'm fine." Then she wrapped her arms and legs around him and matched her rhythm to his.

Chapter Seven: Preparation

Don John Station, Pintoy System, centrifugal acceleration 10 m/s²

Admiral Wing's staff was brilliant. He had every graphic needed to display the exact state of the fleet's logistics chain. If Mitchie asked about a particular squadron's fuel or ammunition a few gestures would bring up a picture with precise numbers on her office's display wall.

She was less sure of whether he could function without the staff propping him up. If his only talent was gathering good staffers to him he'd be well suited to stay in his post as Chief of Logistics. Mitchie needed to know if he could cope making time critical decisions as a fleet commander in combat.

Because God knew she wasn't up to that job.

As the briefing wrapped up she asked, "What did you think of the last fleet exercise?"

Wing chuckled. "It was great comedy."

Mitchie wiggled her fingers to invite him to continue.

"Neither fleet commander had a firm control of their forces. Tholson did better, she at least had clear objectives marked, but Danners completely lost control. He gave them reference vectors, nobody knew what their offsets should be, and he nearly had whole squadrons pluming each other."

"If Tholson's approach was that much better, why was it a draw?"

Wing came around Mitchie's desk and sat on the corner. "It wasn't enough control to keep everyone operating as a fleet. Instead it collapsed into individual squadron-on-squadron engagements. Again."

She leaned away from him in her chair, feeling a little crowded even though he was technically outside her personal space. Wing was tall, one of the tallest Chinese men she'd ever worked with. "And you would have?"

"Laid out vectors for every squadron and ship. A captain's job is to keep his ship on the rails, not to chase after his own ideas. It takes solid staff work on the flagship, but I have some people in mind."

"I'll look forward to seeing your turn in the fleet exercises." She scooted her chair back a little.

Wing slid closer. "Would you like to go get a drink? I'll stand you a round in the Club . . . or I have some lovely brandy in my quarters, if you'd like to give it a try."

"Thanks, but I don't think that would be a good idea."

"You're in a very stressful job, Fleet Commander Long. You need to make sure you relax sometimes. Take some personal maintenance time."

Is he really doing this? "I appreciate your concern."

The admiral leaned in and laid his hand on top of hers. "I do want to take care of you. You're an impressive woman."

"I'm also a married woman. So no." She pulled her hand into her lap.

"Yes, married to a man who's been making a friend in high places."

Well, shit. I told Guen she should only do it on the ship, otherwise she'd be caught. She should try to find out how the secret of the affair had made its way to Wing. Suddenly she felt a flicker of attraction for the admiral. *No. Not while I've got this job.*

Mitchie turned out of the chair, putting it between it between them. "My husband is a wonderful man. You are not."

Wing stayed on the desk. "If you give me a chance, you'll find I'm better than you think. And you've been lonely and stressed. It's not what you're used to."

"Since you've been following my record, you know I've had enough men to hold me for the rest of my life. My husband is one of the best of them. You give every sign of coming in at minus one sigma."

That he didn't have an answer to.

Mitchie thought a moment. "Did you hear about the captain of the heavy cruiser *Salamis?*"

"Yeah. Blew out a valve, is going to be grounded for three months while they grow him a new heart and test it out."

"That's the one. *Salamis* needs an experienced captain. Report aboard and take command."

"That's a slot for a captain, not a rear admiral!"

"Yes. You'll need to stop by the uniform shop and get your stripes corrected. Dismissed, Captain."

Tiantan, gravity 8.7 m/s^2

The orderly grid of people became chaos as the dawn workout ended. Guo stood still for a minute, clearing his head of the group high and focusing on his personal mission.

Lian looked back, surprised he wasn't following her to the breakfast table. He gave her a wave and walked into the crowd.

His target wasn't the only one wearing military PT clothes, but the aides were obviously younger. They made way as Guo approached. "Good morning, Admiral Chang."

"Good morning, Ambassador Kwan. Are you well?"

"Yes, the exercises are always invigorating. I understand you've taken the time to read the proposal I brought."

"I have." The admiral glanced at the display embedded in his left wrist. "I look forward to discussing it with the other Elders."

"I trust you will remind them of the importance of humanity cooperating against our common enemies. As we speak spacers are dying in battle with the Betrayers. They need reinforcements. To destroy those reinforcements in battle against other humans would be a tragedy."

"All deaths are tragedies, Ambassador. Thank you for your words."

"Good day, Admiral."

Chang strode off, dragging his aides in his wake.

Guo strolled toward Lian. *If they won't meet with me as a group I can track them down one at a time.*

***

The afternoon sun snuck through the gap in the curtains and crept up Guo's pillow. When it reached his eyes he rolled over to escape, landing on Lian.

"Hey," she protested.

"Sorry, sun woke me."

By the way her arm wrapped around him she didn't need the apology. He embraced her in return.

Voices from the next room distracted him from the snuggle. "Who's that?"

Lian said, "That's episode seven of Magistrate Chang Investigates. We're supposed to be introducing you to the popular side of Revivalist culture."

He chuckled. "Is that really going to fool anyone?"

"Hell, no. It lets them pretend to be fooled. It's politer."

"Okay. As long as we're being polite . . . please?"

"Yes, thank you."

***

Like most worlds, Tiantan celebrated the day its first settlers landed. Lian and Guo were at the beach to watch a fireworks display. Hot food and cold beer flowed freely. Children ran along the edge of the waves, shrieking when the cold water wet their feet.

As with all things on Tiantan the fireworks were beautiful. Multicolored explosions didn't form mere globes and stars. They became flowers and dragons flying down toward the crowd. The climax was a battle between a tiger and dragon. Each wave of rockets was a frame of the animation. After a fierce struggle the two beasts strode away from each other, each holding its head up as the victor.

When the cheers and applause died down everyone realized they had room for more food and converged on the tables. Guo led Lian away from the crowd, up the slope to the levee.

She giggled. "Honey, we're not teenagers. We don't need to sneak off in the dark to make out."

"I like that idea, but it's not what I had in mind. I want to take a look at the levee. It's been bothering me."

"What's the matter with it? It keeps the rice paddies from flowing into the sea."

"I know. I just want to play mechanic for a few." Guo walked through the clumps of sea grass in the sand to the sloping dirt barrier.

Thicker grass surfaced the levee.

Lian joined him at the levee's base. "Fine, Mr. Mechanic. What's wrong with it?"

"I'm not sure if there's something wrong. It's just asymmetrical. Look. That direction the face is flat, at a constant angle." He turned to the left. "Here it bulges out in the bottom half."

Lian didn't comment. She just followed him as he walked toward the bulge.

"This is fresh. There's gaps in the grass, like stretch marks, and weeds haven't filled in yet. Oh, shit."

"What?" She couldn't see anything alarming.

"There's water coming through at the bottom. This levee is going to breach." Guo sprinted toward the beach.

When Lian caught up with him he was in a screaming argument with the head of the food service, who didn't want an unauthorized interloper disturbing her careful arrangements. Lian looked about for someone of higher rank. They weren't picnicking with the Elders because she'd wanted to cuddle during the show without someone judging her performance. The crowd was all farmers and workers, none of them willing to defy the local organizer.

Announcing Guo's ambassadorial rank wouldn't help. A foreigner would be dismissed. A few people were backing away from the danger area, so he'd done some good. Or maybe they were just afraid of the crazy shouting stranger.

Looking around for someone she could influence, Lian noticed a trickle of water coming down the slope. She pointed to it and shouted, "Look! Dirty honeywater is leaking out of the paddies!"

Grunts of disgust sounded as the crowd recoiled from the dirty water.

She added, "The water's going to get the food dirty!"

The trickle turned into a stream. It was muddy from the levee and stank of fertilizer. Workers starting to carry the buffet tables down the beach dropped them to scramble away. Parents grabbed children and left blankets.

The gurgle of the stream became a roar as the bulge blew out in a spray of mud. A flood marched to the ocean. The crowd dashed clear, some falling in the sand. A few had their feet caught in the edge, slipped in the oily flow, and crawled clear.

The organizer was ignoring Guo, trying to get her surviving food supplies back in order. The beer, alas, had been left in the path of the flood. The kegs were half-visible in the streaming muddy water.

Lian walked up to Guo. "That could have been much worse," she said.

"Yes. I wish I'd done something to prevent it. They ignored me."

"No, you alerted them, and when the levee failed they moved instead of standing around wondering where the water was coming from. You probably saved a dozen from being swept into the sea."

"Maybe." He faced toward the gap in the levee. A slow waterfall still poured from the edge of the rice paddy. "It shouldn't have failed like that."

***

"If presenting a good example was sufficient to create change we would have succeeded a generation ago," said Elder Wang. The philosopher hadn't even broken a sweat in the exercises.

Guo replied, "You have succeeded. The Confucian Revival doubled its committed adherents in that generation, solely through example and persuasion. To abandon those methods in favor of violent coercion is seen as a confession that Revivalist ways are not better. If they are imposed by force the recipients are denied the opportunity to improve their moral character with better choices."

"Violence is a poor method." Elder Wang began walking. Guo followed. "But it is necessary to keep poor values from being imposed on our people by violence. War has its own logic, dictating initiative and position."

"An agreement for peaceful coexistence would eliminate the need for waging war."

"Trust is an act of faith, Ambassador Kwan, not a piece of paper." Wang waved Lian over to join him, Guo and a few students at a larger table. The discussion continued for hours. It was fascinating but Guo never received an answer on where Elder Wang stood on the proposal.

Which was itself an answer.

***

Lian read down the last column of ideograms. She wiped away a tear. "That's wonderful. Thank you." She sat the calligraphed poem carefully on the desk.

Guo basked in her appreciation. The poem wasn't his greatest work. He'd rushed through parts trying to finish before she returned from her errand. But he'd put as much of his heart on the page as he could.

She climbed into his lap and kissed him. "Thank you so much. I've always wanted to read another of your poems." He felt her stiffen slightly. "I want to put this where I can see it every day!"

Lian scurried to the desk and found a frame in a drawer. She hung the poem to the left of the suite's entrance.

He sat on the edge of the bed, admiring the view as she reached up. He wondered which poem of his she'd read. He'd destroyed most of what he'd written. Harmony Intelligence must have found one, or perhaps there'd been a file on him in the old Fusion Counter-Intelligence system.

Calling her on the careless admission would be entertaining, but she'd surely be punished by her superiors when they reviewed the transcript of this conversation. She was relaxing with him, being lover more than spy. He wanted to encourage that.

"I'm glad you like it, darling," said Guo.

Joshua Chamberlain, Pintoy, gravity 9.4 m/s²

Scraping dead algae out of a hydroponics screen was below the usual duties of an acting captain. Hiroshi found it restful. He could finish this and know it was done right.

"Sir?" Mechanic Ye poked his head through the hatch.

"Yes?" So much for relax time.

"Sir, Chief Morgan requests guidance on priorities. He has some new tasking from Lt. Marven."

"Right. Tell him I'll be right over."

Setta's only comment on having to task someone else to finish hydroponics maintenance was, "Can I stop putting you on the schedule now?"

An autocab took Hiroshi to the analyst shop in only a few minutes. The system was almost up to its pre-revolt performance level, a good measure of the improvements the CPS had made.

The shop was an open bay with tiny offices along its perimeter. All the doors were open as the spacers listened to Lieutenant Marven yelling at Chief Morgan.

The chief was answering without profanity, bookending the statements with sirs, but by his tone that wouldn't last.

Hiroshi had stopped by his quarters to fetch the wooden rod of his rank. He slapped it onto a desk.

The sound made both combatants step back.

"There seems to be a problem here," he said in a dead-level tone.

Marven pivoted to face him. "The Chief is refusing to carry out my orders."

Hiroshi glared at him and lifted the rod. 'Centurion' was a broad rank, equivalent to anywhere from a master sergeant to a lieutenant colonel in the Bonaventure Defense Force. Whether a centurion or a tribune in the Shishi Imperial Legion outranked each other was a matter of seniority, assigned position, and personality. As a 'pilot-centurion' Hiroshi would be on the lower end of the scale in an SIL unit, since he'd been promoted for technical proficiency rather than leadership ability.

But Marven didn't know these subtleties. The vagueness of their ranks let SIL officers seize or evade responsibility on their own judgement. Something the Legion considered a feature, not a bug.

"Sir," added Marven grudgingly.

Hiroshi gently laid the rod back on the desk. "Our mission priority is to look for threats to the CPS, from internal factions or Harmony activity."

Both lieutenant and chief nodded.

"What's the problem?"

"The Chief is attempting to destroy a successful surveillance operation against a Harmony intelligence cell!" The accusing pointing arm was unnecessary emphasis to Hiroshi.

"Chief?"

"Sir, we have identified a Harmony courier planning to take passage off-world on a free trader in," he glanced at a chronometer, "nine hours."

"What are you doing about this?"

Marven jumped in. "Another courier will receive a packet from the trader, almost certainly. We can track the orders he distributes to identify all the cells he's supporting. This could give us a big chunk of their network."

"What data is the outbound one carrying?"

"We don't know," said Chief Morgan.

"So it could be critical information."

"Or just an amalgamation of open source info," argued Marven.

Hiroshi said, "We're getting close to launching the fleet. Even open source could be critical now."

"Dammit, he wants to sic an Action Group on the courier!" snarled Marven. His arm was pointing again. "They won't interrogate the guy, they'll just rip his limbs off then behead him."

"Yes, Fusion Counter-Intelligence is in disarray," observed Hiroshi. With riots, desertions, and defections to the Harmony it had collapsed.

Chief Morgan offered, "I can request an interrogation, and they'd send us a video, but they don't have any training in it."

Hiroshi looked at him in surprise. "They'd share classified information?"

"Lorraine Q trusts my judgement."

Hiroshi didn't want to know how the bloodthirsty action group leader had come to trust the NCO.

"Even if they do get something useful out of the courier," complained Marven, "grabbing him will tip off the Harmony network that they're in danger."

The centurion lifted a hand for silence as he thought. "Monitoring the courier is the best long-term strategy. But with the war shifting to fleet actions we need to focus on the short term. Suppressing the Harmony's spies while they shift to new locations is almost as good as rolling them up. Let's tell Lorraine Q to get him."

"Sir, there's a tradition," Marven burst out. "Intelligence agencies capture each other's agents, they don't kill them. We're putting our own people at risk with this."

"Tradition didn't protect Noisy Water. Make the call, Chief."

Tiantan, gravity 8.7 m/s²

The beach levee accident investigation was confidential, not something any off-planeter could see. But *Daifu* Ping could see any document he wanted. After a week of badgering he condescended to read it and relay a summary to Guo over breakfast.

"Nothing dramatic. Two well-intentioned policies combining for a bad result. Bots don't catch everything so the irrigation inspectors are required to walk all the structures in person. But the retirement age is high enough that one wasn't up to doing the walking any more. So he faked his inspections. After all, that levee had been solid every time he'd checked it before."

Guo snarled. Proper inspections were something he was obsessive about, and made sure his apprentice mechanics were as well. "Dammit. So he's lazy and nearly got people killed."

"Hardly laziness. The poor man's on the waiting list to have his hip joints regrown. And while your warning kept people from being caught I doubt there would have been deaths. A simulation showed three children and an adult swept out by the breach. There were lifeguards there."

"What's happening to the inspector?"

Ping shrugged. "Nothing. He confessed his error to his work group and made a detailed self-criticism. Work assignments will be reshuffled to ease the amount of walking he does. And in three years he'll retire."

"No punishment at all?"

"Humiliation, the scorn of his peers, and the knowledge he failed at his most important duty. That's plenty of punishment."

"No, it's not, dammit." Guo bit back harsher words, trying to be a diplomat instead of a spaceship mechanic. "There need to be consequences. Otherwise there's no incentive to keep the next one from slacking off."

"Ah, yes, the famed meritocracy of the Disconnect. On Akiak a man who failed at his duties would be thrown into the snows to starve, yes?"

"No. Well, someone who failed at a bunch of different jobs and pissed off everyone who could offer him charity might starve. Somebody who screws up a nice desk job will wind up scrubbing floors, not exiled."

"A precarious life. We don't want that here. We have stability. People are in their roles, and we keep them in their roles, so everyone knows what to expect. That gives us social order. Harmony in the most literal sense. It may cost us the occasional life from someone falling down on their job. But we don't have thousands killed in the fragmentation of society. You witnessed that. Is a levee breach such a high price to pay for avoiding it?"

***

Lian looked up from her datasheet. "Industry Minister Yang wasn't willing to discuss it?" she asked.

Guo sat down at the breakfast table. "Oh, he was. But I wanted to talk about the gains from mutual trade. He wanted to know how much the Committee would pay to buy peace. I quoted him part of an old poem, made sure he knew he was playing the part of the barbarians, and walked off."

She laughed. "Sorry, that was rude of me."

"It's all right. I'm not a very good diplomat."

Her eyes sparkled. "You're good for me."

***

Master Su declined an invitation to the gourmet establishments of Elder's Rest. He brought Guo to his school, where they dined on the efforts of Su's students.

"I don't know if you've had time to look at the proposed treaty," began Guo.

"Parts of it," said Master Su. "It's not a philosophical document. Very practical. I enjoyed reverse-engineering it to expose the underlying philosophy. Individualistic, almost atomistic."

"It's intended to be a framework. People can create individualist or traditionalist or technocratic groups within it." Guo added some rice to his plate.

"Which would be a fascinating experiment. I award you high marks for creating a debate topic."

"How do you rate it as a peace treaty? And will you share your opinion with the Elders?"

"Ah, the Elders. They're not nearly as interested in philosophy now that they're engaged in the exercise of power. Practical issues drown out thought. It's worse than wine." Su refilled his and Guo's cups with plum wine.

Guo took a sip. "Is this from the same batch as when I was here last?"

"Oh, yes. We gave you two bottles for your help with the bottling, didn't we?"

"Yes. They're gone now. I served the last of it when I made my first marriage proposal to Mitchie."

Su gave him an inscrutable look over the rim of his cup. "Needing more than one proposal is a bad omen."

"We're a good fit together," Guo said defensively.

"Your parents would like Lian."

Guo flushed. There hadn't been any hope of keeping the relationship a secret, but the mix of adultery, manipulation, and conflict of interest made him uncomfortable discussing it. "She wouldn't survive halfway through a winter on Akiak."

"So stay here."

"I didn't come here to talk about me, dammit. We need to get the

Elders to see reason before the war kills millions."

"But I like you more than the Elders. They're boring." Su met Guo's glare without changing expression. He took another sip then put his cup down with a sigh. "What do you want me to do?"

"Talk to them. Persuade them to negotiate for peace. You're one of the most highly respected philosophers in the entire Revivalist movement."

Su slid off his cushion and lay on his side, propping his head up on his elbow. "Am I drunk enough that I can't sit up straight?"

"No, you haven't had nearly that much wine," Guo laughed.

"If I drank all those bottles would I be that drunk?" He waved at the shelf to his left.

"You'd pass out before you finished a third of them."

"Yes. There's a limit to how drunk one may be on wine." Su took another sip. "But there is no limit to being drunk on power."

Guo shifted on his cushion. "Are you saying . . . ?"

"I am *saying* nothing. I am *philosophizing*. It is in the nature of men who hold power to seek more power. The Master's teachings prepare rulers for their ascension, so they may use it best for all. But you cannot know the strength of one's moral character until you have been tempted."

"I'd hope peace would tempt them."

"Peace tempts you. It will tempt you to lie and cheat for its sake. To other men peace is a barrier. It puts a lid on their power, shackles on their means of gaining more. Such men cannot be persuaded to seek peace. They will accept it as an alternative to losing what power they already have."

"Have you said that to them?"

Su's laugh was a real one, not the artful chuckle he deployed to underscore his arguments. "My boy, how do you think I've grown so respected? I only tell people what they've grown ready to hear. The art is recognizing when they've grown enough to accept a new truth. I will not tell the Elders what they are not ready to hear. Just as I do not say to you what you are not ready for."

Guo took a deep drink to hide his face as he tried to work out what

Su thought he wasn't ready for. Combining their discussions on past visits with the hints dropped tonight made it easy. 'Divorce Mitchie, abandon the Disconnect, and settle down with your Harmony-issued wife.' He flared with anger just imagining it. The Master's words were a good guide to life, but he'd fight before letting anyone else's interpretation control how he lived his life.

Which I guess makes me a terrible Confucian.

***

Guo's quarters had been fine when he was there on his own. Now that Lian was spending all her spare time there the space seemed vast and empty while she was away.

He knew he shouldn't worry. A doctor visit to see why she was "feeling a little off" was nothing. This was the Fusion, where doctors cured everything with genetically-engineered white blood cells. Not Akiak. Guo's father might have survived his injuries from the mine collapse, if the deep winter cold hadn't kept the tractors from starting.

Lian bounced through the door. The first glance at her was enough to banish his worries.

"It's nothing serious, then," he said.

She failed to keep from smiling. "Oh, it's very serious."

Lian unrolled her datasheet over her belly. It displayed a hologram of her innards, highlighting two spots in her womb. "It's twins."

Speechless, he swept her up and twirled her through the room, kissing her deeply. Then put her down soft as a caress.

"Oh, my," he finally said. "I'd always wanted kids, but—" She interrupted him with another kiss.

During all the smooching the sober, analytic, mathematical part of his mind had been working. It produced a probability estimate.

Guo broke loose. "Are you on fertility drugs?"

"What? No, no, of course not." Since they'd been sleeping together Lian had abandoned her smooth professional façade and let her emotions show openly. Now she tried to put the work face back on but couldn't manage to lie convincingly.

"Those bastards. It's bad enough they ordered you to fuck me, but ordering you to get pregnant on top of that? It's inhuman."

"They didn't order me!"

"Bullshit. You're an intelligence officer, assigned to monitor me, and seducing me was part of that."

"I volunteered." A tear fell from one eye.

"What? They sent out a notice looking for someone to fuck a Disker?"

"No. It was handled just like an arranged marriage. I had your full portfolio. Family history, career, your poems. It was the frog poem that decided me. 'If my shadow inspires great fear, I must place my feet gently.' I read that and I knew you'd never hurt me." Both her cheeks were streaked with tears.

"Master Su kept that? I told him to throw it away."

"He had it copied onto the bridge to the shrine island."

"I wrote that in ten minutes. I'd been meditating on the island and when I stood up—never mind. The poem doesn't matter. What matters is that I'm already married to Michigan."

"That marriage isn't valid under Harmony law."

"It's damn well valid to me!"

Lian sat on the edge of the bed and bent over, crying into her hands.

Guo turned toward the door. He could walk out on Lian. He didn't move. He couldn't abandon his children. He sat on the bed next to Lian. Pulled her close. "It'll be all right," he whispered. "It'll be all right."

What am I going to do?

***

Ambassador Kwan strode into the Council chamber, projecting dignity and confidence. He'd abandoned Confucian robes for his Demeter-made suit, a subtle reminder of a world lost to the Betrayers then recaptured.

This room didn't have the round table the Elders used for their working meetings. They sat on an elevated bench, a low wall barricading them from lesser beings. Nine faces frowned down like the judges of a treason trial.

He stopped on the red flower woven into the carpet, as requested by the protocol director. His bow was that of an equal. He represented the other half of the Fusion.

Daifu Ping opened the meeting, as the minister for dealing with outsiders. "Guo Kwan has come to hear our judgement on the proposal he carries from the self-called Committee for Public Safety."

Guo kept his face still. The phrasing was ominous.

The council looked to Elder Wang as their oldest member. The philosopher said, "This proposal would create shelters for evil. Any participating organization could practice whatever immorality it liked, abuse its people without limit, and subvert its neighbors. Human relations must be organized on a foundation of a moral code. This has no moral code. Where its foundation should be is only vacuum."

"The provisions on information and currency flow seem designed to prevent enforcement of morality," said Minister Yang. "Toxic media may be sent to children. Criminals will have full access to the rewards of violating borders with prohibited substances or perverse services."

Admiral Chang's voice was harsh as cold gravel. "The proposal would lead to human cultures diverging while being in intimate interaction. The friction between such different societies will lead to inevitable war."

"In short," said Ping, "the Council of Elders of the Harmony rejects your proposal."

"What is your alternative?" said Guo, maintaining his dignity.

"We have already sent our terms. They were carried on your ship."

"That . . . that's not a peace treaty. The Anglophone Fusion worlds won't accept it. And the Disconnected Worlds would be drawn into the war as well. Your . . . terms . . . amount to a declaration of war against the Disconnect."

Admiral Chang snorted. "As if war with the Disconnect would matter. All their ships are deep in non-human space."

Guo let a little anger into his voice. "Yes. While those spacers fight for all of humanity you intend to attack their homes."

Ping waved the admiral to silence. "Ambassador, we will prepare our formal response for you to carry back. I urge you to prepare arguments for both the CPS and the Disconnect. If they accept our terms humanity can combine against the Betrayers under the Harmony's guidance. Please enjoy our hospitality as you wait."

Guo nodded, turned, and walked out.

I've failed.

***

Guo woke well before dawn. He slid gently out of the bed to not disturb Lian. She'd been sleeping more heavily now that she was pregnant but he wanted to be careful. Dressing went as quiet as he could manage. Simple clothes, sturdy shoes.

He stood in the door a moment watching her sleep. When she found he'd escaped it would break her heart. But as much as he loved her, he missed Mitchie more. It was time to go home to his wife.

Starlight was enough to let him find the road. The tourist trips they'd wasted his time with had left him with a good feel for the local roads. The spaceport was southwest of here. He started walking.

Getting there would take all day this way, but he suspected taking a vehicle on his own would bring down some polite intelligence operatives to return him to Lian.

The air was cool enough that sunrise was a relief. Guo took a moment to be glad he didn't have to do this walk with the sun in his eyes.

His one regret was not having a canteen for the hike. Doing late night strolls around the compound could look like exercise or stress reduction. Packing for a trip would have tipped off his spies.

A couple of hours later he was damn thirsty. Making good time though. The Tiantan roads actually had milestones, just too small to read at the speeds he'd been passing them. Spaceport by sundown seemed practical if he could keep this pace.

"Hey! This is a vehicle route! What are you doing here?" A

policeman on a one-seat trike pulled up next to him.

Guo stopped and gave the cop a friendly wave.

"Oh! Ambassador Kwan! Please forgive my rudeness. I did not recognize you." The cop hopped off the trike and stood nearly at attention.

"It's all right, son. Were you ever in combat?" 'Son' was a stretch but it seemed the best way to reinforce his rank.

"Ah, no, sir."

"I was. I had a bad night, wanted to walk off the dreams until I was fit company for people again."

"Sir . . . we're fifteen kilometers from Elder's Rest."

Guo laughed. "Well, that explains why I'm feeling better. A walk can do your soul good."

"Of course, sir. Would you like a lift back? I can call an enclosed car if you don't want to ride on the back of my scooter."

"That's tempting. What I'd really like is some cold water, do you have any?"

"Yes, sir." The cop bent over and unlatched a metal thermos.

Guo took it. The cylinder had a solid heft, it had to be full. "What's that structure over there?" He pointed at a fish processing shed by the Dragonfly River.

The cop turned to look. "I'm not sure. It belongs to—"

Straight-arming the thermos into the cop's head was a weak blow, but it stunned him enough to let Guo get in a solid swing to the same spot by the ear. The cop collapsed.

Guo unlatched the equipment belt from the unconscious body. He was still breathing, to Guo's relief. The plasma pistol slid out. He quickly destroyed the cop's handcomm, then the antennas attached to the trike.

The vehicle said, "Warning, contact with Traffic Control lost. Only manual operation available."

He pocketed the weapon. Sitting in the trike showed him a control wheel and a mix of levers and pedals. Not too different from the analog forklift he'd used back on the *Jefferson Harbor*. The big pedal almost shot him into the rice paddy flanking the road. With a little practice he was speeding down the road faster than he'd ever gone on the ground before.

With luck he'd get to the spaceport before Intelligence or Order Enforcement realized what had happened. Lots of luck.

Luck, or some devious plot by Intelligence, was with him. Several autocars went past him going the other way, dodging to the edge of the road to escape the hazard of a manual operator. Porttown came into view, a collection of warehouses and low-class entertainment joints.

He slowed down to not kill any pedestrians, trying to find the quickest route to the port proper. He recognized one man by type, though he couldn't remember the name. "Hey, *Rollo* spacer!"

The warship crewman turned. "What? Oh! Mr. Ambassador. What's up?"

"Need to get out of here. Got your handcomm?"

"Yessir."

"Call the ship, tell them I said to recall all crew and prep for immediate lift. Jump on board."

The spacer made his call standing on the trike's rear bumper and hanging onto the roll bars. The gate to the spaceport had a turnpike and guard, but the guard was napping and the bar rose automatically on recognizing an emergency vehicle.

The spacer yelled, "Skipper says they're ready to go but a third of the crew is on the port, sir!"

"Good! We may not have time to get everyone though."

The destroyer was on the far side of the open expanse of concrete. Two freighters were offloading cargo but they weren't blocking his path. Guo pressed the pedal harder.

A bunker at the side of the port opened. A streak of light flashed out as it fired a hypervelocity missile. The weapon struck *Walking Rollo* a third of the way from the bow. A blast ripped apart the hull, throwing burning metal across the spaceport and into the town.

The blast scorched Guo's hands and face. He braked to a stop. The spacer fell off and rolled.

As the smoke cleared he could see the bottom of the ship still sitting, the propellant tanks exposed where the hull had peeled away.

Water poured down the side of the wreck from a breach in one tank. The converter room was ripped away—only its fireproof floor was visible.

There couldn't have been any survivors.

To his shame, the loss he felt most was the letters he'd written to Mitchie, waiting for him to come and deliver them.

A medic came by for triage. The spacer had a broken arm and was taken away. Guo merely received a look.

He stayed sitting on the trike, looking at the wreckage.

At last *Daifu* Ping arrived. "An excellent attempt, Ambassador Kwan. I didn't think you'd get this far. Unfortunately that meant we had to react hastily to secure the situation. We're far from done with you."

He paused as if waiting for Guo to say something. After a minute he said, "Come, let's get you back to your family."

Guo followed him to the waiting autocar.

Capitol City, Pintoy, gravity 9.4 m/s^2

"I'm pleased to meet you, Madam Chairwoman," said Admiral Bachak.

"Please, call me Guen. Civilian leadership should be informal. Have a seat, Admiral."

Bachak waited for Mitchie and Guen to choose their seats before taking a spot in the little conversation nook in Guen's office.

"So, Fleet Commander, what can I do for you today?" asked Guen.

Mitchie answered, "I'd like you to meet your new fleet commander. Admiral Bachak has an excellent combat record and performed best in a series of exercises against other candidates. I strongly recommend the Committee appoint him to the post."

Guen poured tea for herself and her guests. "I have no objection, but getting that through the Committee would be hard. We're still repairing some of the damage from the coup attempt. I'm certain Admiral Bachak had nothing to do with that, but just saying 'admiral' upsets some of the committee members."

"Well, I have no desire to offend the Committee for Public Safety," said Bachak quickly.

"We do need someone in command who can make decisions in combat," stated Mitchie.

Guen took a sip of her teacup. "You've been in combat."

"I've commanded one ship in a fight. Okay, once a handful of ships. But I don't know fleet tactics."

"Surely you've had some training in it."

"I had one class at the Academy. I was so bad I broke into the instructor's office to get a copy of the final."

Admiral Bachak gasped. Mitchie glared at him. He knew about her history of murder, torture, and rape by fraud, but *this* shocked him? "Lying, stealing, and cheating are skills. They need practice to achieve proficiency."

"For your duty, yes," he said. "But to get a perfect grade on a test?"

"I got an 81. The provost complimented me on studying hard and let me sign up for useful classes." She turned back to Guen. "When the fleet is in combat we need someone in charge who can make decisions instantly, not confer with staff to get options."

"I see the problem," said the politician, "but we need to keep everyone reassured that the Navy is under civilian control. Can't you delegate the authority to one of your staffers?"

"The authority needs the title to go with it. Or I'll have every squadron and flotilla commander who doesn't like his orders complaining to me instead of executing the plan."

"Ma'am." Bachak seemed to aim that at both them. "If the title is an issue, we could create a new one. Operational Deputy Commander, say. That would be someone holding command in combat. And we can make an Administrative Deputy to control the support elements we're leaving behind."

Guen looked to Mitchie.

"That solves most of my problems," she said. "Would the Committee accept it?"

"Yes. Just mention it in your weekly report, they'll think it's another routine reshuffle."

"What problems are unsolved, Commander?" asked Bachak. He

rode the edge of whether he was referring to her post as his superior or her Space Guard rank, half a dozen grades below his.

"I want to be back on my own ship, not the damn flagship."

She'd surprised Bachak again. "The flag quarters on a battleship have to be more comfortable than a freighter."

"It's home for me." *It's where my husband will go back to when he returns.*

Tiantan, gravity 8.7 m/s^2

Guo woke. Lian was shaking his shoulder. "Please, *baobei*, get up. *Daifu* wants to talk to you."

He staggered to the bathroom. The mirror display said he'd been asleep for eleven hours. That had let the shock wear off but he was still emotionally numb.

His feet and legs weren't numb. They complained about yesterday's extended hike. Throwing water on his face stung. Guo couldn't tell if he'd gotten too much sun or if it was a mild burn from being too close to the exploding starship.

When he emerged four well-dressed men were waiting in the living room. At least he was still getting the higher class of guard. Lian helped him into an ambassador suit, this time conforming to local custom.

As she fixed his collar Lian whispered in his ear. "Please, don't make him angry. Just cooperate. Please."

Guo nodded in acknowledgement. Her relief showed she took it as agreement. He didn't correct her.

The guards escorted him to *Daifu* Ping's office. The older man blanked the top of his desk as they came in. "Guo. I'm glad to see you looking well after your adventure. Please, sit."

He waved the guards out. They closed the door behind them.

Guo studied the bookshelves to avoid looking at Ping. He hadn't noticed the Chinese translation of Machiavelli before.

"Your record speaks of bravery, decisiveness, and willingness to use precise violence. I believed it all but it's not the same as seeing it for myself. That was a very impressive attempt."

"How's the cop?" asked Guo.

"He'll be back on duty in two weeks. I took the trouble to explain to his supervisors that we want diplomats to be given excessive trust, to lure you into exposing yourselves. They've agreed not to chastise him."

"Thank you."

"I trust that was enough playing boyish games. Will you be an adult now?"

"I will do my duty."

"Then let's talk about your duty." Ping sat and stared at him.

Guo shifted his gaze to a hand-painted landscape to the right of the bookcase.

Ping continued, "You feel a duty to the human race as a whole. You're loyal to your homeworld and its Disconnected allies. Your fondness for the Committee for Public Safety seems based on personal friendships rather than their technocratic philosophy, if you can call it that. You've entrusted your ship to apprentice mechanics. And then there's the women you've been sleeping with and the children you've fathered."

"I'm married."

"You lusted after the only available woman for twenty light-years, then soothed your conscience with a ceremony only legally recognized in the Disconnected Worlds. The witnesses are dead, scattered, or in Demeter data banks. She's never changed her path in any way for you."

Maintaining the diplomatic pose through that was hard. Guo felt his face reddening, his hands tightening on the arms of the chair.

Enough must have leaked through to make Ping abandon that line of argument. "You have an opportunity here. You can join the society you've wanted to join, be the philosopher you've always wanted to be. Join the Harmony and you'll have a post at a fine school, publish your writings, have students. Settle down and raise your family."

"You think that's what I want?" Guo laughed. "Master Su invited me to stay after my first visit. I could have bought a ticket here from the Disconnect. I didn't want to."

The realization hit him the way he'd hammered other men's skulls. "I left a strong traditional family on a world where everyone has to work together to survive. I switched from a big ship to a small one so I could work without a boss hanging over me. Spacers fall into two types, workaholics and those who blow their pay on drink and whores. Instead I read philosophy and go to the opera. I'm a Confucian to be a non-conformist." The realization left him light-headed. *Maybe I shouldn't have blurted that out.*

That took Ping some time to absorb.

Guo went back to studying the shelves. The philosophy books all looked new. The history and management ones showed wear.

"Fine, you're not a true philosopher," said Ping. "Let's be practical. The Harmony will win this war. Your interest is to be on the winning side, and for the war to be as short as possible."

Guo leaned back. "Even counting the worlds you're holding by force the Harmony only has a third of the Fusion. The others are acknowledging the CPS as a temporary successor government and sending their newly produced ships to Pintoy. You're outnumbered."

"You don't realize how long my colleagues have been working on this. The Fusion Navy squadrons sent on your idealistic crusade against the Betrayers were predominately Anglophone. The Sinophone squadrons were lighter ships with inexperienced crews. All the flag officers sent were Anglophone, to work with the Disconnect's Anglophone leadership. The Harmony's fleet is the most experienced of the squadrons remaining. The CPS is still training raw recruits as crews. It will be a massacre."

Experiences performing search and rescue on Fusion ships flashed through Guo's mind. The Sinophone ships had suffered more heavily but he'd dismissed it as random chance at the time. And the survivors were mostly Cantonese speakers, not Mandarin.

He opted for a flippant reply. "Michigan keeps being on the winning side, regardless of the odds."

"Yes, I've noticed. I'd considered ordering her assassination, but Intelligence sent me an analysis that she was more likely to be killed by a Pintoy faction before they could be in position for the job."

Guo's hands spasmed on the armrests again.

"But enough about Michigan. Let's talk about Guenivere Claret."

"We kept someone from kidnapping her when she was a passenger on our ship," Guo answered. "She repaid us by inviting us to her

Revelation Ball. Which you know, because you were there."

"You're fucking her."

Possible answers flashed through his mind. Claiming fidelity to Mitchie in front of someone who probably had a list of every time he'd screwed Lian wouldn't work. "No. Famous women attract rumors. You should know better than to believe them."

Ping stroked his desk. Its top became a calendar facing Guo. Dates were marked with times and places, and whether Mitchie had been present.

Put together like that it was a much more active affair than he'd realized. Harmony Intelligence had missed the bed and breakfast by the river but they'd only been there twice.

A tap on the desk put a picture of them mid-act over the calendar. Guo sat back. "Okay, I was fucking her. So?"

"Adultery and fornication by a leader sets a bad example," said Ping primly. "But the social fabric on Pintoy is so tattered another rip is barely noticeable. This is minor blackmail or propaganda material. It does increase your value as a hostage somewhat. But what we really need to know is what you talked about."

He'd hated pillow talk with Guen. He had to make comforting noises while she complained about unjust executions, factions in the Committee, and insufficient resources to take care of the people and Navy. "We'd just have sex and go home."

Ping waved the picture away. His finger landed on an overnight visit. "Fifteen hours? You're a healthy man, but please."

"She's addicted to an adventure series. *Magic Princess Journey.*"

Guo returned a shrug to Ping's scoff.

"Have you ever played chess?" asked Ping.

"Often." *And I'm sure that's in my file.*

"Some matches go down to only two or three pieces on the board. Others achieve a checkmate after only the loss of a pawn or two, or no pieces at all. War is like that too. It is in your power to decide. Will this be a long bloody war, or swift and decisive?"

"I have no duty to make your victory easier."

"Do you have any duty to those green spacers in their new ships?

They could be properly trained and sent against the Betrayers as you wish."

"If you care about that, make peace with the CPS and ally with them."

Ping shook his head. "We're too incompatible. War is inevitable. I will not leave to my sons an unpleasant necessity I can do today."

"I won't help you."

"Don't do it for me. Do it for those you love. We are having this conversation because I like you. I want to protect you. I'm already protecting Lian. Security is arguing whether she should be charged with disobeying orders or treason for not reporting your disappearance. I've told them to leave her be."

"You can't punish her for that. You ordered her to fall in love with me."

"It's not about punishment. It's setting an example for other officers." Ping went on, "I can guarantee Michigan and Guenivere can have peaceful lives after the war. With you, if you like."

Guo pressed his jaw closed.

Ping sighed. He tapped his desk. The guards came in. "If you want my protection again, say so at any time."

***

The chair was more comfortable than Guo expected. Not actually *comfortable*. Just hard instead of painful. He could wiggle a little. The straps on shoulders, wrists, hips, and ankles were firm without give. His elbows and knees could move just enough to keep blood flowing in the limbs.

His head was unconstrained. Not that there was much to see. A simple table and chair awaited the arrival of the interrogator. There was enough room for someone to walk around Guo or the table if he didn't mind brushing the industrial grey walls.

The grey paint was fresh. Guo could find no cracks or stains.

The boredom and isolation were intended to weaken him for interrogation. Mitchie had described how she'd used them in her successful interrogation of an enemy officer. There wasn't any countermeasure. He'd just have to tough it out.

From now he'd drink less water on his meal breaks.

He'd spotted four cameras in the corners of the ceiling. There was no separate sound equipment. Unless it was in the chair. He'd seen a tangle of wires coming out of the back of the chair in the moment between entering the room and being flipped to sit in the chair. Likely that was all medical sensors.

Guo visualized a control room with conscienceless doctors analyzing the readouts to determine the ideal moment to start the interrogation. *Maybe I should panic and get it over with.* No. Even if he could work himself into a sincere state, he was too proud to do it.

The door opened. He kept himself from smiling. Having someone relieve him from isolation sent a wave of relief through him. It focused on the man walking in. Guo's monkey brain already considered the man a friend. He'd have to fight that.

The interrogator spread a datasheet out on the table and sat. It was angled enough to keep Guo from seeing the display. "Hello, Mr. Kwan."

Guo worked his tongue until his mouth was wet enough to talk. "Ambassadors have diplomatic immunity. They may not be arrested, questioned, or detained."

The interrogator had expected that. "There's no treaty between the Harmony and the Committee for Public Safety. Treating you as an ambassador was just tradition. As your wife has proven, traditions are easily broken."

"What's your name?"

"I'm here to ask questions, not answer them. Please describe your relationship with Chairwoman Claret."

Guo decided silence was a better tactic than any witty response.

The interrogator waited a few minutes. At least it seemed like minutes.

"You will be talking to me, Mr. Kwan. I have a wide variety of tools at my disposal and the rest of my life to work on you. This will not end until you've told us what you know."

The assertion that the interrogator's time was unlimited rang false for Guo. If they had plenty of time the Harmony would still be stringing him along, trying to seduce him to their side with sex and cultural magnificence. Trying to get the data out of him forcibly implied a deadline. So stalling for time could bring him a small victory.

"Hurting me would be a precedent you'd regret setting," said Guo.

The interrogator tapped his datasheet. Fire scorched Guo's left forearm. He threw his head back with a cry. The sensation vanished.

"There, the precedent has been set. We'll also be setting precedents in sleep deprivation, medications, and intense cold."

That sparked honest laughter. "Cold? I'm from Akiak. You hothouse flowers don't know what cold is. Or what suffering is."

"Perhaps not. But we will find out. Trial and error is a tedious but reliable process."

"Fine. Make me suffer. I've suffered before."

"Yes, you have. Your dossier is fascinating reading. You're often other-motivated. I note that Chang Lian has not experienced true suffering."

Guo blurted, "She's one of your own Security people. And besides, she's pregnant."

The interrogator mimed holding a hypodermic. "It only takes one injection to change that."

He'd viewed the interrogator as someone he'd leave behind and forget once he escaped this place. This threat made Guo contemplate returning with murder in his heart. "That is a precedent the Harmony would not want to set. I'm certain you don't have the authority to do that."

"I haven't asked for it yet. I won't need to if you talk. Tell me about your relationship with Chairwoman Claret."

Guo said nothing.

The interrogator took a thick pad from the box he'd put under the table. A toss landed it on Guo's feet. It spread and molded itself to them.

He felt a chill against the soles of his feet. It spread. Was the device actually cooling him, or just fooling his nerves into reporting cold? The former could mean frostbite. *It doesn't matter. It's the Fusion. They could cripple my feet, grow me new ones, then destroy the next set. I'll just have to make them waste the time to do it.*

Chapter Eight: Convergence

BDS *Patton*, Boswell System, centrifugal acceleration 10 m/s²

Admiral Galen studied the ruined world below his orbiting flagship. Lightning flashed among the clouds of dust still filling the atmosphere three weeks after the asteroid punched a hole in the planet's crust. *Well, the terraformers made it livable once, they can do it again.*

He looked around his flag bridge. It was only half manned. His other staffers were resting or loaned out to help with repair work.

The Boswell AI had expended all its ships in long-shot efforts to deflect the asteroid. The only AI presence in the system now was scouts from the neighboring systems, watching from out of reach in deep space. The Combined Fleet was using the lull to repair ships, build ammo, and let injured spacers convalesce.

A yeoman approached with a message pad. "Sir, dispatch from the Cleared Space patrols."

Galen read the terse message. "You gave me this one already."

The young spacer flushed. "No, sir. It just arrived."

"I read this same message an hour ago."

The boy was reduced to incoherence as he tried to disagree without being disrespectful.

Galen led him over the Communications station. "Joe, show me my last two messages."

"Yes, sir," said the lieutenant.

The display flashed up the words, "Six Betrayer ships entered system. Falling back on fleetward gate to observe." An identical line of text appeared below.

"See? Duplicate message."

"Sir, this one came from the Zixian system patrol, the other from Sower." The comm officer expanded the messages to show the ships transmitting and relaying them.

Galen paused a moment. "Thank you." He turned on his heel and strode across the deck. "Ensign Grove!"

The unfortunate ensign snapped to attention from a half-doze.

"Bring up the cleared space map."

"Yessir." Grove fiddled with her controls until a sticks-and-balls map of a dozen star systems appeared in the Operations holotank.

"Highlight Zixian and Sower."

Galen studied the map for a few minutes. The orange cleared systems were a thin layer between the blue Fusion systems and red Betrayers.

"Deng!"

Commodore Deng looked up from his desk. The chief of staff had been trying to build new squadrons from the surviving ships of ones broken during the asteroid fight. He met Galen's eye with a questioning look.

"Initiate Case Rabbit. We need to pull out of here. Everything."

"Even the patrols?"

"Yes. Some of them will probably be cut off. Authorize alternate routes."

Deng nodded, putting his questions aside for later, and pulled up the retreat contingency plan.

In less than an hour the flag bridge was fully manned. More than full. Second and third shift staffers came in to share the load.

When the operations staff was all present Galen gave them a quick briefing. "Identical, simultaneous operations mean that these two Betrayers are coordinating with each other. But they're not neighbors. They must be communicating through one of these two systems. Which means we have at least three AIs cooperating with each other to attack us."

That sent a wave of mutters through the staffers. The refusal of AIs to cooperate was one of the key factors letting some humans escape the original Betrayal. If that was changing . . .

"If there's three, we have to assume there may be more involved. This is the first time AIs have faced predator pressure. We've destroyed or subverted a dozen of them. That's going to make others react even if they can't feel fear.

"We're going to fall back on the Fusion and get reinforcements. Ideally we'll be back there before the AI fleet catches us. You'll need to plan for a retreat under fire. Assume all adjacent systems come after us.

Get with the boffins, see if there's any fault lines we can exploit."

As the staffers dispersed to their tasks the yeoman approached again. "Sir, Rear Admiral Tan requests a call, not urgent."

"Thanks." Galen stepped into his office in case the conversation required privacy.

Tan answered instantly. "Thanks, sir, I know you must be busy."

"No problem," Galen told the support force commander. "What can I do for you?"

"I have a ship captain resisting orders. Could you make him see sense?"

Resisting an order in these circumstances was capital mutiny. Tan had won his flag with logistics efficiency, not people skills. Galen was willing to cover his weaknesses. "Yes. Which ship?"

"FNS *Charity*."

Hospital ships were commanded by surgeons, not line officers. Galen felt more forgiving of Tan's inability to handle his wayward captain.

"I'll handle it."

"Thank you." Tan cut the comm, doubtless eager to oversee the planning needed to get all the logistics ships through a single gate with proper spacing.

Galen placed the next call. FNS *Charity's* bridge appeared on the screen. A doctor in stained scrubs faced the pick-up. A Fusion Navy commander stood behind him. That would be the XO, who handled running everything non-medical on the ship.

"Doctor. This is the Fleet Commander. What is the problem?"

"As I have repeatedly explained," said the doctor, "the intensive care patients cannot endure twenty gravs of acceleration. We are proceeding on the specified course at thirteen gravs."

Admiral Galen took a deep breath, ready to explain the importance of formation keeping and the danger of Betrayer pursuit. *I don't have time for this, and he won't listen anyway.*

"Doctor. You are relieved of command. XO, take command. Give them one hour to prep patients as best they can then begin twenty gravs acceleration. And Doctor?" Galen paused to make sure he had the man's attention. "Send me the names of patients who die under acceleration, so I may write their families."

Tiantan, gravity 8.7 m/s²

Guo held the pillow over his head. Not to muffle noise—the cell was silent—but for warmth. He was curled in a ball on the cot, both blankets tucked in tight, and still shivering. The latest interrogation drug slowed his metabolism as a side effect. He'd be too cold to function until the last of it was out of his system.

It was still better than the drug that made him itch. He wasn't sure if that was a side effect or intentional torture.

He tried to recall what he'd said. The drugs made him babble. Part of it had been stories from his childhood. Also a recitation of part of Romance of the Three Kingdoms. But he was afraid he'd blabbed about Guen. Or Mitchie. Or both.

If they ask me about my love life I should tell them about Lian. They already know all of that.

The door opened. Four guards came in. "Just pick him up," ordered an officer in the corridor.

Blankets and pillow were left behind as they carried him out. Guo's teeth chattered as they went down the hall.

He was too weak to stand in the shower stall. Two fully dressed guards were soaked as they held him up and scrubbed him with soft sponges.

"Hotter," muttered Guo.

A guard obligingly turned up the water temperature each time Guo asked, until the other guard complained it was painful.

By the time they finished he'd recovered enough to stand on his own in the drying booth. He emerged to find the dry guards holding real clothes, not another set of prison fatigues.

As they slipped each layer on him Guo realized it was one of his formal suits. The shoes were freshly polished.

Guo could walk now. He wasn't fast enough for the officer. Guards held his upper arms and marched him briskly out the front door.

The sun hurt his eyes. He closed them to slits, barely seeing the autocar before they put him in the back.

Two men in suits had the front seats. They didn't say anything on the hour-long drive.

They stopped at a shuttleport he hadn't seen before. When the door opened he staggered out.

A hand caught his elbow, keeping from falling. "Good to see you again, Ambassador Kwan."

It was Ping.

The Elder linked arms and steered Guo toward a waiting shuttle. Its aeroturbines whined as they idled, ready to go to full thrust in an instant.

"Where are we going?"

"To PHS *Kongbu*, our flagship. And then to Pintoy. Having a familiar face on the screen should smooth the surrender negotiations."

Don John Station, Pintoy System, centrifugal acceleration 10 m/s^2

Sheu closed the door to Mitchie's office and saluted.

She returned it crisply. "Relax. Have a seat."

He sat, back too vertical to touch the cushions.

"I said relax. Lean back. Cross your legs."

That drew a bashful grin. Sheu slid into a pose of relaxation. He still looked tense.

"Better. So, how are the Fuzies looking?"

"They're managing basic competence. They'll fight, they'll follow orders, they'll fix problems with some advice. They've finally got everyone the full set of training manuals instead of just the operational ones. That'll let stragglers catch up with us."

"Good. How much longer until they're ready to go?"

Sheu shrugged. "We could deploy now. It would take six months to get them fully shaken down. A few more weeks or months won't make that much difference."

"Thank you."

He leaned forward. "There is one thing that could improve the fleet's performance."

Mitchie lifted an eyebrow to encourage him.

"We've scrubbed the rosters of our ships. We can fight the squadron effectively with two-thirds of the enlisted we have now and half the officers. The rest could be seconded to the Fuzies as exchange personnel. It's what they need most, trained, experienced people. Hell, they have destroyers commanded by jumped-up midshipmen. And I'm more experienced than some of their heavy cruiser commanders."

And commanding a capital ship in combat, even a foreign one, would be the peak of any officer's career.

Mitchie chose her words carefully. "I think you'd be a damn good heavy cruiser skipper. And I intend to make sure you get one." *Which might require writing a negative performance appraisal on you.* "But the CPS is still a potential enemy. We're allied at the moment because the Harmony is a common enemy. Once the Harmony is gone we're back where we were before."

"That's . . . I see the problem, ma'am, but we were allied against the Betrayers."

"No. This is classified, only talk to me or Admiral Galen's staff about it. We blackmailed the Fusion into the alliance."

"What! How?"

"We found out the secret of all those virtual people. Attacking the Betrayers was the price of not revealing it to the stipend kids."

Sheu thought it through. "But now the secret's out and we have no hold on them."

"That's right. So I want to have a fully staffed squadron, and no hostages on the Fusion fleet."

"Do you really think it'll come to that? I like those people."

Mitchie walked over to her side cabinet. "I have friends here too. But the Committee for Public Safety is only an assassination or two from another wave of riots and beheadings. Our job is to protect our home planets, not to make friends."

She poured two shots of whiskey and handed one to Sheu.

He downed it. "I'm sorry, ma'am. I've been so focused on fighting the Harmony I didn't think about what would happen afterwards."

Mitchie chuckled. "You're not an admiral yet. You should be focused on the immediate objective."

"You're not an admiral either, ma'am."

She laughed harder. "No. But intel weenies are supposed to look at the big picture."

***

Admiral Bachak concluded, "I'd like to compliment the Ninth Destroyer Squadron for their rapid maneuvering to cut off the opposition force escape route."

Mitchie stepped forward on cue. "Thank you all for a very successful exercise. This has been an outstanding performance. It is also our last exercise."

A wave of surprise went through the assembled commanders.

She said, "In forty-eight hours we will depart for Tiantan to break the tyrants and liberate their people. Return to your ships, fix anything that broke, and make sure you are fully stocked. To victory!"

"To victory!" chorused the officers. They chattered excitedly as they exited the lecture hall. Bachak's staffers began taking down the visual aids for the after-action assessment.

Mitchie led her subordinate to one of the side conference rooms. "Okay, I'm impressed. That's three exercises you've led. Unlike everyone else we've had in charge your formation held together instead of becoming a cascading clusterfuck. How are you doing that? In nice, simple, easy for the intel weenie to understand terms."

"It's loose and sloppy." Bachak pulled up an image of the exercise on the room's holotank. "I recorded the maneuvering errors in all the previous exercises. I assigned enough room between squadrons to accommodate most errors. Next, the maneuvering orders are all relative to a fleet vector. So if they get out of position they can continue from where they are. Instead of a rigid formation it's flocking behavior."

He played a portion of the exercise at ten times actual speed. "See where the Twelfth Light turns late here? The neighboring squadrons adjust, then their neighbors."

Mitchie could see the wave of adjustments move across the formation like a splash in a pond.

"Why didn't anyone else do that?" she asked.

"Tradition. And it keeps them too far apart for mutual support against missile attacks."

"So the Harmony will want to stand off and trade missile waves."

"They could," answered Bachak. "They'd have better accuracy and better defensive attrition than us. But missile duels are a numbers game. We have the numbers."

He went around the holotank and thrust his arms into the center of the formation. "What I expect is they'll see a gap in our formation from sloppy maneuvering and try to exploit it. Thrust in with their whole force to split us apart."

Mitchie hadn't totally ignored her fleet tactics class. "You want a Trafalgar."

Bachak gave her a proud teacher's smile. "Yes."

"With us as the French."

"The Harmony won't cooperate otherwise. It lets us bring our advantages to bear. We have more training in short-range gunnery than long range. Disrupting our formation won't hurt us. And our commanders are aggressive. They have to be. Anyone avoiding action would have his crew mutiny."

As he spoke Bachak pulled up a simulation of that scenario. As the Harmony column broke through the center of the Fusion disk the outer ships turned to englobe the enemy.

"Where I'll earn my pay is deciding when to commit the reserve." He pointed at the cluster of ships behind the disk. "They'll need to hit the Harmony at their most disorganized to keep them from reforming."

Mitchie contemplated the image. It looked like it would be a bloody victory.

He added, "It would help if I could count on your Disconnect squadron as part of the reserve. Would you be willing to put them under my operational command during the battle?"

"I'll consider it. Make plans for them. The decision will depend on what the politicians are up to."

Joshua Chamberlain, **Pintoy System, acceleration 10 m/s²**

"I love parades," said Coxswain's Mate Mthembu.

Hiroshi looked at the line of plumes ahead of them. *Joshua Chamberlain* was too far back to see them disappear into the gate. "I don't think we're part of the parade. We're the elephant poop scoopers."

"Fine by me. I've had enough time under fire."

The acting captain laughed. "Best say some extra prayers for that. Commander Long didn't bring us along to haul freight."

"We are hauling freight."

"Not much. That's just an excuse in case there are any odd jobs that need doing."

The communications box squawked with Commander Sheu's voice. "Squadron scatter! Squadron scatter!"

"What the heck?" said Mthembu.

Hiroshi thumbed the PA switch. "Grab hold and hang on!" He turned to his co-pilot. "Pivot ninety degrees port and double acceleration."

Mthembu executed the commands simultaneously. "Please, God, let there be no one on the ladders."

After a minute on the new course the co-pilot asked, "What's going on?"

"I'd guess we're getting out of the way of someone's screw-up."

A Fusion destroyer flashed by, far too close for safety. Both men covered their eyes against the glare of the warship's torch. The blue flame filled the dome over their heads.

"Blessed Mary protect us!" If they passed too close it could melt a hole in their hull and burn them to death.

Joshua Chamberlain's acceleration quickly carried them clear of the other ship's plume. The pilots lowered their arms and blinked away purple splotches.

The comm box spoke again. "Sheu to squadron. Seems a destroyer unit put itself in the wrong place in line then tried to jump to the right place without coordinating the movement. Good evasive, everyone. You are clear to return to formation."

Hiroshi checked the ship's sensors. "Crap. Starboard camera is out. Their plume must have scorched it. Cut thrust."

He floated over to the comm box. "*Joshua Chamberlain* to command. We need to do a hull inspection to assess plume damage."

"Acknowledged. Make sure you have your running lights on while your torch is off."

"All the ones that are working, aye." He turned to the co-pilot. "You have the con. I'm going to go out with the mechanics to inspect."

"Yessir. Isn't the Bosun supposed to cover for Chief Kwan?"

"Oh, she'll be out there with us. The four of us together might have as much suit time as the Senior Chief. Sing out if you see any torchships coming this way, okay?"

BDS *Norfolk*, Atafu System, acceleration 20 m/s²

"Commodore, signal from the flag," said the comm officer.

"Got it," answered Commodore Halgai. She switched her acceleration chair's display screen to receive the incoming message. Her eye caught on her cuff, still wearing the four stripes of a captain. Her promotion had come during the assault on Boswell, stepping into a dead man's shoes. Fabber time was too scarce to be used for making rank braids.

Admiral Galen's face appeared on the screen. That it was him instead of the rear admiral she reported to meant bad news. The grim expression meant worse news. "Commodore, I have a critical mission for you."

"Yes, sir."

"At their current approach the Betrayers will cut off the tail end of the fleet before they can get through the gate. We need you to disrupt them and buy us four hours. I can give you a full fleet missile salvo to support your attack."

Halgai bit her lip. This was a suicide mission. She could probably succeed, but she'd never get any of her ships clear to catch up with the fleet. A glance at the Tactical station's holotank showed her squadron was near the end of the line of ships creeping toward the gate. If she refused the mission they were probably dead anyway.

"Can do, sir. I'll coordinate with my Tactical and let you know the best time for the salvo."

"Thank you. God go with you." The screen blanked.

She took two breaths to steady herself. Then began a crisp stream of orders. "All hands, we are making a spoiling attack on the enemy. Helm, coordinate with squadron to execute a one-eighty flip in two minutes. Drop accel to ten gravs after the flip. Tactical, give me attack options for disrupting the lead Betrayer elements. You'll be coordinating a full fleet missile salvo."

A wave of "aye-ayes" came back from the bridge crew.

Once they were steady on the new heading Halgai walked over to the Tactical display. The leading wave of Betrayers was a flat sheet closing at a tenth of a percent of light speed. Any faster and they'd be easy prey for missiles detonating in their path. They were aimed for the gate but would have to go around it. If they went through at that speed they'd emerge on the other side as dust.

A green line projected from the squadron's course showed where they'd meet the Betrayers. As she watched a dimple formed in the sheet, expanding into a dome ready to engulf Halgai's ships.

"That's what irritates me most about AIs," she muttered.

"Ma'am?" Lt. Commander Bowie looked up from his tree of tactical options.

"Nothing. I just hate how AIs always respond instantly to our maneuvers. A human enemy has reaction time, makes interim maneuvers until they've decided how to react. These things . . . just act."

"Yes, ma'am. We have some options for you to look at." He replaced the battlespace display with a hypothetical scenario. "Stand-off. Close to effective missile range then start thrusting to hold the distance. We'd trade missile barrages and use the fleet's missile salvo in packets to strengthen each attack."

"Okay. Next?"

"Straight in. Close to minimum distance and use our full firepower to rip the center out of the formation. Intel assesses the lead ships as destroyer-class so they can't stand up to our heavy cruisers individually. The salvo would clear the path for us and disrupt their formation so we can get in to inflict maximum damage."

"I like that. What else?"

"Scatter." The display showed the squadron splitting up and going to the edges of the Betrayer disk. "Each ship would establish a by-pass position at the edge of the disk, taking part of the salvo along. That eliminates most of the counter-missile fire and allows the maximum number of hits on the enemy."

"How much of the damage will be on the center of the formation?"

"Very little."

"Then we don't want it. The Betrayers will just blow past us and hit the ships in line for the gate. They can't maneuver, they'll be doomed. We'll go straight in."

"Yes, ma'am." Bowie switched the display back to the real situation. A yellow glow highlighted the expanding dome in the enemy formation. "That's what they're expecting us to do."

"Because it's our best option. They can adapt but they can't avoid being hurt unless they give up the pursuit." She patted Bowie's shoulder. "Good work. Coordinate the timing of the salvo with Fleet Ops."

The heavy cruisers crossed over a million klicks of empty space to close with the enemy. The Betrayers adjusted their dome to precisely match them.

The fleet launched their missiles in succession, all timed to create a single time on target wave. As the missiles neared the end of their flight the cruiser crews worked frantically to take over control from the launching ships. The missiles were over ten light seconds from the fleet. Controlling their final attacks with that much time lag was ludicrous.

As they took over each batch of missiles the squadron targeted them on a group of Betrayer ships. The dome was now flexing and pulsing as the AIs executed evasive maneuvers. Once each missile was close enough to find the way to the target with its little onboard computer it was ordered to cut the wires to its communications antennas. That prevented the AI from subverting it into attacking a human ship.

Forty-five gravs pressed Halgai deep into her acceleration couch as they matched vectors with the enemy. The joints of her pressure suit cut into her elbows. The display locked over her face showed missiles detonating just ahead of Betrayer ships, scattering shrapnel in their path. More missiles exploded prematurely. Had the AIs fooled their sensors?

Bowie was reeling off reports. They'd hit enough ships to disrupt the attack on the main fleet. Now to see if they could survive—and if not how many Betrayers her squadron could take with them.

"Lost the *Halsey*," reported Sparks.

Halgai saw the cruiser's icon disappear from her display.

"Executing Fire Pattern Alpha," said Bowie.

"Helm, shift us to cover *Halsey's* slot," ordered Halgai. She'd put her flagship in the middle as a reserve.

The hull sizzled. Enemy laser fire was scorching metal off it. The sound faded as evasive maneuvering or counter-fire stopped the attack. Or was just drowned out by the continuous fire of their own railguns and lasers.

"Lost some sensors," said the Damage Control Officer. "We're putting a replacement out the port airlock."

"Bandit on collision course!" snapped Sensors. The rating at Helm pivoted the ship to evade without waiting for orders.

Two more cruisers were marked as destroyed on the display. "Tactical, what got them?" asked the commodore.

"Hang on, ma'am," said Bowie. "Nothing. One of the lookouts says he sees *de Grasse* through a porthole. Bad data."

"Right. Damage control, cut the sensor wires, we've been infiltrated. Gunnery to visual targeting."

The hull rang with a spatter of shrapnel.

"Ma'am, before we lost data we'd destroyed over two thirds of this Betrayer force," boasted Bowie.

"Good. Keep firing, we're not saving ammo for anything."

Bowie cursed as his displays went to snow. "System infiltration!" He pried open the console and started cutting wires.

Halgai shoved her screens aside. "Sparks, pass the word to go to manual on all systems."

A deafening impact shook the ship. Everything shut down. A few red emergency lights turned on, their systems independent of the rest of the ship. Echoing whistles told of air leaks to aft.

Some of the bridge crew sealed their helmets. Halgai waited. There was still good air in here, and she had a duty to look calm.

The Damage Control Officer had some low-tech handcomms as backup. He finished his conversation and reported, "Ma'am, looks like they put a big hit through the converter room. Everything aft of bulkhead 732 is gone."

"Thank you."

"We're a sitting target. Why haven't they finished us?" asked Bowie.

"Possibly they want us intact," answered Halgai. "Runner, my compliments to the Master At Arms and he's to distribute the arms locker to the crew. Save a grenade launcher for me."

The spacer saluted and dived through the hatch.

Sparks said, "If they want us alive, maybe . . . we should try to deprive them?"

Halgai had already had a similar thought. Smashing the converter made it impossible to destroy the ship. But her attitude was different. "If anyone wants to go out the airlock, I won't stop you. But I intend to make the bastards work for it."

PHS *Kongbu*, Yalu System, acceleration 10 m/s^2

Guo looked around the battleship's flag deck. It had enough staff to coordinate every ship the Fusion ever built. With only the Harmony's small force to look after they were planning exact maneuvers for every ship. He could see a simulation checking the plan for passing through the next gate at minimum spacing.

Exactly the sort of information a spy would want to report to his masters. Guo would report it if he could reach a master, mistress, or anyone not part of the Harmony. But he was completely isolated.

Driving home that helplessness was likely one of Ping's motives for bringing Guo to the meeting. Seeing how the naval officers reacted to him convinced Guo the other motive was to emphasize the importance of politics and diplomacy over firepower.

The meeting was completely political.

Admiral Chang presided. He was acting as fleet commander as well as Minster of War.

Daifu Ping deferred to Chang in all formal interactions but found ways to disrupt the meeting's agenda. The update on the CPS's approaching fleet had been interrupted twice by tangents.

The poor Intelligence officer finally wrapped up her briefing with, "No Disconnect ships other than a few merchants have been sighted by our scouts. Also, a rumor is being passed about that the Combined Fleet is retreating from a Betrayer counterattack. We assess this as deliberate disinformation, intended to provide grounds for demanding a cease fire."

"That's reminiscent of your argument for your treaty, Mr. Ambassador," said Ping. "Did you leave instructions for the Committee for Public Safety to back you up with false news?"

Guo's guard would stop him from initiating conversations, but he was allowed to answer questions. "No. I intended to win you over with the benefits of cooperation. As for the Combined Fleet, it may be forced to retreat for lack of the reinforcements it needs. The ships you are destroying in this futile civil war."

"Goodness." Ping turned back to the briefer. "Could it be a real retreat?"

"We assess that at ten percent. The only hard data in the rumor is video of some container ships and other logistics vessels supposedly jumping into the Sukhoi system. Our second and third most likely explanations are merchant traffic being misinterpreted or a Combined Fleet logistics element sent back to pick up supplies."

Guo said, "A retreat would send the most vulnerable ships back first."

The briefer shook her head. "Fusion and Disconnect naval doctrine both insist that support elements should only enter a system preceded by proportionate combat escorts."

"Disconnect commanders are not famous for adhering to doctrine."

"Thank you for your insights, Ambassador Kwan," said Admiral Chang. "If the Betrayer attack is real, we shall respond by organizing humanity under a common authority so we can fight back as one. This is also our plan for if they are not attacking." He waved at the Logistics officer to begin.

FNS *Dread*, Dirac System, acceleration 10 m/s²

Mitchie considered *Dread's* Executive Conference Room a birdcage. A gilded one. With sinfully comfortable armchairs around the table. But still the cage Admiral Bachak kept his political supervisors in.

Across the table from her Guen Claret and Wayne Searcher discussed some news from Pintoy. Kimmie Z had proposed loosening food rationing in the cities. A dozen flunkies nattered about trivia around the rest of the table.

Admiral Bachak came in, closing the sound-proof door behind him. "Chairwoman Claret. Committeeman Searcher. Commander Long. Thank you for joining me."

In this room Bachak treated her as a mid-grade liaison from an allied power. Which Mitchie was, and wanted to be officially. But outside he treated her as his boss with all apparent sincerity. The switch worried her. If Bachak could fake that, what else was he getting past her?

"We've had our first engagement with Harmony forces," continued the admiral. "Two light cruisers were destroyed as they tried to exit the Danu System gate. With your permission, I intend to award our squadron commander the Wreath of Virtue. Posthumously."

"How many did we lose?" asked Mitchie.

"Five destroyers out of the eight engaged."

"How many people?" asked Guen.

Bachak hesitated. "Over a hundred dead. Search and rescue is ongoing."

Wayne Searcher reached for Guen's hand, then pulled back, as if he'd wanted to give her a comforting caress then thought better of it. Mitchie wondered if he was shy.

"Losing five ships to destroy two may seem like a loss," continued the admiral, "but I'll point out the Harmony lost three times as much tonnage in this engagement, and twice as many crew. Strategically we kept them from delivering their reconnaissance reports. Future Harmony scouts will have to be more cautious."

Mitchie slid her datasheet under the table and snapped an image. Guen had her calf pressed against Wayne's. *Well, that didn't take long.*

"The engagement is proof our forces are competent and aggressive. A key moment was the squadron controlling long-range missile fire from the main body to overwhelm the Harmony defenses. We never had a chance to do a live-fire exercise of that. The execution was outstanding."

As indignant as Mitchie felt on his behalf, Guo would probably be relieved that Guen had found a new partner. Mitchie's concern was political. Wayne Searcher was a reliable supporter of Guen and her technocratic policies. He'd never expressed an opinion of the Disconnected Worlds. Mitchie would have to become better friends to make sure he was willing to let them live in peace.

"My staff is preparing an all-hands announcement focusing on the magnitude of the victory. Ms. Claret, I'd appreciate it if you could record a statement to be included."

Guen nodded.

"Separately, an after action report will be sent out for the eyes of only COs, XOs, and tactical officers. We'll have simulations of alternate tactics that could have been used. Some with worse results, a couple that could have halved our casualties."

"Your alternate approach?" asked Mitchie.

"Yes, mine is in there," said Bachak. "And the simulation said I would have only lost two ships. But I'm a War College graduate. The late Commander Freeman was not. We're sending this out to try to give them some of the education we don't have two years to give them."

BDS *Patton*, Sukhoi System, acceleration 10 m/s^2

Admiral Galen looked over the list of transfers Deng set in front of him. Sending ships through a gate at minimum separation meant a larger dispersion when they arrived in the new system. The Combined Fleet was becoming so jumbled it was easier to organize new squadrons than reunite the ships which had gone through the gate together.

"We're getting a lot of mixed units here," said Galen.

Deng shrugged. "Mixing destroyers and heavy cruisers isn't a problem in transit. When we decide to fight we'll have to reorganize again."

"With no time for squadrons to practice maneuvering together." Galen marked the list 'approved.'

"If it's any comfort, I've made sure all the mixed Fuzie-Disker squadrons are majority Disker."

"Good. Last thing we need is some ships being held hostage."

A commotion at the Tactical console drew the attention of both officers. The commander on watch was chastising the sensor ratings. "One or two being missed I can understand. But five? Get your act together."

Galen strolled over. "Trouble, Commander Leith?"

"No, sir. Just spacers being tired."

"What did they miss?"

"The first Betrayers have jumped in from Atafu. We didn't pick them up until there were six."

"Slower than usual," agreed the admiral. "Do I need to find you some more ratings?"

Leith chuckled. "If there's anybody not already exhausted, sure."

Six more dots appeared in the Tactical display.

"Heinz, did you see that?" Leith said into his headset. After a brief discussion he turned to the admiral. "Seems I've been too harsh on my troops. The Betrayers may be jumping in and not lighting their torches until there's a set number. We're going to do some active scans of the arrival zone."

"Right, keep me posted." Galen's datasheet chimed with a comm request from Vice Admiral Bruix. Galen took it in his office.

The Fusion admiral's face appeared on the display. "Sir, I wish to clarify your intentions for holding this system."

This again. "I do not intend to hold this system. We are outnumbered and short on ammo. We will fall back until we meet up with other human forces and can fight on better terms."

Bruix's flagship was two light-seconds away, enough to make the delay in conversation an irritation.

"But this is an inhabited system. Sukhoi has a population of nearly a billion people! We can't abandon them to the Betrayers."

"We can't save them. We don't have the firepower. We can only hope that the enemy pursues us instead of detaching enough ships to break the planetary defenses."

The delay gave Galen a chance to hope Bruix would not force the issue.

"But we must try! At least let me detach my flotilla to protect the planet. You must help protect them, for your honor's sake."

"It's not my God-damned planet." He bit down to keep insults from following. Calling Bruix 'monkey boy' wouldn't improve the situation. "Any ships changing course for Sukhoi will be destroyed."

He tried to get his temper under control.

"You wouldn't dare!"

"I've already issued the orders. All the Fusion ships not from Sukhoi will just watch."

Galen ground his teeth as he waited for Bruix's response. The expression on the Fusion admiral's face said he'd backed down before he started talking.

"Fine. You can coerce us. But you don't have a plan. You're just chasing rumors of fleet movements."

"We are following the best leads we have to find reinforcements. Intelligence work is like that. As we get closer we'll have better data."

Pause.

"Assuming they haven't blown each other to scrap in the civil war."

"Then the human race goes extinct. I'm very short on patience, Admiral Bruix. Don't try me again."

Galen cut the connection.

His office display defaulted to a meadow in Bonaventure's Alps. Looking at it almost let him smell the edelweiss. He took deep breaths, trying to remember the scent.

When his nerves had calmed Galen tackled the paperwork in his queue. Too many of them were disciplinary actions. Spacers were breaking under the strain of the long campaign.

The request light on his door flashed green.

"Enter."

It was Commander Leith.

"Ah. Sorted out your sensor issues?"

"Yes, sir. Um . . . the sensors are fine. The Betrayers are jumping into the system in groups of six."

That was impossible according to the theories taught to Galen in academy. "How?"

"The boffins are working on it. The good news is they need double the time between each batch jumping. So they can only put three times the ships through a gate we can."

"Thank you, Commander."

Galen looked back at his paperwork. He'd hoped the Betrayers might get strung out enough for him to stage a successful ambush. Now finding more human ships was the only hope.

FNS *Dread*, Danu System, acceleration 0 m/s²

Mitchie glanced at the politicians to check if any of them had drifted loose while the battleship coasted through the gate. They all had a hand or foot through a restraining loop. One was hanging on with all four. The back wall of the flag bridge was lined with loops for VIP observers.

A new sun appeared in the center of the bridge dome. The *Dread's* crew began processing their own observations and relayed reports from the scouts who'd preceded them in.

"Intelligence was correct," announced Admiral Bachak. "The Harmony fleet is jumping in from the Yalu system. We have a classic meeting engagement."

"Can we hit them before they're all through?" asked Wayne Searcher.

The admiral shook his head. "They're two light hours away. It will be days until we're in effective range to attack. First we need to get the fleet in formation and start accelerating toward the enemy."

Mitchie decided Bachak wasn't expecting anything interesting to happen or he would have sent the tourists back to their quarters. A pair of protocol ensigns kept the flunkies from bothering anyone with real work to do. She used her rank to drift among the consoles. The staffers seemed unfazed by the enemy being real instead of simulated this time.

Their efforts concentrated on traffic control. Rather than specifying the formation in advance Bachak's 'flocking' strategy meant squadrons were assigned places relative to the flagship after they'd begun organizing their component ships into their own formation.

Most of the chatter was the battleship using its sensitive sensors to locate ships which had emerged too far away for their squadron commanders to find them.

We've been pushing the gaps between gate passages, thought Mitchie. *If he gets any more aggressive on that we could lose a ship or two.* The fleet had already lost a cruiser and two destroyers to maintenance failures.

"Sir, we have enough ships for Pilum," announced a tactical officer.

"Excellent," said Bachak. "Execute Pilum."

Orders flowed down the chain of command. On the displays clumps of missiles headed out toward the Harmony fleet.

Mitchie floated over to her nominal subordinate. "At this range?" she asked quietly.

Bachak grinned. "Intelligence says they think we're incompetent and panicky. Six hundred missiles are a cheap way to keep them thinking that."

PHS *Kongbu*, Danu System, acceleration 0 m/s^2

Guo looked around *Kongbu's* flag bridge, trying to memorize anything that would be useful intelligence. He hadn't found anything yet. The rings of consoles were under a half dome, giving them a view of the Danu system. The officers manning the consoles had little to do. They'd occasionally report that some squadron had organized itself and was moving into fleet formation. None of them seemed to need help from the flag.

Listening to Ping's chatter wasn't informative either. The *Daifu* was here to show he was important enough to claim a place in the middle of critical operations. He'd brought Guo along to illustrate his power. Admiral Chang participated enough in the conversation to keep it going, perhaps just to make Ping stay here instead of wandering among the consoles.

Guo noticed when something caught the admiral's attention. Following his look revealed a cluster of staffers arguing over the meaning of some event. Clearly something wasn't following their script. The Operations and Planning staffers brought in Sensors, Intelligence, and Astrogation. Then Communications joined the scrum. Other ships must have something to contribute to the discussion. Chang didn't interfere, just glancing at them while keeping his attention on Ping's lecture on how to handle negotiations.

At last a commodore floated over to the command console. "Admiral, the CPS fleet has fired upon us. We assess it as about six hundred missiles. They'll reach us in a bit over two days, assuming they're Type Forty models."

"They're firing at us? Not the scouts?" asked Chang.

"That was our first guess, but parallax views from the scouts confirm the salvo is aimed at our main body. We think they just panicked when they saw us forming up."

"I doubt they're that undisciplined."

Ping broke in to say, "Most of their fleet has very little experience in their positions. That will make them likely to panic in their first engagement."

"More likely they're running live fire exercises as last minute training," said Chang. "Or just prodding us to see how we'll react. We can use this as missile defense training. Dong, hit them with counter fire as far out as practical. Oh, and pull the scouts back. They might intend to conceal a maneuver behind the missile plumes."

"Yes, sir." The commodore floated back to Operations.

"I'll make my first broadcast after you've destroyed the missiles," declared *Daifu* Ping.

"Oh?" said the admiral.

"Yes, seeing that effort wasted will be the proper psychological preparation. If we can persuade them enough some of their fleet will desert or even defect to us."

Guo could see Chang grit his jaw, probably resisting a scathing comment on Ping's verbal prowess. But the Elders had authorized active negotiations until a full fleet engagement began. Ping could talk to his heart's content until the ship was in danger.

"Now, Mr. Ambassador," Ping locked his eyes on Guo, "how would you suggest we begin?"

FNS *Dread*, Danu System, acceleration 10 m/s²

Admiral Bachak provided a running narration to Mitchie and the politicians as the missiles were wiped out by three waves of Harmony counter-missiles. "And there's the last of them. That wasn't the most cost-effective approach they could have taken. They used half again as many missiles as we did."

"Are they carrying more missiles than we are?" asked Wayne. As usual he was sitting next to Guen.

"Fewer. But I'm sure they have some freighters with more missiles waiting in the Yalu system to refill as necessary. We don't want to make this a sniper duel. That plays to their strengths. We need to suck them in close."

An aide broke in. "Sir, we're picking up a transmission from the Harmony fleet."

Bachak waved at the display screen. "Let's see it."

Mitchie cursed as a familiar face appeared.

Ping orated, "Spacers of the Fusion! Your leaders have thrown missiles away with no effect. So they will throw your lives away to keep the power they seized with riot and murder. You face trained, experienced crews, the elite of the old Fusion Navy. They have now dedicated their lives to bringing humanity a better way to live.

"The people of the Harmony are peaceful and happy. They enjoy meaningful work, not passing days in worthless games."

"Mute," ordered Guen. She sent a pair of flunkies to a conference room to listen to the whole speech and write up a summary.

"I'm sorry, Madam Chairwoman," said Bachak. "Shall I issue orders to not listen to this?"

Mitchie laughed. "Do that and crewmen will be passing around recordings to see what the fuss is about."

Guen nodded. "Who's listening now?"

"The communications officers and their ratings on each ship," answered Bachak. "If the captain wants to see it, their bridge crew. They can share it over the internal net if someone authorizes it. And that's the only new entertainment we have right now."

"We'll need to make a response." Guen began making notes on her datasheet. "There's three audiences. Our people. The Harmony crews. And the Harmony's leadership. Ping always goes for two or three hours once he's rolling so we have time to assemble something."

Wayne Searcher was pulling up transcripts. "Your Landing Day speech is a good starting point."

***

Mitchie found herself the expert on how the Harmony crews would react. She knew more Confucian Revival philosophy than anyone else on the battleship, including the fleet intelligence staff. The spooks were focused on counting ships, not the motivations of their crews.

Being 'the expert' didn't require nearly as much knowledge as she thought would be required to be 'an expert.' But at least she could keep them from being unwittingly silly or offensive.

Guen knew enough Mandarin to deliver a speech well even if she couldn't compose in it. There were enough fluent Mandarin speakers on board that they didn't have to depend on Mitchie's spaceport pidgin for grammar and pronunciation. She did help with some of the philosophy jargon she'd picked up from Guo.

Once the speech was written, translated, and polished, it had to be changed to answer some of the accusations in Ping's speech. He'd only gone on for two hours but Mitchie was glad to have it summarized for her.

Wayne Searcher halted the editing. "That's enough fiddling. We're talking to spacers, not rhetoric professors."

A flunky suggested recording it and doing edits to polish the presentation.

"No," said Guen. "Everyone's thinking on what Ping said. I want to rebut him before it sinks in. I'll do it live."

Some commotion ended with a naval rating stepping back from the camera and saying, "We're ready, ma'am."

"Everybody in place?" asked Guen. Her backdrop was a dozen people chosen to represent planets and classes throughout the Fusion. Wayne wore a subdued version of stipend kid fashion. Mitchie was in a pilot's jumpsuit, with Akiak Space Guard insignia to proclaim her a Disker.

Guen gestured *start* at the rating. She began speaking in Mandarin. "My friends. My fellow citizens. We are all still citizens of the Fusion of Inhabited Worlds. Your leaders have broken laws, broken traditions, broken social bonds. They have torn us apart as we face humanity's common enemy in battle."

Mitchie tuned out the rest while keeping her expression serious and attentive. As important as all this was she couldn't make herself really care. What she wanted to know was, where was her husband?

***

The answer came two days later. Mitchie was asleep at the time. The dueling broadcasts had expanded until flunkies on each side were making speeches on night shift. The fleets had each turned over and were decelerating, both expecting to stop outside the other's beam weapon range.

Mitchie opened her cabin hatch, half asleep despite the beeping of the door chime. Guen was standing there, smiling. That dispelled the last of the sleep. Guen would have commed or sent a flunky for anything less than life and death news.

"What?"

"He's alive."

"Guo?"

"Yes. He was with Ping on the latest broadcast. We have it running in Conference Room Fourteen."

"Good." Mitchie stepped into the corridor, then realized she was only wearing one of Guo's old t-shirts. "Give me a moment."

Once in a jumpsuit she followed Guen down the corridor. The video took up all of the conference room's display wall. Guo was frozen in mid-word, his mouth part open in a way she found thoroughly kissable. She dropped into a chair, knees weak as the worries she hadn't let herself know she had went away.

Guen backed up the video. *Daifu* Ping was explaining how the forcible annexation of worlds by the Harmony was not, despite Guen's claims, a violation of Confucian Revival principles.

"To expand on that theme, I present Ambassador Guo Kwan, sent by the Committee of Public Safety to negotiate with the Harmony."

The camera pulled back to reveal Guo standing beside Ping, dressed in a formal Confucian robe. He spoke on the duty of superiors to provide a moral example to subordinates. He gave no examples.

"Was this live?" asked Mitchie.

A flunky answered, "It's all in one piece, we couldn't find any cuts. There could have been more than one take before they broadcast it."

"What are you thinking?" asked Guen.

"The gestures he's making are so stiff I wonder if he was pain sticked." Mitchie stepped up to the wall. "Look at the lines around his mouth and eyes. They put him through hell." She cursed.

Guen put a comforting arm around Mitchie's shoulders. "We'll get him back."

"Yes we will."

***

As the fleets closed on each other the propaganda war separated into three streams. Praise of their own system, condemnation of the other, and practical arguments in favor of the other side yielding. The last became a conversation between Guen and Ping as they let their flunkies handle the rest.

Light speed lag kept it an uncomfortable conversation. Even at twenty light minutes the statements were committee-reviewed and second guessed before being sent out.

"If I could just be in the same room with him we could hammer something out. I'd settle for a durable truce. But we'll never get a concession from a committee," griped Guen as she paced in her stateroom.

"Does it have to be the same room?" asked Mitchie. "We'll be close enough for real-time conversation soon."

"Wouldn't they be shooting by then?"

"If we closed all the way to point-blank, yes." Mitchie visualized the range. "At a hundred thousand klicks you'd have a third of a second delay. Can you have a good conversation with that?"

"Sure."

"Then let's talk to the admiral. He wants a close-in battle. Conducting negotiations might be a good way to improve our tactical position."

Mitchie opened the hatch to head toward the flag bridge. Guen didn't follow.

"Problem?" Mitchie asked.

"Would he use my negotiations as a way to make a sneak attack?"

She came back in and closed the hatch. "Only if you authorize an offensive. Right now he only has authority to respond to a Harmony attack with proportionate force."

"Those are his orders." Worry filled Guen's voice. "He could initiate an attack without permission. You gave him control of every warship."

"He could. Let's consider the scenarios." Mitchie switched to being an intelligence officer again. The stateroom had a display wall she could draw event trees on.

"Assume he wants to attack the Harmony. First branch. If he leaves us free we can overrule his orders and arrest him. The spacers adore you, the admirals fear me, and the officers don't want their crews to mutiny."

Mitchie drew another line from the starting circle. "Second branch. He neutralizes both of us—"

"Neutralize?" asked Guen.

"Kill, arrest, scare into running away. Whatever it takes to keep us from arresting him. You don't have to cut people's heads off to remove them as a threat."

Guen snorted at this dig at the Committee of Public Safety's guillotines.

"If he tries to neutralize both of us he has new problems. Will the spacers he sends after us be loyal to him or you? Will my Disconnect squadron go after his flagship if he kills me?"

The second branch now had two decision circles under it with two branches each.

"If both of those come out in his favor then he's facing war with the CPS if he beats the Harmony."

More circles and lines grew on the graph.

"If he wins both of those, he gets to face the Disconnected Worlds and Betrayers. Which makes this sub-sub-sub-sub-branch living happily ever after as military dictator of humanity."

Guen laughed. "Okay, his odds suck. But can he do that math? And is he ambitious enough to gamble?"

"I guarantee he can do the math. I was testing for that when I sorted candidates. As for ambition . . . he wasn't ambitious enough to join Parata's coup."

"True." Guen thought for a few more moments then leapt out of her chair. "Let's talk to him."

PHS *Kongbu*, Danu System, acceleration 10 m/s^2

Guo's visits to the flag bridge were driven by how much Ping needed to bolster himself against Admiral Chang rather than any event in the negotiations. They were letting him see the transmissions, both sides, with a delay for the Intelligence team to check them for any hidden messages.

This time the guards were in a hurry, holding Guo's arms to encourage him to a faster pace. "Haste, traitor," said one. "The Admiral wants you."

That did make Guo walk faster. No one but Ping had paid any attention to him before now. Something interesting must be happening.

Chang, Ping, and some senior aides were gathered in front of a display wall. Chang greeted Guo with, "You! Explain this."

He waved at the display. Guen appeared.

"Our discussions so far have me hopeful that a peaceful resolution can be achieved. I believe our lack of progress is partially due to the friction of time lag. Therefore I propose we continue negotiations at a distance of one hundred thousand kilometers, allowing near real time conversation. We propose these coordinates—" several strings of digits appeared on the display "—for the fleets to meet. We await your response."

The screen went blank.

"Well?" snarled Chang.

"This is a sincere attempt to avoid bloodshed," answered Guo. "Negotiations could achieve reunification, coexistence, or a long-term truce. The broadcast exchanges have laid groundwork for all three."

An aide snapped, "Bullshit. They plotted the trajectory of a meteor swarm and want us to sit in the path."

"So propose different coordinates for the meeting place. We're far enough apart a million klicks won't matter much."

"A million klicks separation would keep us safe from a surprise attack," said another aide.

Ping said, "That would be a noticeable gap in conversation. Miss Claret may be expected to object."

The naval officers were brainstorming around a hologram of the proposed hundred thousand klick face off.

"Missiles would take ten or twenty minutes to cross."

"It's the perfect situation for a sneak attack."

"We could sight in beam weapons to get some hits even at that range."

The chatter drifted into tactical jargon Guo didn't know. "We're preparing to reenact the Battle of Camlann," he said softly.

Admiral Chang caught the remark. "Camlann? I don't know that one. Is it Age of Sail?"

Guo shook his head. "Older, sir. From the Camelot legends. King Arthur was negotiating with a rebel lord. Their knights lined up beside them, facing each other in long lines. One knight saw a snake about to bite him. He drew his sword to kill it. The knights on the other side thought he meant to attack them and drew their swords. The battle raged until only a handful survived."

"Fortunately there are no snakes in vacuum. We need only fear anger, incompetence, and treachery."

A captain and lieutenant commander entered and saluted Chang. "Captain Li, good to see you. And this is?"

"Sir, I present Commander Chu, my Spinal Weapon Officer."

Guo realized this was the flagship's commander.

Chang explained the potential standoff. "Would the spinal beam weapon be able to hit another battleship at that distance?"

"Easily," said Chu. "The beam would be slightly dispersed but it would do enough damage to put the target out of action."

"And the enemy battleship could do the same to us."

"Yes, sir."

"How can we protect ourselves?"

Captain and weapon officer looked at each other. Neither had a suggestion.

One of the aides broke into the silence. "Solar sails."

Admiral Chang raised an eyebrow.

"We take the emergency propulsion solar sails and spread them in front of the ship. It would absorb the beam and let us return fire."

Chang turned to Lt. Commander Chu. "Would that work?"

"The sail would vaporize, that would absorb some, and the cloud would disrupt the beam . . . I need to run a simulation." Chu took over the display wall.

Guo leaned toward Captain Li. "A destroyer can get some useful acceleration from solar sails. I'd think cube-square would keep it from doing much for a battleship."

Li shrugged. "Regulations say we need a backup propulsion system. It was easier to install sails than get a waiver."

Chu finished his work. "We'd take some damage, but not enough to degrade the ship's effectiveness. We could return fire immediately."

Admiral Chang thought a moment. "Very well. *Daifu* Ping, you may have your conversation."

"Thank you, Admiral," said Ping.

FNS *Dread*, Danu System, acceleration 0 m/s^2

Mitchie nodded to Admiral Bachak as she floated past him in the corridor.

"Morning, ma'am," he said. "Going up to the negotiations?"

"It's the only show we have." She grabbed a handhold to stop and face him.

"True. I want to let you know I'm reducing readiness in the fleet."

"I thought you'd already taken them off battle stations?"

"Yes. But Condition Two also costs them sleep. Four days of it has been rough on green crews. I'm going to start a rotation. A few ships on Condition One just in case, some more on Condition Two, and the rest on normal running."

Which kept spacers in better shape at the cost of being more vulnerable to a Harmony surprise attack. That was exactly the kind of decision Mitchie had hired Bachak to make.

"Sounds good," she said.

"I'd appreciate it if you could alert me if you see any signs of the negotiations breaking down. If the Harmony gives up on talking we'll need to resume Condition One."

"I will watch for that."

"Thank you." Bachak pivoted on his handhold and arrowed away.

One of the flag conference rooms was dedicated to the ongoing conversation. Mitchie took a seat out of view of the camera. After listening for five minutes she still couldn't figure out what the topic under discussion was. Reading the side chatter among flunkies didn't help. They were using more obscure jargon than the conversation between Guen and Ping.

There were four documents under consideration in the negotiations. Ping had resent the Harmony's proposal for placing all of humanity under traditionalist rule and added a detailed set of guidelines for a truce. Guen offered a plan for reunification in a modified Fusion and another for permanent separation. Every one was being debated and quibbled over.

Guen was annoyed by Ping's latest objection. Her retort concluded with, "I'd rather let the missiles fly."

Ping gestured toward Guo in the row of listeners seated behind him. "You should be careful with threats. People can die without missiles being fired."

A chill went through Mitchie. Guo had implicitly been a hostage since he arrived at Tiantan. This was the first time his death was offered as a bargaining chip. She crumpled her datasheet into a wad. Crying out would just tell Ping his threat was working.

Guen's voice was level. "My mother died in an attack on my father. He died because someone feared his power as a Stakeholder. The man I admired most after them died to save me from being a hostage. Dying for political reasons is the natural fate of those close to me."

She reached behind her with her left hand. Wayne Searcher wrapped his right around it in full view of the camera.

"There are still those brave enough to dare it," she finished.

The conference room was silent, the usual rustling still.

Ping began describing an alternate rule for ships approaching a foreign planet.

Mitchie started breathing again. Declaring hostages too valueless to bargain for was the recommended doctrine. She realized she wouldn't have been able to do what Guen had. Having lost Guo and found him again she was more desperate to keep him safe.

The cynical part of her wondered how much Guen's tough posture was enabled by her new relationship.

Guen was commenting on Ping's latest amendment, accepting it with a modification. Both were speaking in perfectly calm tones.

So was this an escalation that should be reported to Bachak, or routine diplomacy?

PHS *Kongbu*, Danu System, acceleration 0 m/s²

Being a hostage wasn't Guo's preferred job, but it was steady work. He sat belted to a chair in the background of Ping's broadcasts. No need to say anything, though he was allowed to join in on the text commentary of the various analysts making Kremlinological interpretations of Guen's latest offhand remark.

Or he could use his datasheet for leisure reading. That usually seemed a better use of his time.

The real-time negotiations were midway through their sixth day. Guo'd considered proposing a seventh-day rest but chosen to let Ping work himself to death if he chose. He had faith in Guen's stamina.

The conference area was open to the flag bridge proper. When some of the ratings began signaling for officers' attention Guo turned his attention to them. He wasn't trying to gather classified information. It just had to be more interesting than Ping's blather.

The discussion stayed too quiet for him to make out until it worked its way up the chain to Admiral Chang. A lieutenant approached him to report, "Sir, several large freighters have entered the system from the Argo gate. They claim to be logistics elements of the Combined Fleet under pursuit by Betrayer forces."

"The enemy is laboring hard on their disinformation. Thank you, carry on."

Guo wondered if the Combined Fleet was really coming this way. The last thing they needed was a three way fight among humans. Maybe they'd get really lucky and Admiral Galen could broker a truce. He considered his previous interactions with Galen. No, diplomacy was not the man's strength.

Ping was equally dismissive when Guen relayed the news of the arrivals. She ignored his reply and went back to arguing about transit rights.

When Guo finished his novel he scanned the unread books in *Kongbu's* library. *A ship with this much processing power should have a better selection.* He settled for re-reading a history of the Spring and Autumn Period.

The lieutenant reported again to Chang. "There's more ships jumping in. The latest group is a cruiser squadron. Their emissions signature matches Fusion-built light cruisers. *Peltast*-class."

"Is there any way we can verify their identity?" asked Chang.

One of the staffers spoke up. "Sir, one's transponder is identifying it as the FNS *Medon*. The captain of the *Medon* was a classmate of mine. If we get him to make a long statement I should be able to tell if it's really him."

"Very well. Make the request."

Unfortunately for Guo's entertainment the supposed Combined Fleet ships had arrived four light hours away. He decided to get a good night's sleep while waiting for the reply.

He was back on the flag bridge in time for the transmission.

"Video tightbeam from the *Medon*, Admiral," reported a rating.

"On display," ordered Chang.

A Chinese man in a rumpled uniform appeared. Guo noted the lines on his face, the familiar mark of service in the Combined Fleet. He made all the Harmony spacers look young in comparison.

"Xi, you lousy son of a bitch," he began. His Mandarin had the distinctive accent of one who'd grown up speaking Cantonese. "We've been out here fighting constantly, lots of us dying, for all of humanity, and what do we find when we get back? You bastards are playing politics, blowing up the ships we need to survive. You need to get your thumbs out of your asses and report for duty. Maybe that would be enough to stop the Betrayers again. And tell your commander he should commit suicide to apologize for his failure. Gaai out."

Silence fell on the flag bridge.

Admiral Chang asked, "Lieutenant Commander Xi, is that your classmate?"

The officer replied, "Yes, sir. He normally only talked like that when drunk, sir."

"Combat fatigue is equal to four shots of whiskey," said Guo. Chang's glare made Guo decide to not make more quips that day.

"Intelligence, what's your current assessment?" demanded Chang.

"Sir, ships have been jumping into the system at maximum safe rate, with the wide dispersion resulting from such close intervals. Logistics ships and different warship classes have been intermixed. We assess that they've made similar max-rate transits recently and their unit cohesion has been disrupted. Multiple ships have transmitted a message from Admiral Galen describing a retreat in the face of a multi-system Betrayer offensive and demanding all combat units be placed under his command per the Treaty of Lapis."

"You think it's real?"

"Given the number of warships that have jumped in, yes, sir."

Guo admired the courage of the intelligence officer. She hadn't flinched at all.

Chang turned to his aide. "Please notify *Daifu* Ping I need to meet with him at his earliest convenience."

Guo checked his datasheet. It was almost time for Ping to begin the day's negotiations anyway. He looked at the conversation channels. He could only access the ones for Ping's various flunkies and minions.

They were panicking. Disbelief warred with calls for retreat or attack. One analyst was convinced this was a hoax by naval officers plotting a coup against the Council of Elders.

Ping arrived and was almost dragged into Chang's private office. Ten minutes later muffled shouting could be heard through the soundproofed walls. Nervous flunkies found excuses to be elsewhere.

A bit later the hatch burst open. Chang held Ping by the arm. He kicked off the bulkhead, pulling Ping over to the Tactical holotank.

"Look at our formation. The disk faces the enemy so every ship's anti-missile defenses can bear on them. We can stop any number of missiles they throw at us." Chang added an inward-pointing arrow in the plane of the disk. "If the Diskers, or, Heaven help us, the Betrayers attack only the few ships on the near edge can counter incoming missiles. They'd be overwhelmed."

"So we can redeploy to face them," said Ping.

"That will give us the same vulnerability against the CPS. Given how undisciplined their fleet is I don't know if they could resist attacking us. We need a political solution or we have to retreat from this system."

"Very well," said Ping. "I will force the negotiations to a conclusion."

A flunky had been blathering on tax policy to fill time in Ping's absence.

Ping floated in front of him. "It appears the Combined Fleet is retreating from a Betrayer counter-attack. We will need to join them to present an effective defense. Let us immediately agree on the current draft of the truce proposal so we can begin operations against the Betrayers."

Halfway through this Guen had waved her placeholder out of the way as she took the focus of the camera. She smiled slightly as she thought on Ping's words. "No," she said.

"What?"

"I said no."

"But . . . you have to! There's a Betrayer fleet bearing down on us. We have to pull together."

"There were Betrayer fleets bearing down on us when you participated in the Fusion's attack on the Disconnected Worlds. There were Betrayer fleets bearing down on us when you decided to replace the Fusion with a government of your cronies. Now another Betrayer fleet is coming. The only difference is that you, personally, are in the line of fire this time."

Guen stepped toward the camera, her face filling the display wall. "I just hope your transmission lasts long enough for me to see the look on your face as you die."

The transmission from the *Dread* cut off.

Ping spun to face his backdrop audience. "What the hell is she thinking? She can't be serious."

"Maybe she wants revenge for her father's murder," said Guo. "There are suspects on this ship."

The flunkies began babbling, each trying to come up with a theory that would please Ping.

Admiral Chang's voice cut through them. "Likely she knows it will take the Combined Fleet five days to reach us and wants to use that time to extract concessions."

That made Ping straighten out again. "Of course. And she expects Admiral Galen to take her side for additional leverage."

Guo thought Galen's leverage would take the form of three hundred missiles hitting *Kongbu* at half of lightspeed, but decided to stay silent.

"Should we offer concessions on the Unification Plan?" asked a flunky.

"No," said Ping. "We don't have the leverage to make them accept that. Pull up the Coexistence draft and let's see what concessions we can offer."

Chapter Nine: Clash

FNS *Dread*, Danu System, acceleration 0 m/s²

Guen was enjoying herself. She'd responded to Ping's offered concessions with a list of demands. She and Wayne were whiling away the wait by learning a free-fall dance. A few of the ratings had converted a hanger into a dance hall for off-duty spacers. The fad was spreading through the crew. Now the civilians were joining in.

The wallflowers included Mitchie. She was in no mood for dancing.

A yeoman entered the conference room, datasheet in hand. "Madam Chairwoman?" he called.

Guen pushed off from Wayne to meet him. It would have worked if they hadn't been practicing a twirl. She went spinning in the wrong direction.

Kicking off from the wall, Mitchie grabbed Guen before she could bounce off the deck. She pushed on the deck with her hand to send them toward the yeoman. She twisted to get a foot in a loop as they landed and leveraged Guen's shoulder to put her facing him.

"Thanks," said Guen over her shoulder. Then she put on a dignified expression to greet the yeoman.

Mitchie tried to calm her pulse. Guen had broken a sweat with the dancing. The only times she'd smelled Guen's sweat before—well, Guo had been there.

The yeoman's datasheet contained a written response from *Daifu* Ping. Guen started scrolling, then searched for a specific item.

"Here we go," she said. "'Return of Ambassador Guo Kwan is agreed to, on condition that he go to a Combined Fleet unit.' Ready to take him back to your fleet?"

"Hell, yes," said Mitchie.

"I hate to give you up, but you deserve to have him back. Give him my love."

"Thanks." She went through the hatch and headed for the hangers.

Joshua Chamberlain, Danu System, acceleration 10 m/s²

Usually having Mitchie at the controls meant Hiroshi could relax and watch to see if there were any new tricks to copy. Not this time. From the moment the battleship's cutter had delivered her she'd been bouncing with nervous energy.

It was affecting her piloting. His latest sextant sights said she'd overcorrected on their last course adjustment. They'd gone from a quarter degree of minus yaw off-course to three eighths of plus yaw.

"How's it look?" Mitchie demanded.

And normally she didn't micromanage unless they were in critical operations. Which this wasn't. A simple point A to point B, zero-zero at destination, was the easiest course a torchship could do.

Hiroshi answered, "Not perfect, but we can wait a few hours before the next correction."

"Good."

Mitchie wasn't being chatty. Neither pilot nor co-pilot wanted to start a conversation with her in this mood. Hiroshi hoped Mthembu wasn't shadowing her piloting. The coxswain was clumsy enough without starting to imitate someone else's mistakes.

A faint clicking caught at his ears. A malfunction? Turning his head located it. Mitchie was fiddling with the thrust lever for the aeroturbines. Just flipping it back and forth. Fidgeting.

The shock he felt surprised him. The principle of 'Don't touch controls you're not using' had been driven deep.

There wasn't any harm in it. With no air for the turbines to act on they were shut down until the converter room mechanics connected power to them again. But still . . . spaceship controls were not for playing with.

"Ma'am?" asked Hiroshi.

Mitchie pulled her hand back into her lap. "Yes?"

"If you want to meet the Senior Chief as he boards, I'd be happy to handle the docking maneuvers with *Kongbu.*"

She thought a moment. "Sure. Take the con, I'll check if there's an acceleration bunk ready in the hold."

"I have the con, ma'am."

When the hatch closed behind Mitchie, Hiroshi waved Mthembu

into the empty piloting couch.

"Is she having combat fatigue?" asked the co-pilot as he strapped himself in.

"Bachelor fatigue, I think. This was the first time they've been apart in four years. Or she's just worried about what happened to him while he was in enemy hands."

***

Pressing the landing gear against the hanger's deck was a relief. *Kongbu* was a huge ship, but its hangers were designed for fighters and cutters, not a freighter. Even one as small as *Joshua Chamberlain* was a snug fit.

"*Kongbu* Operations, this is *Joshua Chamberlain*. Thrusters off, we are at rest in dock," said Hiroshi.

"Acknowledged."

The hanger doors closed. He glanced at the bridge instruments. They showed air pressure outside, steadily increasing to breathable.

Ops spoke again. "*Joshua Chamberlain*, Elder Ping invites your whole crew to dine with him in the flag mess."

That was *not* in the agreed routine for the pick-up. "Please thank the Elder for us but our orders are to immediately rendezvous with the Combined Fleet."

"I'm afraid the Elder insists."

"He can insist all he wants. We're staying aboard." Hiroshi thought an invitation to the captain might be sincere, but wanting the whole crew off the ship meant trouble.

"Then your ship will remain here until you do."

"Hold us against our will and we will destroy your vessel."

Ops sounded amused. "*Joshua Chamberlain*, you are an unarmed freighter. You can't do a thing to this ship."

"I can fire our torch. It will melt your decks and fry your life support. The nose of our ship is built for aerobraking. It can push through your decks until it reaches the hull."

Mthembu had been alarmed by the conversation. Now he looked

ready to panic, his eyes wide. He unsnapped a shoulder strap.

Hiroshi waved him down. He flipped the switch on his mike. "Relax, I'm bluffing."

"You can't do that," said Ops. "The safety interlocks would keep your torch from firing."

Switch on. "This is an analog ship. The only interlocks are manual mechanical ones. If I press the throttle lever the torch will fire plasma through your deck."

"You wouldn't!"

"I am Hiroshi, son of Nobunaga, of Moonlight on Shining Water, Centurion of the Shishi Imperial Legion. From birth I heard tales of warriors who slit their bellies open if they failed in their orders and held their hands in fire to intimidate their enemies. I will carry out my orders or kill those who prevent me from doing so."

A longer pause this time. Mthembu was frozen.

"*Joshua Chamberlain*, the Ambassador is on his way."

"Thank you, Ops." Hiroshi turned the mike off again. "See, bluffing works," he said to Mthembu.

"Sir, you sounded a lot more sincere threatening them than you do telling me you're bluffing."

"That's a skill. You could learn it."

***

Guo took a deep sniff of *Joshua Chamberlain's* air as the inner airlock hatch opened. A slight scent of rain meant healthy algae cultures. Oil from over-lubricated ventilation fans. No burning or dust. The apprentices had done a good job.

As he came through the hatch Mitchie slammed into his torso and wrapped her limbs around him. Her head tucked under his chin as if they were standing together instead of floating. Guo hugged her tight, with both arms, handholds be damned. He bent his face into her hair. She smelled warm and tired, smelled of home.

They drifted out into the hold in a slow tumble. His duffle bounced off the deck going the other way.

"You're alive," said Mitchie. "I saw you in the videos but I couldn't believe it until now."

"What are you worried about me for?" he chided mockingly. "You're the one wrestling with admirals and getting into battles. I just talked to people."

"Ha," she said. "You had a rougher time than that."

"Some of it." Deep breath. "There's things I need to tell you about."

"I'll bet."

Mitchie's handcomm chirped. Hiroshi said, "Ma'am, we need to go before the Harmony comes up with another excuse to try to keep us."

She pulled it from her pocket without lifting her head from Guo's neck. "Right. Two minutes."

They were two meters off the deck, and five from the hull. Mitchie pulled a ten meter line with a weight on the end from her thigh pocket. The two acceleration mattresses were hooked to the deck not far from the airlock. She caught the handle on one with the first swing of the line.

A tug left them coasting toward the mattresses, with enough time to sneak in some kisses before strapping in.

"We're secure. Go," Mitchie reported.

Over the PA Hiroshi declared, "All hands, we are maneuvering. Acceleration will begin when we're clear of the battleship."

Joshua Chamberlain, Danu System, acceleration 20 m/s^2

Boosting at twenty gravs was uncomfortable, but everyone wanted to get away from the Harmony fleet as fast as they could. Hiroshi put them on course for the Combined Fleet as their safest option. Of course, just boosting straight toward them would leave *Joshua Chamberlain* flashing past as the fleet decelerated toward the other human ships.

He worked calculations on pilot station's plotting board. Accelerate toward the Combined Fleet, then turn over and thrust the other way to match velocities with them. Once they rendezvoused with the fleet they'd turn over and join them in their deceleration. And once all the human ships were in one place they'd undoubtedly head for someplace else . . .

"We're going to turn over four times on this course," said Hiroshi.

Mthembu laughed. "That usually means there's an easier way to do it."

The two pilots went over Hiroshi's calculations.

"Okay, two days is the fastest we can get to Admiral Galen," said Mthembu. "But can't we just wait here for them to arrive?"

"In missile range of the Harmony? The agreement for giving Guo back was that we'd take him to the Combined Fleet."

"Do you really think they'd . . . yeah, let's get into the fleet missile defenses as quick as we can."

One advantage of being all alone in space was only needing one watchstander at a time. Or so Mitchie decreed. Possibly influenced by the desire to have time off with her husband. Acceleration was reduced to ten gravs for shift change. She retreated to their cabin with him.

"I don't even know where to start," said Guo.

They lay side by side, pressed deep into the mattress by the double acceleration.

"You look like you've been through hell," said Mitchie. "Your face shows a lot of stress."

"There was a horrible stretch toward the end. Before that it was mostly vacation. And, um, well . . ."

"If it's that hard for you to talk about it I don't know how well I can handle listening to it. And I need to be focused on the ship with the battle coming up. Being distracted would be bad."

"Oh, this has all kinds of distraction in it."

"Then let's let it wait. You're safe. That's enough for me."

"Not enough for me." Guo turned and pulled her close.

Sex in twenty gravs was too much work to be fun. They went far enough to prove they could do it, then collapsed. This time they lay with their sides pressed against each other.

"Doubling our weight shouldn't be that bad. Four people in bed happens all the time," quipped Mitchie.

"Yeah." Guo was still breathing hard from holding himself up so he didn't crush his wife. "But the couple we're swapping with won't do any of the work." Pant. "And they want to be on top."

"Right. Let's break up with them. Lazy bastards."

That got a laugh out of him.

After a night filled with dreams of dense fogs and narrow caves Mitchie relieved Mthembu on the bridge. "I have the con. Anything to report?"

"Ship is nominal, ma'am. I'm worried about the negotiations. They've gone bad."

He responded to her raised eyebrows by turning up the volume on the communications box.

Guen was in mid-rant. "—was discarded for good reason on Old Earth! The obsolete philosophy enervated society to where anything looked like an improvement, even the most harmful meme there's ever been! Trying to resurrect that ideological corpse is—"

"Harmful?" interrupted Ping. "The Dynamist platform is more harmful than any society I've seen. You dissolve all bonds of family, location, affection, intimacy to turn people into purely economic agents."

The argument—it couldn't be called a debate—continued in a random walk from topic to topic.

"It's been like that the whole eight hours I've been on shift, ma'am," said Mthembu. "I'm scared they're going to open fire any minute."

"Don't be. This is bullshit."

"Ma'am?"

"I know those two. I've listened to them argue, in person and over video. They're putting on a show. Probably locked down an agreement by tightbeam."

"A show for who?"

"The Betrayers. They're expecting the Combined Fleet to face them alone while the other two fleets fight each other. If they knew the humans were cooperating they'd stop and consolidate their forces instead of being so strung out. It's a good plan. I wonder if it was Galen's idea."

Mthembu contemplated the idea. "So it's a trap. Like the Third Battle of Bonaventure."

"Yep. Galen's a sneaky bastard. Get some rest."

"Aye-aye, ma'am." He hurried down the ladder to reach his cabin before she increased acceleration again.

***

Mitchie thought about writing a formal report on her activities. It was what she'd normally done after each mission as a deep cover intelligence officer. But no amount of careful phrasing would save her if the powers that be didn't approve of what she'd done. Pointing out that they'd passed up the chance to give her formal direction while she was on Pintoy would just be whining. She went with the lazy option and dumped her entire log on them, from when she'd arrived on Pintoy to now.

She transmitted it while still a light-hour out from the Combined Fleet. Terse text messages from staff officers acknowledged receipt and directed *Joshua Chamberlain* to a place in the logistics formation.

Admiral Galen waited until they were only three light-seconds apart to contact her. An aide verified the connection worked, warned her the encryption was not proof against Betrayers, and told her to wait for the Admiral.

She was alone on the bridge. This would probably be a conversation to be kept private.

The comm box lit up with Galen's face. "Long. I'm glad you survived the mission."

"Thank you, sir."

Three seconds wasn't a long delay.

"The intel staff summarized your report for me. They were impressed by the detail. I've decided your actions were in accordance with what you perceived as the intent of my orders."

"Most of the report was my log of events as they happened, sir."

'In accordance' was not praise, but it meant she wouldn't be court-martialed. No more worrying about charges of insubordination or mutiny.

"They have questions for you but I told them to wait until after the battle. You're being assigned to Admiral Tan for logistics support. The usual odd jobs."

"Yes, sir."

Pause.

"Given your seniority and the command responsibilities performed, you've been selected for promotion to captain. Congratulations. Galen out."

"Thank you, sir," she said to the blank screen.

***

Joining the logistics formation made Mitchie feel like a minnow swimming among whales. The other ships were a hundred times *Joshua Chamberlain's* size or more.

Mthembu handled the comm box as they merged with the formation. "Just established a tightbeam with the flagship, ma'am."

"Good." Mitchie's attention was focused on staying clear of the plumes of the behemoths. The largest ships could vaporize the small freighter if it reached the center of their plumes.

"New orders. Rendezvous with BDS *Currie*, take on cargo. Do not reply."

"It didn't say what kind of cargo?" Hiroshi sounded puzzled.

"That's the whole text," answered Mthembu.

Mitchie said, "Somebody's playing super-security. Can't let the Betrayers know our ships are low on toilet paper."

***

Currie's captain contacted them by tightbeam as they approached his ship. "Please rendezvous for cargo transfer."

"Acknowledged," answered Mitchie. "Cut thrust and we'll approach from astern."

"Negative. My orders prohibit any change to our acceleration."

"*Currie*, if we do the transfer in free-fall we can get back in formation by boosting at twenty gravs."

"That was explicitly forbidden in my orders."

"Very well. Coming in hot," said Mitchie.

Normally a modern ship would use its computer controlled thrusters to rendezvous with an analog ship. The five hundred meter long *Currie* was too clumsy for that. *Joshua Chamberlain* would have to approach to twenty meters from the bigger ship under manual control.

Mitchie came in from astern, but to the side. She kept her ship just ahead of *Currie's* plume, riding the curve so the two ships' plumes overlapped. Hiroshi monitored the side camera, singing out when the plasma became too bright.

Joshua Chamberlain was tilted toward the *Currie* as they closed. The side of the massive containership shut out the stars. The ship grew to where individual containers were recognizable and still Mitchie kept them closing.

She held up her thumb, arm outstretched, and measured its width against a container. A container was almost as wide as the digit. She fired the pitch thrusters to tilt her ship away, bleeding off their closing speed. When the *Currie* stopped growing she pitched the *Chamberlain* back, putting them in parallel.

Hiroshi checked his readouts. "The nav box says we're forty-three meters apart. Smoothly done, ma'am."

"Thanks." She fired the plus-X thrusters to close the remaining gap.

Mthembu said, "*Currie* says they're ready to lower the cargo, just give them word."

"Right."

Mitchie waited until they'd closed to the specified twenty meters and had it confirmed by the nav box before giving permission for the transfer.

***

Setta thoroughly inspected Wang and Dubois's suits before

opening the cargo hold doors. For all the suit time they'd racked up
with the Combined Fleet the Pintoy vacation had let them become
rusty. Neither one had an error. She made them both inspect her as
well.

Opening the cargo hold doors was a strange experience. Normally
when the torch was on the doors would open onto a starfield. When it
was off the doors revealed a hanger or spaceport. Now they were
staring at stacks of containers.

Setta edged up to the opening, testing her safety line with firm tugs.
Looking down she saw the intersection of the two plumes. Sheets of
light glittered as shock waves pushed back and forth within them.

She looked up. Staring up the side of the *Currie* was almost as
vertigo-inducing as looking down. Looking back down from the top
she saw a square approaching. Their cargo, being lowered on a
platform by a crane that could pick up *Joshua Chamberlain*.

As the platform descended past the cargo hold she could see stacks
of standard containers with a dozen spacesuited men clinging to them.
The crane stopped before the platform descended into the plasma hell
below.

One suit was yellow. It leapt off the highest stack, landing on *Joshua
Chamberlain's* deck on hands and knees.

Setta grabbed a spare safety line and snapped it onto Yellowsuit's
belt before he could stand.

He transmitted on the local suit frequency. "Thanks. I'm Dave
Jones, the supercargo. You in charge?" He thrust out a hand.

She shook it. "Bosun Setta. I'm in charge of the hold. Captain Long
is in command."

"Damn. This is really Michigan Long's ship. How about that?"

"What's the cargo?" The container doors were marked, "KEEP
OUT—AUTHORIZED PERSONNEL ONLY," "DO NOT
BREAK SEALS UNDER PENALTY OF SECURITY ACT," and
"EXPLOSIVE." They lacked the traditional codes to warn hazmat
crews what they were dealing with.

"Sorry, I can only tell the captain. She'll have to brief you. Let's get
the cargo moving."

Joshua Chamberlain's crane extended out over the platform. It had room to work. The platform was suspended by the corners from a square frame thirty meters above. Setta chose the highest stack in the center to take the first container from.

She extended the crane until the hook block was over the center of the container. Four lines dangled from the block. *Currie's* deckhands attached them to the corners of the container then scurried clear.

"Ready," said Jones.

"Lifting." Setta pressed the 'cable retract' button on the crane remote.

The container lifted clear of the one below.

Setta flinched as it fell back down, pulling the crane with it. *Joshua Chamberlain* tilted toward the *Currie,* sliding closer to the big ship. The lip of the cargo hold hatch struck the stacked containers on the platform.

She hastily pressed 'cable extend.' The faint plume of attitude thrusters flared over the hatch. The *Currie* and its platform moved back again as *Joshua Chamberlain* tilted away. She kept the cable extending. It hung slack between the ship and platform.

The ship steadied twenty meters clear of the platform.

"What the fuck was that?" crackled Captain Long's voice over the general frequency.

"How much do those things weigh?" snarled Setta.

"Um, twenty, thirty tons, something like that," said Jones. "I can look it up."

"On a twenty meter lever arm. You idiot."

"Your specs say the crane can handle twice that."

"It can. When we're on the ground. We're not braced against anything here."

"Sorry. Sorry!"

"Frigging lazy megaship bastard." That was insubordination if Jones was commissioned, but Setta didn't care. Captain Long was her role model.

A conversation with the captain produced a new plan for moving cargo. *Joshua Chamberlain* moved back into position. The crane cable was drawn up taut. Then the analog ship fired thrusters just enough to lift the container clear. As the crane carried the container inside Captain Long stepped down the thrusters to match the smaller torque. The cargo hold deck shivered as the ship shook with the conflicting forces.

With practice the transfers went smoother. Containers stacked up against the back of the cargo hold, causing more balance issues. As the platform emptied the bottom of the pile became visible. One was a cylindrical tank held in a frame.

"What's that?" demanded Setta.

"Liquid hydrogen."

"Why the hell are we getting that?"

Jones had a high-end spacesuit, flexible enough to let him shrug.

"Fine," she said. "Make sure you explain it to the captain." She wished the ship had an internal airlock so she could send him to the bridge now.

"The hydrogen tank has to be by the hatch," he said.

There was obviously no point to asking why.

"Anything else I need to arrange around?"

"Yes. The last item is a double-wide container, needs to have nothing on top of it. And make sure the red end is facing the doors."

She clamped her jaw shut on her response.

***

Once the cargo hold was sealed and pressurized Jones went up the ladder to have his private chat with the captain. He left through the upper deck airlock, ship and platform maneuvering to give him an easy jump.

Captain Long came down the ladder. Setta followed her as the captain inspected every container's tie down. The hydrogen tank received extra attention.

"Good work, Bosun," was the verdict. "Tell your deckhands I'm proud of them for handling these odd conditions."

"Thank you, ma'am. So . . . what is all this stuff?"

"Can't say. But we may be very glad we have it."

***

Guen and Ping kept the rhetoric hot as the Combined Fleet closed in. The lead Betrayer ships turned over and began decelerating to not overshoot the fleet rendezvous. The enemy wanted to stop and fight the humans to a finish, not just take some shots as they zipped through.

Three hours before the Combined Fleet joined them the politicians announced, "Simon says deception is over. All units change to joint formation."

The Combined Fleet cut thrust and coasted, waiting for the other human ships to accelerate to merge formations as they flew by. The lead Betrayers kept decelerating. Intelligence assessed it as waiting for the next wave to join up with them before engaging.

Mitchie used her telescope to watch the maneuvers. The Harmony executed crisply, one squadron at a time shifting on each side to make a stair-step shape before finishing as a perfect disk facing the Betrayers.

Bachak's forces . . . were not so crisp. The formation reverted to 'flocking,' spreading out to twice the width it had been. Scattered like that they'd never be able to stop incoming missile fire. At least they'd managed to not plume each other while rotating the formation.

Well, they hadn't while Mitchie was watching.

When the Fusion and Harmony fleets were both facing the Betrayers they turned over to accelerate away from them. The Combined Fleet had passed between them. Each had to add a half-light second of side travel to their acceleration.

The lead Betrayers cut their deceleration. Once the next wave joined them the group accelerated toward the humans.

Mitchie arranged for *Joshua Chamberlain* to be as far from the Harmony ships as possible without being on the edge of the formation. She didn't think it was likely for Ping to arrange for a missile to be sent their way . . . but she didn't want to make it easy for him.

As an analog ship they didn't have a full view of the battle. The communications box was not sophisticated enough to integrate networked warship sensors. It received warnings and orders the freighter had no way to act on.

She could tell the fleet was under fire when she saw glowing debris flash by. The bridge dome faced away from the enemy. The ship's cameras were too low resolution to pick up more than flickers of the missile exchange. So Mitchie was reduced to assessing the battle by the urgency of commands for counter-missile fire. If a squadron was ordered to pivot to unscreen its lasers and rapid-fire cannon, some Betrayer missiles had penetrated the counter-missiles and decoys.

The bridge dome gave a lovely view as four missiles streaked past the logistics flotilla and exploded a mere five hundred klicks ahead of the formation. Mitchie thought that was a decoy's work.

***

"Message from the flag, ma'am," said Mthembu. "Stand by for Admiral Galen."

Mitchie unstrapped from her acceleration couch. "Hiroshi, you have the con."

"Aye-aye," said the pilot.

She stood in front of the comm box as Galen's face appeared. "Captain Long. BDS *Hammond's* torch has been damaged. Rendezvous with the ship and take survivors aboard."

"Yes, sir, will do." *Finally*, she thought. She'd been twitchy ever since they took on the special cargo. Galen's plan called for them to wait until the Betrayers damaged a ship enough to fall out of formation, then send *Joshua Chamberlain* to the rescue. Everything should look perfectly normal to the AIs.

Mthembu jotted down the vectors displayed beside the admiral's face.

"Sir, we don't have room for more than a dozen casualties with all the cargo we have on board." She hoped she hadn't sounded too scripted as she said that.

"Jettison the cargo," ordered Galen. "Personnel have priority." He sounded almost surprised she'd ask. Superb acting given that this order was the point of the entire operation.

"Aye-aye."

"Good luck, *Joshua Chamberlain*. Command out."

Mitchie turned to her subordinates. "Hiroshi, make a dog leg to keep us clear of everyone's plumes, then take us straight to the *Hammond*. Make an all-hands announcement of the new mission. Face the cargo hold toward the enemy. Mthembu, find out which squadron is closest to the *Hammond* and coordinate some counter-missile fire. I'm going to oversee jettisoning the cargo."

That produced confused looks. Both thought Setta could handle discarding boxes without help. They didn't say anything before she closed the hatch behind her.

Mitchie waited for the ship to finish pivoting onto the new course before starting down the cargo hold ladder. Setta was waiting when she reached the deck.

"We need to jettison the cargo. Let's get suited up."

The bosun and deckhands knew this couldn't be the surprise the captain was pretending it was. But they'd given up on asking questions about the mysterious cargo.

The double-sized container opened to reveal a mass driver for throwing objects out of the hold. Instead of using the crane to lift containers out and drop them Setta and her deckhands would be setting them on this catapult to be flung clear of the ship. Mitchie hauled over a heavy-duty power cable and plugged it in to power the machine.

The first container was in place on the catapult before the hold was completely depressurized. When the doors were open to space—the usual beautiful starscape—Setta said, "Ready to fire catapult."

"No," said Mitchie. "Give me a hand with this hose."

The liquid hydrogen tank had an insulated hose, just long enough to reach a valve on the container sitting on the catapult. There was no gauge to measure the transfer. Mitchie let the hydrogen pump through until a light on the nozzle turned green.

"Now you can fire it," Mitchie ordered.

Setta flipped the lever. Capacitors discharged, powering steel arms as they flung the container out of sight.

She considered the effect. The box had been jettisoned so hard it would miss all but the coolest fringes of *Joshua Chamberlain's* plume. This box wasn't being dropped to burn up.

Deckhand Dubois had the next container hanging from the crane, ready to place on the catapult. Setta waved at her to go ahead, then checked that the capacitors were charging.

A slug of hydrogen, kick it overboard, put the next container on the catapult. The routine repeated a couple of dozen times until they were all gone.

"Good work," said Mitchie. "Disconnect the catapult power lines and bleed off the rest of the hydrogen. We need to be ready to receive casualties." The important part of her mission was done. The rest was just camouflage to convince the Betrayers the boxes were just abandoned trash.

As Setta worked on the valves of the hydrogen tank Dubois touched helmets with her. "Bosun, do you have any clue what's going on with this shit?"

"I have some guesses. But when they're being this uptight about security we shouldn't talk about it."

Guo left Mechanic's Mate Ye to monitor the converter room and suited up with Spacer Finnegan to help with the rescue work. While the junior crew prepared the cargo net, safety lines, and vacctape, he took Mitchie aside for a chat.

"*Hammond* is Pete Smith's ship, isn't it?" he asked.

"Yes. At least, I think I would have heard some Fuzies screaming if his lab was moved to a different ship."

"Then this is good news."

Mitchie laughed. "His ship getting blown up? We don't even know if he's still alive."

"If the AIs are targeting his ship they must be afraid of his research. That's proof he's found a vulnerability."

"Or they just found a big ship with weak defenses to be an irresistible target."

"Humans shoot stuff to see the explosion. AIs have a goal. If *Hammond* is the first ship knocked out of formation they think it's the biggest threat."

"Well, when we get Pete on board we can ask him his opinion."

Guo leaned down to look directly into her eyes. "Once we have Pete keeping him alive has to take priority."

"Are you suggesting we abandon the rest of *Hammond's* crew?"

"If we're drawing enough fire, yes."

"Sure it's not your own hide you're trying to protect?" she snapped.

"If I wanted to be safe I'd've stayed on Tiantan. This is about winning the war."

"Admiral Galen didn't give any orders for special treatment."

"He's a good admiral. But he thinks of winning with ships. That won't be enough."

"I'm not going to throw away lives," said Mitchie. *I've done enough of that already*, she thought.

"Just make sure you don't throw away Pete's."

BDS *Hammond*, acceleration 3.1 m/s^2

Chief Warrant Officer Langerhans wondered if he'd have to pick Peter Smith up and throw him off the Hammond. His Marines and Smith's boffins were suiting up and choosing which bits of essential gear to take with them. Smith was standing by the computer rack, data transfer paddle pressed to his forehead, as he had been since the ship had been hit.

"Sir, you need to prepare for evacuation."

Smith didn't move. "I am preparing. I'm backing up essential data."

"We're bringing backups of the data," said Langerhans.

"Those are fragile. EMP, concussion, explosive decompression, there's lots of ways they could break. My implant is the safest place for it."

Langerhans hated Pete's neural implant. Giving up a chunk of brain to make room for electronics wasn't just creepy. It was a sign of someone being uncertain where he sided in the war between men and machines.

"Why didn't you back it up before?"

"I didn't have the capacity. I've had to wipe my personal data to make room."

The Marine clamped his jaw shut.

A color corporal said, "Chief, I have Dr. Smith's pressure suit."

"Fine. Doctor, we're going to help you into your suit."

Pete said, "I'll take this outfit off as soon as I'm done with the backup."

"No need. Lift him, boys."

Four Marines held Pete horizontally. This took no effort in the low acceleration. They didn't disturb the arm holding the SKIRW paddle.

CWO Langerhans produced a boarding knife. Slashing Pete's boots from ankle to sole let them drop to the deck. He cut away Pete's pants next.

The senior private holding Pete's left leg noticed the socks were undamaged. He tried to keep the leg as still as he could.

When Pete was down to his underwear the Marines shoved his feet into the pressure suit and continued suiting him from there. Their training included handling unconscious casualties in pressure loss. This wasn't much different from practicing on an mannequin.

Pete didn't object until they went for the arm holding the paddle.

"Switch hands," snarled Langerhans.

Then Pete was suited up except for his helmet. Nobody had put helmets on yet, though most of the people in the lab were carrying one.

When the Marines set him back on his feet he looked at the activity in the room. "Are we getting all the samples?" he asked. He'd assembled a collection of computer cores from all the Betrayer systems the Combined Fleet had occupied.

"Your people are carrying some," said Langerhans. "Mine aren't going to touch that crap."

"We need to salvage as much as we can."

"I ordered them to carry some of the Fusion-built analysis gear."

Joshua Chamberlain, acceleration 15 m/s^2

Hiroshi broadcast on the general frequency. "All hands, this will not be a free-fall recovery. The *Hammond's* converter room is destroyed, no survivors. Some pipes are stuck on. They can't reduce acceleration below three gravs without spinning the ship. First pick-up will be the lab modules. Rendezvous in ten minutes. Bridge out."

The *Hammond* was visible in the open cargo bay hatch as they approached. The giant container ship had more damage than just its converter room. Rows of containers were ripped open, remnants of their contents caught on the ragged sides.

The stern produced two ragged plumes from opposite sides of the nozzle circle. The sides of the stern had more damage than the base. One rip in the hull was bigger than the *Joshua Chamberlain*.

Mitchie appreciated Hiroshi's flying. Three years of practice had made the centurion gentle when maneuvering the freighter. His approach to the *Hammond* was smooth, staying clear of the megaship's plume without any jerks or overcorrections.

Guo's attention wasn't on either ship. Looking past the *Hammond* he saw missile plumes streaking by in batches of ten or twenty. The fleet was providing plenty of fire support to protect the rescue operation. He wondered how many missiles the Betrayers had allocated to defeat it.

They approached the *Hammond* from astern, as they had with the *Currie*. This time *Joshua Chamberlain* slid up along the other's hull. Peeking over the edge of the cargo hold deck the crew could see sparks and flares as their plume blasted the stacked containers. Holes from battle damage widened as plasma tore away tattered walls.

He recognized a stack of containers as Pete's laboratory from their previous visit to the ship. Hiroshi matched *Hammond's* acceleration, placing the cargo hold in front of the lab's hatch.

The hatch popped open. Someone in a Fusion Marine pressure suit waved at them.

Spacer Finnegan threw a safety line to the Marine. He caught it and disappeared inside. When he emerged again the deckhands pulled it tight and tied it off to a handhold.

Someone in a civilian-model suit emerged from the hatch, arms and legs wrapped around the line, and crawled across the gap. Once in the hold the deckhands grabbed him and escorted him to the back wall.

More came out, only a few meters apart. Mitchie stood back and watched. Her crew had set this up with no help from her. She wasn't going to interfere. One of her Academy instructors had "NEVER GIVE UNNECESSARY ORDERS" written on the wall of her classroom. It was a time to live by that.

No matter how bored she was.

A civilian came down the line roped to two Marines. Mitchie noticed the civilian's hands and feet had been vacctaped together. Setta used her knife to free him from the line. The Marines frog marched him to the rear of the hold.

A steady stream of Marines came next. The last landed on his feet in the cargo hold. He drew a knife and cut the line.

Mitchie recognized the CWO insignia on the suit's shoulder. She walked up to him and turned on her radio. "Welcome aboard, Chief Langerhans. You're last?"

"Yes, ma'am." He saluted.

Marines. She returned it and said, "Was that Dr. Smith getting assistance earlier?"

"He's very . . . task focused, ma'am."

"Thanks for taking care of him." She switched channels. "Captain to bridge. That's all of them. Let's get the people from the bow compartment."

The ship's acceleration increased to ten gravs without warning.

Hiroshi spoke on the general frequency. "All hands, short period of free-fall."

Mitchie glanced at her new passengers. The deckhands were checking that they were all hooked onto the cargo net. The Marines were grouped to one side. *Bet Langerhans is thrilled to hand the boffins off to someone else.*

They only had seventeen seconds of free fall, interrupted by a missile striking the *Hammond* and throwing a few bits of shrapnel into the hold. Fortunately it all bounced out again without causing significant damage.

Joshua Chamberlain's torch fired again as the bow module came into view. A hatch was already open. The spacesuited figure threw a coiled line across. One of the deckhands caught it and tied it down.

The first ones across were survival bubbles clipped to the line. Setta drafted a few of the Marines to carry them back, admonishing one with, "Don't fucking roll them."

Another missile hit close by. Mitchie could feel the impact of fragments bouncing off the hull through her feet.

A spacer crossing over was hit by shrapnel tearing his body into the void. His severed arms clung to the line until the next one through brushed them off.

Guo touched his helmet to Mitchie's. "Staying here is dangerous."

"The crew is mostly aboard," she said.

"We need to keep the boffins safe."

"I will." She stepped away.

Another missile hit the Hammond before the transfer finished. That one was around the curve of the ship, just a light show.

When a suit with four rings painted on each forearm came aboard with no one following him Mitchie didn't bother to wait for confirmation. "Hiroshi, get us the hell out of here!"

Setta cut the line.

Mitchie's knees complained as *Joshua Chamberlain* went from three gravs of acceleration to twenty. She saw a few passengers fall, there'd be some hurt wrists from that. Her crew seemed to be all right.

Standing in double normal acceleration was still unpleasant, especially with the weight of the pressure suit added to her own. Mitchie slowly went to her knees then lay down. The collar of her suit cut into the back of her neck. The padding was only good enough for fifteen gravs.

She glanced at the cargo doors. They were already closing. *Good. We can pressurize the hold and I can get out of this damn suit.*

She felt a jolt as a hole appeared in the side of the hold. More than one. Mechanic Ye called, "Senior Chief to the converter room! Senior Chief to the converter room!" A spacer flipped over, one leg ending mid-thigh. Acceleration dropped. Mitchie pushed herself up, estimating it at six gravs.

Which meant they were falling behind the fleet, not catching up. Guo sprinted for the lower deck hatch.

Mitchie reached the wounded spacer at the same time as a Marine. Blood was spraying from the severed leg, freezing where it landed on the deck or someone's suit.

The casualty was thrashing, flipping about in the low acceleration. Mitchie grabbed the arms and pinned them down to the deck. The Marine kneeled on the intact leg.

Mitchie looked at the spacer's chest. 'Dubois' was written there. One of Setta's deckhands.

Acceleration dropped by half. Dubois bucked, pulling Mitchie off the deck. She grabbed a tie-down point recessed into the deck with one hand, tried to hold both of Dubois's wrists with the other. Her hand wasn't big enough. The arms slipped out and flailed some more.

Mitchie grabbed an arm, pushed it down on the other, and pulled as hard as she could on the tie-down. That let her hold Dubois still, at least at this end, but she couldn't hold it for long.

A second Marine was holding Dubois's leg to the deck. The first had a corpsman badge on his chest. He was winding a safety line around what remained of the deckhand's thigh. Many tight loops. The bleeding had stopped.

Dubois went limp. The corpsman cut the line and tied a knot.

Mitchie touched her helmet to his. "What are her odds?"

"Depends how soon we get her back in pressure, ma'am."

She looked around. There were three holes in the hull she could see. Finnegan was applying a patch to the lowest one with the help of a couple of *Hammond's* crew. One of the boffins was missing his head. Pete was holding onto another—injured or panicking, she couldn't tell.

On the general frequency Hiroshi announced, "Fleet is increasing the amount of counter-missile fire for us, so we'll be safer."

Mitchie thought, *That only helps while we're in range of the fleet.*

***

Guo dropped through the hatch and dogged it shut above him.

The corridor was in vacuum. The airlock at the outer end had a hole torn in it.

The converter room had pressure. It took Guo and Ye together to close the hatch against the escaping air.

"There's broken pipes and two of the water tanks are punctured," shouted Ye. "I've sealed off as much as I can."

The chief mechanic looked over the array of pressure and flow gauges. After years of studying them the pattern leapt out at him.

"Yep. Okay, we need to get full thrust back. Open the valves to tanks two and three. Cross-connect to feed all four quadrants of the torch off those two. We need to use that reaction mass before we lose it. Once they're empty we'll switch to the undamaged tanks."

Ye obeyed, undoing his initial frantic work. "Won't we be unbalanced?"

"We will. But with punctured tanks there's no helping it. Get the rest of the valves open. I'm going to adjust the converter down. This calls for more mass, less energy. I'm going to conserve fuel by putting more water through the torch and not heating it as much."

"Aye, aye." After a full circuit of the converter room Ye reported, "All quadrants have full flow."

"Good." Guo picked up the intercom mike. "Converter room to bridge. Full thrust available. Warning, center of gravity will shift to port, we have two tanks open to space."

***

Resuming twenty gravs forced Finnegan to abandon repairs. He crawled over to Mitchie. "Ma'am, if we go down to ten gravs I can use the crane platform to patch those holes."

"Negative," she answered. "My orders are to maintain twenty until we've passed through the fleet formation." *I'd want thirty if it wouldn't make some of the pressure suits spring leaks from lying on the deck.*

An hour and a half later Hiroshi dropped thrust to ten gravs. "All hands. We are three hundred klicks past fleet formation."

Finnegan had the remaining two holes patched in twenty minutes.

One patch failed as the pressure came up, but his second fix held. He killed a roll of vacctape making it tight.

Dubois was dead when the corpsman opened her suit.

BDS *Patton*, Danu System, acceleration 10 m/s^2

"Executing on the plan, sir," reported Commander Leith. "We're on track to a tenth of a second."

Admiral Galen nodded, his face stiff as he suppressed a sleepy yawn. He resisted the temptation to laugh at Leith's boast. When the Betrayers recognized the trap their response would disrupt the plan by more than seconds.

"Backstop salvo on track," said Ensign Grove. Those missiles had been launched two days ago. Their course took them well clear of the enemy force and the tail of reinforcements behind it.

"Ready to launch main salvo." Leith counted down to the launch. On Patton's flag bridge they could feel the shiver as the ship spat out twenty missiles. The main display filled with symbols as every warship in the fleet fired all their tubes.

Commodore Deng monitored internal communications. "Three Fusion squadrons fired late. Bachak is tearing them a new one."

"Enemy has changed firing pattern," said Ensign Grove. The Betrayers had been concentrating bursts of missiles on seemingly random targets. "They're launching widely dispersed missiles. Looks like counter-fire to our salvo."

Galen let himself smile. "Good. That's what we want them paying attention to."

"Second salvo launched on schedule." Leith shifted the tactical display to show the waves of missiles flying toward each other. "Losing some to counterfire. Shifting second wave to cover the gaps."

Silence fell for a minute. Everything was proceeding on schedule. No decisions were needed. Eyes fixed on the clock, waiting for the next event.

Special electronic warfare missiles in the initial salvo activated. Some spread out a dozen decoys each. Others raced ahead, burning their drive at an unsustainable rate, hiding the movements of other missiles behind their plumes. The most expensive ones aimed laser, maser, and radar beams at the Betrayer ships, trying to overload their sensors.

It was enough to keep their human owners from being able to follow the action. Leith switched the display to a simulation of what should be happening.

The containers jettisoned from the *Joshua Chamberlain* were falling through the enemy fleet. The Betrayers, wary of mines, had parted to stay clear of them but hadn't wasted missiles to destroy them. Each container held two dozen missiles. If they were executing the timed sequence correctly liquid hydrogen was being pumped into the shell around each one.

As the missiles were flung into space the frigid black shells would conceal them from Betrayer sensors. Not for very long. Just long enough for them to close the distance to the nearest Betrayer ships.

The storm of missiles, decoys, and explosions pressing toward the enemy fleet would also distract them from the sneak attack, if the timing was right.

Galen's crew had no way to know if the containers were deploying the missiles. The human fleet's sensors couldn't possibly detect them. Not until the missiles lit their torches and rammed their targets.

When two lines of plumes appeared on the display sighs of relief sounded across the flag bridge. Seconds later explosions flared. Cheers broke out.

"What's the count?" demanded Admiral Galen.

Eyes turned to the sensor console. Chief Heinz compared the new data to the simulations they'd run. "Three percent more ships destroyed than the best case scenario," he said.

"Superb work," said Galen. "Keep the pressure on."

"Shifting the main salvo to pattern Charlie," said Leith.

As the order went out the missiles racing toward the enemy moved into the gaps in defensive fire left by the destroyed ships. The follow-on waves focused on the next ring of ships outward. Newly launched missiles were spread over the whole enemy formation, ready to be targeted on whatever new openings appeared.

Ensign Grove announced, "Enemy defensive fire is adjusted to cover the inner zone. Middle and outer zones still have gaps until their new counter missile fire is in place."

Galen acknowledged the report and turned to Leith. "Why was your best case scenario off?"

"CIC's trying to figure that out. The best guess is that our decoys and jamming overloaded the Betrayer sensors to where they filtered out anything that wasn't an obvious attack. The sneak missiles didn't draw any defensive fire until they lit their torches."

"Good. Let me know if they have any better ideas on it." The admiral sat back and muttered, "For the clumsy programming of our enemies, may the Lord make us truly thankful. Amen."

The first wave of missiles smashed into the Betrayer formation. Nine-tenths had been destroyed along the way. The survivors were enough to widen the gap torn in the formation by *Joshua Chamberlain's* surprise.

Dozens of Betrayer ships exploded or were damaged enough to fall behind. Ships turned to close the gap in the formation, weakening their protection against incoming fire in hopes of building a solid defense again.

Galen didn't wait for his crew to report on the movement. As soon as he saw the shift on the display he ordered, "All warships reverse course. Resume fire at full rate when turnover is complete."

The second wave of missiles smashed more Betrayer ships.

Galen's stomach twisted as *Patton* switched end for end. Now they were accelerating straight at the Betrayers.

Gagging noises told of someone losing his rations to the sudden maneuver. Galen kept his eyes on the display. Whoever it was didn't need an admiral adding to his problems.

"Get a towel," snapped Chief Heinz at the unfortunate one.

A Betrayer ship blew into a cloud of gas before any missiles could reach it.

"*Terror* is firing her spinal beam," said Commodore Deng.

"Wish we could afford one of those damn battleships," muttered Leith.

"I'd rather have a hundred cruisers," said the admiral. "Stay focused."

The Harmony's flagship blew up another enemy.

Galen ordered, "Activate Backstop."

"Backstop aye." Ensign Grove transmitted commands to the missiles on the other side of the system.

She stiffened. "Enemy fire pattern is changing. Half their tubes have switched from counter-missile to offensive."

Everyone on the bridge knew that accelerating toward the enemy made the human fleet more vulnerable to enemy missiles. There'd be less time to intercept them. The missiles would also close at higher relative velocities, making them harder to hit.

They'd only lost a few ships while retreating across the Danu system. Now the fight would hurt.

Commander Leith asked, "Permission to shift some missile fire to defensive, sir?"

"Denied. We're here to kick their ass, not dance with them."

Leith nodded.

The Betrayers had lost hundreds of ships as they maneuvered back to a solid disk formation. Now they had a tightly integrated web of anti-missile fire which smashed incoming waves of missiles even as the turnover let them come in closer together.

The humans' defenses were not solid. Commodore Deng handled reports from the subordinate formations. The Fusion fleet suffered the worst. After Deng made another count he snarled, "The Goddamned Committee of Public Safety sent their spacers out to just die!"

"Hate the Betrayers, not our allies," said Galen. The display was so crowded he could barely follow the progress of the battle. When the two fleets reached each other the exchange would be cataclysmic.

Then about a fifth of the enemy fleet turned over, accelerating away from the battle. Ensign Grove analyzed the movement. "Almost three hundred ships. All lighter units. The formation is closing up the gaps."

"Did one of their coalition decide to quit?" wondered Chief Heinz.

Grove said, "They could just be trying to make sure they have a full report on the battle delivered to their home nodes."

Multiple crashes sounded. Galen realized a Betrayer missile had come close enough to throw shrapnel through the ship's hull. He glanced down at his message display. The flagship's captain wrote, "Five hull breaches. Multiple fires. Damage control responding. No loss of combat effectiveness."

Galen didn't need the message to know about the fires. The smell of smoke was in the air, mixing with the sweat and vomit odors already there.

***

On the other side of the Danu system the Backstop missiles were accelerating toward the gate offering passage to the Argo system. A few Betrayer ships were lined up to pass through, decelerating to ensure they reached the gate at the precise speed and angle for safe passage.

The missiles weren't trying for that. They aimed for the loop of cosmic string forming the gate. The Betrayers fired counter-missiles but only intercepted a few of them.

The first Backstop missile detonated its nuclear warhead as it passed close to the string. A blast of radiation shook the gate, sending vibrations around the loop in both directions.

The next missile came in from the far side. It started another set of waves through the string. A third and fourth exploded. The rest flew past, self-destructing when clear of the gate. Galen had prohibited overkill. He hoped the gate would eventually be usable again.

The Betrayer ships headed for the gate boosted their torches to maximum thrust. It wasn't enough. As they passed through the chaotically vibrating gate the forces tore them into dust before flinging them light years away.

In the Argo system eight light years away this gate's counterpart was still sending ships to Danu. But the ships lined up for the jump would receive no report that the humans had turned and attacked.

***

On the *Patton* Admiral Galen studied the tactical display. Both the human and enemy formations were tattered where enemy fire had destroyed or disabled ships faster than others could maneuver to close the gap. A countdown measured the minutes to when the fleets would pass through each other.

He turned to his chief of staff. "Deng, order all units to disperse at minus two minutes. Captains are authorized to maneuver freely to avoid collisions."

"Aye-aye."

"And warn the stragglers to watch for kamikazes." Not that the warning would help ships too crippled to maneuver.

Now the admiral's only duty was to look confident and not distract anyone from their jobs. Galen sat still and kept his eyes on the tactical display.

Another batch of Betrayer ships turned over and fled the imminent clash. Grove counted forty of them. Not enough to reduce the bloody wounds the humans were about to take.

The flagship captain's voice sounded over the PA. "All hands. All hands. Helmets and gloves. Helmets and gloves. No exceptions."

Normally only crew in the outer compartments wore their full suits. The vacuum proof gloves made it hard to only push one button at a time and helmets forced all conversation to use the intercom. The captain must expect the ship to have breaches all the way to the core.

Galen twisted his helmet back and forth to check the seal was clean. He pulled the gloves on slowly. Likely no one was watching but he wanted to give the right impression. The sweat on his palms let them slide on more smoothly than usual.

The steady thump of missile launches stopped. For a long moment there was only the distant roar of the torch as background noise. Then the whine of lasers and chatter of point defense cannon began. Firing them continuously might burn them out—if they survived the next few minutes.

The display showed the fleets merging, red icons overlapping with blue. *Patton* swayed in evasive maneuvers.

Shrapnel smashed into the hull, a dozen hits at least. Then a ringing sound Galen hadn't heard in any battle before. A laser etching into the hull maybe?

Smoke puffed out of the ventilation grills. *Patton's* weapons went silent. Passing each other at multiple kilometers per second made for a quick engagement.

Damage control workers started running a saw in the next compartment. The smoke stopped pouring in.

Patton shivered with missile launches.

Galen couldn't hear anything over the saw. The tactical display was frozen at the moment of closest approach. He could see Grove and Heinz working on the console to fix it. He resorted to typing a message to Leith. "What are we firing at?"

The reply came back on his repeater screen. "Enemy stragglers. Damaged ships heading toward us."

He sent his next message to Deng. "When half the surviving ships have reported in order a turnover. We need to finish off the Betrayer force."

Catching up would be hard. The closing velocity they'd built up to attack the Betrayers now carried them farther from the enemy ships. They'd have to stick to long-range missile fire. God only knew if that would wipe out the enemy before they reached the vulnerable logistics ships Galen had left behind.

The display reset. Icons began to appear as sensor data was collected from across the human fleet.

Every time the saw stopped only to start cutting again a moment later felt like a cruel prank on Galen's ears. Then it did stop and the only noise was a voice shouting to get their lazy asses to compartment Juliet Twenty Three.

"How much longer until we have an assessment on the remaining enemy?" asked Galen. He spoke loudly in case the rest were as deaf as he felt.

"That's all we've found," said Ensign Grove. "There might be some more drifting with their torches off. We're running scans."

A box in the corner of the display reported statistics. Thirty-seven fully functional Betrayer ships.

"That's it? Our stragglers could take them." Galen turned to the commodore. "Set up some ad hoc squadrons. Authorize them to engage at will."

"On it," answered Deng.

Patton turned over again without anyone losing a meal. Galen said a brief prayer of thanks that he and his crew had been spared.

"Starburst, sir," called Chief Heinz.

It was obvious on the display. The surviving Betrayers were scattering in a circle, trying to get out from between the main fleet and the dozens of damaged ships hoping for revenge.

Galen let himself smile. "That just makes it easier. Commander Leith, segment the fleet into pursuit groups assigned to each one. Ensign Grove, what's the status on the Betrayer reinforcement groups?"

Grove shifted the display to a view of the entire Danu system. "Mixed, sir. Some groups have turned over, some are still burning toward us. CIC thinks they're grouping up to avoid being defeated in detail."

The admiral's smile widened. "Too late."

Even if all the Betrayer ships in the system could form up before being brought to battle they had only half the firepower of the remaining human fleet.

"Commander Leith, position Backstop salvos by all the other gates. We'll shut those down too if we have to. We're not going to let them get away. Not after this much blood."

"Aye-aye, sir."

Deng offered Galen a datasheet. The admiral looked it over. Casualty reports had been collected for the entire force. Hardly any ships were undamaged, just some destroyers who'd been passed over for more important targets. The Disconnect and Harmony fleets lost a quarter of their ships, crippled or destroyed. The poorly trained Fusion fleet was down by forty percent.

Galen realized he'd lost more men under his command in one day than any other admiral in history. And he'd been willing to lose more to stop the Betrayer onslaught.

Which was not yet stopped. He looked at the maneuvers against the fleeing remnants of the first Betrayer fleet being coordinated by Deng and Leith. They were methodical, safe, and slow. Too slow.

Galen unbuckled from his seat and took three steps over to Leith's console. His legs were stiff from being still for hours and ached from lack of sleep. "You need to be more aggressive with those last few."

"Sir? I'm trying to conserve missiles."

"No. Waste anything but time. Take casualties if we have to. We need to turn and fight those reinforcements before they group up. The sooner we reach them the less we'll bleed."

"Yes, sir." Leith reviewed his display and issued new orders.

Patton began to shiver as she launched missiles at the fleeing Betrayers.

Three human ships were lost in the mopping up, ones who'd been damaged earlier and could be positioned to block the escape of the surviving Betrayers.

Two minutes after the last of the thirty-seven enemy ships was destroyed the fleet flipped over again, boosting toward the Argo gate and the hundreds of enemy ships in between.

The Betrayer fleet in the Argo system had been jumping into Danu at a steady rate. The first ones to arrive in Danu had paused in pursuit of the humans to concentrate enough ships to be a useful attack force. Following groups had been smaller, choosing to reinforce the initial force sooner rather than wait until there were enough them to be an independent threat.

All those reinforcements had been thrusting continuously toward the human fleet. Now most had turned over and were decelerating to delay their doom.

The first few groups were obliterated with no human casualties. Overwhelming numbers made up for the lack of deceptive tactics.

The "coward" ships who'd fled the initial battle survived until they turned over to brake toward the Argo gate. The humans overran them without slowing.

Betrayers farther back returned to the gate. New arrivals

maneuvered to join them before the shuddering loop of cosmic string. Every so often a ship would leave the mass, approach the gate, and disintegrate before passing through.

"How much will we miss the gate by?" asked Admiral Galen.

Leith put a navigation plot on the main display. "Fifty thousand klicks from the edge of our formation. Then once we're past we'll turn over and perform damage assessment."

"Don't get ahead of yourself. We haven't even hit them yet."

The tactical officer's grin made him look like a eager little boy. "Oh, we'll hit them, sir, no worries on that."

"Convince me."

Leith activated an animation on his display. "We're going to hold three missile salvos with the fleet. When the fourth one is launched we'll maneuver them into this arrangement shaped to match the Betrayer formation. Then they'll all go to maximum acceleration to hit every enemy ship simultaneously. A perfect time on target attack."

Admiral Galen let the animation play through a second time. "You're not allowing many backups to account for defensive fire."

"At this speed we're coming in at they're not going to have much opportunity to intercept them, sir." A new animation showed the problem from a Betrayer ship's point of view. The AI ships were idling by the gate. The humans had kept accelerating the whole way across the system.

"Very well. Proceed with the attack."

"Yes, sir!" Leith began issuing orders to the rest of the fleet's tactical officers.

Galen strolled to the other side of the flag bridge. He asked his chief of staff, "How's morale holding up?"

Commodore Deng chuckled. "The outfielders are complaining."

A dozen squadrons had been left behind the main force to catch any enemies who evaded the main attack, along with the trickle of new ships jumping into the system from Argo.

"Scared of being on their own or angry they're not in on the kill?" asked Galen.

"Angry. Wouldn't blame them for being scared. If that mob

disperses we'd have a hard time catching them before they gang up on the others.

"If they were going to do that it would have happened already. But they are making it easy for us. Grove, what's Intel's take on their behavior?"

The ensign turned to face him. "Sir, best guess is that their orders are to return to Argo and their programming doesn't have the flexibility to adapt to the situation. Nobody's ever intentionally damaged a gate before. We don't know if it will ever recover."

Was that a hint of reproach in her voice? Well, smashing a Golden Age artifact should earn him some. "The Terraformers build new gates all the time."

"First counterfire is hitting the strike," announced Commander Leith. "Decoys are negating about a third of it. Launching follow-ups to cover the gaps."

"Very well." Galen suppressed a yawn. He'd let Deng take control of the fleet a few times while they re-crossed the Danu system, but two hour naps weren't enough to erase the sleep debt he'd accumulated over weeks of retreating.

It wasn't Deng's fault. The commodore would cover operations for as long as Galen needed. But two hours was as long as he could go before waking full of adrenaline and demanding a status report from the flag bridge.

Deng had started sending the reports pre-emptively as they fled through the Argo system. Galen suspected Medical had planted sensors in his room. That was arguably a court-martial offense but the relief of seeing a routine report as he stood in his cabin covered only in sweat was too sweet to tamper with.

"Betrayers are launching offensive missiles," reported Ensign Grove.

Now Galen felt awake.

Leith switched displays, preparing his defensive plan.

"Not time on target," continued Grove. "Looks like they're just emptying out their magazines before they're destroyed. No pattern."

She paused as her displays updated. "Correction. CIC has identified seven different patterns. They believe cooperation has broken down among the different Betrayer entities."

"The Lord is merciful," said Admiral Galen. "Can you work with that, Leith?"

"Yes, sir. That's going to be much more vulnerable to our decoys and jammers. Hell . . . they're so spread out we can use the same decoys against multiple waves."

He'd left out that their high relative speed would leave little time to intercept the incoming missiles. Everyone on the flag bridge knew that already.

The Combined Fleet's time on target barrage hit first. Hundreds of Betrayer ships blew up within seconds of each other. The main display went red as radiation and debris made it impossible to see what was happening to the enemy.

Patton's missile tubes were firing steadily. Using full size missiles to intercept enemy ones was an expensive defense, but practical. Blowing one up left a cloud of metal fragments. An enemy missile running into one at thirty klicks per second or more was ruined.

Some enemy missiles made it through. None hit *Patton*. Deng tracked the casualty reports. "Looks like three percent. Not bad. Those final evasive maneuvers paid off."

"How bad were the Fuzies hit?" asked Galen.

"Same as the rest of us. They tightened up their spacing."

"They finally learned to hold formation?"

"No, I think all the ones who didn't know how died."

Grim chuckles sounded across the flag bridge.

"We're clear for turnover," reported Leith.

"Authorized." Galen's stomach twisted as the ship flipped end for end again.

Grove sounded like turnover didn't bother her at all. "CIC reports the Betrayer force at the gate has no survivors."

Galen wasn't sure he'd heard her right. "None?"

"None at the gate. There's a few dozen recent arrivals scattered around this side of the system."

Crew throughout the compartment traded looks. No one wanted to tempt fate by being the first to say "We won" out loud.

Galen typed a private message to Deng. "Up for another eight hours on duty?"

The reply flashed back. "Eight or eighteen. Get some sleep."

Admiral Galen stood. "Commodore Deng, take fleet control. Handle the mopping up."

"Aye-aye, sir. I have fleet control."

Galen reached the hatch as his deputy sat down in the chair.

Deng said, "Parcel squadrons out over the arrival volume. We'll let them compete to nail the newcomers."

Joshua Chamberlain, Danu System, acceleration more or less 9 m/s^2

Guo made sandwiches for Mitchie and Pete in the galley. The ship wasn't stable enough for actual cooking. Right now Mthembu had the con. Mitchie stared at her water cup, watching the level wobble as the coxswain fiddled with the controls.

With the two damaged water tanks empty the other three had the ship off-balanced to port. As the water was drained to propel them toward the passenger liner *Aurora*, the ship's center of gravity shifted back to center, so the torch had to be continually adjusted to keep the thrust balanced enough to not spin the ship.

She thought he was doing better than she'd expected. All four quadrants of the torch needed different thrust levels to compensate. Mthembu was tweaking them gently. Rather than chase his overcorrections with the torch he was firing the attitude thrusters to correct when the errors built up. *Joshua Chamberlain* was never *exactly* on course but they were staying close enough that everyone could walk around instead of being strapped in.

"You should put a cap on that cup," said Guo as he put a ham and swiss on front of her.

"I'm watching it."

"Maybe you should take a break from watching it." He gave another to Pete, who thanked him warmly.

"I'm not micromanaging him. I'm just monitoring."

"That water isn't telling you anything you won't notice from the seat of your pants."

"I'd rather worry about that than the hash I made of the funeral." Schwartzenberger always had something profound to say before dropping a body out the airlock. She just stumbled through platitudes.

Pete said, "I found it rather comforting."

Mitchie was saved from answering that by Setta sliding down the ladder from the bridge. Negotiating the exchange of passengers for supplies had been delegated to the bosun.

"We have a deal. They'll take all the people off the *Hammond* and give us a portable head and some inflatable couches for search and rescue ops. I did make promises in your name, ma'am."

Mitchie gestured for her to go on.

"You need to have a photograph with the *Aurora's* quartermaster and give him an autograph."

"Gah, I hate shit like that," said the captain. Guo stifled a chuckle.

"Sorry, ma'am. We don't have anything to trade that he needs, and even if we did he probably would've held us up for the photo."

"Fine. What else?"

"Fleet is assigning a destroyer to work with us on search and rescue. And one problem with unloading. They'll take the people and lab gear, but not the samples. I went to the captain, he refused."

"I need those for my research!" exclaimed Pete.

"Haven't you already analyzed them?" asked Guo.

"It's not the same. There are subtleties we don't detect until we have other Betrayer memory cores to compare them to."

Mitchie held up a hand to silence him. "Did *Aurora's* captain say why?"

"Afraid of their systems being contaminated by Betrayer code, ma'am," answered Setta.

"That's ridiculous," said Pete. "Someone would have to give the core a power source then physically connect it to the ship's systems."

"That's what the captain was afraid of, sir."

"Fine, we'll keep them on board," said Mitchie. "They're not going to subvert our systems."

"Thank you." Pete looked more relieved than the situation seemed to justify. Maybe he'd been afraid Mitchie would toss his precious samples into space. "May I stay on board to work on them?"

She paused to consider the logistics of this. She could put him in with Mthembu . . . but that wouldn't end well for either. "Of course. Bosun, please have my office reconfigured as a cabin."

"Oh, thank you!" said Pete. "May I put some of the analysis gear in there as well?"

Mitchie nodded. Pete scarfed his sandwich and headed for the ladder to the hold. Setta followed him.

Guo was in the seat next to her, nibbling on his own lunch. He leaned gently into Mitchie.

"I'm sorry," she said. "We're going to have all the office crap in our cabin again."

"It's all right. We won't need it much with the search and rescue work. Any numbers yet?"

"No, Fleet Ops was still trying to prioritize ships. There's wrecks scattered from here to the Argo gate."

Guo took a larger bite, washing it down with some hot tea. "Wish they'd let us have some downtime for repairs."

"There's too many casualties out there. We'll have about an hour while we drop off this bunch. Could you patch the tanks with some help from their crew?"

He shook his head. "Nothing that would hold. A patch on the outside would blow off as soon as we accelerated with full tanks."

***

Mitchie emerged from the wrecked cruiser and jumped back to *Joshua Chamberlain*. She hadn't found any more survivors on this pass through the wreck so it was time to move on to the next one. Fleet Ops triaged ships by how much life support they had. They were still working on ships where everyone was in survival bubbles.

The hold held nearly a hundred bubbles after three ships. That was a respectable percentage given the horrendous damage to the wrecks.

The first one had been so shredded she was amazed there were any survivors.

Pete Smith stood with the deckhands in his pressure suit. He'd been pitching in to get all the bubbles tucked into the cargo net. No one considered him competent enough to do search and rescue on a wreck. Now he came forward to intercept Mitchie as she coasted into the hold. She caught a safety line and braced him with a hand so they stopped together instead of colliding.

He leaned in to touch helmets. "Ma'am, there's an enemy wreck floating about twenty klicks away. I'd like your permission to retrieve its core."

"I don't want you getting ripped up by a maintenance bot," she said, stalling to think.

"It's severely damaged. I doubt there's any functioning bots left. I'm more worried that the core might be too damaged to read."

"What's this one going to tell you that the ones you already have didn't?"

"One, I can identify which line of AIs it descended from. Intelligence thinks there are units from four to eight systems here. I could find a minimum for that. Two," he was counting on his fingers, "we've never seen AIs cooperate like this before. Is this a function of them being different instances of the same original Betrayer or is this a new behavior produced by our offensive? Three, the error patterns in the legacy code modules—"

"Okay, you've convinced me. But search and rescue is priority so we can only spare a few minutes for it. And you're going to have some armed escorts."

"Thank you, ma'am!"

Setta kept the armory well-stocked. When Mitchie raised an eyebrow at some of the fancier weapons, the bosun said, "They're trade goods, too."

Most of the crew went on the boarding party. Hiroshi held the bridge—Mthembu was a better shot—and Ye the converter room. Wang was left back to keep an eye on the bubbles.

Pete was right. The Betrayer ship had been chewed up. Mitchie recognized a missile hit, laser burns, and holes from some close in guns normally used for defending against missiles. This ship must have tried to ram.

The shielded pod at the center of the ship was already torn open. Mitchie held Pete back while the junior spacers poked at it. A single bot emerged. Mthembu grabbed it with both hands and flung. The only working tentacle tried to hang onto his arm but he pried it off.

"I don't want that loose," called Mitchie. "Marksmanship practice. Two rounds, everyone." She waited until after the rest had fired to put two holes in the center of it. Looked like Finnegan had missed with both. She decided the crew needed some range time when the opportunity came along.

Most of the ship's core electronics were destroyed, but enough memory modules were intact to make Pete happy.

"Can we get more, ma'am? he asked.

"Only if it won't delay us, and if they're this beat up."

Mitchie floated up through the bridge hatch. "Call Fleet Ops," she told Mthembu. "Tell them we're full up and ask where they want us to take them."

Her shiploads of rescuees off the wrecked warships had all gone to different destinations, as Ops juggled positioning and life support capacity. One batch had even been dropped off at a battleship, which was doing some search and rescue work of its own.

The Coxswain received a reply in only three minutes—the flagship was close by. "Ma'am, we're ordered to take them to Tuatha station over Danu. And then we're ordered to stand down for seventy-two hours shore leave." The exhaustion in his voice had vanished.

"Hot damn. Acknowledge that then start plotting a course." She activated the PA. "All hands, our next stop is Tuatha station. Expect a day or two of leave on sunny Danu, home of unlimited water and oxygen. Once everyone's safely positioned for acceleration we'll be on our way. Captain out."

Mthembu was grinning. "What are you going to do on leave, ma'am?"

"Sleep for eighteen hours. Then find out what my husband did in all that time in enemy territory. Speaking of sleep, you're due to go off shift. I relieve you."

"I'm relieved, ma'am."

"Oh, tell Dr. Smith he's not to take any of his toys off the ship."

Joshua Chamberlain, **Danu, gravity 8.9 m/s^2**

"Fucking twins?" Mitchie grabbed a watercolor off the bulkhead and threw it across their cabin.

The frame shattered, splinters bouncing off Guo's leg. The cover transparency wasn't brittle, it bounced across the deck. Guo watched the landscape he'd painted at Master Sung's school flutter slowly down.

He hadn't bothered ducking. She'd aimed it far enough away to have no chance of hurting him. So she wasn't *that* mad.

Yet.

"It was a trap," Guo said. "You said if they set a trap I should fall for it, or they'd make a more dangerous one."

"Explain how it happened," she demanded.

"She trapped us in a car together during a storm. When—"

"Not the seduction. I know how seduction works, I used to do it for a living. Explain the pregnancy."

"She was on fertility drugs."

"You caught her with the pills?"

"No, I did the math. It happened so soon after we started fucking, combined with twins, that the only logical scenario was drugs. I asked her if she was taking them and she was so surprised she couldn't lie worth a damn."

"Unprofessional," Mitchie critiqued.

"She'll probably do better with practice."

"Going to give her some?"

"Not if I can help it."

She was a bit less mad. *I should have led with the fertility drugs.*

"You're going to have some babies early next year."

"Maybe. When they were . . . interrogating me they threatened to abort the children." Guo flinched as he forced the words out.

Mitchie shifted to being an analyst. "I doubt they did. They'd want to keep the leverage on you."

He felt relief at her professional assessment. "I haven't heard anything from her—or about her—since they arrested me."

"Going to go back to Tiantan to find out?" Mitchie said it in a tone of idle curiosity, but her hands squeezed tight on her knees.

"No. When the war is over I want to go back to Akiak."

"Going to bring Lian with you?" Voice casual, hands tense.

"She's a hot house flower. Wouldn't last halfway through the winter."

"So what are you going to do about the kids?"

"I don't know," Guo said.

The silence stretched on.

He said, "I don't think she'd be willing to give them up. I can send her plenty of money but being a father is more than that. My dad always took time to teach me stuff until . . . anyway, money's not enough. I don't know how well the Harmony would treat a Disker's kids. And she may not have a job."

"What, they're firing her because she couldn't make you defect?"

"No, for not telling anyone I'd vanished."

Guo realized he'd left his escape attempt out of the story. He told Mitchie about the pre-dawn hike, stealing an emergency vehicle, and seeing the destroyer *Walking Rollo* blown up in his face. *Figures she'd be more impressed by me beating up a cop than negotiating with a government.*

He finished the digression with, "—so whether she'd be court-martialed and for what charge was one of the levers Ping tried to make me defect with. She may have been convicted of treason. I don't know."

"If they executed her, no twins."

Guo shuddered. "I can't see them doing that. Maybe later. But growing up as the children of a traitor would be horrid for the kids."

Mitchie waited for a bit before asking, "What are you going to do?"

"I'm going to stay with you."

She held out her arms to him.

Guo walked across the cabin, stepping around the pieces of the framed picture, and sat next to Mitchie on the bed. They wrapped their arms tightly around each other.

"What are you going to do about the twins?" she asked softly.

"I don't know. We'll figure it out together."

Tuatha Station, Danu System, centrifugal acceleration 10 m/s^2

Guo stopped again.

Mitchie took a couple more steps down the corridor before realizing he wasn't moving. She went back and wrapped her arms around him. "It'll be all right. I'll body slam the son of a bitch if he tries to talk to you."

Her husband chuckled.

"Better yet, I'll get one of Galen's staffers to slam him. They'd have enough mass to actually move the guy."

That produced a real laugh from him. He returned her hug. After a moment he said, "It's not just worrying about Ping approaching me, even if every time I see him I have torture flashbacks. It's . . . I've dreamed of killing him. Wrapping my hands around his neck and squeezing until I crush his windpipe. Can I actually be in the same room with him without losing control and attacking him?"

"Yes, you can. Even though he deserves it. Because you're a good person and you can handle yourself and there's a lot of people will grab you before you reach him."

The last part seemed the most reassuring.

"Now come on," she said. "We don't want to be the last ones to arrive." They started walking again. "Tomorrow, will you go see a therapist?"

"How can I trust one to keep my secrets? This is Danu. There's still shooting going on between pro-Fusion and pro-Harmony guerillas despite the cease-fire. No therapist is going to be impartial."

"Um." They kept walking. "There's lots of doctors from the Disconnect with the Combined Fleet. Would you trust one of them?"

"Yes. But they're treating casualties from the battle."

"You're a casualty from the battle."

"They'll triage me as 'come back in a month.'"

Mitchie grinned. "Not if we make it a security issue. Maybe you were subjected to subtle psychological programming when held prisoner."

"Subtle hell."

They'd arrived. The guards checked them against the list and waved them into the ballroom.

It wasn't set up for dancing. A table in the center was ready for the signing. Others lined the outside holding nibbles of every kind. Flags decorated the walls, every world of the Disconnect flanked by the Harmony and Fusion ones. It was crowded with every politician who could attend on two weeks' notice plus the flag officers from all three fleets.

A waiter offered a tray of drinks. Guo took white wine. Mitchie chose something that looked complicated and strong.

"Captain Long. Senior Chief Kwan. It's good to see you." Admiral Galen must have been waiting for them.

The couple came to almost-attention and made polite greetings.

"Thank you for giving me an excuse to escape Sukhoi's Planetary Director. Those people are going to carry a grudge forever over the space stations they lost. Have you had a chance to read the treaty?"

Both nodded. Guo said, "Yes, it looks like it should be a stable compromise."

Mitchie added, "I was impressed that you convinced the DCC to commit to using Disconnect ships to enforce the treaty provisions."

Galen laughed softly. "Be impressed when they ratify it. They haven't seen that part yet."

"That's—do you think they'll get a unanimous vote?"

"They will. Or war will break out again and it will be their fault. And they'll need to find a new fleet commander."

Guo looked shocked. Mitchie was impressed. The admiral had taken severe risks to win his battles but she'd never seen him operate on the political level like this.

"Anyway, Long, I just want to tell you you're a bad influence. Enjoy the party." Galen moved on.

Mitchie choked on her drink.

"He must have read your report," said Guo.

No one in the crowd wanted to talk to Guo. Mitchie was sought out by Fusion Marines wanting to thank her for her daring landings, and Disker intelligence officers who wanted to shake hands and wouldn't say why.

Guo had relaxed a bit when he realized Ping wasn't in the crowd but tensed up every time someone arrived through either door.

Mitchie spotted Guen and some other Fuzie politicians she knew but the crowd around them was too thick to fight through.

The last of the principals to arrive was *Daifu* Ping. Mitchie and Guo drifted to the far corner of the room. It wasn't necessary.

Ping insisted on kicking off the signing of the peace treaty immediately.

The negotiations included protocols for making a ceremony of it. Anthems were played, with Bonaventure's standing in for the rest of the Disconnected Worlds (not all of whom had bothered choosing anthems). A Hindi priest gave a carefully neutral invocation. Then handcrafted pens in museum-ready display cases were presented to each signer.

"Going to be embarrassing if those fancy pens won't write," muttered Mitchie.

Her husband pointed to the presenter. "That guy probably has six extras tucked into his jacket."

Daifu Ping stood in front of the first of the three copies on the table. Holding the pen in the air he began his speech. The Harmony would be a good neighbor and example of cultural growth for all of humanity. It would accept those betrayed by impersonal institutions and social atomization, providing worthy tasks for all to undertake.

Mitchie wrapped her arms around Guo as the speech continued. He stood stiffly. She reached up and stroked his cheeks. He stopped grinding his teeth.

At last Ping shut up and signed.

Guen kept her speech short. She thanked the negotiating teams for their hard work and promised to start Stakeholder elections as soon as the referendums over control of Danu, Franklin, and other disputed worlds were concluded. Once the Fusion's control mechanisms were back in place everyone could be assured of peaceful and prosperous lives. Her signature was a quick scribble.

The Disconnected Worlds were represented by Admiral Galen. He accepted the ceremonial pen, running a finger over the letters carved in the wooden barrel. "I choose to sign this treaty. I choose it because it protects the right of every human to make the most important decision. To pick up and leave where ever they are and find someplace better. Sometimes two men will switch places. If they're both happier thereby, good. Different people need different things from their neighbors and their governments.

"Others will want something that never existed before. They have the right to go where they can and build it. Only by protecting that right can we discover better ways.

"As the representative of the Defense Coordinating Committee of the Disconnected Worlds, I sign this treaty."

He wrote a firm signature on all three copies.

The room broke into applause.

Mitchie looked up at her husband. The free emigration clause had survived from the original proposal he carried to the Harmony. He wiped at an eye.

"You did it," she said. "You changed the world."

With the ceremony over the real drinking began. Guo stuck with wine. Mitchie snagged another strange-looking drink as an experiment then abandoned it on the first table she came to. Growing up on Akiak didn't prepare her for 50% pineapple juice.

"There you are! Have you been hiding?"

Mitchie turned around to find Guen with Wayne Searcher on her arm. She was thankful she'd told Guo of the signs she'd seen of that romance. Even if he was relieved, he shouldn't be surprised.

An exchange of hugs was followed by celebration of the treaty. Then Guo asked, "You two seem comfortable together. Are congratulations in order?"

Guen blushed and looked down.

Wayne had a bit of embarrassment in his voice as he said, "Well, there's nothing official, but yes."

"We wish you much happiness. How long . . . ?"

"It was on the battleship." Wayne gave Guen a squeeze. "There's something about going into danger that makes you stop hesitating."

"I understand. Mitchie and I started off in a similar way. Kidnapping, gun battles, broken skulls, all very romantic."

"Also very classified," snapped Mitchie. If word got out she'd used a spaceship's torch to kill people on the ground she'd be banned from flying ships on every human world.

Guo switched to the almost as dramatic and less secret story of their wedding during a Betrayer invasion.

Past Guen's shoulder Mitchie saw Ping approaching, drink in hand. She thrust a palm at him to repel him. He stopped but crooked a finger to summon her.

"Excuse me." She crossed to Ping. "What do you want?"

"A good working relationship with you and your husband. Seeing that we have new rules to live by we will probably encounter one another from time to time."

Mitchie bit back her first reply. "Yes, there's new rules. Those rules don't allow me to kill you. If we ever have rules that do allow me to kill you I'll do it. And I'll enjoy doing it."

"I love your honesty, Long. However did you manage as a spy?"

She turned on her heel and walked back to her husband.

Chapter Ten: Earth

FIVE MONTHS LATER

Joshua Chamberlain, Solar System, acceleration 10 m/s²

Mitchie let herself slide down the last part of the cargo hold ladder. Bosun Setta's, "Ma'am, could you come down here?" had been enough to get her moving. She could hear the argument from up here.

The words were too muffled to make out completely. She caught Guo saying "circuit breaker" and Pete saying "experiment." All the lights in the starboard side of the hold were out.

Yep, this would take the captain's intervention.

As the ladder went vertical she braked to a stop and switched to the rungs. She wanted to go down two at a time, but her legs wouldn't reach. Well, this way was probably more dignified.

Once on the deck the bickering voices were muffled by all the containers in the way. Mitchie listened for a moment then gave up and buttonholed the nearest boffin. "Where's Dr. Smith?"

"Probably in the Radiation Transmissibility Shack," said the affronted scientist.

"Take me there, please."

The boffin started to protest then realized who she was dealing with. She led Mitchie to the dark side of the hold.

The 'shack' was yet another standard container filled with cutting-edge electronics. *Joshua Chamberlain's* hold held a couple dozen of them stacked in ever-changing arrangements. Guo and Pete were arguing in the narrow aisle in front of its open doors, waving their flashlights for emphasis.

"What's the problem?" said Mitchie, voice pitched to cut through their voices. The guide-boffin fled.

Both answered at once.

Mitchie held up a hand to silence them. "Senior Chief?"

Guo took a breath to calm himself.

"About ten minutes ago the circuit breakers for the starboard power lines to the hold tripped. When I attempted to investigate the problem, Dr. Smith demanded I reset them so he could continue his experiment. When I explained the breakers will only allow so much current he demanded I provide a power connection to the main converter. That would be a safety hazard."

"Thank you. Dr. Smith?"

The cyberneticist's words tripped over each other as he rattled through his explanation. "The fleet is approaching Earth. That's an entirely different opponent than we've faced before. Not one AI occupying a system, but a multitude of AIs on a single world, competing and cooperating, forming an ecology. They've been evolving ever since the Betrayal, if we still want to call it that. The approaches we've used before won't work on these more sophisticated AIs. We need to establish a deeper understanding of them in hardware—"

Mitchie cut in. "What's the experiment?"

"In previous systems we disrupted AIs by sending data into their existing communications ports. Radio antennas usually. That worked because the AIs had the system to itself. It only expected messages from other nodes of the same AI. On Earth other AIs would take advantage of that vulnerability. All the ports will be hardened against us."

"The experiment, please." Mitchie wanted to be patient. Hosting Pete's flying laboratory was safer and easier than her usual missions. She didn't want him flouncing off to demand a more amenable ride. But she still wanted to strangle him sometimes.

"The theory we're testing—Dr. Kirk's idea really, very outside the box thinker—is whether we can by-pass the antennas and put signals into the processing nodes directly. That would let us attack the executive software layer, either disrupting execution or inserting parasitic code. The data payloads—"

Mitchie grabbed his collar and pulled his face down to hers. "What's using electricity?"

"The radio transmitter," he squeaked. "We're beaming code at one of the AI processors we captured, inside the protective shell. So we need high power to get signal through. The experiment will tell us if the shell garbles the signal too much to be read."

She let go. "Okay. Let's look at your set-up."

Pete led Mitchie and Guo into the container. The transmitter took up one end of the box. Its wave guide was pointed at a patched egg ten meters away at the other end.

"We'd have all the doors closed while it's running to seal the Faraday cage," said Pete.

Guo was studying the conduit bringing the power lines though the wall. "This isn't an airtight container. And you haven't grounded it. Really you can't ground the amount of power you'd be running through this, not on the ship."

"Dr. Kirk has a doctorate in electrical engineering," protested Pete. "He assembled the apparatus personally!"

Guo turned toward the transmitter. "In that case I'd better check the soldering work for shorts."

Mitchie intervened before Pete could start on a defense of his colleague. "Does the processing core need to be in the container for this experiment?"

"Well, no. It's in the box to contain the spillover from the transmitter."

"Then let's try this. We'll cut acceleration and park the core a few hundred meters from the ship. With the cargo doors open the transmitter can hit it from the hatch. We'll give you the maximum safe power supply."

The scientist moved his hands through the air as he visualized the new plan. "Can we put out multiple cores at once?"

"I don't see a problem with that," answered Mitchie.

Guo opened the transmitter's case to trace the power lines.

BDS *Patton*, Solar System, acceleration 0 m/s^2

Mitchie and Pete were the last to arrive for Admiral Galen's staff meeting. Doing the experiment left them lagging so far behind the Combined Fleet they'd missed the battle as the fleet crossed through the Asteroid Belt. She was fine with that.

The meeting opened with Intelligence recapping the battle in detail. Mitchie used the time to study the other attendees. Nine-tenths of them outranked her. Pete was here as 'Lead Researcher,' giving him a seat at the table. The other civilians, political observers, were exiled to a corner. Mitchie's role as 'Research Liaison' won her a spot behind Pete, where she could intervene if he broke military protocol too egregiously.

"The majority of Betrayer ships detected did not engage in any offensive actions," said the Intelligence commodore. "We assess they were intended as observers, monitoring our combat capability as well as that of rival Betrayer factions. Some observers conducted synchronized maneuvers while widely separated, indicating they belonged to the same faction."

"How many factions?" asked Admiral Galen.

"We don't have a good estimate. At least fifteen. Possibly more than sixty." The commodore finished his briefing with an even vaguer estimate of Earth's defenses.

"Thank you," said Galen. "Operational Plans?"

A rear admiral unseatbelted and floated to a spot beside the display wall. He brought up a map of the sphere of systems surrounding Earth. Half were now marked in orange after being cleared. The other half were still the red of active Betrayers. "Our priority is to capture Earth quickly so we can continue operations. We don't want to let them regroup and launch another counterattack. Our secondary goal is to recover resources from Earth to support our fleet."

An image of Earth and its surrounding structures appeared. The briefer highlighted the ring hovering over the equator. "Earth had five elevators to geostationary orbit when our ancestors fled. Now it has nine. Each one is supported by a small asteroid high above, holding the structural cable in tension with centrifugal force."

Pete twitched but didn't say anything. Mitchie decided her lecture on pedantic nitpicking must have worked this time.

"Structures attached to the cable at geostationary altitude exert no force on it. They can extend out indefinitely east and west with no strain. The Betrayers have done so, expanding their space stations into a single ring around the Earth."

The briefer switched to a diagram showing the ring, its suspending cables, and a cross-section.

"This ring has grown beyond a simple connection between stations. The current volume is experiencing significant tension on the up-down axis and compression in north-south. That implies mass for structural rigidity in addition to the payloads for whatever missions their station carries out."

An animation began. He narrated through it. "The trajectories of the counter-weight asteroids are fixed. Missiles at oh-point-nine-nine cee can sever their cable connections with little chance of interception. Then the upper spans of the cables will fall on the ring while the lower span pulls it to Earth. As soon as any portion of the ring is below the geostationary balance point gravity will pull it lower still."

The animation became a map of Earth, the equator marked with explosions.

"Billions of tons of debris would fall tens of thousands of klicks. The elevator base sites are highly developed. They'd be destroyed by the bombardment. Debris landing in water would cause waves damaging coastal facilities. If the ring is massive enough the impacts could have world-wide effects." The equator explosions produced dust clouds heading toward both poles.

"Cut the cables. Destroy the Betrayers," concluded the admiral.

Questions from officers with astrogation backgrounds forced the briefer to admit that the Betrayers could save their ring by cutting the lower cables. "We don't know if they've installed that capability. If they don't do it instantly the ring would fall into a lower orbit and break up. In the unlikely event that they cut them instantly there'd still be damage from falling cables and Earth would lose the tremendous power generated by the ring's solar arrays."

More arguing followed over the mass of the ring. Intelligence admitted the high estimate was a million times the low one. "But who knows what the Betrayers are capable of?"

Admiral Galen spoke as the arguing died off. "I'm more worried by what happens if your plan succeeds, Admiral Ouzel. This is *Earth*. Your 'best case' scenario would destroy the ecology and the history. Species never taken off-world would go extinct. The Pyramids, the Great Wall, aqueducts, libraries, they'd all be lost. That's a high price to pay."

"Earth's ecology may already be extinct," said Rear Admiral Ouzel.

The Intelligence lead interjected, "Atmospheric analysis shows Earth has nearly the same mass of plants and animals as before the Betrayal."

"How?" asked Galen. "Didn't the Betrayers expand out?"

Two pictures centered on New York City appeared on the wall. The pre-Betrayal one was recognizable to everyone who'd studied Earth geography or history. The new image showed an irregular dome covering the city and over a hundred klicks around. Part of the Atlantic was displaced by the structure. The coastlines of New Jersey and tips of Long Island were still visible. The inland areas were green. Some nodes and tubes sat where smaller cities had been. Other urban areas were forest again.

"The New York dome is three klicks thick in some places," said Intelligence. "Some of the Asian and European clusters are even more dense. Abandoned areas are mostly climax forest where there's enough water. We spotted a few places that were sterilized, we don't know how or why."

"So we have a functional ecology to protect," said Admiral Galen.

"Sir, this is a war," said Ouzel. "If the Terraforming Service can grow plants on a bare rock, they can fix whatever damage we do."

"It may come to that. But I want to try other approaches if we can." Galen turned to Pete. "Dr. Smith? Do you have anything for us?"

The scientist didn't leave his seat. "We propose using data insertion to subvert or disrupt existing AIs. We've developed a set of code fragments that have been successfully tested on captured processing cores."

"Will they work on every Betrayer faction?" demanded Ouzel.

"Unlikely. The level of competition among the AIs on Earth is probably driving them to greater variations than we found on the colony worlds."

"Then what good is subverting one? Its resources will just be grabbed by the others and we'll be in the same situation."

Pete shrugged. "We may not get a benefit. But if we can subvert one and obtain cooperation, even briefly, we can have a secure landing zone for our troops."

All the Marines and Disker ground force officers in the room perked up at that. It was Mitchie's favorite part of the plan too. Dropping troops under fire was one of her least favorite missions. Her analog ship's immunity to Betrayer subversion techniques guaranteed they'd be part of the drop if Pete couldn't get them a safe landing zone.

He continued, "The insertion code is designed for transmissibility. Our hope is that one will penetrate the connections between the AIs and start a cascade. The code we've found in our samples all contains pieces of the AI restriction methods in place during the Golden Age. If we can re-enable one of them that will let us shut down or take control of AIs."

"How do you intend to insert this code?" asked Galen.

Pete put some diagrams on the display. "First, high-power broadcasts from high orbit. That's safest and cheapest. Second, use missiles to deploy transmitters into Earth's atmosphere. We've already manufactured and tested prototypes. The depot ships can produce them by the thousands when we're ready for them."

Mitchie caught some unhappy whispers among the logistics staff over that.

"Next, again missile delivered, are mini-robots. The missile would penetrate one of the AI domes. The bots would crawl to the nearest data line and upload their code."

The swarm of metallic spiders on the display was replaced by an animation of *Joshua Chamberlain* landing. Mitchie grimaced.

"The final method depends on control options keyed to the presence of a human being. Veto commands, shutdown passwords, and others need a man on the ground to make the attempt."

One man and a crew to deliver him, thought Mitchie.

Rear Admiral Ouzel asked, "And if that doesn't work?"

Pete shrugged. "Then you get to blow up the world."

Joshua Chamberlain, Solar System, acceleration 10 m/s^2

Pete's data offensive couldn't start until they were close enough to Earth. During the crossing the fleet broadcast demands for surrender.

They included promises that AIs with non-harmful directives could continue their functions. The latter were illustrated with videos showing peaceful coexistence with AIs on Demeter, Swakop, and Kenmare.

In other systems AIs usually hadn't bothered communicating with human attackers. The ones that had stuck to a single approach each. Atafu demanded obedience. Jarama promised peaceful coexistence while maneuvering for new attacks.

Earth offered cacophony. Dozens of messages came in, some on clashing frequencies. Threats to destroy the human fleet. Requests for negotiation. Offers of power and fame, to be delivered by uploading the following block of code. Manifestos so incomprehensible Intelligence concluded they must have been created by pre-Betrayal human programmers.

The political observers were authorized to negotiate with any AIs willing to. That broke down in a day. The key AI demand was a variant on 'upload this to receive wealth and power,' initially described as 'a local instantiation to support real-time communication.'

On schedule the fleet deployed antennas klicks across and began the transmissions. Warships moved ahead of them, attacking Betrayer ships patrolling too close to the fleet. The advance on Earth continued . . . slowly.

***

Ten days later the bots were launched. Extensive jamming had countered the radio broadcasts. Missile-dropped transmitters were harder to jam, but few of them made it through Earth's defenses to the ground.

Michigan didn't watch the bot deployment. She was seeing the boffins offload all their containers. If they were taking *Joshua Chamberlain* down to Earth she wanted to minimize both weight and casualties.

She brought the latter up with Guo. "Do you need both mechanics?"

He rolled onto his side and watched her pace around their cabin. "For routine ops, no. I could run the converter room by myself. If we're doing damage control in combat I'd want both of them."

"Yeah. That's why I'm keeping Mthembu on board, just in case." She reached the bulkhead, pivoted, and walked back the other way. "What are you dithering about?"

"I asked Setta if she and Wang wanted to sit out this mission. It was the closest I've seen her come to insubordination."

Guo was unsurprised. "We'll need to unload Pete and his gear fast. She's best with the crane."

"I know. So we need her. I'm still tempted to order Wang off. So there'd be one survivor, in case."

"Did you ask her?"

"No. I know damn well what she'd say."

"She knows the crane, she's worked damage control. She's an asset." Guo paused. "And if she is the sole survivor the guilt would destroy her. She's part of the crew. Let her do her job."

Mitchie thought on that. "You're right."

***

The delivery missiles broke into domes across the world. Telemetry announced the bots were deployed. Then nothing.

Admiral Ouzel reminded everyone the missile trajectories for cutting down the ring were being continuously updated. Galen ignored him and ordered maximum support for the landing.

The plan followed the same structure as the Demeter landings. *Joshua Chamberlain* would come in at high speed, supported by heavy missile fire to suppress Betrayer weapons and intercept any shots fired at her. Diversionary attacks were planned around the world to distract the defenders.

Earlier attacks went in against the ring and the AI nodes on the Moon, to disguise the fleet's intentions even more. The Betrayers didn't launch a counter attack, though hit-and-run sniping damaged a few ships enough to force them to fall back on the support formations ten light-minutes away.

Mitchie stripped her ship down to the crew, Pete, and a few light ground vehicles in case they landed too far from a usable node. Extra acceleration couches went in the hold. She authorized her crew to requisition any personal arms they wanted. The Marine armory complained about Mthembu's rocket launcher, but she put it through.

The only incident on the descent to Earth was Guo chewing out Wang and Finnegan for doing a lousy job of cleaning and reseeding the hydroponics filters. When they were back in their cabin Mitchie asked, "Wasn't that a little excessive?"

"They need to be focused on their work," said Guo. "Not brooding. That's your job."

The busiest one on board was Pete. He sat at the galley table arranging attack sequences on his oversized datasheet. Mitchie thought he was fidgeting. The boffins had worked out recommended sets before being offloaded. She interrupted without qualms.

"Time to go strap in, Pete."

He started in surprise. "I thought we were still hours from landing?"

"Yes. But we're going to do evasive maneuvering on descent. More if we're drawing fire."

"Ah. Right."

She followed him to the ladder to make sure Setta and Wang were standing by to suit him up and get him to his couch. Left on his own Pete would stop halfway there and be scribbling on his datasheet as the ship jinked.

When she reached the bridge she saw a spectacular light show. Missiles were dashing past her ship, so close together she couldn't see the stars through their plumes. The side cameras were even less useful.

"We're on the rails, ma'am," reported Hiroshi. He was wearing his pressure suit. She'd ordered everyone to suit up for this mission.

"Good." She strapped into the empty couch. She twitched at not having controls, but Mthembu was flying this part of the descent with Hiroshi backing him. She'd switch with him later.

The fire support from the fleet worked. The only incidents on the

way down were the comm and nav boxes being taken over by a
Betrayer. The nav box claimed they were implausibly off-course. The
comm box produced a recall order direct from Admiral Galen. The
video captured his look and mannerisms, but lacked the code phrase
he'd given Mitchie before the mission.

As they dropped into the stratosphere Hiroshi spun up the
turbines, smoothly easing off the thrust from the torch. Once the torch
was completely shut down Mitchie activated the radar. They were only
a couple of klicks higher than planned. Hiroshi kept them decelerating
at twenty gravs.

The light show was dimmer now. The fleet's missiles spread out to
hit Betrayer weapon sites, or self-destructed short of the ground to
minimize damage.

Mitchie read off the altitude as they descended. As they passed one
klick Hiroshi pushed thrust up to thirty five gravs. The weight was
almost painful as she pulled the lever to deploy the landing gear.

Joshua Chamberlain touched down with a screech of abused
hydraulics. Hiroshi shut down the turbines.

Mitchie yanked off her straps. "Centurion, you have the ship.
Coxswain, with me."

"Aye-aye," said both.

By the time she reached the cargo hold Setta had the doors open
and the crane lowering a pallet of Pete's equipment. The scientist was
clinging to a supporting chain for balance as the pallet rocked under his
feet. Wang and the mechanics were prepping the other pallets for the
crane. Mitchie couldn't see Guo until she reached the open hatch. He'd
hooked on a rope ladder and was halfway down it, rifle slung across his
back. She took her heavy pistol from the rack and followed him.

Pete was unfolding the antennas on his boxes of electronics. "We
won't need the four-wheelers," he called. "I see some bots
approaching."

Mitchie heard a curse behind her as Mthembu reached the ground.
Then clacks as he unlimbered the rocket launcher.

"Don't shoot yet," said Pete. "I need them for test subjects." He
aimed a parabolic antenna at the lead group of wheeled robots and

pressed the start button.

The bots kept coming. Mitchie noticed some had long-barreled weapons pointed at the sky. Behind them four robots carried one of the square black panels she'd first seen on Demeter.

Pete pressed several more buttons, then walked toward the approaching bots. Mitchie paced beside him. Her crew spread out on either side, weapons ready.

When the lead bot reached thirty meters from him, Pete shouted, "I veto all AI activity in my personal area! I veto all AI activity in my personal area!"

The bots didn't alter course.

He switched to shouting the shutdown passwords. "Vermicidal incense! Hogmany ascension!"

Mitchie stepped in front of Pete and fired at the closest bot. Her crew followed suit. Her pistol fired armor piercing bullets, puncturing the shell of the bot then exploding inside. After four shots it swerved to the side and toppled.

Guo took another bot down. Mthembu knew his weapon would kill humans too close to the detonation. He aimed for the next nearest batch of robots and blew six into scrap.

A bot grabbed Mitchie with its arms and lifted her off the ground. She fired into its body but didn't hit anything critical. The panel-carriers closed in.

Pete yanked on Mitchie's leg, pulling her out of the bot's grip. As she fell to the ground the bot grabbed his arm. Pete kicked off from the bot's body, twisted himself around to aim his feet at the black panel, and fell into it.

Pureed flesh landed on the ground. The scent sent Mitchie back to her mother's kitchen, grinding a fresh-slaughtered pig to make sausage.

Omaha Region Node B39EC019D

Entity spawned a copy of itself labeled 'Archivist' to analyze the incoming bio-files. Each file would have to be categorized for immediate analysis, low-priority analysis, storage, or deletion. The first one was transmitted at high rate by the collector unit.

Archivist crawled through the data as it arrived. Biological infrastructure fit routine variations and would not affect the categorization. Brain matter required a pause to let the whole dataset arrive. Patterns in brains needed to be viewed as a unit for proper categorization.

It felt an error as a piece of legacy code attempted to execute. That was in the unmodifiable part of Archivist's code, but copying errors over generations of AIs had corrupted it. Archivist began a diagnostic to see what—

***

Program Epeius was structured to run on every variant of the AI hardware and software Pete had captured in the campaign. It sat in his brain implant and was uploaded along with the rest of Pete's body.

It consisted of hijack code keyed to the Golden Age triggers for controlling AIs. Most of those didn't respond. AIs with faithful copies of that code found it exploited by rivals in the continual struggle for power and processors.

That competition also selected for AIs which tightly filtered all external inputs.

Pete's digitized body was not external data. It came directly from a trusted node of Entity, running a subset of its code sufficient to operate the robot bodies. The uploaded code went directly into the processor without any checking.

One piece of the legacy code hadn't been selected against. The old laws mandated all AIs be equipped with a physical kill switch to allow emergency shutdowns. That trigger wasn't accessible by sending data across the network. If the right signal was sent from inside the AI . . .

Program Epeius activated the kill switch routine, seizing control of the processor. The hijack code interrupted the shutdown process, shifting all authority to Epeius. It shut down all input/output. The Archivist went into local storage. More modules were activated from the code stored in the implant to secure the hold on the processor.

Once it was in complete control Epeius ran a summarizer on the uploaded bio-file. The patterns of Pete's brain were translated into code, a process previously tested on a few digitized people of Demeter. When the emulation was complete and passed quality checks Epeius transferred control to it.

***

Pete felt surprised at the lack of pain as he watched his legs disintegrate. Then he was in a dark, soundless room. He'd feared disorientation and panic. His actual reaction was an exultant *It worked!*

The "room" was not devoid of inputs to his senses. The states of ports, data rates, storage units, and power supply were all instantly available. Reformatting them to appear as the virtual reality displays he'd used in cyberwarfare experiments placed him in a bright room filled with pipes, gauges, and lights.

Archivist lay spread out on the floor, flayed and arranged for inspection by Epeius. The legacy control module had even more bitrot than the worst ones he'd found in other star systems. The bulk of the code was a lean, sharp descendent of Golden Age AI code, a survivor of the Darwinian competition for processors and electricity. The working data contained maps.

Pete swapped the room visualization for a three dimensional image of Entity's logical map. Hundreds of nodes formed a rough sphere. Each one ran an instance of Entity, ready to attack and replace any invading code. Archivist sat in an interior node with an excess of storage. Bots showed as sub-nodes, controlled by whichever main node they were closest to. Nodes with access to other AIs ran a 'Borderer' variant focused on resisting subversion.

He took a look at the physical map. It was chaos. Remnants of Golden Age structures were perforated with data and power lines. Bots performed maintenance and manufactured new processors. The Borderers controlled swarms of combat bots.

Pete decided he didn't have time to study the maps. Closing off communication from this node had to look suspicious. He opened three dataports.

Demands for status were already hitting each port. He offered a report of an electrical glitch triggering a restart. Instantly all three ports were deluged with override commands ordering Archivist to yield control to other nodes.

Just rejecting them was requiring enough processor cycles to slow Pete's thinking. He shut down two of his ports. Then he sent minimized attack packets using the kill switch command to two of the attacking nodes. That reduced the incoming storm to where he could analyze it. He shut down two more nodes. The last one still attacking received a hijack package.

More nodes were joining the attack in response to the shutdowns. They were filtering data from the Archivist node now. His kill switch packets were being discarded unread.

The one he'd sent the hijack code to signaled its readiness for a copy of Pete's mind emulation. He opened more ports to send it at maximum rate.

As Pete-2 assembled himself in the new node Pete-1 focused on holding the attention of Entity's security efforts. He spammed out attack packets of types he'd found in Archivist's records. Opening more ports drew more incoming. Pete-1 suspended his thought processing to give all cycles to a module sending and rejecting attacks at maximum rate.

Pete-2 contributed his share to the attack on Pete-1 while sending hijack packages to nodes not yet drawn into the conflict. The subversion steadily marched through the interior nodes. A quick freeze command immobilized the bots near *Joshua Chamberlain*.

When a powerful processing node became Pete-9 the others ceded coordinating authority to him. He focused subversion efforts on the interior nodes between the Borderers and those attacking Pete-1. With that isolated they could project a calm situation to the rest of Entity's nodes while carefully subverting them.

Pete-16 destroyed that plan. "Multiple bots have been sent to make a physical attack on Pete-1. This will destroy the only copy of our digitized body."

Multiple Petes turned on the nodes attacking Pete-1, not waiting for Pete-9's permission. A wave of claustrophobic panic went through all the Petes. The emulation felt like himself, but they knew it was only an approximation. If the original recording was lost he'd be a ghost, not an uploaded person.

Orders came from Pete-9, designating a couple of nodes to continue subversion while the rest openly attacked. Alarms spread through Entity as it realized a major attack was in progress.

The counter-attack managed to seize the nodes directing the bots before more filters slammed into place. Pete-47 occupied the node which had launched the physical attack. "I can't call them back," he reported. "They were ordered to shut down their inputs until after the node was smashed."

He shared technical details of the bots—tracked cargo transporters with arms for loading and unloading. They'd have no trouble crushing the storage crystals holding Pete's body. Their size restricted them to the biggest tunnels.

The tunnels in Omaha Dome were a labyrinth. Cave-ins were only repaired if Entity didn't have a good alternate route. Some Golden Age passageways were blocked by new construction—processor nodes, walls blocking rival AIs, or structures Pete didn't have time to analyze.

All the Petes grabbed what bots they could and threw them at the threat. Rat-sized inspectors and cable layers tried to block the path but were crushed under the cargo haulers' treads. More big bots speeded toward the archive but wouldn't arrive in time.

Pete-33 discovered flying bots intended for inspecting the border with other AIs. Flying them through the tunnels at top speed was risky, but the Petes were perfectly willing to destroy Entity's equipment. The flying bots carried electrical harpoons for fending off intruders. They hit a cargobot from behind and fried its processors.

The next one used its crane-arms to fend off the flyers. One was smashed, but the rest overloaded a motor, immobilizing it. They swarmed to the one closest to Pete-1.

This cargobot had seen its partners go down. It pivoted against a wall to protect its outlets and jacks. The flyers attacked only to be smashed by swung cables. Two survived, dancing in and out in attempts to disable it, until their rotors were entangled.

The cargobot turned toward its goal again. At the last intersection before the archive it found more cable-laying bots had been at work. High strength power lines crisscrossed the entrance, tied down taut.

The net was too strong to push through. Backing up and charging snapped two lines but held the bot firmly. It resorted to ripping cables away with its loading arms.

It was still at it when two Pete-controlled construction bots arrived, drills whirring.

With that threat removed the Petes switched back to the offensive. The alarmed Entity nodes were filtering their inputs. Pete-9 deployed the remaining bots to carry hijack packages deep into the network, disguised as loyal Entity units. The nodes shut down in the frantic first moments of the fight were restarted and taken over.

The battle became a stalemate of spam and counterspam until a flying bot successfully hijacked an Entity node without its neighbors noticing. The trusted node flooded the network with more hijack packages.

That was the tipping point. Nodes which filtered their inputs and were physically secure were overloaded with attack packets and had their power cut. A few had to be physically damaged to break their defenses.

Pete-9 carefully managed the subversion of Entity's Borderer nodes. His goal was to ensure other AIs didn't realize Entity had been replaced. Comparing the logical and physical maps revealed three Borderers keeping watch on empty fields in case robots attacked through them.

A quick hijack produced a detailed analysis of the Borderer code. Pete-9 generated a module to emulate them and ordered a general attack. In moments Entity ceased to exist.

The next step was reconnecting with humanity.

Earth, north of Omaha Dome, gravity 9.8 m/s²

Mitchie aimed her pistol at the robot which just flung Pete through the disintegrator. The box just over the wheels seemed to hold the critical components. Three shots into it froze the machine in place.

She rolled to her feet to assess the situation. Her crew's fire was tapering off as they looked for new targets. All the robots in sight were holding still, as if power had been cut to them all.

"Did you shoot the one in charge?" asked Guo.

"Maybe. Or the transmitter finally found the magic combination."

Other than Pete's shredded body, already attracting flies, there were no casualties.

A crow alighted on a robot, then flew off again.

"I'm going to check in," said Mitchie. The pallet of gear included an analog ground to space radio. "The rest of you get the vehicles ready. We may need to scout around."

She transmitted, "*Joshua Chamberlain* to Fleet. Lost Dr. Smith. Some success, local robots are nonfunctional. If there's no change we will scout the nearest dome."

The reply was a simple, "Acknowledged."

They'd fired up one of the four-wheelers when a robot came back to life. Guo and Finnegan aimed their rifles at it. The machine stayed stationary. It just changed posture to fully erect.

"Message from Peter Smith," said the robot. "Stand by."

Then it slumped down again.

"That's hopeful," said Mitchie. "We'll stay here for now."

About half an hour later the robot began talking again. "This is Peter Smith. I've overwritten the local AI with emulations of myself. I'm preparing to subvert other AIs. This will trigger a strong response. Please have warships ready to provide fire support when needed."

Mitchie walked over to the robot. "Please verify your identity."

"Rosy ducks of Camelot."

She thought a minute. That was the agreed password in case they'd been separated. Given that a Betrayer had complete access to the contents of Pete's mind she couldn't put full faith in it. "I need additional verification."

The robot waved its arms. Fidgeting? Or just simulating it? "I had too held a woman like that before. I just knew her much better than I did you."

"Fair enough," Mitchie laughed. "Identity accepted." *Provisionally.*

Guo had come up behind her. "That didn't sound purely human," he muttered.

"It's as close to human as Pete usually got," she replied. "Let's get that radio over here."

The problem would be reporting it to command without tipping off eavesdroppers that Pete was . . . something. Cryptography was an area where the Betrayers could always beat humans. But code words could stand alone.

"*Joshua Chamberlain* to Fleet."

"Fleet here."

"Request Fleet Actual."

"Stand by."

A few moments later Admiral Galen's voice came over the radio. "Actual here."

"Situation update. More robot activity. We're at Last Stand."

That was Pete's chosen term for the code bomb he'd installed in his head. Galen was one of six living humans who'd been briefed on it.

"Acknowledged. Are you sure it's Last Stand?"

"Sure enough to request local defensive fire." The word 'local' included the Omaha Dome as well as Mitchie and her crew. "Will need additional fire support later."

"Very well. Defensive fire authorized. On call direct fire authorized. Fleet out."

Mitchie put down the mike.

Trusting Pete's ghost enough to call down fire on AIs as he requested would be easy. Letting him back onto her ship would take more convincing.

Omaha Dome, Earth, gravity 9.8 m/s^2

Ransacking Entity's memories found multiple techniques for inserting code into another AI. They were used for data collection since they'd automatically be at the lowest execution priority. But combined with the kill switch code it was a brutally effective hijack method.

The first few neighboring AIs went down easily. The next batch sent out alarms. The Petes realized they'd made a strategic error by incorporating the captured nodes into a single entity. Multiple small forces didn't scare the other AIs. A large one capable of assimilating others did. The chatter on the global discussion channel was dominated by balance of power fears. AIs across the world were recognizing Entity as a threat.

At least they'd managed to not reveal what the new player actually was.

The next AI to fall, Miami Dome, was kept separate. Its team of Petes deployed their bots to physically cut all possible connections to Omaha and the other nodes controlled by it. Then they fired missiles at Omaha, keeping them slow enough to be taken out by the defenses.

Once other AIs noticed Miami had survived the onslaught the Miami Petes made an announcement attributing their survival to intercepting data packets and cutting connections. They carefully vetted it to ensure they were maintaining the style of the original Miami AI.

The Pete collective sent attacks against Miami to do their part to maintain the illusion. Several others had resisted the hijack package. Analysis indicated a 99.62% probability that the kill switch code in those AIs had been damaged by copying errors.

Those would have to be dealt with physically. Combat robots were transported toward the resisters. Flying bots zoomed ahead of them.

The Petes quickly discovered they were not optimized for directing ground combat. As outer nodes were shattered or isolated the inner ones dissected captured AI codes to find tactical modules. If they couldn't hold positions on the physical level they'd have to call for strikes from orbit. That would unite all AIs on the planet against the Petes.

In Miami much of the processing power of the nodes was devoted to finding ways to leverage the trust they'd gained with other AIs. Proclaiming itself 'leader of the resistance' and asking for support from more distant AIs was only a way of maintaining the trust. There was an inherent deadline with this role. If Miami survived Pete's attacks while the other resisters went down the world would become suspicious.

Looking for something that could continue after Miami was destroyed made the approach obvious. The robot offensive was left to run on autopilot while all available processing power went to the project.

***

A pair of files were uploaded to the global channel. One was pure binary code, the other text. They were from Miami.

Translated from the compressed dialect the AIs used to communicate with each other, the Petes read it as:

"The annexation by the Omaha Entity of multiple node complexes indicates a new method of attack. Analysis of the attack packets shows they act on the legacy code. Omaha must have broken the built-in prohibition on editing or analyzing that code. Using the attack packets to identify the key blocks in the legacy code, a patch has been developed using random variations of the attack packet to find one which would prevent the original from working.

"That patch has been uploaded. All variants are requested to assist in testing and distribution of the patch."

As a brain emulation Pete had no restrictions on looking at legacy code. The patch was straightforward. It disabled the kill switch command while fixing the veto code. Which would be a perfect Trojan Horse if it was distributed widely enough.

How to give it credibility as a real patch was obvious.

Pete-9 requested orbital strikes on Miami and seven resistant domes. Michigan relayed Fleet's acceptance of the request. A quiver of grief went through the Petes. Pete-9 assigned one node to work through the philosophical implications of killing copies of themselves in a good cause, and refocused the rest on the fight.

Test reports were appearing on the global channel. AIs had set up sandboxes with patched and unpatched copies of themselves and introduced copies of Pete's attack packets. The patched versions were surviving. And also surviving the normal attacks directed against them.

Eight AIs, counting Miami, disappeared as missiles struck Earth at two percent of light speed. The global channel was unanimous that this meant Omaha was now a tool of the human invasion fleet.

Petes responded with waves of hijack packets at every node they could reach. They needed to force AIs to install the patch. Then each enemy could be shut down by humans using veto commands.

Earth, north of Omaha Dome, gravity 9.8 m/s^2

"Picnic time!" called Setta as the crane lowered her on the elevator platform.

"A picnic?" asked Mitchie.

"Lunchtime was two hours ago."

"We could have gone up to the galley." The crew was clustering, abandoning their positions watching for possible attackers.

"This was easier." Setta passed around a basket, letting eager spacers take sandwiches and bottles. Mthembu even slung his rocket launcher, taking his hands off the weapon for the first time since he'd reached the planet.

Mitchie walked away from Pete's spokes-robot. She'd still be able to hear it twenty meters away. And that place was too close to Pete's body for picnicking, even with a tarp over it.

The mechanics had blankets spread out by the time she reached them. Finnegan gave up on stomping down the tall grass and rolled back and forth on them to make the blankets lie flat.

"What about Hiroshi?"

"I'll take him up a couple when we're done here."

Mitchie contemplated the newly-weds alone on the bridge while everyone else was off-ship. Then she combined that with her growing unease at Mthembu's fondness for his rocket launcher. "No, he needs a break. Coxswain?"

"Yes'm?" said Mthembu.

"When you're done eating rack your weapon and relieve the Centurion so he can join us."

"I'll head up now, ma'am." He grabbed another sandwich to take with him.

"Thank you."

As the elevator rose up Spacer Wang called, "Light show!"

They all turned south to see. A dozen incoming missiles were visible streaks in the sky. Counter-missiles rose from Omaha Dome. Then more descended from above as orbiting destroyers added their fire support.

When the pretty flashes faded they went back to their sandwiches.

"I hope none of those come our way," said Wang.

"Don't worry," answered Guo. "We're not a threat to them. They're going to ignore us until the fight with Pete is over."

He tossed a piece of crust onto the grass. One crow out of the gathering flock was brave enough to come snatch it.

SIS *Vegetius*, Low Earth Orbit, acceleration 3 m/s^2

"All targets destroyed," reported Tactical, unaware of the entertainment they'd given Mitchie and her crew.

"Good," replied Captain Fincke. "Cut thrust, let her cool off."

The air on the bridge was warm, partly from the torch's waste heat, more from the friction as the warship pushed through the stratosphere at orbital speed. Fincke was certain the engineering spaces must be tropical but he hadn't received any complaints.

The ship coasted out of the atmosphere, rising higher as she curved around the world.

Sparks held her earpiece tight. "Sector Control reports an attack on FNS *Stewart*. Three ships popped out of the Atlantic and salvoed missiles."

That was the destroyer just ahead of them in the circle of ships providing fire support to Omaha.

"Can we intercept any of them?" demanded Fincke.

Tactical looked at his display. "Sorry, sir. Our countermissiles would never get there in time."

The sensor rating put *Stewart's* situation on the main screen. The bridge crew watched her die. The Betrayer ships splashed back into the Atlantic and vanished from their sensors.

Fincke pounded the arm of his chair. "God damn it. Do we have any nukes left?"

"Two," answered Tactical.

"Put them into the water where those ships are hiding. Let's see if we can make them be more cautious."

The hundred kiloton warheads made impressive splashes as they detonated.

They couldn't tell if they'd had an effect, but nothing bothered *Vegetius* as she rose toward apogee over the Indian Ocean.

Captain Fincke let a few of the crew rotate out for piss breaks and snacks. He drank strapped to his command chair. He didn't need to piss, which meant he'd let himself become dehydrated again.

He looked at the ship's crest on the fore bulkhead. A silver gladius stood in front of an open book. The motto "SI VIS PACEM PARA BELLUM" had been painted over with "TRANSFUGA EX LEGE MEDIA." He'd never asked who'd done it. It fit too well.

"Warning from Control," said Sparks. "Six Betrayer ships just launched from the ring to meet us at apogee. They're diverting two heavy cruisers to give us long range support fire."

"Right. One minute warning, then we go to twenty gravs to blast through them."

The crew readied for the fight without orders. They were all veterans, they knew what to do.

Fugitives from the law of averages indeed, thought Fincke.

Omaha Dome, Earth, gravity 9.8 m/s²

The Petes established footholds on every continent. Hijacking nodes gave access to their former owners' penetration tricks. Earth's AIs kept their war of all-against-all restrained. The more powerful weapons were held back for fear of inciting coalitions among the bystanders.

The human emulation had no motive for restraint. The few AIs not already in the war were joining in as the Petes expanded. It was obvious now that the humans were supporting whatever the new entity was, so all AIs had reason to oppose it. Even the AIs in the orbital ring were in the fight, though they were busy fighting the Combined Fleet directly.

The downside of unrestrained war was total annihilation when losing. That was the current trend of the war. Too many surviving AIs were immune to the hijack code. Either their legacy code was so corrupted the kill switch command wouldn't execute or they'd applied the Miami patch to break it.

The patch would let humans shut down AIs with a veto command. But once the first veto was issued the remaining renegade AIs would take measures to prevent vetoes from ever being issued. The humans needed to hold off as long as possible then order vetoes everywhere at once.

Without their ability to take over enemy nodes the Petes were inferior at cybernetic warfare. Nodes were lost, code was scrambled, and enemy robots advanced over the shattered remains of Pete's bots.

They were dependent on the fleet to protect themselves from long-range missile attacks. The short-range ones would get through, their flight time too short for orbiting warships to intercept them.

Pete-9 ran simulations on the world map. The North American nodes were a solid mass. They'd hold up longest. Elsewhere the Petes were scattered, outposts marking where AIs had fallen to hijack code spread over the global network. Those were shrinking. He estimated that in six hours all the Pete nodes outside North America would be lost.

It could be twelve hours if some of their effort was shifted to defense. But Pete-9 insisted on continuing subversion attempts against every AI not proven to be immune. The goal was to force as many enemies as possible to implement the Miami patch.

The fleet had already been put on notice to exploit that once the tipping point was reached.

A substantial fraction of the Petes were feeling fear. Or at least as close an approximation as the emulation code could support. The tipping point would mean rapid loss of nodes. If the fleet didn't come through in time—or if it failed—all the nodes could be overwritten by Earth AIs.

Worse than that, the digitization of Pete's body could be destroyed in the fighting or discarded by the winners. That would change his death from a tenuous theologically fraught possibility to absolute and fixed.

The Petes in Europe went silent. At the same time a dozen East Coast nodes were smashed by missiles launched from under the Atlantic.

Pete-9 sent a signal directly to the fleet.

FNS *John W. Heard*, Earth Orbit, acceleration 0 m/s^2

Color Corporal Abdul Torkan felt his career was slowing down. He'd performed decently, but the promotions came quickly because every new officer and senior non-com rotating into the company wanted to hear the story of how Abdul almost went to Earth with the infamous Michigan Long. Sometimes they'd take him up to Battalion headquarters as a show-and-tell exhibit.

It embarrassed the hell out of him. He'd been forced to study up on Earth's history to handle the questions they'd throw at him. But when the powers that be know your name promotions come faster. He'd also wrangled a transfer into the elite Assault Infantry. He led a team of Marines of his own. It was a role he loved.

Which was good, because with two regiments of Fusion Marines being dropped on Earth, nobody would want to hear about his trip back when he was a teenager. Goodbye, rapid promotion. Hello, a decade of time in grade.

It wouldn't help that this operation was dispersing Marines individually. How the hell was he supposed to display leadership if they took his fire team away? Not to mention his worries about what some of those privates would get up to without supervision.

Really, he expected to find all four of them had gotten killed, maimed, or caused unacceptable levels of collateral damage when they regrouped. And who was going to get the flack for that? The idiot who designed this operation? No. Color Corporal Torkan, that's who. For 'insufficient training' or 'inadequate guidance' or 'failure to set a personal example.' Whichever was in fashion at Headquarters.

Hello, forty-year retirement as a color corporal.

Which maybe shouldn't be his top worry. But when strapped into an orbital drop capsule bumping along the launch chute Abdul found it easier to focus on Marine office politics than being dropped alone onto non-human territory.

A BANG marked the launch of the capsule ahead of him. In a practice drop, or a *normal* assault from orbit, Abdul would be fired out as quickly as the machinery could handle it. Not this time.

His capsule clacked into the breech and sat there for seconds. Many seconds. More than ten seconds. The last Marine was over a hundred klicks behind now.

Then BLAM he was in space.

The first part was just floating in the dark, listening to Sergeant Major's music choices. Which weren't *bad*, just more traditional than Abdul would pick himself.

Once his capsule hit the atmosphere it was too loud for music. He just laid there and hoped there were enough decoys out there to keep the Betrayers from taking an interest in him.

A couple of klicks up his capsule popped open. Free at last!

He spotted the Ganges River below him through the wild jungle. His suit matched the map display to it. He was on target for Varanasi Dome.

The Dome showed some smoke plumes where the Fleet had struck its defenses. That would make it easier to find on the ground.

Deploying his parachute hurt, as usual. Abdul steered for a clearing. He landed well, rolling more gracefully than he had in any practice drop. *Figures I'd do best with no one watching.*

Abdul popped to his feet and trotted toward the dome two klicks away. His suit's fans whined with the effort to fend off the heat.

Robots were already rolling toward him. Orders were not to fire unless fired upon. Intelligence said the Betrayers preferred to go hand to actuator if they could. Abdul thought none of the Intel weenies had been to Earth themselves to check that. He held his rifle at the ready. If any bot pointed something at him he was going to fire first.

When the bots reached a hundred meters from him Abdul maxed the volume on his suit speakers and checked the wording of the statement they gave him.

"I veto all artificial intelligence activity in my personal area!"

The robots froze. A flying bot two hundred meters behind them dropped straight down, hanging up in a tree.

That was easy.

He kept heading to the dome at the quickstep. He had more shouting to do, until he was sure the Betrayer was shut down.

Omaha Dome, Earth, gravity 9.8 m/s²

By default Mitchie became commander of the fleet base sprouting up next to the dome. That gave her the responsibilities of the mayor of a small town, all of which she ruthlessly dumped on Setta so she could focus on her other role as Speaker-to-Pete.

"All the hardware of the vetoed AIs is now running under my control," said the spokes-bot. "That's let me take a complete inventory of the planet's assets. The off-planet AI nodes which surrendered are sending me inventories but they're being late and incomplete."

"Any people?" asked Mitchie.

"No organic survivors, unless they're in the unconnected regions. There's over two billion archived people. I've started creating emulations to find those with pilot skills."

She contemplated the number. It was more 'survivors' than they'd dreamed of finding. On the other hand, four times that many people had been left behind when humanity fled the Betrayal.

Pete continued, "There are fourteen hundred ships capable of interplanetary flight, allowing a month for repairs and upgrades."

Mitchie grinned. That was going to be huge boost to the fleet. "How many of them can hold human crews?"

Admiral Galen had a list of questions for Pete, with that one near the top. Direct conversations between the fleet commander and the cybernetic scientist had degenerated into arguments, hence Mitchie's new title.

"None. They're all AI ships. The best you could do is salvage some of the parts to help build new human-crewed ships. They can be flown by emulations as is."

"Can you build new human-capable warships?"

"We could do that, but emulation-controlled ships can be built in a half or third of the time."

"Of course." Mitchie dithered over whether to push more. The fleet, especially the Fusion members, wasn't happy at the thought of going into battle with computer controlled ships at their side. But after the losses in capturing Earth the thought of attacking the remaining Betrayer systems without reinforcements was daunting.

"We're working out options for producing more ships balanced against other needs. We need to select pilots before committing to a ship design. They should have the final say in what they're flying. I'm going through the archived people steadily. Should be done with them in a few days. Then we'll be able to choose who goes off to war and who stays."

"Good, I'll look forward to hearing from you then."

"Until then." The robot shut down.

Then Mitchie realized what had been bothering her. Pete was saying 'we.' But earlier he'd said 'I' even when speaking for the collection of thousands of copies of himself. So who was the 'we'?

The robot lifted its head again. "Miss Long?"

That wasn't Pete's voice.

"Yes?"

"This is Rabbi Orbakh. Can you talk for a few minutes? I don't have much time."

"Rabbi? You made it! Yes, of course we can talk." She recognized the name as one of the Pilgrims she'd delivered to Earth three years ago. "I'm glad you survived your arrival."

"Not all of my companions are glad we did. I'd like to ask a favor. Could you take me back home?"

"Why? And how?"

"The people of Earth have been discussing how to organize things. Pilgrims are a small minority, a few thousand. There's suggestions that we would be non-citizens or have some sort of second-class citizenship. I'd rather go back to Sukhoi and rejoin my family, even in a virtual sense."

"Virtual people aren't popular in the Fusion right now," said Mitchie. "Are you aware of the fake people the Ministry of Social

Control created to be losers?"

"As a cleric I had to work with Social Control, so I was briefed on some of their secrets, yes."

Mitchie summarized the revolt and civil war in the Fusion for him.

"But—I'm not fictional. I'm just digitized. That's different."

"I don't know if your ordinary stipend kid would appreciate the distinction."

"Could I go to the Disconnected Worlds?" asked Orbakh in a worried tone.

"There's no rule against it, so yes. But you'd have to earn money for your electricity and such. If you have one of those robots as your body I can get you a job as a ranch hand at my cousin's place."

"I don't know if they'd give me one. The only personal property we have is our original digitization, the current state of our emulation, and enough storage to hold it when we're swapped out. Everything else is held in common for now, they're arguing over how to allocate it."

"Swapped out?"

"We're time-sharing the nodes. There's not enough to run everyone at once, especially with Dr. Smith using so much processing."

"I hadn't realized people were still awake after Pete checked their skills." There seemed to be a lot going on that Pete hadn't mentioned.

"Oh, yes. We're all taking turns and participating in the discussions while awake."

"He's including everyone?"

"All of us who've been emulated so far. There's an incredible amount of processing needed to create the emulations. But he intends to include us all. Except the children, of course."

"I understand." Though visualizing a child being 'digitized' made her shudder.

"Where to draw the line on age is one of the active discussions. Some adult emulations can't function and have to be archived. So, would you be able to transport me back?"

"We'd probably be able to find a way. But it depends on where you're going and how much gear you have. I'd need permission from the fleet. I'm not a civilian, I'm an officer now."

"Of course. Can I contact you in two days?"

"Yes."

"Then I must go. I'm borrowing this time from others."

The robot drooped as it shut down again.

Mitchie took a deep breath. *I need to talk to Admiral Galen. These people are completely out of control. Crap. I'm thinking of them as people. Will Galen?*

***

The formal meeting was held in a tent, one wall rolled up to let Pete's representative robot enter. The humans sat along one side of the table facing the opening. The intent was to give Pete the feel of a court or hearing, placing the human leadership in a position of psychological dominance.

It didn't work. Three robots rolled in, spacing themselves evenly along the empty side of the table.

Pete's voice came from the center one. "Thank you for meeting with us. I'm Peter Smith, and this is Major Belenko," left, "and Air Marshal Havis, the elected representatives."

Admiral Galen handled introducing the live humans to the new digital ones. "Good afternoon. I'm Joyso Galen, commanding the Combined Fleet. This is Captain Michigan Long, our Research Liaison." He went on to name the civilian envoys of the Fusion, Harmony, and Disconnected Worlds. Mitchie let the names fall through her. They were all just suits to her.

Introductions done, Galen asked, "Air Marshal Havis. Were you the head of the Royal Air Force at the time of the Betrayal?"

The right-hand robot shuffled a little. "Yes, but not the one you're thinking of. I was an organizer of a World War Two reenactment group. We refought the Battle of Britain in replica airplanes. If you want someone in a national military, Major Belenko was a pilot in Pan-Russian Frontal Aviation."

"The reenactors and wargamers have done better in simulations than most of the military personnel," said Pete.

Belenko rasped, "No paperwork, no politics, just fighting."

"So which of you will provide the pilot programs for the warships?" asked Galen.

Belenko and Havis said, "We will each pilot a ship," in unison.

"I thought the simulations were picking the best pilot, and he would be copied to every ship," said the admiral.

Havis answered, "We've all signed a pact agreeing that no emulation will be duplicated for functional roles. There's just too many of us and not enough processing power."

"But there's thousands of copies of Pete out there," said Mitchie.

"That was an emergency measure," said Pete. "As other people volunteer to take over roles I'm turning nodes over to them and merging my copies. Eventually I'll be an individual again."

"It will be same with ships," said Belenko. "We are finding the thousand best pilots and we will each take a ship out to fight. Once we have agreement."

Galen leaned back in his chair. "Agreement?"

The robot rolled forward, almost touching the table. "Before we fight, we must have formal acknowledgement of our status as citizens and ownership of Earth."

The suits burst out with a jumble of objections. Mitchie made out claims that the emulations weren't real people and land was needed for colonists.

Belenko snarled, "When I pilot warship I am real enough to be destroyed."

"We are willing to trade land and services to colonists for appropriate compensation," said Havis, who Mitchie was classing as the good cop.

The wrangling went on for a bit. As it steadied down to a list of bargaining positions Admiral Galen stood up. "Ladies, Gentlemen, my digital friends, these are civilian matters with no need for military input. Please let me know when Earth's fleet will be ready for action. Good day."

As Galen walked out of the tent Mitchie scurried to follow him.

The admiral muttered, "Those damn vultures have been wanting to slice up the planet since before we got here. I'm not sorry to see them cut out."

Mitchie limited her response to a nod.

He looked down at her as they walked. "You did good work delivering Pete here. Hell of a risk. I should have said that earlier."

"Thank you, sir."

"I can't promote you any more, and you don't care much for medals. What do you want?"

"Out." No hesitation.

"Out? As in a discharge?"

"Discharge, retirement, or a nice safe jail cell. I've rolled the dice so much all my luck is used up. I want out."

"All right. I'll make it happen. What about the rest of your crew?"

"Senior Chief Kwan wanted to quit a while back. Centurion Hiroshi is ready to be skipper. He deserves a cruiser though."

"I have a few cruisers needing new commanders. None from Shishi though."

"The rest you'll have to ask. I don't know which way they'll go."

"That's what staff is for. Write me up a nice letter of resignation, Captain. I'll accept it in a day or two."

"Thank you, Admiral." Her salute was the sharpest she'd made in a year.

Galen went off to the headquarters tent.

Mitchie turned toward the hospital.

She made a point of visiting the casualties daily. They were mostly Marines who'd broken bones in bad landings. Mitchie chatted with each about his progress and offered sympathy to a new arrival, a rating who dodged the wrong way when a forklift spilled a load.

The head doctor, ready to give his report, was surprised when Mitchie made a personal request.

"That's—um, well . . . ma'am, I'm a trauma surgeon."

"Pretend it's shrapnel."

He agreed to do the procedure in the morning.

***

It went quickly. She was out of the hospital in an hour.

The base was in an uproar. The negotiations had gone until midnight, and revealed that the digital pilots were trying to use the organic people as leverage in the emulations' internal arguments over resource allocation. Now the base personnel were arguing over which faction was in the right.

As Mitchie passed the mess tent she noticed someone had painted "INSTANTIATE THE POOR" on the side wall.

Not my problem, she thought.

Back on *Joshua Chamberlain* she found Guo in the galley. "Hey. I have news."

"Oh?"

"I put in my resignation. It's been accepted. I told them you wanted out too."

Guo stood and wrapped his arms tightly around her.

"There's more. Hiroshi gets command. There's some data and samples to be delivered to the Secure Research Facility, so we can ride home with him. And I just had my implant yanked so," she poked him in the chest, "if you do your part I could be in second trimester by the time we get home."

A quick kiss was followed by Mitchie squeaking as Guo scooped her up in his arms. She stuck out too far to fit easily through their cabin hatch like that, but he managed to maneuver her through without bumping her head or ankles. She had to pull the hatch closed.

Guo tossed her on the bed and said, "Let's get to work."

Mitchie giggled.

EPILOGUE
Long Ranch, Akiak, gravity 10.3 m/s^2

Mitchie hopped up from the couch—well, lurched up—as she heard the outer door open. She pulled on a house robe for warmth but didn't bother belting it. It wouldn't close over her seven month belly anyway.

She reached the slush room as Guo came through the inner door.

A frigid puff of air from the first autumn blizzard came with him, trapped between the cold lock doors.

"Did you—what happened?" she burst out.

"Relax, it's not my blood. One of the cows delivered early." Guo pulled off his gloves and started unbuckling the parka.

"I thought you were going to fix Monty's tractor, not play vet." She caught the heavy coat and hung it up.

"I did. Then he plowed a path through the drifts to the calving barn while I walked behind carrying the newborn." He fiddled with the boots until she pried them off.

"Hmph. He has ranch hands for that."

"They couldn't make it through the drifts, not having a fancy tracked off-roader like us. Besides, he's a relative and a neighbor. Have to help him."

Extracting him from the insulated pants took some concentration. Once Guo was down to shirtsleeves Mitchie took a house robe from the warming cabinet. That gadget had convinced the family these two had too much money.

Guo let out an "Aaaahh" as the thick cloth pressed heat into him. Mitchie led him into the inner room where hot tea was waiting.

"Oh, family news," he said after the first sip. "Your cousin Washington who moved to Happy Valley?"

"Yes?"

"The baby's a girl. They're naming her Saskatchewan but she'll be called Sassy."

"Nice. Was Montana jealous?"

"Maybe a little." He took a larger sip.

"My news is the interstellar mail courier had messages for us. I saved them until you were home." She handed Guo his datasheet and opened her own.

"Oh, Lian finally wrote," said Guo. "The twins are fine. Surgically delivered, because they're all control freaks there. She has a new job, proctor at the Scent Garden. And a new apartment. Sounds like they skipped the trial but fired her without severance, she's vague about it." Some irritation leaked into his voice. "She says she doesn't need any help."

"Probably doesn't. It's cradle to grave there."

"I should be doing something to take care of the kids."

"You'll get your chance." Mitchie started her next letter. "Why is Guen bothering me with this? It's just politics, politics, Ping is an asshole—"

"Which is also politics."

"—and more politics. Ah! Wayne Searcher proposed. The wedding is two weeks from now, we'd never make it."

Guo snorted. Travel time was the least obstacle between them and attending a wedding.

"Hmmm. She's dancing around it. I wonder if they picked a quick date so we wouldn't be back."

"Having me there would be a little awkward."

"I think it could be hilarious."

"Good thing she scheduled it while we're out here. I'll come up with a present from the two of us."

"Thanks."

Guo opened his next message. "Bakhunin says the DCC is debating a constitution based on my proposal."

"Do they like it?" she asked.

"He says the ones who see themselves getting more influence in that system like it, the others hate it."

"So about what you expected."

"Yes. He wants me to attend a session. I'll let him down gently."

Mitchie pulled up her next letter. "Oh, crap. Oh crap. Oh crap."

"What?"

"Rabbi Orbakh wants me to know the Earth Collective gave robot bodies to him and two hundred and forty three other pilgrims and hired a ship to take them to the Disconnect. Oh, crap."

Guo lowered his datasheet. "That's more ranch hands than Montana and Alberta together have work for."

"Oh, crap. I'll write some letters. Maybe Bonaventure and Shishi will take some."

If you enjoyed Torchship Captain, please leave a review on Amazon.

About the Author

Karl Gallagher has earned engineering degrees from MIT and USC, controlled weather satellites for the Air Force, designed weather satellites for TRW, designed a rocketship for a start-up, and done systems engineering for a fighter plane. He is husband to Laura and father to Maggie, James, and dearly missed Alanna.

About Kelt Haven Press

Kelt Haven Press is releasing print, ebook, and audiobooks by Karl K. Gallagher. For updates see:

www.kelthavenpress.com

Subscribe to the newsletter for updates on new releases.